THE DARK POWER

For a moment, the thing that called itself Nicholas Bonner gripped the young girl's shoulders and swung her to face Sia, saying, "Do it the way I showed you. Do it now, Aiffe!"

Aiffe wriggled under his arm, refusing to look at the old woman. "Nick, I want to go home. Let's go home." Nicholas Bonner took her limp arm, holding it out, making her point at Sia.

Farrell heard Sia's voice, full of terrifying pity. "Child, no!" The air suddenly smelled violently of lightning.

He felt the old house lunging and aching in the ground, while the walls curtsied slowly to each other. The chair and fire tongs hurtled into his legs. He heard the girl cry out in bitter shock and pain.

Then chaos came to an end. The only sound was Sia's rasping sigh. "You see," she told Nicholas Bonner, without triumph. "You cannot come in. Not even with her to make the way."

A MASTER STORYTELLER

By Peter S. Beagle
Published by Ballantine Books:

THE FANTASY WORLDS OF PETER S. BEAGLE
A FINE AND PRIVATE PLACE
THE LAST UNICORN
THE FOLK OF THE AIR

THE FOLK OF THE AIR

PETER S. BEAGLE

A Del Rey Book
BALLANTINE BOOKS • NEW YORK

A Del Rey Book
Published by Ballantine Books

A portion of this novel appeared in *Phantasmagoria: Tales of Fantasy and the Supernatural*, edited by Jane Mobley.

Library of Congress Catalog Card Number: 86-7936

ISBN 0-345-34699-8

Printed in Canada

First Hardcover Edition: September 1986
First Mass Market Edition: January 1988

Cover Art by Romas

For Colleen J. McElroy
without whose aid, advice,
comfort,
cocoa at midnight,
and maddening refusal to understand
that some books just don't get finished,
this book would never have been finished.

I

*F*arrell arrived in Avicenna at four-thirty in the morning, driving a very old Volkswagen bus named Madame Schumann-Heink. The rain had just stopped. Two blocks from the freeway, on Gonzales, he pulled to the curb and leaned his elbows on the steering wheel. His passenger woke up with a sad little cry and grabbed his knee.

"It's all right," Farrell said. "We're here."

"Here?" his passenger asked, still dazed, peering ahead down the street at railroad tracks and truck bodies. He was nineteen or twenty, brown-haired and pink-cheeked, neat as a new ice-cream cone. Farrell had picked him up in Arizona, near Pima, taking the sight of a V-neck pullover, tobacco-tan loafers and white Exeter windbreaker hitchhiking across the San Carlos Indian Reservation as an unquestionable sign from heaven. After two days and nights of more or less continuous driving, the boy was no whit damper or grubbier than before, and Farrell was no nearer to remembering

1

whether his name was Pierce Harlow or Harlow Pierce. He called Farrell *mister* with remoreseless courtesy and kept asking him earnestly what it had been like to hear *Eleanor Rigby* and *Day Tripper* for the first time.

"Avicenna, California," Farrell announced, grinning at him. "Museum of my twisted youth, vault of my dearest and most disgusting memories." He rolled down his window and yawned happily. "That good stink, smell it, that's the Bay. Must be low tide."

Pierce/Harlow sniffed as instructed. "Uh-huh. Yes, I see. Really nice." He ran his hands through his hair, which promptly sprang back into one sculpted piece, polished and seamless. "How long did you say it's been?"

"Nine years," Farrell said. "Almost ten. Since I made the mistake of actually graduating. I don't know what the hell I was thinking of that morning. Just got careless, I guess."

The boy chuckled politely, turning away to rummage in his Eddie Bauer knapsack. "I've got the address of the place I'm supposed to go in here somewhere. It's right up near the campus. I can just wait." In the smudgy pre-dawn light, the nape of his neck looked as thin and vulnerable as a child's.

The sky was the color of mercury, mushy as a bruise. Farrell said, "Usually you can see the whole north campus from here, the bell tower and everything. I don't remember it getting this foggy." He stretched until he ached, locking his hands behind his head and feeling stiff muscles crackle and sigh and mumble to themselves. "Well, I can't go rouse up my buddy yet, it's way too early. Might find ourselves some breakfast—there used to be an all-night place on Gould." One bright little sparkle of pain remained when he relaxed, and he glanced down to see Pierce/Harlow smiling diffidently and holding a switchblade knife against his side, just above the belt.

"I'm really sorry, sir, " Pierce/Harlow said. "Please don't do anything dumb."

Farrell stared at him so long and so blankly that the boy began to fidget, tensing every time a car hissed by. "Just put your wallet down on the seat and get out. I don't want any trouble."

"I guess we can assume you didn't go to Exeter," Farrell said at last. Pierce/Harlow shook his head. Farrell said, "No point even asking about the programmer trainee job."

"Mr. Farrell," Pierce/Harlow said in a flat, gentle voice, "you think I won't really hurt you. Please don't think that." On the last word the knife dug harder into Farrell's side, twisting through his shirt.

Farrell sighed and drew in his legs, still resting one arm on the wheel as he reached slowly for his wallet. "Shit, this is embarrassing. You know, I've never been held up before. All those years in New York, walking around at night, everywhere, taking the subway, and I never got robbed." *Not in New York, at any rate, and not by an amateur who doesn't even know where you're supposed to hold the knife.* He made himself breathe as deeply and quietly as he could.

Pierce/Harlow smiled again, beckoning graciously with his free hand. "Well, you were due then, weren't you? It's just an occupational hazard, no big deal."

Farrell had the wallet out now, his upper body turned to face the boy, feeling the knife's pressure lessen slightly. He said, "You should have pulled this back in Arizona, you realize. I had more money then. Not having had to buy meals for two people up to that point."

"I hate driving a stick shift," Pierce/Harlow said cheerfully. "Anyway, come on, I bought gas a couple of times."

"Seven dollars' worth in Flagstaff," Farrell snorted. "Be still, my heart."

"Hey, don't, don't get snotty with me." Pierce/Harlow was suddenly trembling alarmingly, blushing in the dimness, stuttering wet-lipped, crisp consonants turning mealy. "What about all that gas I bought in Barstow? What about that?"

Halfway down the block a young couple came jogging toward them, perfectly matched in their jouncing plumpness, their green sweat suits, and their huffing clockwork pace. Farrell said, "No, you didn't. Barstow? You sure?" *Is this a clever plan? What do we do if this is not a clever plan?*

"Damn right, I'm sure," Pierce/Harlow snapped. He sat up very straight, the knife licking snaky ellipses in the air between them. Farrell stared over his shoulder, hoping to catch the woman's attention without angering him any further. She did turn her head in passing and actually halted, holding her companion's arm. Farrell widened his eyes and flared his nostrils discreetly, tyring earnestly to look distressed. The couple looked at each other and huffed on past the bus, out of step for only an instant. Pierce/Harlow said, "And it was nine-eighty-three in Flagstaff. Just so we have that clear, Mr. Farrell." He snapped his fingers for the wallet.

Farrell shrugged resignedly. "Dumb argument, anyway." *Oh lord, here goes baby.* He tossed the wallet so that it bounced off Pierce/Harlow's right knee, falling between the seat and the door. The boy reached for it instinctively, his concentration flickering just for a moment, and in that moment Farrell struck. That was, at

4

least, the verb he preferred to remember, although *lunged, clawed,* and *scrabbled* also presented themselves. He had been sighting on the knife wrist, but got the hand instead as Pierce/Harlow pulled away, crushing the boy's fingers against the switchblade's rough bone handle. Pierce/Harlow gasped and snarled and kicked Farrell's shin, yanking his hand free. Farrell let go as soon as he felt the blade sliding moon-cold through his own fingers, then heard it worrying his shirtsleeve far away. There was no pain, no blood, only coldness and Pierce/Harlow's mouth opening and closing. *This was not a clever plan.*

Unfortunately, it was the only one he had. His natural gift for fallback positions and emergency exits never showed up for work before seven o'clock; absolutely all he could think of at this hour was to duck away from Pierce/Harlow's frantically menacing flourish of the knife and throw Madame Schumann-Heink into gear, with some vague vision of driving her into an all-night laundromat on the corner. As an afterthought, he also screamed *"Kreegaaahh!"* at the top of his lungs, for the first time since he was eleven years old, jumping off his parents' bed, which was the bank of the Limpopo River, onto his cousin Mary Margaret Louise, who was a crocodile.

The most immediate thing that happened was that his worn sneaker slipped off the clutch pedal. The second was that the rearview mirror fell into his lap, as Madame Schumann-Heink rose up on her back wheels and danced ponderously into the middle of Gonzales Avenue before she came down again with a smash that threw Pierce/Harlow face-first against the dashboard. The switchblade sagged in his fingers.

Farrell had no chance to take advantage of the moment; he was half-stunned himself, and Madame Schumann-Heink was frisking in second gear toward the left-hand curb, heading straight for a parked van with MOBILE IMMENSE GRACE UFO MINISTRY stenciled neatly on its sides. Farrell hauled desperately on the wheel and found himself veering under the nose of a garbage truck that bore down on him like a ferryboat through the fog, glowing and hooting. Madame Schumann-Heink spun in a surprisingly agile U-turn and scurried before the truck, rocking cripplingly on dead shocks, her tail pipe farting in tin-can bursts and something Farrell didn't want to think about dragging just back of her front axle. He pounded on the horn and kept howling.

Beside him Pierce/Harlow, sand-pale with shock and rage, knuckled blindly at his mouth, sputtering blood. "Bit my tongue," he mumbled. "Christ, I bit my tongue."

"I did that once," Farrell said sympathetically. "It's a real bear, isn't it? Try to put your head back a bit." Without turning, he began walking his hand shyly toward the knife lying forgotten on Pierce/Harlow's lap. But his peripheral vision was also sleeping in this morning; when he struck a second time, Pierce/Harlow made a sound that was all inhale, snatched up the switchblade, and missed medical immortality by cringing inches, getting the seat cover instead. Farrell swung Madame Schumann-Heink hard to the left, cutting in front of a bellowing semi, and careened down a side street lined with office furniture warehouses and bail bondsmen's establishments. He heard everything loose in back go booming from one side of the bus to the other and thought *oh, sweet Jesus, the lute, sonofabitch.* The new worry kept him from noticing for two blocks that such traffic as there was was all coming toward him.

"Well, shit," Farrell said sadly. "Wouldn't you know?"

Pierce/Harlow crouched on the seat, elbows flapping absurdly as he tried to brace himself against everything, including Farrell. "Pull over or I'll cut you. Right here, I'll do it." He was almost crying, and color was puddling grotesquely under his cheekbones.

A Winnebago the size of a rural airport filled the windshield. Farrell whimpered softly himself, hung a fishtailing right turn on the wet pavement, and bucked Madame Schumann-Heink up a parking-lot driveway. At the top of the ramp two important things happened: Pierce/Harlow grabbed him around the neck, and Madame Schumann-Heink popped blithely out of gear— her oldest trick, always most judiciously employed— and began to roll back down. Farrell bit Pierce/Harlow's forearm, somehow contriving while chewing to wrench the Volkswagen into reverse and send her shooting back out into the street, well in the wake of the motor home, but squirting like a marble straight through a sawhorse barricade around a pothole. *The lute, oh please, goddamn.* A taillight exploded, and Pierce/Harlow and Farrell let go of each other and screamed. Madame Schumann-Heink popped into neutral again. Farrell pushed Pierce/Harlow away, fumbled for second gear, which was never quite where he had left it, and stood on the accelerator.

Madame Schumann-Heink, who normally required a tail wind and two days' notice to get up to fifty miles an hour, was doing sixty by the time she hit Gonzales. Pierce/Harlow chose that moment to try another frontal assault, which was unfortunate, because Farrell took the corner, and a "Swingers Exchange" vending machine along with it, on the far side of two wheels. Pierce/

Harlow ended up on Farrell's lap, with the knife curiously snuggled into his own armpit.

"I think you should have taken that computer job," Farrell said. They were tearing back down Gonzales, nearing the freeway. Pierce/Harlow disentangled himself, wiped his bleeding mouth, and got the knife pointed the right way. "I'll cut you," he said hopelessly. "I swear to God."

Farrell slowed down slightly, gesturing toward the approaching overpass. "You see that pillar coming up, with the sign? Yes? Well, I was just wondering, do you think you can throw your knife out the window before I hit it?" He smiled a shut-mouth crescent smile, which he hoped suggested a syphilitic picking up weather reports from Alpha Centauri on his bridgework, and added in a serene singsong, "Her tires are all bald, her brakes suck, and you are about to become sticky stuff on the seat."

The knife actually bounced off the pillar as Farrell swerved away from it, the wheel slugging and whipping like a game fish in his hands, the back tires keening coldly. With the rearview mirror gone, the old green convertible was a sudden clubbing blow out of nowhere, yawing wildly under the window, fighting for traction, sliding sideways into the bus like an asteroid being slowly raped by the pitiless mass of a larger planet. There was a moment for Farrell in which nothing existed but the underwater languor of the driver's face, rippling and folding silently with terror beneath his great oil-drum helmet, the heavy golden chains and ornaments cascading down the rather pink body of the woman beside him, the rosette of rust around a door handle, and the broadsword in the hand of the young black man in the back seat, who seemed to be casually fending Madame Schumann-Heink away with it as she hung above him. Then Farrell had sprawled across the wheel and was dragging the bus to the right with all his strength, tucking her into a squealing circle around another pillar, finally slamming to a stop almost behind the convertible as it righted itself and gunned ahead toward the Bay. Farrell saw the black man waving his sword like a conqueror in the mist until the car vanished up a ramp onto the freeway.

Farrell exhaled. He became aware that Pierce/Harlow had been screaming for some time, piled haphazardly on the floor, rocking convulsively. Farrell cut the engine and said, "Knock it off, there's a cop car." He was shivering himself and wondered distantly if he were going to throw up.

There was no patrol car coming, but Pierce/Harlow did stop wailing, as abruptly as a child might, with a gulp and a sleeve rubbed across his face. "You're insane. I mean, you are really insane." His voice was a snuffly, aggrieved hiccup.

"Keep it in mind," Farrell said heavily. "You try to get out and find your knife and I'll run you over." Pierce/Harlow jerked his hand back from the door and stared at him. Farrell ignored him, letting his vision swim and his body shake itself still. Then he started Madame Schumann-Heink up again and turned her slowly, peering anxiously in every direction. Pierce/Harlow drew breath to protest, but Farrell forestalled him. "Be quiet. I'm tired of you. Just be quiet."

"Where are you going?" Pierce/Harlow demanded. "If you think you're taking me to the police—"

"I'm too damn beat," Farrell said. "My first morning here in ten years, I'm not about to spend it in a station

9

house with you. Just stay cool and I'll drop you off at a hospital. You can get that tongue looked at."

Pierce/Harlow hesitated, then sank back, touching his mouth and looking at his fingers. He said accusingly, "I'm probably going to need stitches."

Farrell was driving in low gear, listening intently to new scraping sounds under the bus. "With any luck. I'm counting on rabies shots, myself."

"I don't have any health insurance," Pierce/Harlow said. Farrell decided that he couldn't reasonably be expected to reply and turned sharply left on Paige Street, suddenly recalling the clinic somewhere around there and the soft, rainy night much like this one when he had dragged Clawhammer Perry Brown into Emergency, crying with the certainty that he could feel Perry's body chilling every moment on his shoulder. *Skinny old Clawhammer. Car thief, great banjo player, and the first serious pillhead I ever met. And Wendy in the back seat, bitching all the way because he'd gotten into her stash again, telling him the wedding was off. Ah, lord, them days, them days.* He reminded himself to tell Ben about Perry Brown when he got where he was going. *He got fat later on, somebody said.*

By the time he pulled up in front of the clinic, the sky was showing a runny, gray-mustard stain off behind one pewter corner. A stranger would have missed it, but Farrell still knew an Avicenna dawn when he saw one. He turned to Pierce/Harlow, who was slouched against the door, eyes closed, fingers in his mouth, and said, "Well, it's been real."

Pierce/Harlow sat up, blinking from Farrell to the clinic and back. His mouth was badly swollen, but his style was already beginning to regenerate itself, spinning pink-and-white self-assurance before Farrell's eyes, as a lizard grows new limbs. He said, "I'm going to look pretty silly, coming in for a chewed-up tongue, for God's sake."

"Tell them you cut yourself shaving," Farrell said. "Tell them you got French-kissed by the Hound of the Baskervilles. Good-bye."

Pierce/Harlow nodded meekly. "I'll just get my gear out of the back." He rose and squeezed past Farrell, who turned to follow his movements. He picked up his sweater and groped unhurriedly for the authentic Greek fisherman's cap and the pocket stereo. Farrell, bending to recover his wallet, heard a sudden sweet clunk and straightened up quickly, making a sound like Madame Schumann-Heink's transmission.

"I'm sorry," the boy said. "That's your mandolin thing, isn't it? I'm really sorry." Farrell handed him his knapsack, and he opened the slide doors and started to step down, then paused, looking back. "Well, I thank you very much for the ride, I really appreciated it. You have a good day, okay?"

Farrell shook his head, marveling helplessly. "Do you do this a whole lot? I ask out of some concern."

"Well, I don't do it for a living, if that's what you mean." Pierce/Harlow might have been a college golfer defending his amateur standing. "It's more like a hobby, actually. You know, some people do underwater photography. I just get a kick out of it."

"You don't know how it's done," Farrell said. "You don't even know what to say. Somebody's going to kill you, you keep this stuff up."

Pierce/Harlow shrugged. "I get a kick out of it. The look on their faces when it finally starts to sink in. It's really addictive, just knowing I'm not what they're so sure I am. Sort of like Zorro or somebody." He

11

dropped to the curb, turning to give Farrell a reminiscently affectionate smile, as if they had shared an adventure long ago, in another language. He said, "You ought to try it. You're practically doing it anyway, right now. Take care, Mr. Farrell."

He slid the doors carefully shut before he sauntered away toward the clinic. Farrell put Madame Schumann-Heink in gear and eased her into the thickening San Francisco commuter traffic that seemed to be starting far earlier than he remembered. *What would you know? Back then, everyone in the world lived on Parnell Street and slept till noon.* He decided that whatever Madame Schumann-Heink was dragging would keep until he got to Ben's house, as would thinking about the events of the last half-hour. His skin felt stiff with dried sweat; his head had begun to thump with each heartbeat. The Volkswagen smelled of feet and blankets and cold Chinese food.

Driving north on Gould Avenue—*where the hell is the Blind Alley? It couldn't be gone, everybody played there, I must have missed it*—he did allow himself to consider, though with some wariness, the matter of the green convertible. At the time, his mind—having promptly skipped town, leaving no forwarding address but only those weary, cynical old suckers, his nerves and reflexes, to settle his debts and post bail one more time—had registered nothing but the driver's huge helmet, the black man's jaunty toy sword—*was it a toy?*— and the woman dressed entirely in gold chains. *But the black guy was wearing something like a mantle, a bearskin?* And the back seat had been tossing with velvet cloaks and stiff white ruffs and plumes like firelight in the fog as the old rag-top hurtled by. *Doubtless the*

Avicenna Welcome Wagon. The one with the chains must be from the Native Daughters.

Gould was a long street, stretching from one end of Avicenna nearly to the other and effectively dividing student country and the hills beyond from the hot, black flatlands. Farrell drove until the used-car lots gave way to antique shops, those to office buildings and department stores—*damn, what happened to that nice old fish market?*—and those in turn to one- and two-story frame houses, white and blue and green, with stairs on the outside. They were old, thin houses, most of them, and in the dour morning air they looked like boats abandoned on the beach, unsafe to take to sea. Farrell's breath tightened, just for a moment, at the southwest corner of Ortega; but the gray, bulging, fish-scaled house was gone, replaced by a Tas-T-Freeze.

They were trying to condemn that place all the time I lived there. As unseaworthy a house as ever I went deep-sea sailing in. Ellen. Even after so much time, he touched the name cautiously with his tongue, like a sore tooth, but nothing happened.

Ben had been living on Scotia Street for a little more than four years, almost since his move from New York. It was not territory Farrell had ever known well, and he was flying blind when he turned right arbitrarily on Iris and sweet-talked Madame Schumann-Heink up a triple fall of short, steep hills. The houses were changing within a block, becoming larger and darker, with shingly New England angles supporting California sun decks. The higher he drove, the further they drew back from the street, keeping to the shadows of redwood, eucalyptus, and ailanthus, except for a few corner stuccos, parrot-bright. *No sidewalks. I can't imagine Ben in a place without sidewalks.*

The sky was still overcast behind him by the time he found the house; but up on Scotia Street the sun was already clambering around in the vines and bushes, purring, rubbing itself against bougainvillaea. Scotia was a shaggy, cranky jungle, winding and crimped as a goat path—a street meant for broughams, post chaises, and ice wagons, where Madame Schumann-Heink and a descending Buick briefly got wedged into a curve like fighting stags. Unlike the tame lawns and gardens of the slopes below, the Scotia shrubbery was voluptuously brazen, spilling across garage roofs and over low stone walls to link properties in defiant wrong-side-of-the-blanket alliances. *A long way from Forty-Sixth and Tenth Avenue, boy.*

He recognized the house from Ben's letters. Like most of its neighbors, it was an old, solid, two-story structure with the majestically shabby air of a buffalo shedding its winter coat. What made it unique on Scotia was a porch roof that ran all the way around the house, wide and level enough for two people to walk comfortably abreast. "Nothing at all to do with sea captains' widows," Ben had written. "Apparently the guy who built the place in the nineties was trying for a pagoda. They took him away before he got the corners turned up."

When he parked the bus and scrambled in back to get the lute, he discovered that his cooking kit was missing. Momentarily enraged as he had not been during the entire holdup, he was quickly fascinated, amazed that the boy could have gotten away under his eyes with something that bulky. The electric razor was gone too. Farrell sat down on the floor with his legs straight out in front of him and began to laugh.

After a little while he drew the lute to him from the

corner where it had ended up. Afraid to remove the cloth and plastic swaddlings to check for damage, he only said, "Come on, love" to it and got out of the bus, sneezing sharply as the smell of damp jasmine and rosemary tickled his nose. He glanced at the house again—*birdhouses, I'll be damned*—then turned and walked slowly across the narrow street to look back down the hills at Avicenna.

The Bay took up half the horizon, rumpled and dingy as a motel bedspread, with a few sails frozen under the bridge and San Francisco beyond, slipping like soap through a dishwater mist. From where Farrell stood in the private sunlight of Scotia Street, treetops and gables broke up his line of sight; but he could make out the university's red-brick bell tower and the campus plaza where he had first met Ellen hustling chess games with freshmen. *And if that's the corner of Serra and Fox, then that window has to be the Nikolai Bukharin Memorial Pizza Parlor. Two years waiting tables and breaking up fights there, and I still always got him mixed up with that other one, Bakunin.* The only movement that he could see anywhere was the green wink of a streetcar sliding down through the flatlands, vanishing between the naked pastel roofs that seemed to overlap one another like lily pads all the way to the freeway. He stood on tiptoe for a moment, looking for the Blue Zoo, the warty indigo frog of a Victorian in which he and Clawhammer Perry Brown and a Korean string trio had shared the top floor rent-free for almost three months, before the party downstairs ended and the owner noticed them. *Did I dream all that, that time, those people? What begins now?*

Walking up the stump-flagged path to Ben's house, he unwrapped the lute, his chest aching with gratitude

15

to find it whole. He sat down on the porch steps, marveling as always at the sight of his own hand on the long golden curve of the instrument, as he had once caught his breath to deny the miracle of his hand touching a woman's bare hip. He hugged the lute gently into his belly and held it there, and the coupled strings sighed into the air, though he had not yet touched them.

"Come on, love," he said again. He began to play *Mounsiers Almaine*, too fast, as he often took it, but not trying to slow it down. After that he played a Dowland pavane, and then *Mounsiers Almaine* again, properly this time. The lute grew warm in the sun and smelled like lemons.

II

*T*he old woman said, *"You had better be Joe Farrell."*

Afterward, at odd times and places, he liked to think about the first time that Sia and he ever looked at each other. By then he remembered no single detail of the moment, except that both of them had instinctively clutched something close—Farrell his lute, and Sia the belt of the worn blue robe, which she drew tight under her heavy breasts. Sometimes he did recall being instantly certain that he had just met either an old friend or a very patient, important enemy; more often he knew that he was making that up. But he felt strange trying to imagine not knowing who Sia was.

"Because if you are not," she said, "I have no business being out here at six in the morning listening to a strange lute player on my front porch. So if you are Joe Farrell, you can come in and have breakfast. Otherwise I am going back to bed."

She was not tall, actually, nor was she very old. Ben

had described her hardly at all in his letters, and Farrell's first vision had been of a great, drowsy monolith standing above him, a menhir in a frayed flannel bathrobe. As he stood up, he saw that the broad, blunt-featured face was no older than sixty, the dark-honey skin almost without lines, and the gray eyes quick and clear and imperiously sad. But her body was as lumpy as a charwoman's—waistless, short-legged, wide-hipped, bellied like the moon—although she carried it with all the vivid rigor of a circus wire walker, even in bedroom slippers like heaps of fluffy slush. The bathrobe was too long for her, and Farrell shivered slightly to realize that it must be Ben's robe.

"You're Sia," he said. "Athanasia Sioris."

"Oh, I know that," she answered, "even this early. What about you? Have you decided if you're Joe Farrell yet?"

"I'm Farrell," he said, "but you can go back to bed anyway. I didn't mean to wake you."

Her hair was very thick and a little coarse, gray and black together, like a winter dawn. It fell down between her shoulder blades, caught, not in a ribbon, but with a gnarled silver ring. Her eyes had almost no white to them. Farrell could see the pupils breathing slowly in the morning light, and he fancied that he felt their full weight testing his strength, as boxers will lean thoughtfully on each other in the early rounds. She said, "Am I afraid of you?"

Farrell said, "When Ben first wrote me about you, I thought you had the prettiest name in the world. I still do, except maybe for a woman named Electa Arenal de Rodriguez. It's a close thing either way."

"Am I afraid of you?" she asked again. "Or am I glad to see you?" Her voice was low and hoarse, the

Greek accent less of a sound than an aftertaste; not unpleasant, but not an easy voice, either. He could not imagine it teasing, consoling, caressing—*Christ, she's older than his mother*—or telling lies. It was a voice suited only for asking nettlesome questions with no safe answers.

He said, "No one's ever been afraid of me. It would be grand if you were, but I don't really expect it."

She had been looking at him, so it was not that the dark regard suddenly shifted or focused on him more intensely, but rather as if he had managed to attract the attention of a forest, or of a large body of water. "What do you expect?" Farrell stared back at her, too tired and uncertain even to shrug, almost peacefully at a standstill. Sia said, "Well, come in, good morning."

She turned her back; as she did so, Farrell felt a curious desolation pass over him—a fox-fierce little autumn wind of abandonment and loss that might have blown out of his childhood, when sorrows were all the same size and came and went without ever explaining themselves. It was gone instantly, and he walked into the house, following a middle-aged woman in a blue bathrobe who moved cumbrously on legs that he knew must have varicose veins.

"Sia's house is a cave," Ben had written to him three years ago, having lived with her then for more than a year. "Bones underfoot, little clawed things scampering in the shadows, and the fire leaves greasy stains on the walls. Everything smells of chicken blood and skins drying." But that morning Farrell thought the house was like a green tree, and the rooms were branches, high and light and murmurous with the sounds that wood makes in the sun. He stood in the living room, studying the manner in which the toast-colored boards of the ceiling went together like the back of his lute. There were books and big windows; mirrors and masks, small, thick rugs, and furniture like drowsing animals. A chess set stood on a low cast-iron table in front of the fireplace. The pieces were of wood, worn almost as round and featureless as the spindles of the staircase. Farrell saw a tall old windup phonograph in a corner, next to a wicker basket full of pampas grass and rusty spears.

She led him to a small kitchen where she scrambled a lot of eggs and made coffee, working swiftly with brown, rather stubby hands, saying very little and never looking at him. But when she was done, she brought their plates to the table and sat down across from him, settling her chin between her fists. For a moment the gray eyes—clear and savage as snow water—regarded him with an earnest, personal hostility that seemed to lick along his bones, scouring them hollow. And then Sia smiled, and Farrell took a very quick breath before the mischief of the women and smiled at her.

"I'm sorry," she said. "May I take the last fifteen minutes back?"

Farrell nodded seriously. "If you leave the eggs."

Sia said, "Frightened lovers are hideous. I have been dreadful to Ben for a week, just because of you."

"Why? You sound like the Pope receiving Attila the Hun. What have I done to deserve all this terror?"

She smiled again, but the deep, secret amusement was gone. She said, "My dear, I can't tell how used to this sort of situation you are, but you should certainly know that no one really welcomes the old best friend. Don't you know that?" Farrell felt the kitchen sunlight stir against him as she leaned forward.

"Oldest friend, maybe," he answered. "Best, I don't know. I haven't seen Ben for seven years, Sia."

"In California, oldest is best," she answered. "Ben has good friends here, people at the university, people who care for him, but there is no one who knows him except me. And now here you are. It's very silly."

"Yes, it is." Farrell reached for the butter. "You're Ben's best friend now, Sia." An enormous Alsatian bitch came and barked once at him; then, with that over, put her head on his knee and drooled. Farrell gave her some of his scrambled eggs.

Sia said, "You knew him when he was thirteen years old. I can't ever catch up with that. What was he like?"

"He had a high, shiny forehead," Farrell said, "and I used to call him Rubberlips." Sia began to laugh very quietly. Her laughter was almost too low for him to hear; it played at the edges of all his senses, like whale song. Farrell went on. "He was a hell of a swimmer, a really rotten actor, and in high school he got me through trigonometry one year and chemistry another. I used to make faces at him in math class, trying to get him to laugh. His father died, I think when we were juniors. He hated my plaid winter hat with the earflaps, and he loved Judy Garland and Joe Williams and little night-clubs where they'd put on a show with five people. That's the kind of stuff I remember, Sia. I didn't know him. I think he knew me, but I was too busy worrying about my pimples."

She continued to smile, but the expression, like her laughter, seemed a part of some other, slower language, where everything he understood meant something else. She said, "But you had a room together, later, when you lived in New York. You would play music together, and nothing is closer than that. You see, I am jealous of anyone who was before me, like God. I can be jealous of his mother and his father sometimes."

Farrell shook his head. "No, you aren't. I'm reasonably stupid, but you're playing with me. Jealousy is not your problem."

"Get down, Briseis," Sia said sharply. The Alsatian left Farrell and trotted clicking to her. Sia fondled the dog's muzzle, never taking her glance from Farrell.

"No," she said. "I am not jealous of anything you know about him, or anything you may have of him. I am only afraid of what comes with you." Farrell found himself turning solemnly, so truly did she seem to see the sullen companion at his shoulder. Sia said, "Being young. He forgets how young he is—there's nothing like a university to make you do that. I never try to make him old, never, but I let him forget."

"Ben was always a little old," Farrell said. "Even shooting paper clips in home room. I think you must be younger than Ben."

The playfulness came back—again somehow shocking to see turning lithely in her eyes. "From time to time," she said. The big dog reared up suddenly, putting its paws in her lap and pressing its cheek against hers, so that the two faces confronted Farrell with the same look of impenetrable laughter, except that Sia kept her mouth closed. He turned away for a moment, looking out of the window at the squat gathering of oaks behind the house. The glass reflected, not his face at all, but the single figure seated in the chair across from him. It had the vast stone body of a woman, and a dog's grinning head.

The vision endured for less time than it took his eyes to translate, or his mind to sidestep, promising to write. When he turned again, Briseis had started after the

22

butter, and Sia pushed her to the floor. "You are hurt." There was neither alarm nor what Farrell would have called concern in her voice; if anything, she sounded slightly offended. He looked down at himself and noticed for the first time that his right shirtsleeve was ragged from wrist to elbow, the edges of the cut dappled rust-brown.

"Ah, it's just a scratch," he said. "I always wanted a chance to say that." But Sia was beside him, rolling up his sleeve, although he protested earnestly, "Farrell's Fifth Law: If you don't look at it, it doesn't hurt as much." The wound was a long, shallow gouge, clean and uncomplicated, looking like nothing but what it was. He told her about Pierce/Harlow, carefully spinning the whole unlikely event into a harmless, idiotic tall tale, while she washed his arm and then drew the cut closed with butterfly bandages. The more he tried to make her laugh, the more tense and abrupt her hands became on him; whether with sympathy, apprehension or only contempt for his foolishness, he could not tell. He chattered on, helplessly compulsive, until she finished and stood up, muttering to herself like any ruinous ragbag lost in a doorway. Farrell thought at first that she was speaking in Greek.

"What?" he asked. "Should have known what?" When she turned to face him he realized in bewilderment that she was furious at herself, this odd, sly, squat woman, as intensely and unforgivingly as though Pierce/Harlow were her personal responsibility, the holdup all her own absentminded doing. The gray eyes had darkened to the color of asphalt, and the airy morning kitchen smelled like a distant storm. She said, "It is my house. I should have known."

"Known what?" he demanded again. "That I'd

23

shove my arm onto some preppy bandit's knife? I didn't know it myself, how could you?" But she stood shaking her head, looking down at Briseis, who crouched and whined. "Not outside," she said to the dog. "No more, that is gone. But this is my house." The first words had fallen as softly as leaves; the last hissed like sleet. "This is my house," she said.

Farrell said, "We were talking about Ben. About his really being older than you. We were just talking about that." It seemed to him that he could feel her anger crowding the silence, see it piling up around them both in great drifts and ranges of static electricity. She stared at him, squinting as though he were drawing steadily away from her, and finally showed small white teeth in a cold sigh of laughter.

"He likes me to be old and wicked and clever," she said. "He likes that. But I feel sometimes like a— what?—like a witch, like a troll queen, one who has enchanted a young knight to be her lover, but he must never hear a certain word spoken. It is nothing magic, just a word out of the kitchen or the stables—but if he hears it, it is all up, he will leave her. Think how she would guard him, not from magicians, but from horseboys, not from beautiful princesses, but from cooks. And what could she do? And whatever she did, how long could it be? Someone would come along and say *straw* or *dishrag* to him sooner or later. And what could she do?"

Farrell flexed his arm cautiously and reached a second time to touch his lute. "Not much. I suppose she'd just have to go on being a queen. There's a shortage of queens these days, trolls or any other kind. People are complaining about it."

She laughed so that he could hear it then, the slow,

disheveled laugh of a human woman in the morning; and suddenly they were only themselves at the table, and nothing in the kitchen but sunlight and a dog and the smell of cinnamon coffee. "Play for me," she said, and he played a little, sitting there: some Dowland, some Rosseter. Then she wanted to know about his wanderings, and they talked quietly of freighters and fishing boats, markets and carnivals, languages and police. He had lived in more places than Sia, but never as long; he had been to Syros, the island of her birth, that she had not seen since girlhood. She said, "You were Ben's legend for a long time, you know. You acted things out for him."

"Oh, everybody has one of those," he answered. "People's dreams dovetail like that. My own legend was running around Malaysia on a bicycle, the last I heard of her."

The mischief flared again in Sia's eyes. "But what a strange sort of Odysseus you are," she said. "You keep having the same adventure over and over." Farrell blinked at her uneasily. Sia said, "I have read your letters to Ben. Wherever you wake up and find yourself, you take some stupid job, you make a few very colorful acquaintances, you play your music, and sometimes, for one letter, there is a woman. And then you wake up somewhere else, and it all begins again. Do you like such a life?"

In time he learned almost to take it for granted, that moment in a conversation with Sia when the ground under his feet was gently gone, like a missed stair or curbstone, and he invariably lurched off-balance, as violently as when he twitched out of a falling dream. But just then he felt himself blushing, saying with hot flatness, "I do what I do. It suits me."

"Yes? How sad." She got up to put the dishes in the sink. She was still laughing to herself. "I think you allow yourself only the crusts of your experiences," she said, "only the shadows. You always leave the good part."

The lute breathed like a creature waking slowly as he picked it up. "This is the good part," he said. He began to play a Narvaez pavane that he was vastly proud of having transcribed for the lute. The translucent chords fell slowly, shivering and sliding away through his fingers. Ben came in while he was playing, and they nodded at each other, but Farrell went on with the pavane until it ended abruptly in a gentle broken arpeggio. Then he put the lute down, and he got up and hugged Ben.

"Spanish baroque," he said. "I've been playing a lot of it, the last year or so." Ben put his hands on Farrell's shoulders and shook him slowly but hard. Farrell said, "You look different."

"You don't look any different at all," Ben said. "Except the eyes." Sia sat watching them, one hand closed in Briseis' fur.

"That's funny," Farrell said softly. "Your eyes haven't changed." He stared, wary and fascinated and truly alarmed. The Ben Kassoy with whom he had waited for buses in the New York morning snow had looked very much like a dolphin and moved as sweetly and frivolously as any dolphin through the acrid waters of the high-school pool. On land he had tripped over things, tall and slouching, nearsighted, stranded in this stingy, unkind element. But he carried himself with Sia's fierce containment now, and the glassy skin had weathered to the hard opacity of sailcloth, the round, blinking face—dolphin-browed, dolphin-beaky, dolphin-naked of shadows—grown as rough and solitary

26

and rich with darknesses as a Crusader castle. Farrell had been casually prepared, after seven years, for a cleared-up complexion and the first gray hairs; but he would have passed this face in the street, turning a block later to look after it in wonder and disbelief. Then Ben knuckled his mouth with his left forefinger in the old study-hall habit, and Farrell said automatically, "Don't *do* that. Your mother hates that."

"As long as you crack your toes in class, I can chew my finger," Ben said. Sia came silently to stand beside him, and Ben put an arm around her shoulders. He said to her, "This is my friend Joe. He takes his shoes off under the desk and does terrible things with his feet." Then he looked at Farrell and kissed her, and she moved against him.

Later she went to get dressed, and Farrell began to tell Ben about Pierce/Harlow and the green convertible; but it kept getting scrambled, because Farrell had not really slept for thirty-six hours, and they had all suddenly caught up with him at once. Halfway up the stairs to the spare bedroom he remembered that he had wanted Ben to hear the two Luys Milan pieces he had just learned, but Ben said it could wait. "I've got a nine o'clock class and office hours. Sleep till I get back, then you can play all night for us."

"Which one is the nine o'clock?" Farrell had curled up in his clothes and a quilt, listening to Ben's voice with his eyes closed.

"My all-purpose monster. It's an introduction to the Eddas, but I get in a little Old Norse etymology, a little Scandinavian folklore, a little history, related literature, and a key to the Scriptures. The Classic Comics version of Snorri Sturlesson." His voice was unchanged—slow for New York, and light, but broken as erratically as an adolescent's by a deep, random jag of harshness, strangely like interference on a long-distance call. *When you hear somebody talking to Wyoming or Minnesota, just for a moment.*

Farrell fell asleep then—and woke promptly with Briseis washing his face. Ben turned quickly to call the dog away, and his words came out in a soft sidelong rush. "So what do you think of her?"

"Overdemonstrative," Farrell grunted, "but very nice. I think she's got worms." He opened his eyes and grinned at Ben. "What can I tell you? Living with her has given you cheekbones. You never used to have cheekbones before, I never could figure out what was holding your face on. Will that do?"

"No," Ben said. The kind, brown, dolphin gaze regarded Farrell almost without recognition, admitting to no shared subways, no Lewisohn Stadium all-Gershwin concerts, no silent old jokes and passwords. "Try again, Joe. That won't do at all."

Farrell said, "I was doing my old charming bit, and she pulled me up so short I think I ruptured my debonair. Remarkable woman. We may take a while." His arm had begun to throb, and he blamed Sia for not leaving it alone. He said, "Also, I'm sorry, I can't imagine you together. I just can't, Ben."

Ben's expression did not change. Farrell noticed the scar under his left eye for the first time—dim and thin, but as ragged as if it had been made with the lid of a tin can. He said flatly, "Don't worry about it. Nobody can."

Downstairs the doorbell rang. Three-quarters asleep, Farrell felt Sia move to answer it, the heavy steps trudging in the bed. He mumbled, "Piss on you,

Kassoy. Stand around like a junior high school girl full of secrets. I don't know what you want me to say."

Ben laughed shortly, which startled Farrell as much as anything that had happened so far that morning. When they were children, Ben had seemed most often to be straining on the edge of laughter, digging in his heels against the terror of finding everything funny. Farrell had seen the ghosts of murdered giggles burning along the perimeter of Ben's body, like St. Elmo's fire. "I don't really know either. Get some sleep, we'll talk later." He patted Farrell's foot through the quilt and started out of the room.

"Can you put me up for a bit?"

Ben turned back, leaning in the doorway. *What is he listening for, what is it that has all his attention?* "Since when do you ask?"

"Since it's been seven years, and unemployed company with no plans is not a good thing. I'll start looking for a job tomorrow, see about a place to live. Take me a few days."

"It'll take longer than that. You better bring all your stuff inside."

"Jobs and parking spaces, remember?" Farrell said. "I always find something. Canneries, fry cook, hospital work, tend bar. Check out the zoo up in Barton Park. Fix motorcycles. Lay linoleum. Did I write you about that, how I got into the union? Ben, the people you let in your house to lay down your linoleum!"

Ben said, "I could probably get you a guitar class at the university in the fall. Not a master class or anything, but not *Skip to My Lou* either. It couldn't be any worse than teaching out of the Happy Chicken Bodega on Avenue A."

Farrell held out a hand to Briseis, who came and

plopped her head in it and went to sleep herself. "I don't even have a guitar anymore."

"The Fernandez?" The Ben he remembered stared at him for just a moment, unprotected, always a little startled, and endlessly, maddeningly honest.

He said, "I traded it to the guy who made the lute for me. I had to be sure I was serious."

"So you actually did something irrevocable." Ben spoke softly, the fortress face expressionless again. Farrell heard Sia's voice on the stairs, and under it a younger voice, muddy and sexless with pain.

"Suzy," Ben said. "One of Sia's clients, pays her by doing housework. Married to a surfing thug who thinks cancer's contagious."

"Is she really a psychiatrist, Sia?"

"Counselor. She has to call herself a counselor in this country." The voices went into another room, and a door closed. Farrell asked, "Is that how you met? You never exactly said."

Ben shrugged in the old lopsided way, ducking his head crookedly, like a fishing bird. He began to say something; but Sia was talking to the woman, and the slow, near-wordless pulse of her voice in the other room was beginning to wash Farrell gently back and forth, here and gone and here. With each lulling swing across the darkness, something he almost knew about her left him, the stone woman with the dog's head last of all. Ben was saying, "So I thought you might as well be working at something you enjoyed."

Farrell sat up and said with urgent clarity, "No, teeth. A purple in the back seat with teeth." Then he blinked at Ben and asked abruptly, "What makes you think I enjoy teaching?" Ben did not answer. Farrell said, "I mean, I don't *not* enjoy it. I dig anything I do well enough. All that stuff, those stupid little jobs, I just don't want to start liking any of them more than enough. I like them stupid."

Then Ben smiled suddenly and lingeringly, the comforting phosphorescence of suppressed delight flaring around him once more. Farrell said, "Now you're thinking about my goddamn hat with the earflaps."

"No, I'm thinking about your goddamn briefcase, and your goddamn incredible looseleaf notebook. And I'm thinking about how you could play, even then. I never did understand how that notebook could go with that music."

"Didn't you?" Farrell asked. "Funny." He turned on his side, to Briseis' considerable distress, and burrowed down in the quilt, resting his head on his arm. "Ah, lord, Ben, the music was the only thing that ever came naturally. Everything else I had to learn."

III

Nothing in Farrell's considerable experience of frying eggs and hashbrowns had quite prepared him for Thumper's. His work here was the opposite, the denial, the absolute negation of cooking: it consisted almost entirely of reheating dormant fruit pies, periodically adding water to the stewing vats of coffee, chili, and something orange, and filling red plastic baskets with sandy gobbets of fried rabbit, prepared in Fullerton in accordance with a secret recipe and delivered by truck twice a week. He also had the responsibility of steeping the chunks, either in Thumper's Meadow Magic Sauce, which smelled like hot blacktop, or in Thumper's Forest Flavoring, which Farrell had renamed "Twilight in the Everglades." For the rest, he mopped the floors, scoured the ovens and the deep fryer, and, before he left in the evening, pulled the switch that lit up the grinning, eye-rolling, foot-flapping bunny on the roof. The bunny was supposed to be holding a Big Bear Bucket of Cottontail Crispies, or it might have been

Jackrabbit Joints or Hare Pieces. Farrell was entitled to one Big Bear Bucket a day, but he took his meals at a Japanese restaurant around the corner.

So did Mr. McIntire, the manager of Thumper's. A hulking, silent man with a red face and hair as gray and sticky as old soap, he winced visibly to serve Wabbit Wieners and pushed the bright baskets of Bunny Buns across the counter with his fingertips. Farrell felt sorry for Mr. McIntire and made an omelette for him his fifth day on the job. It was a Basque *piperade*, with onions, two kinds of peppers, tomatoes, and ham. Farrell added a special blend of herbs and spices, acquired from a Bolivian lawyer in exchange for the lyrics of *Ode to Billie Joe*, and served the omelette to Mr. McIntire on a paper plate with pink and blue rabbit tracks printed all over it.

Mr. McIntire ate half of the omelette and abruptly put the plate aside, saying nothing, twitching his shoulders. But he tagged after Farrell all that afternoon, talking to him in a dry, mournful susurrus about mushroom and chicken-liver soufflés. "I never meant to wind up running a place like this," he confided. "I used to know how to cook burgundy beef, caramel baked beans. Bubble-and-squeak. Remind me, I'll show you how to make bubble-and-squeak. It's English. I used to go with this English girl, in Portsmouth, in the war. I was gonna open a restaurant in Portsmouth, but we broke up."

"My famous mistake," Farrell said to Ben and Sia that evening. "Stirring up the natives. He's already talking about messing with the menu, trying to sneak some real cooking in among the Thumper Thighs before Disney sues the whole wretched outfit right into Bankruptcyland. No more omelettes for Mr. McIntire."

He had been tuning the lute to play for them, and

now he began on a Holborne galliard; but Sia's silence made him fumble the first measures and stop. When he turned to look at her, she said, "But you might like that. To work for a man who is still discontent, who cannot quite resign himself to garbage. What's better, if you have to work for someone?"

"Nope," Farrell said. "Not me. When I'm a fry cook, I'm a fry cook, and when I'm a chef, that's another thing altogether. I don't mind giving, but I like to know exactly what I'm expected to give. Otherwise it gets confusing, and I have to think about it, and it troubles the music."

Sia stood up with a movement so decisive that it wiped out all memory of her ever having been sitting. Her voice remained low and amused, but Farrell knew after a week that Sia only moved quickly when she was angry. "Cock-teaser," she said. She took herself out of the room then, and Farrell more than half expected to see the lamps, the rugs, and the stereo go bobbing after her, the piano spinning slowly in the backwash. The strings of his lute were all out of tune again.

Farrell sat with the lute in his lap, wondering if there could conceivably be a Greek word that sounded like the one he had heard. He was going to ask Ben; but then he looked across the room at shaking shoulders inadequately concealed behind an oversized art book and, instead, he retuned the lute once more and launched into *Lachrimae Antiquae*. His attack was a bit harsh in the opening bars, but after that it was all right. Sia's living room was very good for pavanes.

Somewhere in the house, she stood still. Farrell knew it with his eyes on his flowing, melting left hand, as he knew it when Ben put down his book. Outside in the dark, Briseis whimpered at the kitchen window. The bass line was retarding perfectly, treading almost painfully along his tendons, balancing, walking his nerves like a high wire, while the treble danced in his scalp and skirled just under the skin of his cheeks. He thought about Ellen, and the thought was kindly. *I'm nice when I'm playing. I am really a nice fellow when I'm playing.*

When he finished and looked up, she was standing with her hand on Ben's shoulder, the other hand slowly unweaving her long braid. Farrell discovered that his hands and lips were cold. He said, "Sometimes I can do that."

She did not answer, but Ben grinned at him and said, "Hey, you play good." He held an invisible microphone close to Farrell's mouth. "Mr. Farrell, would you talk to us just a bit about the technique required for a proper interpretation of Dowland's music?"

It was an old game, one they had not played since his arrival. Farrell let his face go loose and silly. "Was that Dowland I was doing? Oh, man, I always think it's that other one, you know, what's that other limey? William Byrd, yeah. You sure that wasn't William Byrd?"

"All that kind of fairy music sounds the same to me," Ben said blandly. "Mr. Farrell, what about your legato? I'm sure every young lutenist in the country would be agog to learn the secret of developing such a silky, liquid, voluptuous legato."

"Yeah, I bet they would," Farrell said, chuckling. "Tell them I said they could all suck Clorox." He stood up to go to bed and had almost reached the stairs when Sia called softly, "Mr. Farrell." She had not moved, but was standing with one arm out toward him, gravely offering him her own microphone. *Queen Victoria with a trident,* Farrell thought. Beside her, Ben's face was briefly the old subway face again, gentle and boneless, seeming close now to snickering with embarrassment at a fat, grizzled woman in a long dress. The flesh of her outstretched arm sagged like a raincloud.

"Mr. Farrell," she said. "Could you tell our listeners, please, just what it has cost you to play like that? What you have chosen to give up?"

"Caramel baked beans," he said, and went on up the stairs, turning at the top, though he had planned not to do that. They were not looking after him, but at each other, and Sia was raising her brown fortuneteller's face to Ben's scarred one, as her quicksilver hair came down. From where Farrell stood, her belly's camber appeared as elegant and powerful as the arc of his lute. *What can it be like for them?* He caught himself trying for the first time to imagine the shifting weight of breasts as softly wrinkled as sand dunes, wondering what sort of teasing obscenities that contrary voice could possibly permit itself. *These deeds must not be thought after these ways—so, it will make us mad.* He grinned, shivered, and went to bed.

That night he felt them making love. Their bedroom was at the other end of the house; the only suggestive sound he ever heard from there was Briseis whining vainly to be let in. This was an understanding intensely beyond cries or creaking springs, an awareness so strong that he sat up, sweating in the dark, smelling her pleasure, feeling Ben's laughter on his skin as if he were caught up in bed with the two of them. He tried to sleep again, but the wicked sharing invaded him from all quarters, tumbling him in his own bed like a pebble in a flash flood. Shamed and terrified, he bit his mouth and clenched around himself, but the cry clawed free of him at the last, as his body shook loose from his will, resonating helplessly to the alien joy that used him in order to savor itself that much more and had already forgotten him as it let him go. He fell back to sleep instantly and dreamed that he was being murderously assaulted by the Thumper's bunny. Neon eyes weeping flames, it kept shaking him and screaming, "You're a spy! You're a spy!" And in the dream, he was.

At breakfast Ben corrected exams while Sia sat in the kitchen's small bay window with a newspaper, eating her favorite morning glop of yogurt, honey, mangos, and dry cereal and giggling softly over the comic strips. The one time she caught Farrell staring at her, she asked him to make her a cup of herb tea. She was dozing when he left for work, a dusty gray Persian cat sprawled twitching in the sunlight, and Ben was snapping pencil points and cursing middle-class illiteracy.

So, it will make us mad.

He literally ran into Suzy McManus, coming through the front door as he was going out. It was dangerously easy not to see Suzy; she took up so little space so quietly. She was a thin woman, almost gaunt, pale of eye and skin and hair, and her voice, addressing anyone but Sia, was equally anorexic, starved of all inflection. Only when she spoke with Sia did she even begin to take on color; and on the occasions when Farrell came on them laughing together, he was astonished each time to realize how young she was. He had promptly determined that he would make Suzy laugh himself, but it was all he could do to get her to talk to him, let alone understanding her mumbled responses to his jokes and questions. Now, righting her before she fell, he flirted with her, saying, "Suzy, this makes the third time I've knocked you down and stepped on you. Don't I get to keep you now?"

Suzy answered him in—as far as he could ever tell—

absolute seriousness, in her usual downcast whisper. "Oh, no, it takes much more trampling than that." She ducked her head abruptly, in a way she had, turning so that she almost looked directly at him, yet Farrell never saw her eyes. Then she vanished, which was another way of hers, slipping past him toward the kitchen, but trailing away into air before she reached the door. Farrell had a very bad day at Thumper's.

Farrell had spent a good deal of his adult life hunting up a new place to stay. In any other city he would have set out with the fewest possible expectations. But his image of Avicenna was ten years old and full of big, sunny rooms and flowery, winy, rickety houses where all his friends lived. It took him a week to discover that almost every one of the dear places where he had been drunk and in love and floating were now either parking lots or university offices. The few that remained were happily unchanged, except that their rents had quadrupled. Farrell stood for a while in the fuchsia-blurred courtyard under the window of Ellen's little room. He knew she was long gone from there, or he would never have made the visit, but it was a matter of continuity.

"There were so many good ones," he said to Ben. "Sometimes you couldn't remember whose house you were in, they were all so good."

"They were dumps," Ben said. "We were just too horny to notice at the time."

Farrell sighed. "Was that it? So much for golden lads and lasses." They were alone in the faculty locker room at the gymnasium, stripping to swim. Ben liked to go there at least twice a week, after his night class. Farrell said, "I miss them anyway, those times. Not me, you understand, just the times."

Ben glanced briefly at him. "Hell, you were homesick for everything while it was all going on. You just wandered along backward, fastest nostalgia in the West." He stuffed his socks into his shoes and put the shoes in his locker, and the compressed, delicate violence of the movement made Farrell think of a leopard floating with his ripped prey up to the fork of a tree. Ben had always been deceptively strong, the result of dutiful exercise, but his strength had seemed acquired, rented for the occasion, not a casual fire. He said, "Come on, drag you for beers."

Farrell was a good swimmer, for Ben had taught him, in the old days, all that a dolphin can actually tell anyone about moving in the water. He kept decently even with Ben for five laps, began to wallow a bit on the sixth, and hauled out to sit with his legs dangling and watch his friend working up and down the pool, arms reaping the water in short, flat slashes, head turning only slightly to breathe. Yet it struck Farrell strangely that once or twice Ben lost the water altogether, flailing and gasping in a moment of distorting terror. Farrell decided that it was one of the mysterious games Ben liked to play alone, for each time he caught his stroke immediately and swam on as powerfully as ever. After the second time, he climbed out at the far end of the pool and came around to Farrell, shaking himself dry.

"I'm sorry," he said. "It was meant to be a compliment, actually. You were always so aware of loss—you were missing things before it was fashionable, before whales and old people were in. I remember, you used to know whenever anything anywhere got paved over, or torn down, or became extinct. It wasn't nostalgia, it was mourning. You still doing that?"

Farrell shrugged. "Sort of. Sort of not. I'm getting a little old to go around keeping track of my defeats."

"It's an honorable calling." They sat by the pool, talking quietly, while jets of water from the inlets thumped against their hanging legs and lights fluttered in the Avicenna hills beyond the small wired windows. Ben asked if Farrell had been meeting old acquaintances, and Farrell said, "It's a little scary. Half the people I know are still striding around Parnell, taking anthropology classes and making the parties. They hang in different coffeehouses now, but it's the same faces. I can't go into that new place, the South Forty, without running into somebody who wants me to come over to the house and play *Fishing Blues*."

Ben nodded. "People hang on in Avicenna. This town is a La Brea tar pit for academic types."

"I'm hip. They come out to do graduate work and wind up shoplifting. Dealing. All the cabdrivers came out on the G.I. Bill in 1961 and flunked their orals."

"Of course," Ben said softly, "there's a point in your life when everyone starts to look familiar." Farrell looked sideways and saw him scratching and rubbing at the base of his throat—another habit of the bored, kindly, sardonic boy strayed from nowhere to slump next to him in assembly. Ben said, "I wish I'd flunked my orals."

"You can't fail tests," Farrell said. "You don't know how."

"Didn't know why, more like it." Ben was leaning forward, writing what looked like *Sia* over and over in the water with his toes.

Farrell said, "You like it here?"

Ben did not turn. "I'm a hotshot here, Joe. They work my ass off, but they know who I am. They'll give me tenure next year, and associate, and let me do about what I want to do. Because I mean business. Because I'm a goddamn first-class scholar of Icelandic literature, and there are maybe three others this side of the Rockies. I am aces around here."

"Then why are we both talking funny?"

Ben gripped the side of the pool, staring down between his legs into the water. He said without expression, "I like two of my undergraduate students and one graduate. No, all right, two graduates. I'm starting to cheat on my office hours, and I've been getting into fights with people at committee meetings, when I show up. There's this book I'm supposed to be writing, about style and diction in the later skaldic poetry. There is one hell of a big feud going on in the department, and most of the time I can't remember whose side I'm supposed to be on. Sometimes I can, and that's worse. It's really not too much fun."

"Well, it'll probably be a lot better for you next year." Farrell tried conscientiously to say something useful. "As you said, once you've got tenure, they'll let you alone. Let you write your own ticket, pretty much."

"A ticket to where?" The familiar sweet, shrewd gaze returned to Farrell, and he saw that the thin scar under Ben's eye was standing up, seeming to stir like a muscle. Ben said, "I don't think it is going to get any better. The boredom I could handle, but I hate feeling so contemptuous. I hate feeling myself getting mean. Joe, it's just not what I had in mind."

"I didn't know," Farrell said. "We never talked much about that part of your life, you never wrote how things were. I thought it was what you wanted, committees and all."

"Oh, wanting's different." Ben gripped Farrell's

41

forearm, not hard, but the urgency in the touch set the bones cringing together. "I did get what I wanted, and I probably even still want it, for all I know these days. But it isn't what I had in mind." He peered at Farrell, squinting with the need to make him see, as though he were tutoring him in chemistry once again. "It isn't what I had in mind."

A door yawped and sighed, and they both turned to see a tall, naked, white-haired man enter and stand peering at them down the pool. He had a massive, grainy face that reminded Farrell of the bowls of stone grapes and bananas in the gardens of Scotia Street. Ben said abruptly, "Go do a couple of laps, I want to watch you."

The white-haired man cried out in the thickest Scots accent that Farrell had ever heard, "Now by the rood, 'tis in sooth the guid laird Egil Eyvindsson of Narroway!" Farrell walked to the near end and went in. He dived too deep and came up off-balance, and it took him nearly a length to find his stroke. Each time he turned his head, he saw the white-haired man striding toward Ben, one arm out in greeting, skidding alarmingly on the tiles, but never deigning to grab for balance, so that he progressed at an increasingly rapid lurch. For all that, a kind of overripe stateliness steamed about him, and he bawled nobly in a voice like wooden wheels on a wet wooden bridge, "Egil, hail! Och, I was but seeking ye the noo! News o' Duke Claudio!"

Farrell swam back slowly, gurgling his delight into the water. When he rose beside them, the white-haired man was beaming down at Ben, rumbling and buzzing through a strangle of glottal stops. "I had it frae the laird Morton of Shaws—aye, I ken weel ye'll say he hath ever been but indifferently o' oor party—" Ben was digging at this throat again.

Farrell said, "How'd I do?" The white-haired man neither started nor turned. Ben said heavily, "You're kicking wrong." Then he turned to the white-haired man. "Crof, I'd like you to meet my oldest friend, Joe Farrell. Joe, Crawford Grant, Crof."

Farrell stuck up a hand from the water, feeling a good bit like the Lady of the Lake. Crof Grant said, "Pleased to meet you, Ben's told me a lot," in a clear New Hampshire voice, and his handshake was firm enough; but he never saw Farrell. There was no least stir of consent to Farrell in his face, no belief in the slaty hand that it closed on anything of substance. Before that placid, smiling denial, there was a moment when Farrell trembled for his own presence.

Crof Grant turned calmly back to Ben. "Yet for that reason itself do I believe his rede that the Duke Claudio inclineth ever mair toward the Laird Seneschal's favor—and if Claudio gaes ower, he'll take the best of King Bohemond's ain folk wi' him. Aye, ye'll scoff, Egil, but gin Claudio's for Garth, then the war's ower as we stand here, and ye'll mind I said so." There was more, but Farrell lost a lot of it after that.

Elbows hooked over the edge of the pool. Farrell hung in the water, fascinated and amused now that the blandly annihilating stare was turned from him. But Ben spoke severely across the serene babble, demanding, "Where'd you pick up that thing of kicking from the shins on down? Took me two years to make you get your whole leg into it, and now you just lie there and flap your ankles. Try it again, Joe, that's ridiculous."

Grant had never stopped talking. Farrell began to

swim slowly along the side of the pool, trying to concentrate on nothing but moving his legs from the hip and on feeling the thrust in his shoulders. Crof Grant's paperback medievalese bumbled on in the tiny waves under his cheek and in the wet tiles.

"Aye, Bohemond's no longer for the crown than the Whalemas Tourney, but what of that?" And again, chuckling thickly, "Egil, lad, ye're a bonny hand wi' maul or longaxe, but the craft o' the court still scapes ye." And twice Farrell heard the white-haired man say clearly, "'Tis the wee lassie they all fear. I'll tell ye straight, I fear the girl masel', each day the mair." He could not catch what Ben said in reply.

Grant finally thumped into the pool and began to swim—heaving himself along in a chugging, high-prowed breast stroke—and Ben beckoned sharply to Farrell. They dressed almost without speaking, though once Farrell asked, "What's Grant teach?"

Ben said, "Art history," never looking at him. In the yellow-green light of the caged bulbs, the fragile scar boiled up maroon.

During the steep, silent ride home, Farrell tilted the bucket seat back, stretched his legs out, closed his eyes and hummed *I Belong to Glasgow*. Ben finally sighed angrily and said, "It's like a running gag with Grant. We met at a costume party a couple of years ago. I went as a Viking skald, and Grant was a sort of Jacobite exile, all sporrans and haggis and the *Skye Boat Song*, the complete homemade Highlander. He's been doing it forever, since long before I got here. Rack of old swords in the office, and he walks around campus reciting laments for Falkirk and Flodden Field to himself. They say he's really impressive at committee meetings."

"All those other people he was talking about," Farrell said. "Sounded like mail call in Sherwood Forest."

Ben glanced sideways as the car took one of the Avicenna hills' Russian-roulette corners. There were few street lights here, and the car was crowded with the prickly, fragrant shadows of jasmine, clematis, and acacia. "I told you, he's like that most of the time. It used to turn off for his classes, but I hear it's even getting into the lectures now. He's got his own names for everybody, and when he's talking faculty politics, you're just supposed to know who he means. That's what all that stuff was about, the king and the war and whatever." He grinned then. "I will say, it does lend a certain grandeur to fights over who has to teach the freshmen this semester. Makes it all seem like the Crusades, instead of mud-wrestling."

"He called you Egil something," Farrell said. Ben nodded, rubbing his mouth. "Egil Eyvindsson. It's the name I used at the party. Egil was the greatest of the Icelandic skalds, and there was another man around the same time called Eyvind the Plagiarist. Professors at play."

They had parked in the driveway before either of them spoke again. Ben cut the engine and they sat still, looking up at the wishbone-sharp gables and the pagoda flare of the porch roof. Farrell asked idly, "How many windows on this side of the house?"

"What? I don't know. Nine, ten."

"That was yesterday," Farrell said. "Nine windows yesterday, eleven tonight. They never come out the same way twice."

Ben stared at him for a moment, then turned away to study the house again. Farrell said, "There are usually more of them at night. I'm not sure why that is."

"Eleven," Ben said. "Eleven windows, counting that half-sort of thing in the pantry." He smiled at Farrell, opening the car door. He said, "At my house, when we were kids. You remember how many times you fell down those last few stairs into the basement? All those years, and you never could keep track, you just kept stepping right off into space. Eleven windows, Joe."

He was halfway to the house before Farrell had even gotten out of the car. The front door opened for him, though no one was standing there. Farrell called loudly, following him, "They move around a little, too. Just a bit, but it's unsettling." Ben went on into the house without turning. The warm yellow light curled around him and lapped him up and swallowed him.

IV

*H*e told Sia about Crawford Grant a few evenings
later, while he was practicing. Ben was away at a meeting of the faculty senate. She sat in a chair with an old
newspaper in her lap, carving a block of some dark
wood into the shape of a woman. "I have heard of him,"
she said. "He sounds like half my clients—they just
know they would surely have been happy in some other
time, some other civilization. They play endlessly with
the stars, the Tarot, the ouija board, to find their real
home. Play that one I like again."

Farrell retuned the lute and struck into the Le Roy
galliard that was her current favorite. He loved practicing in the living room; the high ceiling did not dilute
the sound, nor the small rugs absorb it, and the notes
came out as hard and light as arrowheads. Sia said,
"The displaced ones, they are mostly who come to see
me. You can be uprooted from imaginary places too,
you know."

The galliard, being played too fast, lost its center of

gravity and flapped for balance like a child running downhill. Farrell started over. Sia did not look up from her work, but Farrell was coming to believe that her senses were not as stationary and specialized as those of other people. Her living hair watched his hands moving on the lute, if her head was bent away from him; he suspected that the brown, surprisingly delicate wrist that drove the X-Acto knife over wood as if she were caressing a child would have done as well. Thinking about that, he let the Le Roy drift to pieces again and irritably slapped the lute silent.

When she raised her head, he expected her to ask if she were distracting him; but she said only, "There is something wrong with your music."

"I missed practicing last night. You lay off even a day with this kind of tune, and it shows right away."

Sia shook her head. "I didn't mean that. Your music is beautiful, but it has no *place*, it belongs nowhere." Farrell could feel his face stiffening and flushing even before she said, "Your music is like you, Joe."

He made a joke of it. He said, "Well, lute music belongs wherever the acoustics are good. I always keep that in mind as I go along."

She bowed over the carving again, but she was smiling, showing her neat white teeth with the little spaces in between. "Yes," she said, "yes, you are a master at living in other people's houses." Farrell had been trying to float the galliard off the rocks; now he stopped playing for a third time. Sia said, "It is not such a bad thing. It is really quite lovely to see, like a hermit crab fitting himself into an empty shell. You can match yourself to any surrounding."

"That's chameleons," Farrell said. He fussed with the lute, running a cloth under the strings to dust the fingerboard, squinting as he checked the tied gut frets. The lute whispered in his hands, answering his anger.

Sia began to laugh. "But you are so *good* about it all." The knife never stopped its bright stroking. "The way you play in the evenings, every night, after you have washed the dishes. We would have to break your arms to keep you from doing the dishes. And the way you always bring home something extra on Thursday or Friday—wine, ice cream, cheese, pâté. Never cherries, not since the first time when I said they made my mouth hurt. You remember everything like that."

He stood up, but she made him sit again by moving her head. She said, "Oh, Joe, I don't mean to confuse you. There is nothing gone wrong with your radar; you are still perfectly welcome here for as long as you like." She had stopped laughing, but amusement continued to illuminate her voice, setting the words winking at each other. "You are good for Ben, and I like you; and in three weeks I am already in the habit of your little gifts and your music every evening. In another week you will have become indispensable."

Farrell said, "I should have a place by the middle of the month. There's a man supposed to call me at work tomorrow." There came a knocking, heavy and slow; it had a dull power behind it that made the whole house jar and ache. Sia went to the door.

The carving was of a woman growing on a tree like some lovely gall. She was free of the trunk from shoulders to thighs, and one knee was bent so that only her toes touched the tree; but her hair had just begun to emerge, and her hands still trailed in the wood to the wrists. Farrell fancied that he could see them, bending away as if they were shining through water. The woman had no eyes.

Farrell put the carving down as Sia came back, followed by a short man in a dirty overcoat. She passed the doorway quickly, pausing only to say, "Tell Ben I am with a client." Her face was flushed and angry; it made her look young. The man peered into the room and flinched from the sight of him, from the sight of everything, as Farrell had once seen a hospital patient recoil, one who had been so badly burned that the least stirring of the air around her was a firestorm. The man was no taller than Sia, but his shoulders were almost grotesquely wide and thick, and he walked with an awkward, flat-footed stamp, like a hawk on the ground. Farrell had a glimpse of an overshot, downturning mouth under a stiff yellow moustache, of pale reddish skin, and of small yellow eyes vague with terror.

The Le Roy was an unsalvageable shambles by now, and the Robinson fantasia that Farrell tried next came out equally as muddy. He gave up on tunes for the evening and went back to sixteenth-century finger exercises. They gave him the comfort of doing something fluently and room to think about the short man and the other frightened people who came to visit Sia.

She always referred to them as her clients—there was no surer way to anger her than by calling them patients. Farrell had rather expected them all to be pouty undergraduates, but they turned out to range from lawyers to parking-lot attendants, from a dance instructor to a paramedic to a retired policeman. A few seemed almost as withdrawn as Suzy McManus; most passed Farrell on the stair in a smiling frenzy of control. The night visit was in itself no surprise; Sia kept office hours of a sort, but Farrell had quickly grown used to the voices in the next room, crossing each other from all sides of his sleep—Sia talking in her voice that al-

ways made him dream of the ocean, the seabird misery
of the travel agent, and the headwaiter's hoarse complaining. Farrell could tell them apart in his sleep, by
sound, if not by sorrow.

Now, plinking his thirds and fifths and listening to
the sound of the yellow-eyed man's voice, he knew that
he had never heard it before. It was deep and slow,
almost drawling, and it spoke English with a sprung,
halting rhythm that put a dance step in the middle of
the few recognizable words and made them stumble
over weak vowels at the end. And Sia's voice, when
she answered was full of the same limping music, as
powerfully soothing as the man's was fear-tattered, but
no more comprehensible to Farrell, nor less disquieting. He changed his mind about tunes, and began on
Mounsiers Almaine as brightly as he could; but the lute
voice in his lap sounded to him now like a third stranger
singing upstairs.

From that evening, he gave up actively looking for a
place of his own. He began to pay for his board, inventing an amusing new name and reason for the pay-
ment each week; and he took over, little by little, such
chores as walking Briseis in the evening. The Alsatian
had fallen distractedly in love with him and would sleep
nowhere else but across his feet. He continued to bring
home imported delicacies around the end of the week,
to cook dinners occasionally and swim with Ben, and
to stay out of the way with a gracefulness that made
Sia smile. At night he helped Ben massacre slugs and
snails in the garden, convinced that he could hear the
windows snickering behind him as they winked on and
off. The house itself increasingly lured and alarmed
him; certain small rooms upstairs also seemed to come

and go entirely as they pleased, and he hung his clothes and stacked clean sheets in closets that never stayed quite the same size. He told himself that he was overimaginative and needed glasses, both of which were true. He never saw the yellow-eyed man again.

Now and then he still made a telephone call, or put in a few Saturday hours driving in Madame Schumann-Heink to investigate any advertisements that seemed safely out of the question. He no longer spent his free time studying bulletin boards in shopping centers and coffeehouses, but usually let himself be drawn up to Parnell Street, near the campus, where the sidewalks all but met, looping out in cake-icing swirls to protect fragile shade trees—trees had right of way in Avicenna—and constricting traffic to a single furious lane. There he sat outside a cavernous place called the South Forty, drinking bowls of *caffe latte* and watching to see whether the costumes were ever coming back.

Farrell had last lived in Avicenna during a time of half-wit marvels; a short-lived season when all imaginings were amill in the streets, wheeling and shrilling and rolling by like constellations. The country girls and the mountain men, the Chakas and Murietas and the innumerable starveling Christs, the double-breasted Cagneys and booted McQueens, the zombies and Rasputins, the pirates, the lamas, the Commanches—they were mostly gone now, leaving behind them, as far as he could see, only a lot of shaggy-styled businessmen, a lot of children named Cosmos and Startraveler, and the occasional clutch of bald, pale, pimply devotees in robes the color of canned tuna. Farrell missed costumes. He had enjoyed playing for them, whatever they concealed.

The strange part is, they were forever running around

*yelling at people to get naked, to strip off their masks
and let the sunshine in on their most secret faces, their
true and deadly dangerous and lovely selves. Not me,
boy—the more costumes, the better, you want my opin-
ion. Masks on top of masks, images like layers of winter
underwear, that's more like it. Costumes brighten the
air, and they still let you get your practicing done. Naked
people don't do either one, hardly ever.*

The day that he quit his job at Thumper's—early
spring and a new entree called Hippety Haunches prov-
ing an irresistible combination—Farrell spent looking
desultorily for construction work and for someone who
might be able to build a wooden case for the lute. By
five o'clock he had come conditionally to terms with a
cheerful Bengali cabinetmaker and he was feeling lazily
adventurous and pleased with himself when he wandered down to the South Forty for coffee and baklava,
a Holborne tune he had never been able to finger correctly suddenly beginning to explain itself to him.

There never were any empty tables at this time of
day. He sat at a table near the door, next to a young
man wearing white chinos, Hush-Puppies, and a purple
shirt with a map of the Hawaiian islands on it. The sky
was full of little shadow-bellied clouds, but the air was
honey-warm and seemed to have golden bubbles in it,
like honey; and everyone walking on Parnell, from the
backpacking Amazons to the tattooed, expectant mo-
torcyclists, moved as lingeringly as if they were journeying through honey, in that hour.

The young man in the Hawaiian shirt had not even
turned his head when Farrell sat down at his table; but
when Farrell went inside and returned with a glass of
water, the young man looked sharply round at him,
saying in a hoarse Kentucky voice, "I hope you aren't

planning on drinking that water." His square, lumpy face was ribbed lightly with acne scars.

"As a matter of fact, I was," Farrell said. "Got some baklava stuck in my throat."

The young man shook his head violently and actually moved the glass away from Farrell. "Don't you do it, sir. That water is poison. That water is nothing but plain poison."

I still pick them out, Farrell thought. *That hasn't changed, anyway. There could be one Ancient Mariner on the 747, and I'd sit down by him four out of five times, by independent laboratory test.* He said "Oh, I know that, but everything's poison these days. I surrendered way back when they were just painting the oranges."

"No, don't give up," the young man said earnestly. "Look, when you want some water, I'll tell you the best place to go to. Inverness."

He sat back loosely and grinned with freckled teeth. Farrell nodded, gazing straight away over the young man's shoulder. *My eyes get me into trouble. Look directly at this one and he'll follow me forever, nagging me about loving all creatures great and small.* But he said, "Inverness. Yeah, I've heard that's good water around Inverness."

"Go up there all the time," the young man said. "Gilroy too. Gilroy's not as good as Inverness, but it's all right. And Arnold. There's a little town called Arnold, they've got great water, better than Gilroy." His eyes were dark blue, unnervingly tranquil and benign.

For the first time Farrell noticed the empty glass on the young man's side of the table. He raised his eyebrows at it, but the other only smiled more candidly than ever. "I didn't drink any water out of that. You look and you'll see it's dry. I just come here for the glasses."

He looked warily to left and right; then, with a clumsy slapping motion, he swept the glass off the table. Farrell heard it break, not on asphalt but on other glass. He glanced down to see a wrinkled paper shopping bag squatting openmouthed by the young man's foot. In the sunlight the gleaming curved fragments were heaped as close and as brightly as snow. The young man said, "See, I eat glass. I'll eat all the glass there in two days, maybe three days."

Two feet away from them, three children were haggling loudly over the price of a drug designed to sedate the larger carnivores. A white man and a black woman, both middle-aged, strolled very slowly by, formally arm-in-arm, nodding slightly to acquaintances. Farrell saw them on Parnell every day, invariably dressed alike, whether in frayed suits of red velvet or in bib overalls faded to the color of nursing-home mattresses. He knew them to be direly poor and mad; and yet each afternoon at this time, the man's pace and manner reclad him in the grandly perilous dignity of an iceberg, a rhinoceros, while the black woman carried herself as if she were the swaying, murmuring clapper of a bell of crinoline and taffeta. At the table just behind Farrell, several Iranian students were beginning to hit each other.

"This place has the worst water in Avicenna and the best kind of glass," the young man said. "Funny, but that's how it is. Real quality glass."

Farrell cleared his throat. "You know, I really wouldn't eat all that glass. I really don't think you should."

The young man said, "I been struck by lightning two times." Farrell looked up and down Parnell, wishing with a sudden aching fierceness to see someone he knew coming along. "Once in the back, and once right in the back of the head," the young man said. "Two times." He was leaning across the table again, his meaty breath damp on Farrell's cheek. "That's why I eat glass. Good glass, colored glass a lot, like wine bottles. Desert glass, them old mason jars been out in the sun for years and years. I eat all that stuff."

The mention of wine bottles reminded Farrell that it was Thursday, his usual day to pick up some small dinner present for Ben and Sia. He scraped his chair, mentally choreographing his flight to clear sidewalk: a buttonhook around the Iranians to cut between the regular Rastafarian debating society and two women playing Purcell's *Trumpet Voluntary* on musical saws. Vaguely he thought that it might be useful to start wearing a hat or carrying something like a portfolio. *You put it on the table when you sit down, and when you pick it up even the Ancient Mariner knows you have to go.* He looked along Parnell once more, yearning angrily past the street merchants, the record shops and the tiny bead-curtained restaurants down to where the medical office complexes abruptly began. *I'm lonely,* he thought, *this nut's made me lonely. What a dumb thing.*

The young man said against his face, "And when I'm all full of glass, right up full, and it's all in my blood-stream and my bones and in my brain, and I go somewhere it's dark, in a closet or somewhere, how I'll shine! I'll be like one of them pictures you make with little bits of colored stones, tiles, I don't know what they call them—"

"Mosaic," Farrell said automatically. Then Julie Tanikawa drove her motorcycle slowly past the South

Forty, and Farrell got up and went after her without a word, bumping into tables.

Traffic was backed up for several blocks, as always on Parnell in the late afternoon, and the huge black BSA was barely moving at a walking pace. Farrell plowed into the street like a machine himself, bulldozer-blind and deaf to everything that was not Julie. On his way to her, he knocked a board covered with copper brooches out of the hands of a hobbitish young couple, caromed unaware off a pushcart selling hot soft pretzels, and charged straight through an incipient religious conversion. It never occurred to him to call her name.

The BSA was actually at a standstill when he reached it, Julie having braked for a covey of sign carriers who appeared to be picketing a speed bump. Farrell swung his leg over the bike, sat down behind her and put his hands lightly on her waist. "Akiko Tanikawa," he said in the whining beggar's voice of a Kabuki demon. "You wear short dresses and do not go to the ritual baths. You have broken faith with the eight million gods of Shinto. The footless dead will come to you when the grasses sleep and bitch in your ear."

Julie gasped softly and went momentarily rigid, but the traffic was moving again, forcing her to drive on without turning. Out of the side of her mouth she said, "Farrell, if that isn't you, you are in very deep trouble." The motorcycle jolted forward, nearly scooting out from under Farrell, who yelped as the tailpipe singed his ankle.

"Does this bus go to Inverness?" he asked. "I need a glass of water." Julie hit the brakes again, for no apparent reason, and Farrell's nose smacked hard against the back of her helmet.

She said, "This bus is off-duty, the driver carries only five dollars in change, and the first free moment I get I'm going to pound you into an omelette, Farrell. Jesus Christ, you don't just do that to someone, who the hell do you think you are?"

"Your old college sweetie," he answered meekly. "Who hasn't even known where you were for three years." Julie snorted, but the motorcycle accelerated a bit more smoothly, slipping past a low-rider convertible which was blocking traffic like a mauve kidney stone. Farrell said, "Who was so glad to see you that he got a little, as you might say, transported." He paused, and then added, "As someone was pretty damn transported to see him one time. In Lima, was it?"

Julie made a sharp and very sudden right turn, canting the BSA almost onto its side, like a racer, and gunning it uphill for two blocks as Farrell shut his eyes and clutched her. Handling the great machine as deftly as a feather duster, she whisked it to the curb in front of a fraternity house and cut the engine, pulling off her helmet as she turned toward him. "In Lima," she said quietly. "In the market." Farrell dismounted to let her haul the BSA up on its stand, and they stood the bike's length apart, wary and uncomfortable, staring at each other. He saw that she had let her black hair grow below her shoulders again, the way she wore it in college.

"I'm sorry," he said. "I was just grateful, you don't know." Julie studied him a moment longer; then blinked, shrugged, smiled like water breaking in the moonlight, and lunged silently into his arms. She almost knocked him off his feet—Julie was a strong woman and quite as tall as Farrell—and that was entirely proper, that was the only tradition they had ever had time to establish, unless you counted their habit of meeting one another in strange places, always unprepared. Farrell had thought often in the last ten years—though never when he was with her—that, of all the generous things that had happened to him with women, those first thundering embraces from Julie Tanikawa, after a suitable separation, were about the best. *Taking everything into consideration, like the fact that we can't stand each other longer than three days*.

"I was just thinking about you," she said. She leaned back against his arms, resting her own arms stiffly on his shoulders. Farrell nodded smugly. "Of course you were. That's because I called you here. You weren't even in Avicenna until maybe five minutes ago."

Julie raised one eyebrow, and Farrell recalled a long, tipsily innocent spring night she had spent in trying to teach him to do that. "Well, somebody's been feeding a cat on Brendan Way for the last two years." Farrell began an indignant growl, but she interrupted him calmly. "I'm no good about letters, you know that. Anyway, I knew you'd show sooner or later. One of us always conjures up the other."

He stood peering at her, frowning with the effort of relearning her face, as students ambled by, pushing bicycles and laughing through sandwiches. A dishy, merry, barn-owl face, every feature too large for conventional Western beauty, except the nose, which was too small. But her skin remained as clear and translucent as white wine, and the bones beneath were, at thirty, beginning to keep their old promise of pride and steadfastness. *Her face has secrets now, like Ben's face. I wonder if mine does*. Aloud he said, "Nothing changes. You still look like an Eskimo."

"You still haven't seen one." He realized that he had never held her this long before; usually, no matter how joyous the welcome, they let go quickly and stepped away, a single precise pace. This time, both of them trusted their full weight to the strength of the awkward clasp, leaning apart but keeping firm hold. They might have been children playing a street game, swinging each other inside a circle chalked on the sidewalk.

"You didn't marry old what's-his-face," he said. "Alain, the archaeologist."

Julie giggled. "He was a paleoethnologist. Still is, I guess, back in Geneva. No, I didn't marry him. Almost, though."

"I liked him," Farrell said.

"Oh, he liked you," Julie said. "They always do. You're such a nice fellow. They think you're not a threat, and you know they're not."

A couple of fraternity boys were shouting at them from a second-floor window, "Action! We want some action down there!" The night faces were coming on duty now, floating down toward Parnell like Portuguese men-of-war. Pierce/Harlow hurried by—Farrell would have sworn it was Pierce/Harlow—leading two Dobermans; and a woman lugging a huge signboard that likened a local judge, in four colors, to the Horned Beast of the Apocalypse, banged it savagely against Julie's legs to get past. And still they stood within their invisible circle, both gaping absurdly in growing bewilderment. One of them was shaking, but Farrell could not tell which one.

"That record you were going to make," she said, "with Abe and that crazy drummer. Danny."

"It didn't work out." Their voices were becoming steadily softer, cracking thinly.

"I looked for it." A monk shoved a lighted stick of

incense between Julie's fingers, and then asked her in a Bronx accent for a few pennies for Krishna. Farrell heard himself say wonderingly, "Let's go home."

Julie did not answer him. Farrell put his hand on the back of her neck. For a moment she closed her eyes and sighed like a child falling asleep; then, as the hooting from the fraternity house redoubled, she turned in his arms, saying angrily, "No, no, damn, that's absolutely all I need." Farrell began to speak, but she pulled his hand away, brushing it gently across her cheek before she let it go. She said, "No, Joe, I don't think so. It would be sweet and happy, but we'd better not."

"It's time, Jewel. It's exactly time, this minute."

She nodded, still not quite looking at him. "But sometimes you let things go by, even when it's time. Because you don't know what you'll be afterward."

"Hungry," Farrell said. "I'll cook dinner. I've never cooked for you." Two young men wearing mime-whiteface and Danskins passed them, talking about crampons, carabiners, and prusicking. Across the street, a candidate for something gave a printed flyer to a person dressed as a huge parrot. Julie said, "Joe, damn it, I'm going shopping, I have to pick up some drawing supplies, they close in twenty minutes."

Farrell sighed and lowered his arms, taking a step backward. "Well," he said. "Maybe it's not time." She looked straight at him then, but he could not tell whether she felt regret, annoyed embarrassment, or a relief as sour and jumbled as his own. He put his hands in this pockets. "Anyway, it's wonderful to see you," he said. "Look, I'm staying up on Scotia with a couple of friends. It's in the book, *Sioris*, it's the only one there is. Call me. Will you call me?"

"I will," Julie said, so softly that Farrell had to read

61

her lips to make out the words. He kept backing away, knowing—even without the whistles and guffaws of the fraternity boys—that he looked ludicrously as if he were withdrawing from the presence of royalty. But he knew also that she would not call, and it seemed to him that he had once again stumbled across something irreplaceable just at the moment of its extinction. He said, "Check the clutch on that monster, Jewel. It might be slipping a little."

He was striding briskly toward Parnell, shoulders only a little hunched, when she said, "Farrell, come back here," loudly enough that a baying chorus immediately took it up: "Farrell, you get back there this minute! . . . You heard her, Farrell!" When he turned, he saw her beckoning forcefully, ignoring the second-floor gallery. He approached her with some hesitation, wary of old of the half smile playing like a kitten with one corner of her mouth. The last time he had seen that particular smile, they had both been in a Malaga jail fairly shortly thereafter.

"Get on," she said. She pushed the BSA off the kickstand and straddled it, waiting for him. When he only stared, oblivious to highly detailed instructions from their audience, she repeated the command sharply without looking back as she tugged her helmet on.

"Shopping," Farrell said. "What happened to shopping?" Julie started the engine, and the air around the BSA danced to life, this time enclosing them within a roaring privacy—a momentary country, trembling at the curb. Outside, beyond their borders, the honey-slow twilight was thinning and quickening to a cold, dusty lavender. Skateboarders hurtled past like moths, urgently contorted, one-dimensional in the pale headlights rushing up the hill toward them. Farrell sat down behind Julie again.

"Where are we going?" he asked. The street was beginning to swirl around them, as certain protective inscriptions will do when the magic has been spoken right. Julie turned to face him and stood her stick of incense upright in his hair. "Let's wait and see where the bike wants to go," she said. "You know I never argue with my bikes."

V

My," he said, "what kind of motorcycle is a Tanikawa?"

"A dirt bike. Don't move, stay with me." She was propped on his chest, looking at him, her smile lifting as delicately as the corners of her eyes. The pupils were narrowing to normal size again. Farrell said, "You smell so good. I can't believe your smell."

Julie kissed his nose. She said, "Joe, you're thin. I never imagined you'd be so thin."

"Coyotes are thin. That's my totem, the coyote." He put a hand up to touch her cheek, and she let her head rest on it. "I never imagined you imagining me like that. Hussy."

"Oh, you try people on," Julie said. "Didn't you ever wonder about me at all? As much as you wonder?" Now she lowered herself against him, her face cool on his throat, her body surrounding him like water. But when he said nothing, she dug her chin into him and pulled his hair. "Come on, Joe, it's been ten years, eleven years now. I want to know."

"I thought about you," he said quietly. "Mostly wondering where you were, how you were doing." He caught her hands this time. "I didn't want to have fantasies, Jewel. You try strangers on like that, friends not so much."

"But we were always both," she said. "Or neither. Run into each other every couple of years, pal around for a few days until we fight. That's not friendship, that's just nothing. Scratch my back."

Farrell scratched. "Well, it keeps me hopeful, whatever it is. Even if I'm stranded in Bonn, or Albany, there's always that chance—turn one more corner and here comes Julie. New job, new language, new clothes, new man, new bike." He drew his fingernails up and down her hips, shivering with her. "Hell, you're my role model, I've been imitating you for years."

"And you say you didn't fantasize." She slid off him and pulled the coverlet over them, lying on her side with her legs drawn up, and looking suddenly homely and frail. Farrell tried to draw her close again, but her knees held him away.

"Yeah, all my men," she said. "And you were great buddies with all of them, and you weren't ever jealous, not once. Never watched me going home with Alain or Larry or Tetsu and thought about me being like this with them, lying and talking—"

"Larry who? Which one was Larry?"

"The lieutenant in Evreux. At the airbase. You used to play chess with him all the time. Joe, I think you're the biggest hypocrite I've ever known. I mean that."

Farrell lay back, looking around at the room. He

had no sense yet of being in Julie's home with her; it still felt very much as if they had fumbled drunkenly at the first door they came to, found it open, and fallen upon each other in a little free space granted them by an anonymous donor. But now, in the oval of light that the big bed-lamp threw, he began to recognize objects that he had seen with Julie in Evreux and Paris, in Minorca and Pittsburgh and Zagreb. *The three rows of copper-bottomed pots, the painting her sister did of her in high school, the stones and seashells she always has around everywhere; the brown, blood-cracked cape that wheezy old fraud of a bullfighter gave her in Oaxaca. Same red chenille bedspread, same stuffed giraffe, same ankle-munching coffee table she bought at a Seattle garage sale. Julie's a collector. I used to think she traveled light, but it's that men carry things for her and ship them for nothing.* All the same, a sudden spill of half-sorrowful tenderness and comradeship for Julie's friendly belongings made him shiver and take hold of her hair.

"Why did you call me back?" he asked. "I was walking off just sure I'd messed everything up forever."

"Maybe you have, I don't know yet. I wanted to find out what there was to mess up." She shrugged herself deeper under the covers. "Besides, it was time, you were right about that. One way or the other, we couldn't go back to being whatever we were. Kittens."

"Are you glad?" Julie closed her eyes. Farrell licked a sweaty place just below the nape of her neck. He said, "You taste like red clover. Little tiny explosions of honey."

Julie put her hand on his stomach, just below the ribs. "Thin," she murmured; and then, "Joe? Do you remember the time we met in Paris when I was in my car?"

"Mmm. I was dragging along Monsieur-le-Prince. You were just sitting there at the curb."

"I was supposed to take twenty airmen on a tour the next day and I'd forgotten all about it and I hadn't made any arrangements at all. So I was sitting and thinking about that. Then I saw you. You looked like hell."

"Felt like hell. That was my bad winter. I've never been that down again or in that much trouble. Not at the same time, anyway. Sitting in your car with you, that was the warmest I'd been since I got to France."

She patted him, still keeping her eyes closed. "Poor Joe, in your New York topcoat." A large, fluffy, white cat jumped up on the bed and wedged himself inflexibly between them, jacking up his rear and purring like a sewing machine. "This is Mushy," Julie said. "Old slobby Musheroo. He started out to be Mouche, but it didn't take. Did it, you fat fiend?" The cat kneaded her arm, but he eyed Farrell.

"You've never had a cat," Farrell said. "I don't remember you ever having pets at all."

"Mushy isn't really mine. He came with the house, sort of." Her eyes opened a few inches from his own—neither brown nor quite black, but a questioning, elusive darkness that he associated with no one else. "Do you remember that I was counting?"

"What?" he said. "What counting?"

"In the car, writing on the window. One, two, three, four, like that. Remember?"

"No. I mean, I do now, because you tell me, but not really. Move that cat and come see me."

Julie reached up suddenly and switched off the bedlamp. Farrell's retinas, long accustomed to hurry calls, did the best they could, filing away the high contrast of black hair slashing across a shoulder the color of weak tea, the small breast drawn almost flat by her movement, and the shadow of tendons in her armpit. He reached for her.

"Wait," she said. "Listen, I have to tell you this in the dark. I was counting me. Counting my cycle. I was trying to figure if it would be safe for me to take you back to my room with me. You looked so bad."

The white cat had fallen asleep, but he was still purring with each breath. There was no other sound in the room. Julie said, "It was a matter of a day, one way or the other. I remember that very clearly. You don't remember anything?"

The lights of a car slid over the far wall and part of the ceiling of Farrell's hotel room, making the bidet glow like a pearl and turning the half-empty suitcase at the foot of the bed into a raw grave. Beside him, across the snowdrift of the cat—*Paris winters are dirty, the air gets sticky and old*—Julie's round, tumbly-soft Eskimo face came and went again, as Julie herself came and went up and down in the world; as he would learn to come and go lightly too, if he didn't die, if he made it through this long, dirty winter. He said, "I was twenty-one years old, what did I know?"

For a moment he could not feel Julie's breath on his face. Then she said, "I just told you that to show you that I did think about you, even that long ago."

"That's nice," he said, "but I wish you hadn't told me. I don't remember a damn thing about the counting, or whatever, but I remember that winter. I think you could probably have changed the course of world history by taking me home with you. All that dumb misery would have had to go somewhere."

"Aw," she said. "Aw, poor topcoat." She picked up the cat and poured him gently off the bed. "Well, come here right away," she said. "This is for then. Officially. Old friend. Old something. This is for then."

In the morning he woke in bed with a suit of armor. Actually it was chain mail, slumped empty next to him like the gleaming husk of some steel spider's victim; but the great helm that shared his pillow dominated his waking completely. The helm looked like a large black wastebasket with the bottom reinforced by metal struts and with most of one side cut away and covered by a slotted steel plate, riveted in place. Farrell had his arm over it, and his nose pressed into the face plate—it was the cold, rough, painty smell that had awakened him. He blinked at the helm several times, rubbed his nose, then rolled onto one elbow, looking around for Julie.

She was standing in the doorway, dressed and laughing silently, fingers at her lips in one of the few echoes of classical Japanese manners that he had ever noticed in her. "I wanted to see what you'd do," she gasped. "You were so sweet to it. Were you scared?"

Farrell sat up, feeling grumpy and ill-used. "Should see some of the artifacts I've waked up with, the last ten years." He lifted a fold of the mail shirt, finding it surprisingly fluid for all its weight. "All right, I'll say it. What the hell is this?"

Julie came and sat on the bed. She smelled of the shower and of sunlight, and there was still a fuzzy bloom of water on her hair. "Well, this is a hauberk and this is the camail, to guard your throat, and these are for your legs, the chauses. It's a complete suit, except for the gauntlets and the arming coat, the padding. And the surcoat. Most people generally wear some kind of surcoat over their mail."

"Nobody I know does," he said. He thumped the

helm, which responded softly in the tense, eager way that his lute did when he spoke to it. Julie said, "That's not part of the suit. I made that one a long time ago. I just threw it in for effect." She smiled as Farrell blinked from her to the helm and back. "I made the chain mail, too," she said. "Guess what I used."

"Feels like coathangers. What I want to know is why. I know you can do anything, but it seems like a limited field." He fingered the silver-enameled links again; then peered at them more closely. "My God, these things are all welded shut. Did you do that?"

Julie nodded. "They aren't coathangers, though." She stood up, deftly taking the blankets with her. "Did anyone ever tell you that there's no bottom to your navel? It just goes on forever, like a black hole or something. Come on and get dressed, I have to go to work."

In the shower he guessed that she had cut springs apart to make the rings; over oranges and English muffins, she talked freely about interweaving them in a four-to-one pattern and about being taught to weld by a friend whose house she had decorated. But she would not say why she had made the armor, or for whom. "It's a long story, I'll tell you when we've got more time." Farrell could tease nothing further out of her. He let it go, saying deliberately, "Doesn't look nearly as much fun as throwing pots," so that she could escape into her favorite subject of ceramics. He knew just enough about it to ask fairly intelligent questions; but he liked to watch her talk about her skills.

After breakfast he drove her up to the university, where she did medical and scientific illustrating. "Cross-sections of vertebrae, detail studies of adrenal glands. I like it. I'm good at it." She had held the job for more than a year.

70

"You don't paint anymore," he said. "I'll have to take my easel back." He had made the easel for her five years ago, in Oberlin, the semester that she went back to school. Julie smiled slightly at her hands.

"I never painted," she said. "I can't paint. I can draw, so I do that."

Farrell said, "Jewel, you can do anything. It's made a difference in my life, knowing you can do anything."

"No, I can't!" she cried harshly. "Sorry to disappoint you, but I don't fool myself so much these days. Stop *imagining* me, God damn it, it's time for that too." Farrell heard her throat close down and her teeth click. She said nothing after that until he stopped the bus on campus, as close to her office as he could go. He opened the door for her and helped her down in a way that began as a chivalrous joke and ended with them standing in a soggy heap of paper plates and torn political posters with their hands on each other's arms.

"What happens now?'" he asked. "What are we now?"

Julie prodded his stomach thoughtfully. "Goodness," she said. "When I think I might have gone my whole life without ever knowing about that navel." She pulled his shirt down, tucking it in carefully. "I go out for lunch around noon," she said.

"I'll be job hunting. Meet you for dinner."

"There'a a Moroccan restaurant up near the Waverly. We can have couscous. I introduced you to couscous, didn't I?"

"In the Rue du Four. Do you know, we've never eaten in the same place twice?"

"No," she said. "Are you serious?" He nodded, thinking she would laugh, but she looked startled and sad. He said, "It's all right. One thing Avicenna's got, it's got restaurants."

"Don't," Julie said. Pain in her voice was as new a sound to Farrell, as if she had begun to crow or whinny—he hardly recognized it. "Poor topcoat," she said. She took his hands between her own and brought them to her lips, looking at him over them with mocking, marveling eyes.

"Just don't imagine me, that's all," she said. "Seven o'clock at Fouad's." She bit his fingers gently and left him there, watching her calm legs carry her away down a gravel walk and through a door. A momentary intuition that he would never see her again pinched his breath, as it had done the day before. *You can only watch someone go away so many times.* That was why—in spite of himself, in spite of what he had told Ben in the gym—he still mourned, grudgingly and foolishly, for so many doomed creatures and landscapes and ways of being that he had never seen. *To feel the loss, to know what was lost. To remember. That might be what I do best, after all. I hope not.* He got back into the bus and drove up to Barton Park in the hills, to see about the zoo.

VI

There was one job open, driving an electric train in the shape of an alligator around and around the zoo six afternoons a week, lecturing to his passengers about the animals they were glimpsing. Farrell had hoped for something to do with gorillas; but it was outdoor work, at least, and decently mindless. He agreed to start on the following Monday and left with a copy of the route and the recitation to memorize. There were five and a half jokes in it, underlined in red.

When he went home to change his clothes, he found the driveway occupied by a middle-aged yellow Pontiac, with the left front fender mashed into a rusty fist. He parked Madame Schumann-Heink a block further on and walked back to the house. There were skid marks behind the Pontiac where it had spun up the driveway, clipping off two of Ben's birdhouses and grinding a patch of wild rosemary to rags. The driver was still sitting behind the wheel, randomly pushing the tape deck buttons, but he looked up and opened the door as Farrell approached. "Hi there," he said in a cheerful, rather boyish voice. "Hey, you seen my wife yet?"

He was younger than Farrell, with a round, firm, deeply tanned face under a surfer's helmet of crusty white-blond hair. His sideburns were a shade darker, thick and stubbly; his mustache colorless, almost invisible. Farrell saw that his lower lip had been bleeding.

"I don't think so," Farrell said.

The young man got out of the car as he started past it. He was stockily built, Farrell's height but at least twenty pounds heavier. He said, "But you're going to see her."

Farrell stared. The man came closer, smiling. "I mean, if you go in there, into that house, you'll see her. I mean, that's where she works, isn't it?"

"Oh, Suzy," Farrell said without thinking, and immediately wished he hadn't. The young man's friendly expression did not change, but rather became fixed on his face, as if he had died. "Suzy McManus, right, you got it, good old Suzy. Well, I'm Dave McManus. Dave McManus. I'm good old Dave." He caught Farrell's hand and shook it long and gently, looking straight into the eyes all the while. His own hand was cold and wet and hard.

Farrell had seen pure white drunkenness before, but not often enough to recognize it at sight. He knew the thing itself, however—the freight train rattling and lurching comically from hilarity to slobbering sorrow, picking up speed as it passed through wild, aimless anger straight on into wild sickness; and then, running smoothly and almost silently now, into a dark place of shaking and sweating and crying, and out again with no warning to where a dazzling snowy light made everything very still. McManus neither swayed nor mumbled and hardly smelled of alcohol at all, but Farrell began to back away from him. McManus's smile widened with each step.

"I won't hurt you," he said. "I just want to see my wife, the same as you do." He patted his windbreaker pocket, and Farrell saw how heavily the fabric shifted and swung. "You take me on in there. In the house."

Farrell took another step backward, trying to angle himself toward a parked car. McManus patted his pocket again and shook his head earnestly. "Come on, there's a dog. I don't want to hurt the dog."

"She's a trained killer," Farrell warned him. "They had her in the Army, she used to give courses." He was trying desperately to assess the chance of Suzy's being in the house that morning. McManus put his hand in his pocket and whistled two notes. Farrell walked slowly past him and up the porch steps.

Briseis met him at the door, whining nervously at the sight of the stranger crowding in behind him. For a moment Farrell entertained a mad vision of scooping the Alsatian up in his arms and hurling, or at least shoving her at McManus. But the man was too close, and Farrell knew himself just as likely to rupture something important or throw his back out. McManus stooped to scratch Briseis's ears, and Farrell tensed, thinking, *This is not happening*. Then Suzy came out of a tiny sewing room into the hallway.

When she saw McManus, she caught her breath, started to speak, and then shut her mouth and very carefully set down the sponge mop and bucket she was carrying, leaning the mop against the wall. "Dave," she said, and stood waiting.

McManus's ragged lower lip started to bleed again.

Tears sprang out of his eyes in a sudden dreadful spurt, more like shotgun pellets than drops of water. "Bitch, fucking bitch!" he shouted at her, his light voice splintering into shrill fragments. "Bitch, I love you!" Suzy turned and ran for the living room, and McManus shoved Farrell aside and leaped after her, tugging at his pocket. He promptly tripped over Briseis and fell flat, landing with the gun under him. Briseis, who expected the end of the world at any given moment, screamed in confirmation of her worst forebodings. She threw herself on Farrell for comfort, buffeting him so frantically that he almost fell himself. McManus scrambled to his feet and lunged toward the living room. He had torn his pocket getting the pistol out.

"Do you come here often?" Farrell asked Briseis. There was a crash in the living room, and McManus yelled, "Well, shit, don't blame me for that!" Farrell went into the room in a crouching waddle, taking cover behind chairs. Suzy was halfway up the stair; but, as he watched, she paused, turned, and started slowly back down toward McManus, who was standing over the shards of a stoneware lamp. "No," she said, astonishingly loudly. "No, why should I run from you?"

McManus, who had been steadying the gun with both hands, now let it fall to his side. For the first time, he suddenly looked drunk. He chewed his bleeding lip and sniffed, muttering, "Okay, okay, come on." But Suzy shook her head, and to Farrell's amazement she smiled.

"No," she said again. "Go home, Dave. I'm not coming with you, and I'm not running away from you anymore. I just now realized I don't have to. She showed me."

"Bitch," McManus whispered. "Bitch, bitch." Farrell could hardly hear him; and indeed, the words

seemed not to be addressed to Suzy at all, but to someone remembered or imagined. "She showed you. Blow
her fucking head off, she showed you." He raised his
head and smiled suddenly, coldly in touch with his drunkenness again. "I love you, Suzy," he said. "You know
I love you. Look, I threw Mike out, I mean for good,
like you wanted. I just said, 'Out, man, Suzy's coming
home.'" Something in the little shrug and cavalier flip
of his free hand—like a Chaplin back-kick—made Farrell see for a moment what Suzy might have loved.

"But I'm not coming home," Suzy said gently. She
came all the way down to the last step, which put her
on a level with McManus, and she met his eyes with a
frail, compassionate dignity. She said, "Take care of
yourself, Dave. I'll be all right." Abruptly she ducked
her head, kissed McManus on the cheek, and started
past him toward the kitchen. "Cleaning," she said,
"Floors."

Later Farrell thought that she might have gotten
away with it, except for the kiss. McManus blinked after
her and seemed to slump into himself, rubbing his jaw
and mumbling, actually beginning to turn away. Then
his hand brushed the place where Suzy had kissed him,
and without a word, he turned and swung the gun up
at arm's length, pointing it at her back.

Farrell shouted, and Suzy looked back and cried out,
"*Mother, help me!*" The shot sounded like a baseball
bat slamming down on the living room floor. Farrell
went over the coffee table, but McManus was down
before he reached him, clutching his leg and wailing in
a kind of terrible gargle. The room smelled of badly
burned toast. Suzy started toward her husband, almost
stepping on the pistol as she did so, and then halted,

as frozen as a deer in headlights, looking past Farrell. Sia was on the stair.

She was wearing a long, flowered dress that hung on her like a tablecloth, and she carried a red plastic comb in her right hand. The air tightened on Farrell as he stared at her, trapping him as if in thrashed, sweated bedsheets. Her face was without expression, her voice small and colorless when she said to McManus, "Stand up. Stand up on your feet." Her own feet were bare, wide, and quite clearly as flat as bread boards.

"He can't." Suzy protested. "He's hurt himself, he needs a doctor." She knelt beside the gasping, whimpering McManus, trying to keep his hands from the wound. The small distant voice said, "Stand up," and Farrell felt the two words grind together like millstones. McManus stopped crying.

"Stand up," Sia said once more, and McManus climbed upright and stayed there somehow, his open, straining mouth making him look as if he were waiting to belch. The bullet had apparently gone through the calf of his leg; there was comparatively little blood. He moved his lips weakly, saying, "The gun."

"Go away," the voice said. "Never come near this house again. Never come near her again. She is under my protection, and if you trouble her, you will die. She is one of mine. Go now."

Again Suzy declared, "Oh, he can't, don't you see he can't walk? We have to call a doctor." But Sia gave no sign of having heard; she moved her disheveled head slightly, and McManus, as if on wires, made a single lurching hop toward the door. His face was as white and wet as cottage cheese, and the reek of his pain burned in Farrell's nostrils.

A plump figure appeared in the living room doorway, trailed by a tiptoeing Briseis. Farrell recognized the man as one of Sia's more wistful clients. He said, "The front door was open, so I just," peering at the scene with a ruminant's unfocused near-interest. Nothing in his round, freckled face, puckered thinly like an aging balloon, suggested even momentarily that he smelled gunpowder or saw the smashed lamp or any blood.

Farrell, Suzy, and McManus gaped silently at him, but Sia nodded calmly, saying in her normal voice, "Hello, Robert, just go on along." She stepped aside to let him by, and he went up the stairs without looking back. No one spoke or moved until the door of Sia's office rattled overhead.

Suzy went to support McManus, but he pushed her away violently, summoning all his numbed vitality to make himself step toward Sia. Over his shoulder he said to Suzy, "You better go on up there, baby, the man's waiting." Farrell fully expected to see him lunge bare-handed up the stairs at Sia; his voice was slow with pain, and with the loneliness of great hatred, and he looked at Sia fearlessly. "One of yours," he said. "Yeah, I bet she's picked up a few new tricks since you've had her. Hey, I'd pay to learn them, I can pay."

The good leg buckled under him—though Farrell saw nothing that could have made him slip—and he crashed to his knees before Sia at the foot of the stair. Sia neither moved nor spoke. Farrell smelled wet earth, wet crushed grass, something like coffee, something like the fur of a dead animal. He heard a whimpering, took it first for Briseis, and then understood that the sound was happening in his own throat. He could not make it stop.

This was nothing like the reflected image he had seen

of the huge woman with the dog's head. Sia herself was hardly there at all; she seemed to thin and dwindle almost to transparency, even in Farrell's mind. But for one truly unbearable moment—one instant in which names for things had not yet been invented—he was more aware of her presence than he ever had been of his own. He felt her breathing in the stairs and in the old floor under his feet; she surrounded him with her walls and her rooms, moving in the stones of the fireplace, looking at him from the pieces of the broken lamp, speaking in the sunlight's darting scrawl across the living room rug. Beyond the house, there was only more of her, no least refuge inside himself, for she was that place, too, laughing in his bones, teasing his atoms to make them rattle in the dark like dice. However he turned, he fell toward her, terribly content.

Beside him, McManus crouched lower and lower, his limbs spraddling as if a great foot were crushing him to earth. As Farrell watched, the weight seemed to release him, and he rose slowly and half hopped, half hobbled toward the front door, drawing in his breath with every step. Suzy started to follow, but the woman on the stair looked at her, and she put her hands to her mouth and went into the kitchen. Farrell heard McManus stumbling and cursing wearily under a window, and then the sound of the Pontiac's engine.

"I couldn't see what happened," he said. "With the gun." Sia smiled at him in mild puzzlement. Farrell said, "She called you *mother*."

Sia plucked at the front of her dress, the nervous habit of a heavy woman. "I must go up to poor Robert," she said. "He will spend half our time now apologizing for coming in without knocking. Such a strange arrogance they have, the timid ones; how they peep at themselves." She sniffed and rubbed her nose, having had a cold for two days.

Farrell watched her hoisting herself up the steps one at a time, pausing on the landing to sigh angrily, as she always did. Briseis came to shove her muzzle into his hand, and Farrell petted her, saying absently, "It's all right, don't be scared." But Briseis smelled the gunshot and the blood, and she simply lay down flat, too overcome by human confusions even to whine. Farrell said, "Don't think about it, that's all. Just be a dog, that's what I'm doing." He took her outside to sit on the front steps, where she found her favorite ragged beach towel and killed it several times, while he played some of Henry VIII's songs for her.

VII

Julie and Farrell's record for mutual toleration was slightly less than five consecutive days, set almost eight years before on Nantucket. They celebrated their sixth day together by going again to the Moroccan restaurant, where they had couscous and warm, bitter champagne. Farrell spent the first half of the dinner in playing happily with Julie's fingers and grinning at her; and the second half in telling her, headlong and in no order at all, everything he could put into words about Sia and Ben and Suzy's visitor. Julie listened silently, attentive but expressionless, until he ran out of champagne, fingers, and phrases to describe Sia barefoot on the stair in her flowery dress. "She just took up all the room," he said. "All of it, everywhere."

Julie said slowly, "So after that, you went and washed up, you put on a clean shirt, and you met me here for dinner. And you talked about us. You talked about *Barney Miller*, for God's sake, about running into my sister's ex-husband—"

"I didn't think you'd believe me," Farrell said. "Do you? Tell me you really believe one word of all that UFO craziness I just dumped on you. Come on, one word."

He had let go of her fingers, the better to wave his own hands. Julie reclaimed them now, dipped his fingertips in the couscous gravy, and then licked them daintily, one by one, looking at him. She said, "I don't believe words. I believe you. There's a difference."

"Meaning I hallucinate, but I don't lie. Right. Bless you, Jewel."

"Meaning you're scared," she said. "I've never seen you scared before, not even in Lima. Not that you're so wildly heroic—it's more that you're too curious about whatever's going on really to notice the fear. But this one has all your attention. You saw what you saw."

Farrell sighed and shrugged. "Maybe, but I'm losing it. There's something I know, but it keeps slipping and scrabbling further away from my mind, trying to get back to her. Now I can't remember the way it was— just what happened, and that's different, too. I don't know what I saw."

"What about Suzy?" Julie asked.

Farrell rolled his eyes in exasperation. "She was stunned, she was terrified, she was hysterical, and besides she was looking somewhere else at all the interesting moments. That's what she says, anyway, and by now I'm sure it's perfectly true. People are watching you doing that, Jewel."

Julie nodded complacently, smiling against his fingers. A turbaned waiter swept their dishes off the table like frisbees and swept back a moment later with little cups of coffee as hot and slow as lava. Farrell said, "The gun turned in his hand. He didn't drop it, and he wasn't holding it carelessly, God knows. Suzy called, '*Mother*,' and the gun wriggled and pointed at him and shot him. I keep waiting to forget that part.''

"What happened to the gun?" Farrell shrugged again. Impatiently she demanded, "Well, what happened afterward? I mean, it's been five days, do they talk about it at all, at breakfast? Did the neighbors hear anything, did anybody call the police? I can't believe it's all just going along.''

"That's what it's doing, all right," Farrell said. "No cops, no neighbors, nothing's changed. Ben just says he wasn't there, and Suzy pretends she wasn't there, and old Sia, she don't say nuttin'. Believe me, the matter does not come up at mealtimes." Julie let go of his hands. Farrell went on, "The one I'd really like to talk to is Briseis. She saw it all and she believes her eyes. She won't go near Sia.''

Julie said, "Tell me about her. Not the dog. Sia."

Farrell was silent, matching stares with the waiter, who had already greeted two newcomers at the door and was pointing to their table. He said finally, "There's a grizzly bear up in the zoo. It's amazing how small and slumpy that animal can look, until it moves.''

"Does she attract you?" Farrell's mouth sagged open. "Leaving me out of it—and Ben, and anything else. Would you go to bed with her?''

"Jesus, Jewel," he said. Julie kicked his foot lightly under the table. She said, "When you start talking about bears.''

Farrell said very slowly, "The thing about the grizzly, there's no limit to it. You look at it for a while, you think about it, and you can't possibly imagine where its strength begins or ends. And it's fat and swagbellied and sort of pig-faced and it's attractive too.'' He had not tried to tell her about the night when Sia's pleasure in another room had forced his body to connive in its own solitary ransacking. "It's attractive," he said again. "That kind of power always is, especially when it's got a beautiful silvery-brown coat, and it moves just a little like a human being. But it's a bear."

Julie wanted to walk, so they strolled up two blocks to pay their respects to the Waverly Hotel. The Waverly was eighty-seven years old, and had looked just as strange in its own time as it did now. It was supposed to have been modeled after a Burgundian castle, and it did at least look more like a castle than like anything else in the world. There were round towers and square towers, dunce-cap turrets and Moorish arches and galleries, a functioning portcullis and a sally-port, a driveway approach in the form of a drawbridge, and a stone-flagged courtyard with parking stripes. It changed owners every few years, but was still quite popular with certain conventions.

On a clear night, the Waverly could be seen from Parnell Street—a great drowsy bubble, pink and purple and green, floating softly up out of the hills. Farrell and Julie walked with their arms around each other's waists, leaning together, playing a favorite game of singing improbable combinations of songs in counterpoint. Farrell was chanting "*Il était une bergère*," while Julie gleefully ravaged "*Good Morning, Little Schoolgirl*."

In front of the Waverly, they fell silent, standing under the portcullis and looking straight up into the marzipan radiance. Farrell saw only a scattering of cars in the parking lot and a few people clustered at a side door; but even so, the hotel seemed to resound and tremble with light, like an acacia in bee time. Julie said against his shoulder, "It would be lovely if you could give a concert here someday. You'd never have a better setting for the music."

When he did not answer, she raised her head and looked at him curiously, saying, "Now that made you sad. I could feel it happen in you. What is it, Joe?"

"Nothing," Farrell said. "I don't really give concerts much these days, especially in the good settings. They just make the music feel more dead than it is, and I don't need that. I already know."

"Old buddy," she said. "Childhood sweetheart, moon of my delight, I hate to hurt your feelings, but you aren't exactly the only Renaissance musician in town. Since I moved back here, I've never seen so many classical guitarists, so many countertenors, so many little groups tootling away on their recorders every Tuesday night. You can't throw a rock and not hit someone playing Dowland on a street corner. How can it all be dead, with everyone going at it like that?"

"Because that world's gone," Farrell said, "the world where people walked around whistling that music. All the madrigal singers in the world can't make that other one real again. It's like dinosaurs. We can put them back together perfectly, bone for bone, but we don't know what they smelled like, what kind of sounds they made, or how big they really looked standing in the grass under all those fossil fern trees. Even the sunlight must have been different, and the wind. What can bones tell you about a kind of wind that doesn't blow anymore?"

A cab turned in from the street, and they stepped aside to let it go by, bumping along the silly drawbridge. The driver looked dour and embarrassed. Julie said, "Worlds are perishable. Do you want people not to play

Mozart because they can't ever hear the music with the ears he meant it for?"

"I don't mean it just like that," Farrell began; and then, "No, by God, I think I do mean it like that. Music should be daily. They ought to stop playing a composer's music as soon as the last one who knows what it means is gone. The last one who knew the noises. The stuff I play has hawkbells in it and mill wheels and pikes all grounding at once. Chamber pots being emptied out of the window, banks of oars rattling into the water. People screaming because the hangman's just held up somebody's heart for them to see. I can't hear the noises, I just play the notes. Shouldn't be allowed."

Julie studied him sideways, frowning a little. She said, "People miss the whole thing about you, don't they? You're not really a compromising, adaptable type at all. You're a bloody fanatic, Joe. You're a purist."

"No," he said. "It's like the trouble I have when I travel. Wherever I go, I always want to spend a lifetime there. Anywhere—Tashkent, Calabria, East Cicero. I always want to be born there and grow up and know everything about the place and be horribly ignorant and die. I don't approve of flying visits. It's the same thing with the music, I guess. Smells, noises. I know it's dumb. Let's go back to your place."

Julie put her arm through his. Farrell could feel her sudden silent chuckle tugging at him like a kite. The almost-black eyes had turned golden and transparent in the flare of the Waverly. She said, "All right. Come on, I'll take you where the noises are."

At her house, she darted in and out of closets while he stood scratching his head; she foraged briskly through drawers and sea chests, tossing bright, soft garments behind her onto the bed. Farrell fingered in astonishment over a rising drift of tights and tunics, horned headdresses, and heavy painted hoods; long furred and scalloped gowns, split from high waist to hem, with bell-shaped sleeves, square shoes and shoes with curling tips, and stiff short cloaks like *muletas*. He tried on a tall, round-crowned hat, a sort of fur derby, and took it off again.

"I like costume parties," he ventured at last, "but that isn't really what I was talking about."

Julie paused briefly, regarding him across the rainbow heaps with a familiar flash of affectionate irritation. "This isn't costume," she said. "This is clothing." She tossed him a pair of hose with one leg striped vertically in black and white and the other plain white. "Try these on for a start."

"Did you make all this stuff?" He sat down on the bed to take his shoes off, slightly damaging a hat like a Shriner mosque. "You have some expensive hobbies, love."

Julie said, "It isn't as extravagant as it looks. Most of the material is synthetic—I use terrycloth a lot and I've made things out of ordinary blanketing, outing flannel. There's velvet, some silk and taffeta, some upholstery brocade. I use what I've got, unless people want to pay extra for something special. Rats, I don't think I like those tights on you. Try the brown houppelande."

"The brown what?" Julie indicated a high-necked gown, the full sleeves lined in black and the skirts held together in front by an enameled girdle. Dutifully struggling into the gown, he asked, "What people? Whom do you make these things for?"

"All will be revealed," she told him in a hoarse gypsy

whisper. She considered him abstractly as a design of folds and flows, shaking her head slowly. "It would do, but I don't know. I hate to waste your legs. No."

Eventually she decided on plain hose and a dark blue doublet embroidered with green and gold diamonds and *fleurs-de-lis*. The waist was tapered sharply, and the sleeves were split all the way up the inside of the arm. She gave him a pair of low, pointed shoes and a soft velvet cap and said happily, "You're fun to dress. I could play with you all evening. Go look at yourself."

Farrell stood before the mirror for a long time, not at all out of vanity, but only to make the acquaintance of the slender, burning stranger in the glass. Under the high cap, his face was younger than Farrell's and differently made; the nose was longer, the eyesockets notably more arched, the forehead rounder, the wide mouth grown curiously shadowed and secretive, and the whole off-center cast of the face at once as unnervingly tranquil and as deeply, casually ready for violence as that of a knight on a tomb rubbing or an angel on a stained-glass window. *Is that me? No, it's the light in here, it's the mirror, the mirror's warped or something.* Behind him he could see Julie undressing, her head back as she fumbled with a zipper. The man in the glass watched her, looking quickly back at Farrell now and then. *Is that me? Do I want it to be me?*

For herself, Julie chose a long, simple gown, deep green and close-fitting; and over it, she wore a garment like a full-length apron, almost the same clear, pale amber as her skin. The apron had no sides, being joined only at the hips and shoulders. Julie smoothed her hands down the dark ellipses and told Farrell, "They used to call these the Gates of Hell."

"When did they stop?" he asked, and she giggled.

"This is prim, this is inhibited. High medieval clothing is the most sensual stuff anybody ever wore. I made a kirtle for the Lady Criseyde once—" She stopped, and then asked him, "Do you wonder where I'm taking you? What are you thinking?"

"I still think it's a costume party. With any luck, maybe a costume orgy."

Julie did not laugh. She said very quietly, "That happened once. You wouldn't have liked it."

A short green cloak for him, a longer gray mantle over her shoulders, the hood shrouding her loose hair, and she was saying in the milky night, "You'll have to drive the bike. I'll tell you how to go."

Farrell blinked at the BSA lowering at the curb like a cumulonimbus. Julie put her key ring into his hand. "I can't drive in this outfit, and I feel like taking the bike. You always like to drive my machines."

"Not in the Macy's Parade," he grumbled. "It's bad luck to humiliate a BSA." But he was already unlocking the front fork, greedily but with a certain proper deference. He thought of Julie's motorcycles as her familiar demons, a cross between hippogriffs and pit bulls.

Julie lived three blocks off Parnell, almost on the invisible line dividing student Avicenna from the rest of the town. She rode sidesaddle, one arm lightly holding Farrell's waist as he guided the BSA gingerly up to Parnell. "Like London," she said, "when we used to sneak out at night so you could practice. Because you didn't have a permit."

"And you didn't have title to the bike. I was so impressed with you, stealing bikes and all like that. My outlaw."

"Actually, I was just late getting the papers. But the

other was more fun for you." She directed him north, toward the university.

Every record store was open late, and all car radios and portable tape decks were at full volume, speakers bellowing back and forth like rutting alligators. Farrell eased along Parnell, passing like a diver through the shifting currents, temperatures, and textures of sound. The street simmered and banged in its own lemon-butter light—on this Saturday night at least a little like the old times, when every corner had been an Arab marketplace and all doorways were inhabited by lovers, thieves, and businessmen, by troubadours and children with cellophane eyes and faces made of hard candy. Julie leaned against Farrell's back and chanted softly in his ear:

> "The hag is astride,
> This night for to ride—
> The devil and she together. . . ."

An improbably tall, impossibly thin black man was standing in the middle of the street, flouncing gently as he considered the drivers who passed him by, waving them along with an outsized, flowing blissfulness. The BSA was moving almost at a walk as it reached him, and he had leisure to study Farrell and Julie's faces and clothing, to pat their heads solemnly, and to bend down to them. His face was concave and burnished, smooth as an old wooden spoon. They felt the light, lost, mocking touch of his voice: "Remember me to the girl. Oh, tell Aiffe of Scotland to remember Prester John."

Behind Farrell, Julie said sharply, "Turn right here." Farrell nodded to the black man and cut past a movie theater whose marquee advertised a Rhonda Fleming retrospective, gunning the motorcycle uphill into darkness again.

"That's more like it," he said happily over his shoulder. "Prester John of Africa and India, the one whose cook was a king and whose chamberlain was an archbishop. That's where the Fountain of Youth was, in Prester John's country." Julie said nothing, and he went on thoughtfully. "Aiffe of Scotland. I almost know her, too—sounds like someone in an old ballad." What the name actually brought back to him was the warm, prickly sourness of the swimming pool and Crof Grant nattering on about a girl he was afraid of. He said, "This town always did have the most erudite loonies."

"He's not a loony. Don't you call him that." Julie's voice was hard and low.

"I'm sorry," Farrell said. "I didn't know you were friends. I'm sorry, Jewel."

"We're friends. His name is Rodney Micah Willows."

Farrell opened the BSA up a bit, heading into the hills toward Barton Park. Julie's hood blew back, and her hair snapped along his cheek. She tucked herself closer against him, murmuring the witch-poem once more:

> "The storm will arise
> And trouble the skies,
> This night; and, more the wonder,
> The ghost from the tomb
> Affrighted shall come,
> Called out by the clap of the thunder."

They entered the park at the south end, on the opposite side from the zoo. The main road spiraled up-

ward around a shaggy, bulging foothill, widening
occasionally into shaved areas where redwood tables,
benches, washrooms, and seesaws flourished under the
redwoods. Beneath a tarnished-silver sky, the picnic
structures all stood up like great slabs of granite, appointed to guide an extinct mathematics and uphold a
faith, with thin, shallow rills to lead the blood away.
*California Stonehenge. They'll think we used the whole
park for predicting earthquakes.*

Smaller paths ran away from the camping areas down
to baseball fields and cinder tracks or up and in through
groves silted ankle-deep with redwood mold, smelling
like cool, powdered armpits. Julie directed Farrell onto
one of the steep grades, and he followed it slowly down
a black arcade of trees with a mandarin moon brooding
in their top branches, until he came out suddenly into
a meadow and saw lights jigging far ahead.

"We'll walk from here," Julie said as the cars and
motorcycles began to drift into shape on both sides of
the path. Farrell cut the engine and heard owls. He also
heard Gervaise' basse-dance *La Volunté* being played
by crumhorns and a rebec. The tune twinkled across
the meadow, cold as coins, tiny and shining and sharp
as new nails.

"Be damned," he said softly. He parked the BSA
near a Norton and told them to play nicely. Julie and
he walked on toward the lights. She linked her arm in
his, letting her fingers lie along the inside of his wrist.

"Pick a name," she said. *La Volunté* ended to the
sound of laughter. There was a dark tent, floating at
its base like a distant mountain.

"Lester Young. No, Tom a'Bedlam." She stopped
walking and stared. "You know. *With a host of furious
fancies, whereof I am commander—*"

"Be serious," she said with surprising fierceness. "Names mean something here, Joe. Pick a good name, quickly, I'll tell you why later."

But the music had made him pleasantly frisky, rocking him gently in the sweet air. He said, "All right, Solomon Daisy. Malagigi the Dwarf Enchanter. Splendid name." The consort began to play another Gervaise piece, a pavane, giving it the slow, gracious lilt that makes a pavane something more than procession. "How about John Amend-All? Big Jon and Sparkie? You could be Sparkie." The music sounded no closer as they approached the pavilion in the meadow. An owl was overhead, moving like a great ray flying in the deep sea. Farrell put his arm around Julie's shoulders and said, "Sorry. You choose a good name for me, please."

Before she could answer him, a plumed shadow stood up before them, as sudden as the owl. "Who goes?" It was a low voice, hardly louder than the little scream of steel on iron that accompanied it.

Farrrell laughed in disbelief, but Julie stepped in front of him. "My lord Garth, it is Julie Tanikawa and a friend." Her own voice was clear and buoyant, and close to singing. The sword whined back into its scabbard, and the sentinel came toward them, squinting through the darkness, his gait something between a mince and a prowl.

"The Lady Murasaki?" His tone heaved itself up into Elizabethan heartiness. "Now in Jesu's name, give you thrice good den, shield-may. We had not looked to see you soon at these our revels."

Julie dropped him a quick curtsy, a movement altogether marvelous and warning to Farrell. She said, "In truth, my lord, I'd no mind to come dancing this night, but it pleased my fancy to show my friend how

we of the fellowship do disport ourselves at whiles."
She took hold of Farrell's arm and drew him beside
her.

The sentinel bowed slightly to Farrell. He had a narrow, knuckly, intelligent face beneath a feathered cap,
and he wore a stiff crewelworked doublet that, with its
huge shoulders and waistless line, made him look a
good deal like a jack of diamonds. The tips of his stringy
mustache were each waxed and curled into a full circle,
so that he seemed to have fixed a pair of steel-rimmed
pince-nez upside down on his upper lip. It was the only
thing about him that Farrell liked at all. He said, "I am
called the Lord Seneschal Garth de Montfaucon."

Heeding Julie's glance, Farrell groped randomly
through a pale litter of paladins, wizards, and Canter-
bury pilgrims; then fell back on the Celtic twilight.
"Good sir, there is a geas upon me. A taboo." Garth
nodded, looking nearly as offended by the footnote as
Farrell could have wished. Farrell said carefully, "I am
forbidden to reveal my name between moonrise and
dawn, save to a king's daughter. Pardon me, therefore,
till we meet by daylight, if you will." He thought it was
a very good geas, considering the short notice.

Beyond Garth de Montfaucon, other cloaked and
kirtled figures were passing in and out of the dark pavilion's shadow, or standing still in torchlight. Garth
said slowly, "A king's daughter."

"Aye, and a maiden." *What the hell, if you're going
to have a geas, have a geas.*

"Say you so?" Garth frowned down his nose, seemingly sighting myopically in on Farrell through the foolish mustache. Farrell said, "In sooth," and Julie
giggled. "And not until we two—we twain—have
danced a galliard together." Garth looked away to hail

another arriving couple, and Julie drew Farrell quickly past him toward the trees and the music. Farrell could see the musicians now, four men and a woman standing together on a low wooden dais. The men all wore the ruffled white shirts and overstuffed breeches of Rembrandt burghers; but the woman, who tapped strongly with her fingers on a small drum, wore a plain, almost colorless gown that made her look like a chess queen. Farrell stood still to watch them playing the old music for dancers he could not see.

"Be welcome, then." The bleak little voice of the Lord Seneschal carried clearly after them from the meadow. "Dance well, Lady Murasaki, with your nameless follower." Julie blew out her breath softly and showed her teeth.

"His name is Darrell Sloat," she said evenly. "He teaches remedial reading at Hiram Johnson Junior High School. I say it to myself whenever he manages to make me angry."

A huge man in Tudor dress, all crimson velvet, gold chains, and great slabs of pinkish-yellow jowl, pushed between them like a wave of meat, wheezing winy apologies, the basket hilt of his sword bruising Farrell's ribs. Farrell said grandly, "Nay, doth he bug you, sweet chuck? I'fackins, I'll sock him right in the eye. No, I'll challenge him, by God, I'll call him out." He stopped, because Julie was gripping his wrist tightly, and her hand was cold.

"Don't even joke about that," she said. "I'm serious. Joe, stay away from him."

The pavane came to a languishingly dissonant resolution, and Farrell saw the musicians bow, the men comic in their conga-drum pantaloons, the woman making a curtsy like a silk dress falling to the floor. He began to ask Julie why he should beware of Garth de Mont-faucon; but then he said, "Oh my," as they came around the pavilion and he saw the dancers.

There were some forty or fifty of them—perhaps less, but they shone like more under the trees. The last flourish of the pavane had set their hands free to balance above them in the night, and the torchlight—Coleman lanterns hung from branches—made their rings and their jeweled gloves splash fire, scattering tiny green and violet and silver flames like largesse to the musicians. Farrell could not find any faces in that first wonder of brightness and velvet, cloaks and gold and brocade—only the beautiful clothes glittering in a great circle, moving as though they were inhabited, not by human heaviness, but by marshlights and the wind. *The folk of the air*, he thought. *These are surely the folk of the air*.

"What is it?" Julie asked, and he realized that he had pulled away from her and taken a step forward. Ben was standing beyond the far side of the circle, half-hidden by the vast crimson Tudor. He wore a blue, full-sleeved tunic under a black mantle lined with white, and a helmet with a wild boar's muzzle for a crest. Bronze ornaments glinted at his throat, a short axe in his wide copper belt. As Farrell stared, taking another step, Ben turned his scarred shield of a face and saw him, and did not know him.

VIII

Farrell called and waved, but the harsh dark gaze passed over him without returning. A group of young girls, all clad in Disney-fairy gauze, bounded by, hand in hand. When Farrell could see across the clearing again, Ben was gone. The red Tudor stared back at him out of the faraway secrecy of an old bull.

Julie said, "He doesn't usually come to the dances." Farrell spluttered at her. She said, "I didn't know who he was. There are people here whose real names I haven't learned in two years. They don't tell anybody."

"What's his play name, then?" He knew her answer before he heard it.

"He calls himself Egil Eyvindsson." The musicians began to play a coranto, and there was a stir of nervous, challenging laughter. Julie said, "He comes to the tilts, always, and I see him at the crafts fairs sometimes. Mostly he goes where there's fighting." She spoke slowly, watching his face. "He happens to be the best with weapons I've ever seen, your friend Ben. Broad-

sword, greatsword, maul—in the War of the Queen
Mother's Boots, they said it was like having five extra
knights and a gorilla. He could be king any time he
wanted to be."

"I have no doubt of it," Farrell said. "None. I'm
sure he could make Holy Roman Emperor if he'd just
take the civil service exam. With his grades. Are you
going to turn out to be crazy?"

"Dance," Julie said calmly; and without another
word, she slipped off into the tootling rush of the coranto, dancing away with little sharp steps, springing
sweetly from one foot to the other, knuckles on her
hips and her head cocked sideways. Two couples
hopped between them as Farrell stared after her, the
men bowing courteously to him, making it a curve of
the dance, and the women calling. "Welcome, Lady
Murasaki!" Julie laughed back at them, greeting them
by strange names.

Where the noises are. The crumhorns pattered on the
small moonlit breeze, and all around him, boots, sandals, and soft, loose slippers trod down the wiry grass,
skipping and heeling through the same paces that the
dancing queen of England had loved once. Scabbards
clacked against belts, trailing gowns sighed in the
leaves, small bells tingled at hems and wrists. People
who bumped into Farrell said, "A thousand pardons,
fair sir." He could not find Ben anywhere, but he saw
Julie sauntering back to him, walking the music like a
cat on a fence, saying again, "Dance. Dance, Joe."

Beyond her Farrell saw the gristly face of Garth de
Montfaucon watching him with dispassionate, almost
scholarly loathing. Farrell made a reverence to Julie,
pointing his toes out and sinking into a rocking bow,
while his hands inscribed magicianly arabesques at his

breast. Julie smiled, answering him with a graver reverence of her own, holding out her hands.

He had never danced a coranto, but he had played many, and his feet always knew what his fingers knew; conversely, he could never dance anything that he could not play. The steps were those of a pavane, but a pavane created and performed by rabbits in moonlight instead of peacocks stalking, blue as salt on fire, along white walks under a Spanish moon. Farrell went hand in hand with Julie, copying her movements—the impatient little jump just before the beat, the pouncing advances and retreats, the eager, delicate landings. The music had thinned to a single crumhorn and the hoarse, scratchy drum. In the blowing kerosene light, Farrell saw the woman's fingers flashing on the drum like rain.

When Julie let go of his hand and they danced backward, facing each other, he had a moment to study the dancers nearest to them. Most were his age or younger; a surprising number were unusually fat—though their flowing clothes either minimized this or boldly enhanced it—and if none knew less about the coranto than he did, only a few seemed that much better at it or that concerned with precision. A youth in classical greenwood dress wound out of the ragged aisle, advancing toward the musicians, his skinny legs improvising side kicks and caprioles with a kitten's skittery, implacable energy. An older woman, wearing a huge yellow Elizabethan farthingale that made her look as if she were smuggling washing machines, danced tirelessly by herself to sliding steps with a soft-shoe, keeping almost perfectly to the shrill triple time. Off under a redwood at the edge of the clearing, three other couples were footing a practiced pattern of their own, a twining figure in which the men took turns weaving back and forth between the women, each man miming plaintive, respectful urgency. When the coranto ended, they all bowed and kissed one another, formal as china figurines, random and sensual as bending grass. Farrell kissed Julie on the strength of it.

The dancers did not applaud the musicians; rather, most of them turned and bowed toward the rude dais where the woman and the four clown-trousered men were already fallen into deep, slow reverences, the woman's forehead almost touching her knee. Julie said, "The Lady Criseyde. She teaches the dances—everybody starts with her. Her husband's the head of the Falconers' Guild, Duke Frederik of Eastmarch."

"Frederik the Falconer." Farrell had heard Crof Grant speak the name. He spied the white-haired man swaying dreamily near the dais, swathed from throat to shinbone in a voluminous saffron garment the size of a foresail. It was bunched into a great tumbling bundle at the waist and thrown over his left shoulder to fall down his back like a toga. There was a short blue jacket wound into it somewhere, and two or three forlorn suggestions of a white shirt struggling to surface. Farrell said vaguely, "Scots wha' hae."

The musicians were pooting experimentally again; the Lady Criseyde began softly to tap out the rhythm of another pavane. Julie put her arm under Farrell's, and they took their places in a new line, standing between a Cavalier pair, all curls, feathers, laces, and rosettes, and a black couple in Saracen dress. Julie said, "You are attending at the King's Birthday Revels of the League for Archaic Pleasures."

Farrell looked over at the black woman, who smiled back at him, her soft, serious face wickedly ambushed by dimples. She was wearing mostly opalescent veils

101

and a wide woven belt, and her hair was braided and beaded and tipped with gold. With the casual shock of a dream, Farrell recognized her companion from the green convertible; he was the young man who had so airily warded off Madame Schumann-Heink with his broadsword. He winked at Farrell—a swift, glinting fingersnap of a wink—before turning away, stately and alone among Crusaders.

The pavane was danced in the Spanish style, which had Farrell hopelessly adrift within a dozen bars. It was an unfamiliar air, a good deal livelier than the English paces he knew, and he wandered in and out of the measures in lonesome embarrassment. For all that, he went wistfully when Julie led him away to sit on the grass in the lee of the dark pavilion. "I was getting it," he said. "It's just been a while, is all."

Julie did not answer him, but watched the dances, one hand plucking absently at clover stems. Speaking quietly, without turning her head, she asked, "Have you chosen a name yet?"

"Don't need one. None but a king's virgin daughter may know my name until sunrise."

She turned on him swiftly then, saying, "Don't be a fool. I meant what I told you about names being important. Joe, pay attention for once."

Irritated himself, he answered, "Pay attention to what? Come on, Jewel, some fancy folk-dancing outfit calls itself the League for Artsy Amusements—"

"Archaic Pleasures," Julie said. "Incorporated, with fourth-class mailing privileges." Her eyes were on the pavane again, and her fingers had never left their blind work in the cold grass. "And they aren't folk dancers."

"Oh, right," Farrell said. "They have wars over the queen's garter belt. I forgot. What else do they do?"

"It was the War of the Queen Mother's Boots—and it was a very serious matter." She began to laugh, leaning against him. "They stage tilts," she said. "Tournaments. That's what that helm was for, and the chain mail."

"You mean jousting?"

Julie shook her head. "Not jousts. Jousts are on horseback, and it just gets too dangerous. But they have all the rest of it—sword fights, quarterstaff matches, shooting at the wand, even *mêlées*." The torchlight turned the dancers and musicians to slippery bronze shadows; the darkness made momentary candles of kirtles and plumes. Julie went on, "It isn't all fighting, like Hyperborea. Some of the men never fight at all—they join for the music or the dressing up, they become bards, they do research on heraldry, calligraphy, court procedure, even on the way people cooked and the games they played. But there wouldn't be a League without the tilts."

Prowling gracefully by with a very young girl in a plain blue houppelande, Garth de Montfaucon looked over his shoulder at them. Farrell said, "Hyperborea?"

"That's the Sacramento chapter. There's another one in Los Angeles, the Kingdom Under the Hill. We are the Kingdom of Huy Braseal."

She said the name with a slightly mocking flourish, but Farrell felt a sudden odd little shiver inside himself, a dainty tickle of ice under his skin. He had felt it earlier, in the moment when Garth's sword had whimpered from its sheath. He asked, "Since when have you been mixed up with all this? How long have these people been around?"

"Ten or twelve years. Huy Braseal, anyway—the others started up later." Two huge Afghan hounds, one black, one golden, lolloped among the dancers, their grinning loutishness and primrose eyes somehow turning the pavane altogether into a tapestry fragment glowing far away. Julie said, "I've been involved for a couple of years, on and off. Nancy got me into it, the Lady Criseyde. She's in Graduate Admissions."

Farrell said slowly, "The armor on your bed, that was real. What about the swords and axes and stuff?"

"Rattan, mostly. It's like wicker, only heavier. A few people still use regular softwood, I think—pine and so on."

"Not old Sir Turkish Delight," Farrell said. "The boy with the trick mustache. That was a realie he was waving around."

"Oh, that's just Garth showing off," she answered scornfully. "He always brings Joyeuse to the dances. They have very strict rules about all that. You're not allowed to fight with anything that'll take an edge, but it has to hit hard enough so that it would cut armor if it were sharp. The way it works out, the weapons aren't quite real enough to kill you—just to break a hand or a rib now and then. It's a touchy point with the Brotherhood of Swordsmiths."

"I'll bet," he said. "What a thing. Are you a brother swordsmith?"

"No, I'm in the Artisans' Fellowship. We're the ones who make the clothes and the household banners, paint the shields, and whatever else people commission us to do. I don't make armor anymore; I just did that when I began with the League."

The owl was back, moth-gray in the moonlight, wheeling and stooping above the pavane, calling thinly in what Farrell was sure was anger at finding its hunting grounds so utterly occupied. Julie pointed King Bohemond out to him—a stocky, balding, youngish man wearing a long purple tunic and cope, both garments cut and heavily embroidered in the Byzantine manner. He was standing with three other men—the red Tudor was one of them—under a tree just beyond the clearing. Farrell asked, "How do you get to be a king in Huy Braseal?"

"Armed combat," Julie said. "The same way you win your knighthood or become one of the Nine Dukes. There are a few rituals and trials to go through, but everything comes down to fighting. Bohemond's only been king for a couple of months, since the Twelfth Night Tourney."

The pavane ended with a bone-whistle trill of the crumhorns and a lingering sunset flare of cloaks and plumed caps. Farrell saw that Garth de Montfaucon made as long and deep a reverence to the musicians as anyone there; but the young girl beside him stood up in her blue gown with a slender, edged arrogance that seemed to make the kerosene flames bow down together. Farrell could not see her face.

"Who's that?" he asked. The girl turned suddenly, saying something to Garth and brushing back a lion-colored wilderness of hair with her forearm. Beside him Julie said quietly," "Aiffe," and the small sound was like the rustle of wings.

"Aha," Farrell said. "Aiffe of Scotland." At this distance, his only impressions were of the fierce hair, of skin tanned almost to the same dusty shade, and of a slight, long-waisted form whose step on the earth made him remember once watching a rainstorm coming toward him across a mountain lake. It was the most elegant motion he had ever seen—a languorous pavane over the water—and nothing could have stopped it. "I know that name," he said. "There's a story about Aiffe."

The musicians had downed their instruments and were accepting paper cups of wine from all sides, as the dancers dispersed to seek their own refreshments in the pavilion. Julie shook her head and rubbed her arms. She said, "Her name is Rosanna Berry. She goes to high school. She's fifteen years old."

Farrell studied the taut, haughty figure, at once a princess and a skinny golliwog under the splendid splash of hair. "Mustn't forget to give her Prester John's regards. The very throne may depend on it."

Julie stood up abruptly, brushing leaves from her gown, looking away from Farrell as he rose with her. "Let's go home," she said. "I shouldn't have brought you here." She spoke rapidly, almost mumbling. Farrell had never heard her voice so strangely dimmed.

"Why?" he asked. "Jewel, I didn't mean to make fun, I'm sorry." He took her hand, turning her to face him. "I'm just trying to pick up on the rules of the game," he said. "Jewel, what is it? I'm really sorry." Beyond her he could see Garth de Montfaucon making his way toward the musicians, towing the girl Aiffe after him. She trailed along serenely, smiling and shaking her hair.

Julie's hand felt like Pierce/Harlow's knife skidding distantly through his own. Still not quite looking at him, she said, "Of course it's a game. Middle-class white people running around in long underwear, assistant professors hitting each other with sticks, what else could it be? Thanks for reminding me, Joe."

"Do you forget?" She did not answer him. Farrell said, "Old Garth—I'll bet it's no game for that boy. I'll bet Garth forgets a lot." He wanted to ask her about

106

Ben, but told himself that it could wait until they were home. Instead he asked, "Why did you bring me here? Because of the music?"

Crof Grant ambled improbably by, munching on a dripping turkey leg and chanting with the vacant volume of a sound truck:

"Dool and wae for the order
Sent our lads to the Border!
The English, for ance, by guile wan the day;
The Flowers of the Forest,
That fought aye the foremost,
The prime of our land, lie cauld in the clay."

Julie slipped a pale circlet of woven clover stems over Farrell's right hand. "Favor from a lady," she said absently. "You have to have a name and a favor." She smiled at him then and linked her arm in his, as briskly back with him as she had been suddenly gone somewhere cold and narrow. "Because of the noises," she said. "Come on, let's go meet King Bohemond of Huy Braseal."

They crossed the clearing slowly, pausing often for Julie to be greeted as a sister by personages out of Charlemagne's world, and Saladin's, and Great Harry's. Farrell was presented to a bright swagger of tunics, tabards, doublets, and mantuas answering to such names as Simon Widefarer, Olaf Holmquist, the Lady Vivienne d'Audela, Sir William the Dubious, and Don Claudio Baltasar Ruy Martin Ildefonso de Sanchez y Carvajal. They said, "Lady Murasaki, it me rejoiceth to see thee here again," and, considering Farrell, "Well, my lady, and what sweet scoundrel is't you bring us, say now?" Farrell was most taken with the Lady

Criseyde and her husband, Duke Frederik the Falconer—they had almost identically dark, angular, shy faces—and with the black woman, whose companion introduced her as Amanishakhete, Queen of Nubia. Farrell bowed over her hand and was told, "Pay him no mind, he calls me anything comes into his head. My name is Lovita Bird, and honey, there is *no* improving on that." He also met the Countess Elizabeth Bathory, whom he had last seen in the green convertible, wearing nothing but gold chains. Close to, she looked exactly like a blunt-faced, jasper-eyed Persian cat, and she scratched Farrell's palm when he kissed her hand.

There was no sign of Ben anywhere. Farrell would have liked a closer look at Aiffe, but she had vanished, though Garth de Montfaucon was ever present on the edge of all encounters, twiddling his mustache or the hilt of his sword. Then Julie was curtsying demurely before King Bohemond, murmuring, "God keep your Majesty." Farrell dropped enthusiastically to his knees and cried out, "Long live the king! Kings may override grammar!"

King Bohemond said, "What the fuck?" The men standing with him all cleared their throats, and the king mumbled wearily, "Sorry. What bodeth this outlandish manner of exhortation?"

"It's my favorite proverb about royalty," Farrell explained. "The Emperor Sigismund said it, sixteenth century sometime. I think they called him on using the dative case instead of the ablative."

"Way to *go*," the king grunted. He put both hands on Farrell's shoulders, patting him in little tentative dabs. "Rise," said King Bohemond. "Rise, Sir Pooh de Bear, most faithful of all my knights." Farrell rose with some difficulty, for the king was leaning heavily

on him, humming what sounded like *Your Cheatin'
Heart* to himself. Farrell managed it by clinging unobtrusively to the griffin-embroidered silken stole that
crisscrossed on Bohemond's chest.

Julie said, "May it please your Majesty, behold, I
have brought for your pleasure the flower of lute players, the true nonesuch of Huy Braseal." Farrell
blushed, which surprised him very much. He began to
explain about his geas, but Julie interrupted and did it
for him, speaking the moonshine English as trippingly
as if she had been born to it. The king watched her with
grudging admiration.

"Damn castle talk wears me out," he complained
loudly, wheezing nut-brown ale all over Farrell. "I call
it castle talk because you can't call it a damn language,
it doesn't have any *rules*. Just so it sounds like Prince
Valiant would have said it. Pitiful, you know?"

The red Tudor cleared his throat again. "Sire, my
liege, will't please you join the Queen? She waiteth
upon you even now, for to lead the galliard." He had
a high, toneless voice and deepset eyes like pearls.

"Castle talk," King Bohemond said. "MGM talk,
Classic Comics talk—Walter Scott, for God's sake, it's
all bits and snatches of Scott, anyway." His voice rose,
turning sadly spiteful. "Of course, it doesn't matter to
them. They aren't in ethnolinguistics, they don't feel
the slightest responsibility to language. I mean, fuck
syntax, fuck morphology, right? Hey, whatever feels
good."

He spread his arms wide, striking an attitude of grinning, mindless benevolence. His crown fell off, and Farrell bent to pick it up. "Your Majesty, the Emperor
Sigismund may have meant only—"

King Bohemond said, "Nobody is above grammar.

I mean, that's like being above digestion, right?" He grinned messily at Farrell, jabbing a companionable elbow into his side. "See, I'm embarrassing them, look at them." He glowered around him at the amused noble lords and damsels who came drifting up over the grass in their tights and mantles and gently eddying gowns. "Nobody ever expected me to come out of nowhere. They pass that crown back and forth like a fucking basketball. I was *not* expected. So now they're stuck with this goddamn peasant, this peasant king. Because, of course, nobody ever volunteers to be a peasant, some poor, ignorant, shitkicking serf, they use him for the fifty-yard line in their goddamn tournaments. So the king has to do it, the king has to represent the masses. Whole new tradition around here."

A harshly handsome young woman, taller than he, was abruptly at his side, whispering grimly to him as she rubbed with a wet finger at a stain on his *alba camisia*. King Bohemond wriggled away from her, mumbling, "A people's king," but she moved with him, straightening his crown and tucking the trailing ends of his stole back into this girdle.

Julie murmured in Farrell's ear, "Queen Leonora."

"I believe it," Farrell said.

King Bohemond broke loose again and inquired of Farrell with a sudden surprising dignity, "Th'art a musicker, sayest? Play an air for us, then, that we may know thee. For the reeds and the strings say who we are, beyond all misconceiving, and were each of us a man of music, there would be no more falsehood nor treachery in the world, surely."

Farrell heard the black Saracen purr, "Nor no more marrying, neither." His voice was a strange voice, soft

110

and rough at once, sounding just at Farrell's back, though he was standing nowhere near.

One of the musicians provided a lute, another a drum for a footstool. Farrell tuned the lute slowly, looking around the clearing. Among the gathering faces he saw the Lady Criseyde and Duke Frederik standing quietly together, while three children dressed as greenwood ragamuffins—the eldest could not have been twelve— perched stolidly on one another's shoulders to see him. Julie had pointed them out, saying that they did tumbling, juggling and tightrope-walking at all the fairs. The Countess Elizabeth Bathory watched from the musicians' dais, regarding Farrell with pudgy, cheerful voraciousness. Crof Grant, a snowplow in saffron, came cleaving his way through to the front, nodding and beaming upon the laird-haunted air, smiling forgivingly at those who hadn't jumped aside in time. He finally caromed off Garth de Montfaucon and stalled just behind Queen Leonora.

Farrell said, "Your Majesties. My lords and ladies all. Attend, I pray you, to a *canso* of the great troubadour Pierol, who was so sad in love so long ago." He began to play a pattering, spidery prelude, retarding gradually after a few bars to a supple three-quarter time, barely emphasized. He sang in French, knowing better than to attempt the Provençal.

> *"Bien des gens, hélas, me blament*
> *De chanter si rarement.*
> *La douleur flétrit mon âme.*
> *Et mon coeur est en tourment.*
> *Pourrais-je donc chanter gaîment,*
> *Quand il faut que je proclame*
> *Que m'afflige durement*
> *L'amour que j'ai pour ma dame?"*

The lute was less responsive than his own, and the song's pitch was uncomfortable for his voice. He modulated into a different key, taking refuge in modern harmonies, ad-libbing a pattern of octaves over a completely anachronistic moving bass line. *Wes Montgomery goes to the Crusades.* But all such awareness seemed to be sliding rustily away from him like a railroad station as he played and sang a complaint eight hundred years old to fire-striped faces framed and lighted by the tall collars of cloaks, balanced between ruffles and plumes.

> *"Dans un deuil amer me plonge*
> *Sa cruauté sans recours.*
> *C'est grand mal: un doux mensonge*
> *Me serait d'un tel secours."*

Even one sweet lie would have rescued me from this torment. A switchblade flick of a grin passed between Garth de Montfaucon and the red Tudor; but the Lady Criseyde hugged her husband's arm against her, and the green eyes of the Countess Elizabeth Bathory went round and thoughtful. The tall mercenary captain called Simon Widefarer scratched his grizzled bare chest and smiled; the thick, rumpled Sir William the Dubious fussed with his sagging hose; the black Saracen patted his fingertips together soundlessly. Farrell looked for Julie and sang the last lines to her, as Pierol or his *jongleur* might have sought out one waiting fire-striped glance in the cold, sooty hall.

> *"Alors que pleure nuit et jour,*
> *Et ne vois pas, même en songe,*
> *De remède à cet amour*
> *Que mon coeur tenaille et ronge,*
> *Que mon coeur tenaille et ronge."*

The lute pinged into silence on an unresolved chord, leaving Pierol's formal sorrow wandering in the night. *And I see no help, even in dreams, for this love which claws and devours my heart.* Farrell bowed deeply to King Bohemond and Queen Leonora.

He thought he had done well enough, for someone faking it in the wrong key; but when he heard the rustling and raised his head to see them all bowing to him, as they did for musicians—the gowns and cloaks sweeping down like wind-driven rain, the jeweled chains and girdles glinting like rain in the moonlight—then suddenly he found that he was shivering painfully with tenderness and excitement and fear.

The king said gruffly, "Come, pipe a tune to dance to, lad."

Farrell retuned the lute and struck into *A L'Entrade*. Somewhere far away the choice astonished him considerably: he had never been able to domesticate that rowdy *estampie* into a proper concert number and he could not remember the last time he had even practiced it. But his sweating hands took over, attacking the piece as savagely and sloppily as the troubadours' dungbooted patrons had gone at their meals. The strings buzzed, cawed, whined, twangled, and the music lunged up singing with outrageous exultancy to welcome a twelfth-century spring and make wild, heartless mock of jealousy and old age. *Begone, begone far from here! Let us dance, let us dance joyously all together, eya!*

The Lady Criseyde and her grave-eyed lord Duke Frederik were the first who turned to face each other and join hands. They moved like tall birds of plain plumage, and Farrell made slips in his playing, watching them. Other couples followed quickly as the four musicians took up the tune, the rebec replaced by a shawm.

King Bohemond and Queen Leonora shoved and stumbled to the head of the double line, jumping in on the wrong beat, but leading the dance with a kind of desperate pomp, even so. Garth de Montfaucon pounced down on Julie, swooping her under his arm and prancing away with her, feigning jolly goatishness. Farrell saw sourly that he was easily the best dancer among the men.

The horns drowned him out once they got together, the crumhorns burring and humming, the shawm blasting away like a marching band. Farrell put the lute down on the dais after a while. He felt himself becoming, not at all sad, but very still, oddly content to be invisible, watching the dance recede from him. But there was as well a curious prickling deep in his nerves; an eager, elusive disquiet that turned him, almost unknowing, away from the costumed revelers and toward the darkness beyond the clearing. *Where did Ben go? I should look for Ben.*

As the trees drew nearer, the vague fretfulness sharpened in him, becoming something like the mood that seizes on horses when there is a wind rising or rain brooding, or when the presence of lightning sets every molecule of the air on edge. He halted once and looked back, seeing the lights and hearing the music, dainty with distance now, as he had found them when he first walked through the night meadow with Julie. *But here comes the King to trouble our dancing, eya! Afraid lest some youth should carry off his April-drunk Queen, eya!* A fox laughed metallically on his right; from the redwoods gathering before him, some drowsy bird cooed two icy notes over and over. He heard someone singing to herself under the trees.

It was a thin, whining little song, such as a child

drones endlessly at play in the dirt. If there were words, Farrell heard none, but the sound gave a voice to the restlessness jigging inside him, and he went toward it, feeling himself once more warm between the paws of the inevitable. The song rose slightly, more or less repeating itself in a higher pitch, drearily persistent. The fox yapped a second time, and the moon went out and came back on again.

Farrell never actually saw it happen; the moment was so brief that he was aware of it only as he might have sensed an awkward splice in a film—a twitch of color values, a phrase or gesture only partly accounted for. But for just that wink he felt everything inside himself—blood, breath, digestion, the cells greedily feeding and bearing and dying—stop too; and he stood where he was, while a warm breeze that smelled almost pleasantly of rotting fruit flicked past him and was gone.

Just ahead, in the older night under the trees, the woman's song ended in a tiny, crumpled yelp of terror. A man began to laugh, softly at first.

IX

*I*t was charming laughter, but not nice. Farrell had never heard laughter like that; there was a dissolving sweetness in it, and the memory of many good times, and no kindness at all. *Sirens*, he thought, *mermaids*. It hung in the air like the smell of burning.

From where he stood, Farrell could not discern the man's face in the darkness, but he heard his voice as clearly as if the two of them were across a chessboard from one another, or a sword's length apart. "God a'-mercy, and here's poor Nicholas again, all alive-o!" It was a light, curling voice, the words airily poising their feet to dance, and something in the rhythm made Farrell think about the yellow-eyed man who had stumped like a falcon into Sia's house at midnight. He had dreamed of the man twice since then.

"Arms, legs, senses, fancies, follies, and lovesome honey appetites, every one with me still," the stranger announced cheerfully. "Now bless thy weazeny breech and lantern countenance, my sweeting, and may Nicholas Bonner present his unchurched compliments?" Farrell heard a small scuffle, apparently halted by an almost inaudible squeak from the woman, and then the wonderful soulless laughter again. "Nay, so, so there, dear duck—surely thy dam lulled thee to the roll of blessings awaiting for her who's first to lie with springtime Nick, come all chilled and lonely out of old dull dark once more. Thy firstling will know the talk of all animals, thy second-born the cry of gold in the earth—hither, then, swiftly, for I'm cold, I'm cold." For that instant there was such wailing sadness and terror in the voice that Farrell could not breathe.

Brush and twigs crackled again, but the woman called out in a tone mixing near-hysteria with a certain chattering imperiousness, "Away, touch me not, what are you doing? I mean, I have scribed the pentacle thrice round myself, what are you *doing*, you dumb dork?" And those were the first clear words that Farrell ever heard Aiffe speak.

The man did not answer immediately; when he did, his speech had already begun to alter, but the laughter continued to prowl in the shadow of each word. "Actually, one time is quite enough for a true pentacle. It's a circle you're to weave thrice, and then it wards off nothing a maid with such great lean shanks couldn't outrun." A single chuckle sprang past Farrell on soft paws, as though to take up its own independent life in Barton Park. The stranger went on, "Any road—nay, pardon, I'll have it presently—anyway, the matter's moot altogether, since your pentacle bites only 'gainst demons and the like, and good Nick Bonner's no demon. Not even Will Shakespeare ever called me that—and indeed he spent more time than most trying to devise a fitting name for me." His voice had been husky as flame when he spoke first; now, with use, it was taking on color and suppleness like a new butterfly, stretching itself, basking in the moon.

Farrell sidled and crouched and skulked until he could see Aiffe facing him almost directly across a strange small grove of burned-out redwoods. Some forest fire had scorched the trees to standing charcoal, gutting them so that they looked like great, black, high-backed chairs dragged up around a table of air. The man was standing in their shadow with his back to Farrell, who sensed more than saw that he made as slight a figure as Aiffe herself and that he was naked.

Aiffe was recovering herself rapidly, forcing a bold dignity that Farrell had to admire. She said, "The pentacle's there because I happened to be summoning a demon. If you aren't one, you can just go back where you came from. I don't want you." She added several halting words in what Farrell assumed to be Latin.

The laughter flowered brightly between them, and Aiffe took a step backward, touching her face. The stranger said happily, "Dear squirrel, dear coney, dearest little partridge, it would take such priest-cackle as great Innocent himself never knew to send Nicholas Bonner around the block. I've not been for anyone's bidding since Master Giacopo Salvini died at the stake in Augsburg—and there was a man had demons sweeping his hearth and currying his fine horses." He whistled softly and chuckled again. "Ah, but forty men-at-arms came to curry *him*, and he'd not time to ask his lackwit niece what sweet Nick had promised her in the dark of the chimney corner. And with him went up the only words could ever command my spirit, and the rest is all freedom. Child, there's jabber binds Lucifer to obey that wouldn't do up a collar button on Nick Bonner."

Even at that distance, Farrell could see that the thin girl was trembling, but she answered coolly, "You're such a liar. Somebody sent you back out into limbo, or wherever you go, and you had to stay there until I called you. You're nothing, I still want a demon." Her voice was the lute's voice, poignant and shifting, with coins and little drums in it, and a rubber-band whine.

The man dropped lithely down onto his bare heels, hugging himself and rocking as he cried, "Oh, well hit, fair on the mazzard, squash on the old beezer. What an excellent savory talk is this of yours, after all." His own speech was fast shedding its daintily wicked music; Farrell could hear the vowels collapsing like pricked balloons, and the lilting drawl being overtaken by the concrete consonants of Cedar Rapids. Nicholas Bonner said, "Well, you're wondrous foolish, but not altogether fool. True enough, the last flaming breath of Master Giacopo did consign his betrayer to such night and silence as had me near weeping to join him in cozy hell. Oh, he knew how to venge himself, no man better—I'd found that out while he was yet alight." The same freezing, measureless despair blew through his voice for a second time and was gone.

"So if it hadn't been for me," Aiffe said. Farrell was too far away to read her expression, but he saw the difference in the way she stood, pushing back her heavy hair. She said slowly, "So you owe me one, don't you? You really owe me a big favor."

Nicholas Bonner laughed so hard this time that he had to prop himself with his hands to keep from falling over. "Now truly, *that* deserves my best effort at the local tongue." He cleared his throat, still squatting in the moonlight with his hands flat on the ground, like a golden frog. "Kiddo, just by not being a demon I've done you a better turn than anyone's had from me in a thousand years. Let me tell you, if you'd caught the notice of the humblest, feeblest, most wretched midge of a demon that was ever spawned—girl, the least of those would have swarmed up your two-bit charm like a ratline and swallowed you whole before you could wet your pants. Oh, we're more than quits, take my word for it."

"If I took people's words for things, you wouldn't be here," she answered. "Just don't worry about me, all right? I take care of myself, I can handle anything I can summon." Her hands were closed at her sides, and she leaned toward the crouching man. She said, "I've used that spell three times, and each time something's *moved*, somebody's come to me. Not a demon— okay, I haven't got that down yet—but I always get somebody. I'm Aiffe, you snotty dork Nicholas Bonner. I can make things move."

Nicholas Bonner stood up then. His naked body cast a pale, crooked moonshadow behind him. Farrell watched it wriggle toward him past the blackened redwood stumps; when it touched his ankle, he was certain that he could feel himself connected to Nicholas Bonner, spine linked to spine, like electrodes. He tried to step away from the shadow, but it moved with him as if it were his own.

"Aye, so you can," Nicholas Bonner said to Aiffe at last. His voice had turned thoughtful and cautious, and there was no laughter in it now. He said, "Indeed, you do have a sort of skill, and no denying it. But to what end, that's the issue—to what end?" When the girl did not answer him, he continued impatiently, "Come on, sport, talk up. What do you want that you think a demon could give you?"

Aiffe giggled quite suddenly, shrill as a tree frog. "I want to mess with people," she said. "I just want to get even, that's all."

Farrell felt Nicholas Bonner smile then; the warmth spread through him thinly, like one of the tingling guilts of childhood, forcing him to smile, too. Nicholas Bonner said very gently, almost wonderingly, "Why, we are well met." He held out his arms to her and moved lightly across the redwood grove, and his shadow danced after him.

She did not back away this time, but Farrell did, free of Nicholas Bonner's shadow and of any desire to watch them further. He duck-walked clumsily until he was clear of the trees, then stood up, shook himself, turned and blinked straight into the chestnut-brown eyes and small, close-clipped beard of the black Saracen. The Saracen said politely, "Ah. There you are."

"I doubt it," Farrell said sincerely. Behind him, in the redwood grove, Aiffe laughed twice, sounding frightened and happy. The Saracen seemed not to hear her. He said, "Hey, the noble multitude stompeth and yelleth for encores. Time for your second set."

Farrell grinned until his face hurt, absurdly grateful to see him. "What happened to the castle talk? You could lose your union card, talking like that."

"I'm a bard, man," the Saracen said. "They make allowances for me. I give them whole ballad cycles in Gaelic, Arabic, Welsh, Danish, Old English, Anglo-Norman, and great big chunks out of *Carmina Burana*. They make allowances."

Aiffe's laughter ended in a sharp, lonely cry; but the Saracen already had an arm through Farrell's arm and was turning him back toward the clearing, chatting easily and pleasantly all the while. "Bards have it made;

anyhow. Catch one of the bardic festivals, you'll see what I mean. Everybody else has to stay in character, but if you're competing, hell, you get to do *Eskimo Nell, Stagolee*, anything you want. One time I recited this whole huge epic about King Kong, did it all in iambics and *terza rima*. Took me damn near an hour to get through."

He kept up a graceful patter of conversation as they walked, volunteering, among other things, that he had been a charter member of the League for Archaic Pleasures. "Me and Simon, Prester John, Olaf, maybe a dozen assorted Middle Ages freaks, all swashing away at each other in Garth's backyard. No rules, no structure, just get together now and then and go at it. I mean, we had folks making morgensterns out of croquet balls and bicycle chains in those days, using car antennas for flails. So there had to be *some* rules after a while, and then people started in bringing their families, and there had to be something for the women to do. The League would never have happened without the women."

Farrell said, "But the fighting's still what matters."

The Saracen shook his head. "Not the way you mean. We're a theater, we give someone like Elizabeth a stage where she gets to be one bad, sexy, mysterious Blood Countess from Transylvania—and believe me, she is none of the above as a regular thing. Or you take Simon Widefarer. Simon's a lawyer, contracts or something. Hates it. Hates himself for being scared to tell his parents he didn't want to be a lawyer, hates himself for being scared to quit cold and start all over running some shoestring airline in Belize. But here—here he's a *condottiere*, a free captain, best fighter in the League after Egil Eyvindsson, and he's not afraid of anything.

All we do, we give him a place to be Simon Widefarer on the weekends."

"Do you have a place for Nicholas Bonner?" Farrell asked quietly. The Saracen smiled as vaguely and benignly as though he had not quite heard the question and could not bring himself to admit it; but his arm jumped once against Farrell's, and his effortless amble quickened slightly. Farrell asked, "Who are you? What does this handy little repertory company give you?"

The Saracen wagged a forefinger and frowned with such elegant severity that Farrell had no idea whether he was being admonished, reproached, or very strangely teased. "Two entirely different questions, my good minnesinger. Who I am is a black man fool enough to have a classical education, and there are a lot of people at this dance wouldn't even tell you that much about themselves. Sort of like the Gold Rush, you know, you don't want to be asking somebody what his name was back in the States. Names are magic, names are all the magic there is, every culture knows that. Got any sense, you don't even let the gods know your right name."

He halted suddenly and smiled at Farrell in quite a different way—the thin, bulging grin of something that might eat grubs and shoots and blackberries most of the time, but not always. "But who I am here is Hamid ibn Shanfara, poet and son of an outlaw poet, historian, storyteller, Royal Keeper of the Lists and Legends. Some places south of the Sahara, they'd call me a *griot*." His small, smooth bow exactly followed the curve of the dagger hanging at his waist.

"Another rememberer," Farrell said. "We are well met." Only the chestnut eyes showed the least reaction to Nicholas Bonner's words.

Hamid said lightly, "Beats teaching. I guess I could have taught all that stuff I know somewhere, but I never wanted to. I didn't learn it to teach. I just wanted to *be* it, which is hard to explain to people." He began walking again, glancing sharply sideways at Farrell. "Like you and the lute, yes?"

"Like me and the lute," Farrell said. "Like Aiffe and witchcraft, yes?"

Hamid did not answer until they had almost reached the clearing. There was a new dance going on, a branle by the music and the scrambling laughter. Hamid said finally, "Well, that's a role too, same as a bard or a troubadour. Hyperborea, up in Sacramento, they've got one lady who's into *wicca*, the Old Religion, whatever you want to call it. Looks like a filing cabinet and makes witchcraft sound like organic mulching. The Kingdom Under the Hill has witches up the yingy, mostly reading auras, predicting earthquakes. We've got Aiffe." He hesitated, letting go of Farrell's arm to concentrate on resettling his handsome indigo turban. "Now I don't know what you saw her fooling with back there—"

"That's the trouble," Farrell said sadly. "I do." The Saracen was definitely walking faster now, making for the dancers, and Farrell lengthened his own stride to keep up. He said, "Hamid, we don't know each other, I'm just passing through, this is not my concern. But what you guys have there is no cultural-anthropology drop-out planting string beans naked in the full moon. What you have there is Baba Yaga."

Hamid snorted without looking at him. "Man, Aiffe's like a mascot, she grew up with the League. She's been playing sorceress since she was a little kid."

"I think she's about got it down." Farrell said.

"Look, I would really, truly like very much to believe that she and her boyfriend were rehearsing the class play, or even getting in shape for some local fertility ritual. Or that I was hallucinating somehow, or just getting it wrong, the way I do." He caught hold of Hamid's white linen robe to stop him for a moment. "But this one time I can't talk myself into it. I know what I saw."

At the tug on his robe Hamid turned swiftly and struck Farrell's hand away, saying with a sudden menacing sweetness, "Don't grab at a bard, you don't do that *ever*." There was nothing of the scholar, the clown or the courtier about him now; he might have been a desert priest, like a brown snarl of barbed wire, confronting true blasphemy. He whispered, "You don't known what you saw. Believe me." Farrell could barely make out his words under the music. Hamid said, "She shows off, that's all, she likes attention. She's fifteen years old."

"The real witches and wizards were probably young," Farrell said thoughtfully. "I never wanted power as much as I did when I was fifteen." But Hamid was gone, abruptly vanished into a glowing tumble of dancers who overflowed the clearing and spilled around Farrell, gasping and whooping and falling down. Garth de Montfaucon stalked by, mantis-graceful, mannerly as death. Farrell nodded slightly, and Garth smiled like a zipper and moved on along the way Farrell had come.

Julie was standing near the musicians' dais, talking with the Lady Criseyde, but she went to Farrell as soon as she saw him and hugged him quickly. "Where have you been?" she asked. "I was worried, where did you go?"

"Just walking a little," Farrell said. "I'm sorry, I should have told you."

"I didn't know where you'd disappeared to," she said. "You were just gone suddenly, and so was she—Aiffe—and Garth's been sliding around everywhere like butter in a skillet, really hunting for her. I thought you might have gotten kidnapped; somebody might have been sacrificing infants. Virgins." She laughed, but there was a shivering tinfoil sound to it, and she was slow to let go of him.

"Mostly I was hunting for Ben." He hesitated, trying to find a way to begin telling her about the laughter under the trees. The Lady Criseyde said, "If you seek the Viking Eyvindsson, you might do well to find my own lord, the Falconer. They two are as near to being companions as Egil will allow." She had a low, precise voice and the wary grace of a creature hunted only in certain seasons.

"I'll check," Farrell said shortly, startled to feel a mean high-school squeeze at the thought of Duke Frederik being Ben's preferred friend in this world. He said, "Tanikawa, Jewel, I have to talk to you," but both Julie and the Lady Criseyde were staring past him, unhearing, leaning forward with their mouths slightly open. Farrell turned, knowing what he was going to see and hoping he was wrong.

A little way from them, the girl Aiffe was leading a boy of her own age into line for a new pavane. He was as slender as she and perhaps half a head shorter, but he carried himself with a bold lilt that made him appear to look down at her. In the torchlight, his hair was impossibly yellow—dandelion-thick, so ridiculously, insultingly rich and molten as to make the moon look like pale margarine—though his skin was a smooth,

126

sallow, olive color. He was dressed all in green, from his surcoat to his hose, wide belt, and shoes, and Farrell thought inanely, *Of course, if she can call him here from wherever he was, she can damn sure put some clothes on him*. Aiffe was smiling, holding the boy's arm tightly with both hands.

The Lady Criseyde said softly, "Now that's none of ours, that's no child I've seen before." The yellow-haired boy whispered to Aiffe, making her giggle and rub her shoulder against his. They had a curious air of brother and sister about them; they might have been conspiring to play a trick on a roomful of overfed uncles and aunts. Aiffe could not stop smiling.

"The Kingdom Under the Hill," Julie suggested. "They turn up here all the time." The musicians began to play Cutting's *Pavane for Mistress Knollys*, and Nicholas Bonner made a reverence to Aiffe that reminded Farrell of the tense little wriggle of a flame. She snickered again and curtsied like a stork settling down on a chimney.

The Lady Criseyde had slipped away to pick up her drum and join the music. Julie moved close to Farrell, taking his hand. Nicholas Bonner danced with Aiffe like a flame taking a deeper, brighter hold on a log, digging in. As grave and demure as his dance was, Farrell could feel the sweet, burning laughter crackling in each movement, barely contained, roiling joyously under the solemn skin of the pavane. He heard the terrible thankfulness as well, and the husky voice greeting itself under the trees: "*Arms, legs, senses, fancies, follies. . .*"

"He's not from California," he said. "Believe me." When he turned to Julie, her face was the color of city ice. Farrell raised the hand she was gripping to touch her cheek and felt her grinding her teeth in a failing effort to keep them from chattering. He said, "Jewel," but she would not look at him.

The pavane ended, and Nicholas Bonner quickly imitated the other dancers' grand reverence to the musicians; but Aiffe, as before, remained insolently erect, even tugging at Nicholas Bonner's hand to pull him up again. Abruptly she released him and came walking straight toward the dais where Farrell stood with Julie. Nicholas Bonner followed at the pace of the pavane, still dancing serenely by himself. Aiffe stopped before Farrell and grinned at him, pushing her hair back from her shiny forehead.

"Hey, you are just fantastic," she said. "I didn't get a chance to tell you. You are just a fantastic musician." She punched his arm clumsily.

Farrell bowed without answering. Her nose was as bony as that of a much older woman; her mouth was flat and muscular, her pointed chin as abrupt as an elbow, and the tanned skin bore faint swirls and granulations of acne. But her eyes were green and blue and gray, with the pupil shading imperceptibly into the iris, so that looking into them was like lying on his back, watching clouds in the late afternoon. The lids were arched and full in the center, narrowing quickly to the corners, giving her eyes the shape of tapestry diamonds or spearheads.

"What's your name?" she asked. "Are you a professional? I mean, do you play somewhere? Oh, this is my friend Nick Bonner." She paid no attention at all to Julie.

Farrell had never seen anyone as beautiful as Nicholas Bonner. The nearest thing to it was his memory of a battered stone head in a New York gallery—a fist-sized fragment, supposedly a North Indian image of Alexander the Great, with a face that smiled straight into Farrell's skull, as Nicholas did now. The statue's complexion had been scarred and smudgy, while Nicholas Bonner's skin was as perfect as water, and its clump of chipped gray curls would have looked like fossilized mange beside the boy's absurdly glorious golden crest; but he might have modeled for the fullness of the high cheeks, the mouth's drowsy suggestion of a lift at one corner, and the entire air of soft knowing, so sensuous as to be almost sexless. But the stone eyes were the more human. Nicholas Bonner's eyes were the color of champagne, the color of lightning, and to meet them was to look through a summer window into the ravenous old nothing of a black hole. Farrell thought with an odd unexpected sympathy, *Oh, he probably never could do anything about the eyes*. Nicholas Bonner said, in his light, happy, courteous young voice, "I have great joy of our meeting, good my lord."

Does he know that I saw him? Farrell's heart was hiccuping painfully, and he could not make himself look into Nicholas Bonner's eyes again. "I am a poor thumping tunester, no more," he answered Aiffe, "playing everywhere for a night, and nowhere for two." Nicholas Bonner smiled at the moon, continuing to sway from foot to foot, never quite letting go of the pavane. *Well, if I hadn't danced in as long as I guess he hasn't danced*. He squeezed Julie's hand gently and winked at her.

Aiffe's teeth were thin and sharp, fish teeth. She made a prim face, lowering her glance and murmuring in the League talk over joined hands, "Sir troubadour, I am called Aiffe of Scotland, Aiffe of the North, and this night my soul is given altogether to dancing. Tell me now truly who you are, and what estate you claim in your own country, and then, of your kindness, come and partner me a little while. I am Aiffe."

"My lady, there is a geas," he began but she interrupted him swiftly. "Nay, what are such tinpot forbiddances to Aiffe? Be assured, you will come to no harm in revealing your name to me, but only great good." And she ran the tip of her pale tongue deliberately over her slightly chapped lips.

Julie's hand tightened on Farrell's, and he remembered, not only her fierce warning, "Names mean something here," but Hamid the Saracen saying, "You don't even let the gods know your right name." On a strange small impulse, he replied carefully, "Alas, the spell was cast by the mighty wizard-emperor Prester John himself, and who shall defy such a ban? I pray you therefore, ask me no more, or I may well yield to your grace, and I would not have you mourn that you called my doom upon me." In alley and playground football, his specialty had always been broken-field running.

If the name of Prester John provoked any reaction, he did not know how to read it. Nicholas Bonner laughed outright—*if you heard that sound enough times, some damn thing would break, maybe not your heart, but something*—while Aiffe blushed in patches like poison oak. The Lady Criseyde began tapping her drum lightly, and Aiffe took hold of Farrell's free hand. "Well, we can dance anyway," she said. Her hand felt hard and sticky—long fingers bunched around a tiny hot palm. She said, "They will play the Earl of March's Galliard next. Do you know the turns?"

Farrell said, "I think so." Beside him Nicholas Bonner was bowing to Julie, offering his arm. She accepted him calmly, showing no fear and not looking back at

Farrell as Aiffe pulled him away. Nicholas Bonner did, though, and the angelic mouth twitched once, like the tail-tip of a hunting cat.

Dancing with Aiffe was neither a sinister experience nor a particularly exciting one. She was a deft and meticulous dancer, executing her *ruades*, her springing cadences, her fleurets, and her high-kicking *greves* without a flaw or a variation, easily matching her steps to Farrell's less practiced ones. But her brief interest in him seemed to have lapsed completely: she did not speak or smile, and if she did anything further with her tongue, it must have happened while he was trying to watch Nicholas Bonner with Julie, envying, even as it terrified him, the climate of devouring happiness that accompanied the yellow-haired boy. He said to Aiffe, "Speaking of Prester John. He asks to be remembered."

She blinked vaguely at him—a long-jawed adolescent, plain as an adult, almost embarrassing in her stark lack of the menace and mystery for which she was prepared to badger hell. It was only during the last strain of the galliard that she spun violently away from him into a jagged, blazing scurry of half-steps that carried her as far as the dais—himself three floundering beats behind her—then wheeling back to end with a high jump like a cry of rage, and a reverence so dazzlingly scornful that Farrell stood flat-footed, feeling as if every woman he had ever known, beginning with his mother, were laughing at him in the curve of her arm.

The music ended, but no one ever bowed to thank the musicians for that playing of the Earl of March's Galliard, for Aiffe shook her dust-colored hair and cried out, "Now is the geas fulfilled, and now are you free to speak your name to me. For I am a king's daughter and a maiden, and behold, we have danced a galliard together." The pupils of her eyes had gone oval, and there was a faint, pulsing corona of yellow-green around each one.

In the clearing, the bright voices were guttering and going out, two and three at a time. The dancers stared and murmured and sidled closer, most moving heavily now in tunics veined with sweat and gowns too damp to rustle. Farrell looked for Julie, but Nicholas Bonner hid her from him. Aiffe flung one arm wide, without turning, and Garth de Montfaucon prowled to her side, left hand on his sword hilt, right hand fretting with a wilting end of his *pince-nez* mustache. Farrell said, "Sweet Jesus in the underbrush. He's your father?"

"Aye, indeed," Aiffe answered clearly. "King Garth that was and will be, first ruler of Huy Braseal and still the longest-reigning." Farrell liked her just then, for the pride in her voice. He gazed around among the dancers, wondering numbly who her mother might be. *Maybe the kid's a changeling. Maybe he is. Why didn't Julie tell me?*

"My daughter is a princess of many realms," Garth de Montfaucon said quietly, "whether I am king or no." Aiffe put her arm through his, and they stood like that, smiling the same long, supple smile at Farrell. It made him think of Briseis' habit of laying her head alongside Sia's head, so that they could look at everything together.

"Now we will have your name." She spoke with the toneless cheer of a clubwoman at a reception filling out gummed lapel tags. Farrell was certain that he could challenge her on a technicality—*Garth's grandchildren will be terrific with animals and metal futures*—and knew equally well that he had neither the courage nor the meanness for it. Turning, he saw Nicholas Bonner looking on, all golden wonder, and he felt a sudden deep vertigo teasing him to let go of his real name, announcing loudly as he fell, "It's Joseph Malachi Lope de Vega Farrell, Rosanna, you want to make something of it?" *Names don't get stolen, for God's sake, credit cards get stolen. Why should I play by their rules?*

But Julie was pushing past Nicholas Bonner and through the dancers, shaking her head at him as urgently as if his temptation were flashing above him in a bubbly comic-strip thought balloon. Gaping and swaying next to a bemused King Bohemond, Crof Grant hummed *Will Ye No' Come Back Again?* in his nose. A trickle of sweat fluttered down Farrell's side, and the Countess Elizabeth Bathory leaned forward a little.

"Come, fair knight," Aiffe said, "your name." She hugged her father's arm, shivering with delight, looking like a puppy grinning around a stick it has no intention of retrieving. She held out her free hand to Farrell, palm up, wriggling the long, rag-nailed fingers.

There were no names in his head. Later that was to disquiet him as much as anything else; that he—junkman of the lost, curator of the truly useless, random cherisher, keeper, keener—should come to bay without so much as a third string Round Tabler or journeyman superman out of Italian romances at his call. Aiffe widened her strange eyes, attempting or burlesquing seductiveness, and Farrell found that he could not look away from her. The effort made him dizzy and short of breath, almost sick. He felt Nicholas Bonner's smile trailing across his shoulders, burning where it clung. Aiffe said three soft words that Farrell had never heard before. The sickness moved, spilling thickly through him like some spoiled wisdom that he knew he could not bear. She said the words again, and then a third time, and Farrell began to tell her his name, so she would stop.

Close at hand, a man was singing, or rather declaiming in a high-pitched rhythmic drone that sounded like stones and shells rasping back down a beach with the ebb tide. Farrell had no idea how long the man had been doing this.

> *"With a host of furious fancies,*
> *Whereof I am commander;*
> *With a burning spear and a horse of air,*
> *In the wilderness I wander. . . ."*

Aiffe looked up, and Farrell, released, stumbled a step forward, turned his head and saw Hamid ibn Shanfara. The Saracen's voice had again played its trick with distance; he was standing alone on a hummock of bare earth near the pavilion, with his shoulders back and his hands tucked into the sash of his white robe. He nodded very slightly to Farrell, touching a forefinger airily to the indigo turban, which was coming loose again.

Farrell laughed, feeling as though his throat were full of old straw. With the laughter came the next lines of the lonesome, gentle, possessed madman's song. He said to Aiffe, "My geas is still upon me. I may speak my name to no other hearing than yours."

She lowered her eyes to his again, but no power clenched on him this time, and he could tell that she knew it. She did not move until he whispered mockingly, "Come on, Rosanna, be a sport." Then she came toward him, and he half expected to see the ground rise in small surges under her feet, as the surface of the

134

mountain lake had done when the storm came pacing across it.

When she was very near, he said the name, holding it out between them like holy water or a kitchen chair. "I am the Knight of Ghosts and Shadows." Muscles crawled in Aiffe's temples, as though she were trying to lay her ears flat back; her lips all but disappeared. Farrell bowed to her.

Nicholas Bonner was hugging himself rapturously, bouncing on his tiptoes, mouth wide open, tongue floating and preening between strong bluish-white teeth. Farrell looked down and saw that the clover bracelet on his wrist—Julie's forgotten favor—had turned brown and crisp and was a breath away from falling to sharp crumbles. It scratched his skin faintly as he raised his arm to study it. From the look of it, he might have been holding it near a fire.

X

*B*en did not come home that night, nor the day and night after. Sia gave three unrelated explanations for his absence. On the third night, Farrell cooked dinner, and they ate in a tightrope silence in which Farrell's thoughts ticked and clanged and grated as noisily as his Aunt Dolores' insides had bombilated all through innumerable family gatherings. No one was ever allowed to take the slightest notice, even during a volley over a soldier's grave or Tournament Night at the bowling alley; which always meant the death of conversation before dessert, spluttering smaller cousins being hustled out of the dining room, and his mother reciting recipes in forlorn counterpoint to Aunt Dolores' salute to visiting royalty. Now in turn he heard himself chattering helplessly about garlic soup or his work at the zoo, trying to drown out the bowling-alley racket of his mind, while Sia watched him from far across the table, stolid as a sidewalk. She ate and drank whatever he set before her, as if that were her job.

After dinner, she built a fire, hunkering flat-footed to riffle through kindling like a cardsharp, turning the heavy madroña half-logs daintily around each other until they fitted, all but clicking into a perfect snowflake matrix. She snapped a single match at the pile and sat back with a soft little grunt as the flames exploded upward like arterial blood. Without turning, she said, "It is quite possible to die of unasked questions. Why do you never ask me what you want to know?"

Taken off-guard—they had been torpidly discussing the Avicenna City Council's recent motion to prohibit the local sale of war toys, grain-fed beef, and all dolls without genitals—he replied immediately, "How come you never go out of the house?" He had not realized that he was even aware of it.

"What kind of a question is that?" She sounded mildly surprised and amused. "What makes you think I don't go out?"

Farrell said, "Your clients come to you. Ben and I do all the shopping. You don't go anywhere with Ben— not to dinner, not to a party, a movie, a concert, not since I've been here. I haven't once seen you get the mail."

"But when do you ever see me, Joe? What do you think you see me doing?" Her voice remained oddly playful, almost arch. "All you can be sure of, with your schedule, is that I am someone who eats breakfast, receives strange people at strange hours, and likes to listen to your music in the evenings. For all you know, I might spend my afternoons preaching hell and repentance at a bus stop. I might be working with a gang of shoplifters, confidence tricksters. I might have half a dozen lovers or a paper route. You wouldn't know."

137

Farrell laughed grudgingly, and Sia said, "Ask me a real question."

"Where the hell is Ben?" Sia did not seem to have heard, but continued to squat with her back to him. Farrell said, "Sia, forty-eight hours is just too long for a departmental meeting, but it does make him a missing person. I think we ought to call the cops."

"No," she said to the fire. "No, we call no one." She was hugging herself, rubbing her shoulders as if she could not get warm. A song prickled across Farrell's mind: *Last night I saw the new moon, with the old moon in her arms.* He said, "When I saw him in Barton Park, he didn't recognize me. I didn't tell you that part."

"You didn't have to." Farrell heard the calmness as condescension and found that he was suddenly, carelessly furious. "Of course I didn't have to," he mimicked her. "Nothing ever comes as a surprise to Madame LaZonga. The cosmos is wired to that bay window in the kitchen, the gods check in with you twice a week, your rocking chair is shrouded in eternal veils of goddamn mystery. Me, I really don't want to know all that stuff, whether the universe runs on premium or unleaded. I'm just a bit anxious about my friend, that's all."

She was laughing before he had finished, a rough, generous whoop that set the fire tumbling and giggling itself. Realizing that she was trying to rise, he placed his hand under her elbow, letting her lever herself upright against him. The weight on his arm was so much greater than he had expected that he almost toppled over her, momentarily filled with the terror of drowning. The feeling vanished as soon as she was on her feet, and Sia gave no sign that she had noticed his clumsiness, or his fear.

"Ben was right, how nice," she said. "It takes serious

work to get you angry, but it's very rewarding." She gripped his upper arms, not laughing now. "In the first place, I see nothing from that window or that chair but what anyone else might see. That is the exact truth—and bloody annoying it is too, I can tell you. As for mysteries, visitations—" And here she drew her mouth impossibly down until she looked like Winston Churchill burlesquing the Mask of Tragedy. "—I regret, the gods have not dropped me so much as a postcard in a long time. Perhaps they lost my forwarding address." She gave him a gentle shake, grinning with her small white teeth, turning her face as though to bring every scored slackness into the cruelest light for him, like a beaten wolf exposing its throat to trigger automatic mercy. She said, "I am an old woman with a young lover and I don't know where he is. That is all the story, Joe. I told you that the first morning we met."

Standing this close, she smelled of the bitter coffee that she drank continually, and more faintly of the fire-smoke in her hair and the musky madroña slickness on her hands. Farrell asked, "How long has he been doing it? Running around in the woods, playing he's Egil Eyvindsson sacking monasteries."

The mocking, wholehearted smile bent like a broken leg. "If you mean the League, he has only been with them for a year or so, going to their little wars, fighting in their tournaments." Her tone was flat and dismissive whenever she spoke of the League. "But Egil is another matter. Egil is much older than all that." Abruptly she let go of him and stepped away, stumbling over Briseis dozing under the chess table. Briseis uttered the scream she had been saving for an earthquake, scuttled to Farrell, sat on his foot, and went back to sleep. Sia never took her eyes off Farrell.

"And Egil is real," she said softly and clearly. Farrell

139

felt his stomach chill with the familiar apprehension of unpleasant knowledge bearing down on him. Sia said, "Ben—our Ben—would have known you. Egil Eyvindsson doesn't know anyone in this world."

Oh, dear God, I have done it again. The gift is absolutely intact, I've done it again. He concentrated intensely on scratching Briseis' ears, hearing himself mumble, "I believe it, I mean, we were in a play together one time, *The Three Sisters*, and Ben just vanished into his part, Tusenbach, didn't break character for weeks, I mean even after the play. Tusenbach can be a real pain in the ass at a party." *What is it with me and weirdness, how do we find each other? Damn, you'd think one of us would grow out of it.*

"Come and sit down, Joe." It was a command, though her voice remained low. She took his hand and led him to the couch, while he added hopelessly, "I was Chebutykin. The old guy." Sia pushed him down firmly and sat across from him on a footstool, shoulders hunched and her hands hanging between her thighs. Except for the bright regard, gray as the moon, she looked like a sexless peasant sullenly working up to the effort of spitting into the fire. *Maybe it's Egil Eyvindsson who sleeps with her. Ben probably doesn't have the least idea.*

"How far they go back together, I cannot tell you," she said. "You know more than I do. Did Ben speak of him, do you remember him saying the name, even once?" Farrell was shaking his head, but she went on. "You played games, you used to make up voices, imaginary people; I have seen you do it. There was never a voice that could have been Egil?"

"Lord, no," Farrell said. "We did silly stuff, bus-ride routines, something to do waiting for the subway at two in the morning. You're talking about multiple personalities, you're talking about some kind of possession. It's not the same thing."

"What do you know about possession?" Her tone was suddenly so quick and blunt that he was sure he had angered her.

He answered placatingly, "Not much. I've never seen any devils come out of people's mouths, but I did know a Chinese guy in Hawaii who died, and his spirit went into a jeep." Sia growled softly, and Farrell corrected himself. "Actually, I really knew his nephew, it was his nephew's jeep. And I met a man back in New York who used to get taken over by Jane Austen twice a week. Mondays and Thursdays, I think it was. He'd call me up at all hours and read me whole chunks of this novel she was writing through him. Really sounded a lot like Jane Austen."

After a long moment the growl turned into a harsh chuckle, and she said, "I believe you. Those stories are so incredibly stupid that I must believe you completely. But I would be much more interested if your friend had been the one to possess Jane Austen, so that she began to write like him. Did you ever hear of anything like that?"

"No, of course not." He was strangely disconcerted by the idea; it made him physically giddy to think about it. "You can't have backward possession, retroactive possession; that's just silly, it couldn't work like that. You couldn't have it."

"Tell Ben," she said, and it was at that moment that Briseis, sprawled absurdly on her back before the fire, eyes shut tight and one foreleg pointing straight up at the ceiling, began to make the most terrifying sound that Farrell had ever heard an animal make. So high and cold and distant as hardly to be a cry of flesh at all, it was almost visible to Farrell—a petal-thin wire, coated and edged with powdered glass, like the strings of Asian fighting kites, spinning out of the dog's intestines to haul her, step by agonizedly mincing step, toward the front door, as if the other end were in the grip of the darkness beyond. Her neck was wrenched sideways and back, and she stared unbelievingly at Sia as she howled.

Sia was on her feet before Farrell had finished saying, "Jesus, what the hell?" Facing the door, she uttered a wordless cry of her own, raw and piercing enough to make the living room windows buzz and the old spears murmur hoarsely together in their wicker basket. There was no answer from outside, but Briseis abruptly gasped and toppled over, scrambling up instantly to vanish into the broom closet, where she remained for the next twenty-four hours. Sia never looked after her; rather, she raised her left hand slowly to her breast in a gesture of silent-movie shock and wonder. She stood unsteadily, rocking very slightly.

"You," she said, softly but very clearly. "*Thou*." She shook her head once and said something in a language full of creaking, snapping sounds. In English she added, "You cannot come in here. You still cannot come in." The doorbell chimed while she was speaking, followed by Aiffe's unmistakable splintery giggle. "Special delivery. Hey, somebody has to sign for this package." Something heavy thumped against the door, then slid partway down.

Without moving or turning her head, Sia motioned Farrell to the door. He could hear Aiffe snickering impatiently as he crossed the room and, under that, the little shivery rustle of a desperate voice talking to itself.

The words were impossible to distinguish, but Farrell did not need to.

When he opened the door, Ben fell across his feet, curling up convulsively as he did so. The crested helmet was gone, along with the belt-axe and the copper ornaments, and the torn black mantle was as mud-caked as his hair. Farrell crouched beside him, feeling for bruises and worse, relieved to find that the blood drying on Ben's face came only from a couple of long bramble scratches. Ben opened his eyes, and Farrell drew back momentarily from the helplessly murderous gaze of a mad stranger. Then it went out, as suddenly as whatever held Briseis had released her, and Ben said calmly, "The birds were freezing," just before he threw up a weak orange trickle over Farrell's shoes and fainted.

"We found him in the park," Aiffe said. "Right up by the merry-go-round, you know, the playground. He was climbing around on things and yelling." Farrell looked up at her as he wiped Ben's mouth with his handkerchief. She stood directly under the porch light, thumbs hooked into her jeans pockets, all her weight canted onto one flat hip, and a warily mocking grin stuttering across her face like a lit fuse. She was wearing sneakers, a denim vest, and a pale green T-shirt with the legend WHEN ALL ELSE FAILS, HUG YOUR TEDDY. "I think it's a blood sugar thing," she offered. "They're finding out now that a whole lot of people get really weird when their blood sugar drops."

Farrell said, "You know it's got nothing to do with his damn sugar content. What did you do, mug him? What did you do to him?"

The grin fizzed a moment longer, then exploded into a fireball of defiant delight. "You can't talk to me like that anymore. Nobody can." She took a step toward him, shaking with the violence of her exaltation. "I'm Aiffe, and I can say whatever I want, because I can do whatever I want. And you can't, so you don't talk to me like I'm nothing, a baby, a nothing. You just watch your tone, and you just try really, really hard to make friends with me. Because it makes a difference if I'm your friend or not." Her smile burned more trimphantly with each word, but Farrell saw tears in her eyes.

Behind him Sia said, "Joe, take Ben inside." Her voice was the small stone voice that Farrell remembered from the afternoon when McManus came drunk to the house. He put his arms clumsily under Ben and half dragged, half rolled him through the doorway. Glancing sideways, he saw Sia's stumpy legs move past to halt on the threshold, spreading to brace themselves so squarely and precisely that her house slippers did not protrude even an inch over the sill. She spoke again in the language that sounded like wind in the rigging; and from the delicate spring night, Nicholas Bonner's sweet, sweet laughter answered her.

"Speak English, cookie," he advised her, shrugging himself out of the porch shadows as he strolled forward. Dressed like Aiffe in jeans and a T-shirt—his was black, with a silver-sparkling face of Willie Nelson—he looked younger and more vulnerable than she, almost shy. He said thoughtfully, "Now why should I be so quick with any new human tongue, when you can't ever learn to speak even one quite properly? Why should that be, after all?" There was no mockery in his voice, but a strangely companionable wonder.

Ben stirred and whispered in Farrell's arms, his whole body abruptly dank with sweat. Sia said, "You learn. I make. I have created languages that were dust in the mouths of skulls before you were born. Have you forgotten? The gift you have was an apology, because you have nothing of your own. Have you forgotten, then?"

"I forget nothing," Nicholas Bonner said mildly. "I don't think I can." He kept his eyes down, letting the thick bronze lashes hide them. Aiffe draped herself against him, preening on his shoulder with the air of a movie gangster's showgirl mistress. "Nick's staying at my house," she announced. "Private tutor, hey, hey."

Neither Sia nor Nicholas Bonner seemed to have heard her. Sia made a sound in her throat like hard snow underfoot. She said, "In Augsburg. I thought that was the last time."

"Well, you always did underestimate me; admit it." His speech had lost every trace of another time or place; only the hungry humor remained, so cold that it glowed and danced like little deep-sea fish.

Ben was blinking and coughing now, trying to sit up, as Sia answered, "No, never you. Human stupidity, human longing, human madness, I have underestimated those forever." The last word was a flinty whisper, all but inaudible.

Aiffe said, "He's just here because of me. I brought him here, he's staying at my house." Pettishly playful, she tugged lightly at Nicholas Bonner's arm with both hands.

Farrell said loudly, "I'll get Ben on upstairs."

Sia never turned. Nicholas Bonner and she stood together in a shifting circle of light, and Farrell knew, as he knew nothing else in that moment, that past the circle's edge nothing existed—not himself, not whining Aiffe, not even a hurt, half-conscious Ben, muttering her name over and over like a penance. *If he stops doing that, what happens? Don't stop, don't let her forget about us.*

The boy's golden head lifted, and the transparent, insatiable, monstrously despairing eyes of Nicholas Bonner came to bear on Sia across the bright circle. "I always return where you are," he said. "Every time. Have you ever noticed that?" She did not answer, and Nicholas Bonner smiled. "And each time you're that much weaker, that much more imaginary. I could walk into your house now, if I wanted to."

Astonishingly Sia laughed then, no shotgun snort, but a rich, singing chuckle of seductive contempt. "You? Idiot wizards, drunken priests, any tinker woman with a grudge can banish you from this world; any spiteful child can call you back again. The yo-yo of the universe!" Farrell, struggling to keep Ben on his feet, almost dropped him at that comment. Sia said, "In my house, you? To walk through my shadow would destroy you." She added something in the wind-language, and Farrell wondered if she were calling Nicholas Bonner by his real name.

Aiffe, who had been gaping in growing resentment from one to the other of them, suddenly pushed past Nicholas Bonner into the light. Or at least she tried to; it seemed to Farrell that the circle's edge withdrew from her, slipping just far enough out of her reach to make her lurch clumsily after it, *like that circus clown who used to keep trying to sweep up the spotlight.* Even standing directly between Sia and Nicholas Bonner, thin face reddening, shoulders twisted, she was somehow further outside their concern than before, not merely nonexistent but impossible. She said to Sia, "Wait a damn minute, okay? Now. Who the *fuck* do you think you are?"

She blocked Farrell's view of Nicholas Bonner, but he felt the hot smile spreading on his skin. The boy said straight through her, gently, humbly, "Well, then you'll have to come out to me. Come out of your house and talk to me, old love."

For a moment Farrell thought that she would actually do it. The thick figure tautened, the grizzled hair flared in its silver ring like a cobra's hood, and Farrell found that he was sagging marrowless against Ben as the fire in the living room coughed and went out and an inhalation all around him set every door in the house slamming. Very far away, Sia lifted a bunny-slippered foot from the threshold and Aiffe shuddered to her knees; but Nicholas Bonner stood still, the slight body thrumming only a little, like a knife struck into a tabletop. When Sia put her foot down again, not a fraction further into the night than before, Nicholas Bonner winked at her, and the wink made a clicking, toothy sound, although Farrell knew that it couldn't. Too empty even to fall, he heard Ben whispering, "Sia. Sia. Sia. Sia. Sia."

Almost as softly, Nicholas Bonner said, "But you can't, can you? My poor friend, you're trapped in there. All your beautiful names, all those journeys, those glorious dwellings, all your empire, and just see what it's come to." And he clucked his tongue in perfect parody of sorrowful human relish. "Here you are, ruling over your last two lovers and a dog in a house like a stork's nest, and your power stops at your front door." He stretched his arms wide, wriggling his fingers elaborately, making Willie Nelson grin sequins. He said, "But I wonder if I do."

Ben said clearly, "Prester John, she knows," pointed more or less at Aiffe, and fell down with the effort. Aiffe moved to Nicholas Bonner's side, visibly trembling and so pale that her eyes had gone entirely green,

147

the bright, shallow apple-green of a hurricane sky. Nicholas Bonner put his arm around her without looking at her. He took a slow step toward Sia and then another, bringing the girl with him.

The old woman in the doorway said, "If you come any closer, I will not exile you again. Instead, I will change you."

Nicholas Bonner stopped where he was. His laughter broke over her, smoky-cold as the fumes of dry ice. "What I am doesn't change. Who should know that better than you?" He cocked his head, brazenly quizzical, but there was something surprisingly like wariness in the melting voice, something that remembered pain. "You saw to it yourself. I cannot be changed."

"Not for the better," she said. "That was always beyond me, from the first. But I can make you worse than you are." She did not raise her own voice, but the hair stirred along Farrell's forearms. Sia said, "Try, then."

The boy did not move. "Try it, try it, put 'em up," he mimicked her. "Old love, even at your best, even when you were really somebody, the most you could ever do to me was to push me off the sidewalk for a little while. What do you think you matter now, when you don't dare stick a toe out of your burrow? A traffic light has more power over me than you do, in this world."

"Yes?" The single flat syllable cracked and sparked with derision like static electricity. "Well, you might be right. I am certainly less than I was, no hiding that. But if you stick a toe into my house, I will think about you in a certain way, and you will never be able to wear beauty again, whatever form you may take. And who would pay the least heed to you then, or believe that you have any power at all, in this world?"

For a moment Nicholas Bonner's face became as pitilessly lonely as his eyes. He gripped Aiffe's shoulders until she yelped and swung her in front of him, saying in a light, careful voice, "Do it the way I showed you. Do it now."

Aiffe wriggled under his arm, refusing to look straight at Sia. "Nick, let's go, I need some more practice, okay?" Her acne patches were boiling up like stigmata.

"Focus," the boy said. "You can do it, it's just focusing. Just like in the park, exactly the same, now." He turned her body between his hands with a raging precision, aiming her. She neither resisted nor cooperated, but kept whimpering, "Nick, I want to go, let's go home." Nicholas Bonner took hold of her limp arm, holding it out, making her point at Sia.

Farrell gave up trying to lift Ben and began hauling him away from the door. He heard Sia's voice, full of a terrifying pity, "Child, no," and the boy saying, "*Now*," as the air suddenly smelled violently of lightning and the vast inhalation happened a second time. Farrell scrambled toward the stairs, feeling the old house lunging and aching in the ground, while the walls curtsied slowly to each other and the chess table, the chairs, and the fire tongs hurtled into his legs. He held fast to Ben, pulling against a power like the disemboweling undertow of a sinking ship. The floor seemed to be slanting steeply under him, and he knew that he heard the girl cry out in bitter shock and pain, a chattering moan that laid Farrell's spine bare. But it was Nicholas Bonner's voice, not hers; and with that, chaos came to an end almost as confounding as itself. In the tumbled, freezing house, the only sound was Sia's rasping sigh. Ben had finally stopped saying her name.

"You see," she said without triumph. "You cannot come in. Not even with her to make the way."

Aiffe was almost doubled over Nicholas Bonner's supporting arms, her mouth wrenched up at one corner like a hooked fish. Farrell half expected to see the boy drop her; but the dreadfully perfect face had already smoothed itself back into a bright mask of pleasure, and Nicholas Bonner held Aiffe most gently, stroking her shoulders, drawing his fingers down the back of her neck. He was murmuring to her, so quietly that Farrell could not hear the sound of the words.

"She is not harmed," Sia said. "Take her home. And if there is any mercy in you, any—" She struggled briefly to say something that could not even be thought in English, then used a phrase in the wind-language. "—then leave her there, leave her alone. She can never do what you want; she has not that kind of power. You have made a mistake about her. Let her go."

Ben was sitting up with Farrell's aid, speaking calmly and rather cheerfully in Old Norse. The lights of a passing car swam over the porch, and Farrell saw Nicholas Bonner carefully lift Aiffe and turn her toward him to lean her head on his chest. He smiled at her with something so much like tenderness that it chilled Farrell's heart twice over: once because in that moment the boy looked like someone who had always loved Aiffe deeply; and again because Farrell had no doubt that that particular smile was Nicholas Bonner's top-of-the-line model, the very best he could ever do. A dark splotch was spreading slowly on the girl's jeans, and Farrell realized that she had wet herself.

Nicholas Bonner raised his clear eyes to Sia. He said, "But it's what she wants. She called me here, she asked for my guidance—demanded it, really—and if I left her

now, she'd come right after me, she'd come looking."
He chuckled fondly, caressing Aiffe's matted hair.
"Oh, and you *would* find me, too," he praised her,
slipping into a baby-talk singsong. "Oh, yes, yes, she
would, of course you would." He might have been
crooning to a wriggly puppy.

Aiffe was still plainly too dazed to stand, and abruptly he picked her up in his arms, holding her easily
as he confronted Sia. The Sunday-best smile withered
to a cicatrice on the soft golden face. Nicholas Bonner
whispered, "She has no idea how close she came. You
and I know." Sia did not move or reply. The boy said,
"That kind of power. She almost broke you. Ignorant,
unpracticed, frightened out of her few wits, she almost
walked over you. You aren't quite senile enough not
to know."

Ben began to chant very loudly, thumping the time
on Farrell's knee: "*Hygg, visi, at—Vel soemir pat—
Hve ek pylja fet—Ef ek pogn of get.*" The tune was
dull, but it had a fine swing.

Nicholas Bonner said politely, "Till next time. Or
the time after that." He turned and walked away, carrying Aiffe as if she were his partner in one of the old
court dances. On the porch steps, he stopped and set
her on her feet, keeping an arm firmly around her. Aiffe
staggered once, clutching at him. They moved slowly
off down Scotia Street, leaning their heads together like
dreaming lovers.

Sia said, "Joe." Farrell propped Ben against a newel
post and went to her. She made no room for him in the
doorway, and he felt uneasy about squeezing in beside
her, so he stood cautiously at her shoulder, watching
her watch the street.

Behind them, Ben droned, "*Flestr maor of fra—*

Hvat fylkir va," and outside, the Avicenna night flowed past Sia's house, bearing someone's barbecue guffaw and the crackling bustle of a baseball game approaching on a portable stereo. Farrell caught a twinkle that he thought might be Nicholas Bonner's T-shirt vanishing behind a camper truck. His right knee ached where the fire tongs had bruised it.

"I cannot control what you will remember of this," she said. "I don't think I can." She turned to face him for the first time since Briseis had begun her dreadful crying, and he saw that the challenging gray eyes were alarmingly vague and streaked, and that her dark-honey skin had gone the color of scar tissue, all tone and resilience used up. The smell of her exhaustion filled his mouth, rancid, gritty, and clinging as the smoke of a garbage fire.

"Perhaps I won't even try to make you forget." Her voice, at least, was regaining some life, becoming almost comfortingly acerbic. "You work these things out very well with yourself, you will turn all this—" She gestured around them at the porch, at Ben, at spilled books and scattered furniture. "By morning it will have been some distant foolishness between strangers, maybe a little earthquake thrown in. You are doing it now, I can see you." Farrell began to protest angrily, but she walked away from him, saying, "It's not important, do what you want. I have to get Ben into bed."

Farrell helped her, though she did not want him to. Far too weary to command him, she ended by letting him bear most of Ben's weight as they coaxed him up the stairs, to the shoulder-pounding accompaniment of sonorous skaldic jingles. Farrell got the ruined Viking garments off, took them back down to the washing machine, stayed to set the living room to rights, and returned to find Sia sponging Ben's muddy bruises and brushing shreds of redwood bark out of his stiff hair. Ben had toppled into a turbulent doze, still mumbling rhythmically, his eyes slightly open. Sia was making a sound, too, so softly that Farrell felt it, rather than heard it, in his eyelids and the roots of his hair. *I've never been this close to their bed.*

"I was there when she called him," he said. "Aiffe, Rosanna, she called him right out of the air." Sia glanced at him briefly and went on bathing Ben. Farrell said, "The way you knew each other—I don't understand it, but I'm not going to forget it. I don't want to forget it."

Sia said, "Your lute has fallen on the floor in your room. You should go and see if there is damage." Her blunt, freckled fingers moved over Ben's body like cloud shadows.

"Fuck the lute. Is he all right?" The resonant idiocy of the question made him flinch and brace for mockery, but she was almost smiling when she looked at him again.

She said, "No. Nobody is going to be all right. But coffee would be good, anyway."

The lute was unharmed, though two strings had snapped. After bringing her the coffee, he sat on his bed replacing them, listening to Sia singing to Ben in their room on the other side of the house. She sang more clearly now that he was gone, and he could tell that the words were neither in English nor in the wind-language. The melody was bony and elusive, too alien to be ingratiating, but Farrell listened until it began to dissolve into him, note by note, like bubbles of nitrogen in a diver's bloodstream. He fell asleep wanting to learn to play it on the lute, but he never could.

XI

"Gone before I ever got up," Farrell said. "First thing I did, I didn't even get dressed, I went to check on him, and he was *long* gone. She said he ate breakfast, squashed a few snails in the garden, and off to campus. Another typical day down on the bread-and-jelly farm."

"What else did she say?" Julie was seated at her drawing table, working intently over a rendering of a diseased retina. When Farrell did not answer, she looked up and waved a bamboo pen for his attention. "What did you say to her, for God's sake? I refuse to believe you just split the paper and talked about the awful stuff on TV."

"She doesn't have a TV." Farrell had been watering Julie's houseplants, overdoing it as usual; now he leaned in the workroom doorway, pretending to examine a hanging spider fern. "I asked her things, Jewel. I really pushed. I asked her how she could possibly let him go back to work, as messed up as he was, and what

154

the hell is it anyway with him and this Egil Eyvindsson persona of his? And she looked at me and said, how about some nice orange juice, and *I* said, right, how about Nicholas Bonner, where did you and that little sweetheart go to school together? And she poured the orange juice, and that's the way it went. That big jade plant's dying, by the way."

"No, it's just sulking. I moved it from the bedroom, and it hasn't forgiven me yet." She turned back to the drawing, shaking her head irritably as she studied it, but still speaking directly to him. "It sounds as if you'd switched roles overnight, doesn't it? Now you're the one asking impertinent questions, and she's being not there. Very odd."

"She doesn't look good," Farrell said. "Whatever truly went on between her and Aiffe and Baby New Year, it took something scary out of her." He rubbed the side of his knee, which was blue-green and swollen. "At that, she looked a whole lot better than the girl. That's the one I felt sorry for; I couldn't help it." Julie's head came up swiftly, the dark eyes suddenly disquieted, wind-ruffled water. "Well, I did," he said. "She was like a kid at her first grown-up party, she was so sure she was in control, part of everything, the big time at last. Poor little twit, she didn't even know what to wear."

Julie said, "Never feel sorry for her." Her voice was tight and sharp, but it broke upward on the word *sorry*. She asked very quietly, "And you? Do you have any idea what did go on there last night? What games did they play at the party, Joe?"

Farrell looked back at her for what felt to him like a long time. Then he put his hands in his pockets and wandered to the window behind the drawing table, where he rested his forehead against the dusty, sunset-warm glass and watched Mushy the white cat trudging after starlings in Julie's tiny back yard. "I lived with a werewolf once," he said slowly. "Did I ever tell you about her?" Julie raised her left eyebrow slightly and curled her upper lip on the same side. Farrell said, "In New York. It isn't so much that she was a werewolf. What she mostly was, was nice, Jewish, very unhappy, and with a mother. She said, I remember, she said once being a werewolf was actually a lot less trouble than her goddamn allergies. It wasn't, of course. She was just saying that."

"I'm sure there's a reason for your telling me all this," Julie said. "Fairly sure."

"Just that I don't have any particular trouble with the supernatural. It bewilders me about as much as the natural, I can't always tell them apart." He turned from the window to watch her playing with the bamboo pen as she listened, the long, supple fingers gripping the shaft so strongly that it skidded and twisted like a desperate fish in her hand. He said, "Okay, Point A. The girl, Aiffe, she's a witch. A real one—maybe not major league yet, but working on it. Working very hard. How's that so far?"

"Go on." Julie put the pen down carefully, swung her chair to face him, and began clicking her thumbnails against each other. Farrell said, "Lord, I bet she clowns around a lot in school, drives the home room teacher crazy. Point B. Seems she's been trying to summon up demons, three times anyway. I don't know what happened on the first two tries, but this last time she got Nicholas Bonner. Now, he's not a demon, says so himself, so I can't even guess what he is, except old and bad and cute as a button. And clearly a chronic acquaintance of Sia's, sort of like you and me, which leads us to Point C. Am I going too fast, or too weirdly?"

"No." Seeing Farrell looking at her hands, she clasped them firmly together in her calm lap. "I've never met her, you know. She never comes to the League things with Egil. Ben. I think the Countess Elizabeth went to see her a few times."

Farrell considered that, remembering the cat-faced, strudel-bodied woman who had teased his palm at the dance. "The mind reels. Right, okay, Sia. Who is Sia, what is she, that Ben is a completely different man, physically changed, because of living with her? That she can make a crazy drunk with a gun kneel and grovel and shoot himself in the leg, without touching him? That she can mess with your memory, speak languages that I *know* do not exist, and keep a vigorous young witch and a—a person of indeterminate species but great, great strength of purpose from coming into her house? I mean, this is no ordinary landlady, Jewel, it's time to face facts. I will go further and say this is no ordinary marriage counselor. Incidentally, you are aware that we're having our first high-level conference? I just didn't think it should go unremarked."

He was clowning for her to some degree, and she did smile then, with genuine pleasure, but also with too much understanding. She said, "Look at you. Can't ever get you talking about what's really going on in there, and then, when you do start, it's like a flash flood. A little dangerous." Farrell was not sure what she meant; but when she bowed her head for a moment and knuckled wearily at a place at the top of her spine, his own backbone shivered and sparked in greedy tenderness, and he took a step toward her. Julie said, "Point D."

"Point D," Farrell said after a silence. "Ben. She was starting to tell me something, I think, right before the trick-or-treaters showed up." He closed his eyes, trying to hear Sia's rough, sudden voice asking him, *"What do you know about possession?"* Slowly, laying the words out as precisely as Julie had set down the bamboo pen, he said, "I read one time, whenever Mozart feels another flute concerto coming on, he takes over this housewife in Strasbourg, dictates it through her. Chopin, Mahler, Brahms, apparently they all take turns using the some poor woman. She says it's a great honor, but very tiring."

"And you think that's what's happening to Ben? Some ninth-century Viking just borrows him every now and then to run around in Barton Park?" The words were mocking, but the way she sat watching him was not.

Farrell shook his head. "I did at first, I guess because that's the only kind of possession you ever hear about. Now I don't know." He hesitated, remembering the words that had been all but lost in Briseis' terrible crying, and added, "It's not what Sia thinks."

Julie drew breath to speak and then didn't. Her thumbnails were scraping at each other again. "Well, you'll have to bring me over there for dinner sometime," she said at last. "Sounds like quite a crowd."

Farrell looked at his watch. "Dinner. Point E. High-level conference to be continued over *sashimi* and *sake* at the Half-Moon House. Say amen, and let's boogie."

But she was already turning her chair around again, rotating the drawing to sketch the retina from another angle. "Joe, I can't go anywhere, I'm going to be up all night with this stuff. Call me tomorrow."

"I'll cook," Farrell said. He found himself childishly

reluctant to leave her in the quiet, warm clutter of her workroom and walk out into aimless twilight with his mind still bustling with shadows. "You've got that fish in the refrigerator, I'll make lemon fillets. Just work, don't worry about it. Lemon fillets, nice orange and onion salad, I fix. You got any real garlic?"

Julie stood up and came to him, putting her hands in his hair. "Baby, go home," she said gently. "This is what I do. I'm not hungry and I like working at night and I really have trouble working with anyone in the house. It's getting to be a problem with men."

"Never used to be a problem." The sound of his own complaining voice fed his strange fretfulness back on itself. "The first time I ever saw you, you were painting a still life in the middle of a party. In the kitchen, by God—people rampaging in and out, necking, fixing drinks, something going on the stove, smelling like a home urinalysis, and you eating an apple, painting away, not paying no mind to nothing. You remember that? I think I was looking for the paper towels. A whole bunch of paper towels."

"I was eighteen years old, what did I know?" Julie said. "Go home, Joe. This is what I do now. The drawings have to be ready tomorrow morning, because somebody needs them. The Lady Murasaki, that scared, show-offy girl you want back, she's for weekends, special occasions, whenever I need her." She kissed him then, biting his lower lip and shaking her head slightly. "I still do," she said, "once in a while. Maybe it's the same way with Ben."

Farrell asked, "What about Ben? I have to talk to him, I have to do something about Ben. What the hell do you think I should do?" For a moment Julie's hands tightened on the back of his neck, cool as new leaves, but holding him hard enough that he could feel the smooth callouses on the sides of her drawing fingers. But she only said, "Call me at work," and kissed him again, and—as neatly as Sia ever hemmed his memory or Nicholas Bonner made time clear its throat—they were smiling through her screen door; but he turned away first, never knowing how long she leaned against the door afterward, and a pair of early stars were pricking into view above the Waverly as he sat in Madame Schumann-Heink, wishing he were just arriving at Julie's house and wondering what to say to Ben. *I can't go back there until I think of something.*

Eventually he drove away from the university streets, down below Gould, past the freeway, almost as far as the Bay, to eat ribs and sausages hot enough to cause double vision and cauterize polyps, in a diner slightly bigger than a camper truck. The decor was the same as in his student days—framed railroad timetables and signed photographs of almost-familiar singing groups—and the sour-tempered daughters of the sour-tempered black couple he remembered were still yelling at each other in the kitchen. Farrell found this immensely comforting and overate out of several kinds of hunger.

Standing outside the door, breathing carefully to test his charred sinuses, he heard a rough, friendly voice, sounding almost at his ear: "Hey there, old Knight of Ghosts and Shadows." Farrell turned and saw the man he knew as the Saracen Hamid ibn Shanfara crossing the street toward him, in company with Lovita Bird and two of the musicians from the King's Birthday Revels. One was tall, with long, thinning brown hair and the bovinely enduring expression of a Flemish St. Anthony; the other looked like a happy satyr, red-bearded and

160

bowlegged. They bowed formally to Farrell, there in the tarnished light of the rib joint, as Hamid made introductions. "This is Messer Matteo dei Servi, and this here now *mauvais sujet* and generally worthless type is Brother Felix Arabia." Farrell bowed back and asked them whither they were bound.

"Armed combat class," Hamid answered cheerfully. "Come on along with us. Nothing on public TV tonight except cooking and dog-walking, anyway."

"Armed combat," Farrell said. "As in clash of broadsword on buckler. Shivering of lances. Yield thee, caitiff."

The satyr Felix Arabia grinned at him. "Thursday nights, seven-thirty. Best show in town, for the money." He cocked his rowdy head at the saint. "He's serious about it, he's teacher's pet, just about. Hamid and Lovita and me, we're not really in the class, we're just his occasional cheerleaders. Groupies." He made a baton-twirling gesture, which somehow contained the hard twinkle of an invisible sword.

Farrell found that he was walking with them, Lovita Bird's arm through his and Matteo dei Servi saying shyly, "Actually, I'm not that good, not enough time to practice. I think of it like a discipline, like a philosophy. It's great for my concentration." The long, cumbersome bundle that he and Felix took turns carrying kept nudging Farrell's side coldly, like an inquisitive shark.

Farrell asked, "Who teaches this stuff? Where on earth do you find people who know about medieval fighting techniques?" Felix Arabia looked mildly surprised. "Man, everybody in Avicenna is insanely knowledgeable about something. Especially fighting. Any kind of combat master you want—armed, unarmed—they're all over the place these days. Like wandering samurai in Kurosawa movies."

"Lute players, now," Matteo dei Servi said. "Lute players are tricky to find. *Good* lute players."

Felix Arabia said, "Speaking of which," and for the rest of the way they took turns urgently coaxing Farrell to join their consort Basilisk. When he pointed out that he could only play one instrument well, while the rest of the group—except for the Lady Criseyde, their percussionist—were clearly at home with half a dozen, he was reassured by Felix, "Listen, we don't need any more damn sackbuts and serpentines, but we have got to have a lute."

And Matteo said, "People *expect* a lute, anything older than Mozart, they just do. We're starting to play a lot of non-League jobs around town, and they always ask."

"Paying gigs?"

Felix and Matteo nodded eagerly. Hamid chuckled, and Lovita squeezed Farrell's arm, saying, "I'm his agent."

Farrell said, "We'll talk."

The combat master lived in a fat, battered Victorian at the end of a torn-up street, isolated on three sides by construction moonscapes and on the fourth by a half-completed freeway tributary, so that the effect was of a ruinous old molar clinging on in a skeletal jaw. The front door was open, and Farrell's companions led him into a high, cold room, empty of all furnishing or decoration, save for the rubbings and engravings of weapons and armor pinned to the walls. Five men, dressed alike in padded ski clothing, including boots and heavy gloves, were moving stiffly to stand before a goat-bearded little man in a blue polo shirt and faded chinos.

When he turned to nod curtly to the newcomers, Farrell saw that his eyes were a bright yellow-gray, an African parrot's eyes.

Two of the students wore conventional saber masks; two others had on motorcycle helmets with tinted bubble face guards. The face of the fifth man—a slighter figure than the rest, as far as Farrell could judge through the quilted jacket—was entirely hidden under a steel helmet like an upside-down carafe, the lip of which extended down to cover the wearer's neck. Where the handle should have been, the pointed visor jutted out, bucktoothed and blank. There were slits in the visor, but Farrell could see nothing through them.

Lovita nudged him, whispering, "Your Lady Murasaki, she made that one. Big old thing weighs more than she does." The five men were now ranged before the combat master, peering warily at him over the painted shields on their arms. All but one of the shields were kite-shaped and wooden, four feet or more in length; the lone exception, shaped like a flatiron and obviously as faithfully ponderous as the steel helmet, belonged to the same slender man, whose limbs appeared almost too frail to support the rigors of authenticity. Farrell asked Hamid, "Did she make the shield too?"

The Saracen shook his head. "Henryk Tourneysmith made it last year for William the Dubious. William must have gotten tired of dragging it around."

Matteo dei Servi had unwrapped his bundle of medieval paraphernalia and was changing clothes hurriedly as the little instructor moved nimbly among his padded pupils, sharply tapping a bent arm to bring a shield up to nose height, gripping and turning a shoulder until it made a right angle with the shield. "Bend your knees, I pray you, sweet lordlings. We have spoken of this before." He had a dry, hot voice, rich with impatience. "Right hand on the hip to keep the shoulders straight." He walked around the man with the steel helmet and shield and nudged him vigorously behind the knee. "Feet flat, knees right out over the toes. Ought to be like sitting in a rocking chair by now." The man staggered and seemed for a moment about to crumple. The combat master said, "If you were properly balanced, I couldn't do that," and went on to correct the next student.

Hamid said softly to Farrell, "His name is John Erne. He's been doing this for years, and it is the only connection he has with the League. Doesn't dance, doesn't feast, doesn't take part in anything but this. He won't even fight in the tournaments anymore."

"What does he do the rest of the time?"

Hamid shrugged. "No idea. Man could be a dealer, man could be running a day-care center. I think he's a closet investment counselor, but I can't prove it."

The combat master now chose a sword from several leaning in a corner—all made of planed and shaped rattan—and stood gazing abstractedly at the six men, letting the wooden blade rest on the palm of his left hand. Abruptly he swung the sword up and far back behind his shoulders, took two odd, spraddling steps forward, and struck with all his strength at the nearest man's head. Farrell caught his breath; but the student's shield came up to take the blow, which rattled the shield back into his face. The combat master immediately cocked his arm again for a savage cut at the student's legs; when the swiftly lowered shield turned the blade once more, he aimed another stroke at the helmet and followed it with one to the exposed side. The student intercepted the latter attack, but moved his shield out of the perpendicular to do so, and the master promptly whipped his sword through a backhanded slash to catch the opposite leg just above the knee. The leg buckled, and the student gasped, dropping his guard to clutch himself.

"Up and down," the little master said coldly. "The shield moves only up and down, my gentlemen." Without another word, he leaped at the next man in line— Matteo dei Servi—battering the edges of his shield with a wild drumfire of circling overhand blows. The shield jumped and twisted, dragging at Matteo's arm as he struggled to deflect the onslaught, but he managed to keep it from being driven to either side, and the rattan sword never touched his body. The master stalked on, a goateed *golem* in a polo shirt, smashing at the shields with a mechanical fury as they presented themselves— skinny arms swarming tirelessly, bunchy body almost coming off the floor with each blow. The cold room clacked like a windmill.

When he came to the slender man in the huge carafe-helmet, the combat master paused for a moment, his lined, slanting face seeming to hold pity uncomfortably. He struck twice, lightly, pushing the steel shield from side to side, then said something that Farrell could not hear. The student shook his head without answering and raised the shield to a defensive position again. The master sighed, and the rattan sword tinkled and tolled crazily on the painted steel. It was impossible for the slender man to move the shield quickly; he managed to block a surprising number of the strokes, but the rest went home on his body and legs, making a sound like pine sap exploding in a fire. He never flinched, but Farrell did.

The combat master stepped back and lowered his sword. "Ten minutes." He turned abruptly toward Farrell, Hamid, Lovita, and Felix Arabia, walking with the powerful near-waddle of a ballet dancer. When he hunkered down by them, leaning on the sword for support—a Roman campaigner squinting over the tumbled twilight ravines of Pictish country—he might have been thirty-five years old or sixty. His skin and his sweat-stiffened collar-length hair were the same anonymous color, somewhere between smoke and sand. Hamid said, "John Erne, the Knight of Ghosts and Shadows."

John Erne extended his hand, smiling quickly. "Another musician? Yes, of course." His round, shallow eyes went over Farrell's body as if it were a car on the grease rack.

Farrell asked, "How do you know? Just because I came in with musicians?"

"Well, that," John Erne said. "But mostly because you flinched so, every time I came near hitting somebody's hand." He held his own hands out in front of him, palms down, amusedly regarding their pale-furred backs. The knuckles lumped up like Turk's-head knots, even with the hands open, and two nails on the right hand were black and crisp. "I average about a finger a year so far," he said thoughtfully. "Broke a whole hand the spring before last, in a mêlée." His hands were smaller than Farrell's.

The combat students had taken off their helmets and were leaning against the wall, standing and sitting, all breathing with their mouths open. They all appeared to be in their late teens, except for Matteo dei Servi and the slender man, who sat by himself, bowed over the steel helmet in his lap. When he looked up, Farrell saw that he was Japanese.

Felix Arabia protested, "We don't all worry about our hands." He nodded toward Matteo, already practicing feints and countermoves with his shield. "Look at him, he's *ready*. Come the next Whalemas Tourney, he's going to be out there pounding on anything that moves." Matteo looked over toward them and grinned like a summer-camp photograph.

John Erne chuckled unmaliciously, turning away to check the wrappings of his sword hilt. "He won't, you know." Farrell noticed that his teeth were odd sizes—an assortment rather than a set—and that his nose had been broken at least once.

"Musicians have to practice," John Erne said. "I never met a real musician who wasn't a miser with himself. They'll never come all the way with you anywhere." Farrell stared at him, and the combat master went on, "They know how to learn things. Your friend there, I'll teach him how to do a weapons pass, or how to use his shield in close work, and he'll pick it up faster than the rest of the class, because he's accustomed to thinking about technique. But frankly, I wish he wouldn't bother with it. He'll just be learning how to do something; the better he gets, the more I'll get angry, and he'll never understand why. I really wish he wouldn't bother."

"My goodness," Farrell said slowly. He felt himself smiling, thinking of Julie. He said, "You're like me."

The flat yellow gaze considered him more reflectively this time. "Am I? I don't have any room for more than the one seriousness, if that's what you mean." He shrugged gracefully, rolling his beard between two fingers. "I've had a local reputation for a long time as a sort of knowledgeable nut. People invite me to their history classes, and I give demonstrations and talk about extinct attitudes. I talk about chivalry, honor, *prouesse*, and playing by the rules, and I watch their skins crawl."

Farrell was startled to feel his own skin stir with the words. Hamid said easily, "Well, you make them real edgy, John. This is Avicenna, they just like theoretical violence, rebels in Paraguay blowing up bad folks they don't know. They like the Middle Ages the same way, with the uncool stuff left out. But you scare them, you're like a pterodactyl flapping around the classroom, screaming and shitting. Too real." The round eyes seemed to flick without closing, as parrots' eyes do.

"A dinosaur. You think so?" John Erne laughed— a rattle of the nostrils, no more. "This is my time." He leaned forward and patted Farrell's knee hard. "This is the time of weapons. It isn't so much the fact that everyone has a gun—it's that everyone wants to *be* one. People want to turn themselves into guns, knives, plastic bombs, big dogs. This is the time when ten new karate studios open every day, when they teach you Kung Fu in the third grade, and Whistler's mother has a black belt in aikido. I know one fellow on a little side street who's making a fortune with *savate*, that French kick-boxing." Farrell watched the combat master's face, still trying to determine how old he was. He appeared most youthful when he moved or spoke, oldest when he smiled.

"The myriad arts of self-defense," John Erne said. "They're all just in it because of the muggers, you understand, or the police, or the Zen of it all. But no new weapon ever goes unused for long. Pretty soon the streets will be charged with people, millions of them, all loaded and cocked and frantically waiting for somebody to pull their trigger. And one man will do it—

168

bump into another man or look at him sideways and set it all off." He opened one hand and blew across his palm as if he were scattering dandelion fluff. "The air will be so full of killer reflexes and ancient disabling techniques there'll be a blue haze over everything. You won't hear a single sound, except the entire population of the United States chopping at one another with the edges of their hands."

Farrell asked quietly, "Where does that leave chivalry?"

Matteo dei Servi and another student had begun to work out with their swords and shields, circling each other with the peculiar hitching stride that the combat master had employed. They carried the rattan blades well back and almost horizontal, at helmet height, and they struck over the tops of their shields in the rhythm of fencers, turn and turn about. John Erne snapped his fingernails sharply against his own sword as he watched them.

"A dead art form," he said, "like lute music. As unnatural to the animal as opera or ballet, and yet nobody who puts on even cardboard armor can quite escape it—any more than you can escape the fact that your music believes in God and hell and the King. You and I are what they used to call witnesses, vouching with our lives for something we never saw. The bitch of it is, all we ever wanted to be was experts."

Abruptly he turned his head and called to the two warily parrying students, "Single-time now!" They faltered for a moment; then the tempo of their fighting doubled, each man guarding against a cut as he delivered one. John Erne said, "There can't be a dozen fighters in the League who haven't been through this room. I have trained men to use the broadsword, greatsword, dagger and buckler, maul, flail, mace, the halberd, and the war axe. Some of my students could survive now if you dropped them back into Visigoth Spain or the Crusades."

"So long as they didn't drink anything," Farrell said, and Lovita Bird added almost simultaneously, "Long as they could bring their cassette players."

The combat master looked at them without answering. Matteo's adversary aimed a sweeping forehand slash at his head, but Matteo caught it on his shield and moved in to strike where the man's shield had swung away from the body to counterbalance the roundhouse blow. It sounded like someone jumping on a mattress. The student coughed and bent forward slightly.

John Erne called, "You are less by a leg, Squire Martin." The young man stepped back, turning a gasping, angry face toward the three watchers. "It wouldn't have cut through the armor. It has to cut armor."

"Nay, of us two, who's to be the judge of steel?" John Erne replied mildly. "You're down a leg, Martin."

The student shrugged and lowered himself to one knee, slow in the thick clothing. He crouched behind his shield, exposing nothing but his sword arm. Farrell expected Matteo to strike at that, but he chose to attack over the shield, punching blindly for the tucked-down head and almost compelling the kneeling man to cut at his shoulder. John Erne sighed faintly.

There was no need for him to call a wound; Matteo immediately dropped his shield, switched his sword from right hand to left, and came on more cautiously, trying to take advantage of his foe's limited reach. But he was carrying the sword too high against a crouching opponent; when the logical swipe at his legs came, he had to jump back and launch the return blow while still off-balance. The effort brought his head down within range of a desperate lunge and strike, as his own sword whacked home on Squire Martin's motorcycle helmet. John Erne shouted furiously, "Double kill!" and both fighters collapsed in proper style, rolling pitifully onto their backs. Martin, his faceguard knocked loose, rubbed at his runny nose.

"Dear God," John Erne murmured. He stood up, twiddling his beard again. The ropy, boyish body had not slackened for an instant of the conversation.

Hamid said, "John. Tell the man why you won't have anything to do with the League. You could have taken the whole thing over long ago."

The parrot gaze moved from him to Farrell and back again, the face remaining as serene as a clock's face. "I have a better League here," John Erne said. He tapped his forehead just above the tail of one spiky eyebrow. "I like mine much better."

Farrell watched him walk back to his students, eyes down, feet a bit pigeon-toed. The splotched polo shirt clung to his protuberant shoulder blades. He nodded the two fallen fighters to their feet and confronted the half circle of masked boys. Lovita Bird said, "That man is seriously crazy."

Hamid folded his long legs under him and leaned back against the wall, his chestnut eyes looking very far away. "Might be this is what keeps him sane."

"It's strange," John Erne was saying. "The one thing I really know about broadsword fighting you'll all have to learn from someone else. The first man you face in the Whalemas Tourney will teach you that it's very important to use your shield well and also that you don't know how. You've gotten good enough with the sword, all of you, but your idea of shield work is peeking around an ironing board." He sighed and shrugged, twisting his mouth. "One reason I try to avoid watching my students fight."

A large, blond boy with a swagbelly like a laundry bag spoke up. "Sir Fortinbras—the one I'm supposed to be squire to—says a shield ought to be as big and light as you can manage it. Without making it so light it splits right off."

"Sir Fortinbras hasn't improved as a fighter in three years, for just that reason," John Erne replied calmly. "No more has Raoul of Carcassonne or Simon Widefarer. Those kite shields they all use were made for men on horseback—they're pathetic things to be dragging around in close work. They blind you exactly as much as they protect you, they throw your balance off just horribly, and they stop your technique right where it is. I could go through a field of those things with a butter knife. Foolishness."

He jerked a forefinger at the Japanese student, who was scowling avidly at him over his folded arms. "Most of you probably feel a bit superior to the Ronin Benkei, watching him struggling with that manhole cover of his all this time. But the Ronin Benkei dances with his shield, very old dances of attack and defense called *kata*s. He tells me that he does it twice a day. Can anyone here do that? Martin? Arnulf? Orlando? Can you dance with your plywood weapons?" They shrugged, grinning. The Ronin Benkei's expression did not change.

"I'm embarrassed to admit that I can't either," John Erne said. He drew his own shield out of a frayed, green flannel bag that hung on the back of a chair. His shield was made of steel backed with leather, like the Ronin Benkei's, but it was circular in shape and moderately

convex. Two reinforcing steel bands crisscrossed it, sur-
mounted where they met in the center by a heavy
leather boss ornamented with a painted pattern of
leaves and moons.

"We're going to go on to the weapons pass," John
Erne announced. "The idea of the pass—unlike the
overrun, which, as we know, is nothing much but crashing into your man in hopes of knocking him off balance—is to open up the side you're after without
leaving yourself vulnerable. You'll see a lot of clever
maneuvers like these at the Whalemas Tourney. Some
of them will be aimed at you, so you'd better learn how
to guard against them and how to do them yourselves."
He beckoned to the boy called Squire Arnulf. "Approach and have at me."

Arnulf donned his saber mask, adjusted the long
shield on his arm, and set himself to face the combat
master. John Erne, standing indifferently straight and
scuffing his feet, launched an artless, looping head cut
which the boy picked off easily, raising his shield a few
inches. For a moment, the shield's arc blocked his vision; in that moment, John Erne did a stiff little dance
step and rushed him, lashing like a scorpion into the
sudden gap between shield edge and flailing sword as
he went by. Arnulf swayed, and his sword arm rose to
his featureless head. John Erne sprang back, no trace
of triumph on his face, but only a puckered academic
earnestness. "Now how did I do that?" he demanded.

Arnulf did not answer, but the Ronin Benkei shifted
slightly to catch the combat master's attention. "Your
back leg," he said. "You moved your back leg way
around to your left for the first cut, and that lured his
shield out of line, even before you got it up in front of

his eyes. Then you threw your weight back and pivoted and went in." His voice was very soft and uninflected.

John Erne nodded curtly. "The important thing is keeping your own shield in the same position all the way through. Move those shoulders even a little, and you wind up tied in a knot with Sir Gregory the Grungy about to stave in the back of your head." He laughed his soundless laugh again, but his cheeks were flushing rustily as he looked at the students. He said, "Remember, my gentlemen, this is a representation of death. This has no point system, no electronic umpires, no Olympic team. This is a matter of someone trying very hard to split your skull with eight pounds of iron. If you don't know that when you're fighting, absolutely, then you're missing the point of everything, and I really don't want you in my class." Farrell heard a faint whiny rustle as John Erne drew breath and realized that the combat master was an asthmatic.

He asked Hamid about it later, as they were walking away from the old house with Felix Arabia, Lovita, and Matteo. The Saracen nodded, the scattering of silver hairs in his beard glinting in the blue city moonlight. "It's under control now, but I guess it came near killing him when he was young. That's the one truly personal thing I know about him."

Matteo said, "Well, that's probably why he's so obsessed by this stuff, he's compensating."

But Felix Arabia hooted him down. "Fast-food psychology. Lovita's right, the man's crackers, that's all. Functional, pretty harmless—although I can imagine circumstances where maybe he wouldn't be so harmless—but a stone-ground Wheat Thin."

They were still arguing when they parted from Farrell, Lovita, and Hamid, crossing the street to catch a bus. On the corner Matteo called back to Farrell, "Basilisk has rehearsals every Wednesday night. My place—Hamid'll tell you how to get there." Farrell waved and smiled.

"You going to join up with them?" Lovita asked.

Farrell said nothing until they turned down the side street where he had parked Madame Schumann-Heink illegally. "The only thing I've ever joined was the linoleum layer's union. I haven't played with a group in years. Probably wouldn't fit in too well."

Hamid said, "Do it. They play good music and they're a kick to work with. And you can be part of the League or not, nobody expects the musicians to do all that much. Yeah, Basilisk would be just about right for you."

There was a parking ticket flapping like a trapped moth under Madame Schumann-Heink's windshield wiper blades. Farrell put it in his pocket and turned with his hand on the door latch. He said, "I've met Prester John." Hamid's face became very still. Farrell went on, "You're a *griot*, you're a rememberer, you know everything about the League. Tell me what happened to Prester John."

Hamid ibn Shanfara, whose true name Farrell never learned, glanced sideways at Lovita Bird, but it was the Queen of Nubia who looked disdainfully back at him. She had been largely silent during the combat class, paying elaborate attention to her nails and to an imagined stain on her leather skirt. She said to Farrell, "Honey, the man can't tell you. I mean, he won't ever tell *me* what went down about all that, so he damn sure better not just decide to drop it all on you now." Hamid put his arm around her; it was the first awkward move that Farrell had seen him make. Lovita said, "It's that girl, I know that much, anyway. Something real nasty she did, but won't nobody talk about it. Not him, nobody."

"Prester John was a friend of Julie's," Farrell said. "I really need to know, Hamid."

"Nothing to know." Hamid's voice was as quiet and reasonable as the people who climbed the stairs to Sia. "Nothing to tell. Whatever happened, it happened, no way to make it unhappen." He implied a bow without actually performing it and turned away.

"A whole lot of people sure trying, though," Lovita Bird said to the air.

Ben's car was in the driveway when Farrell got back, but Sia and he were already in their bedroom, although it was still early for them. Farrell ate an apple, dialed all but the last digit of Julie's phone number twice, felt morosely pleased with himself for not interrupting her work, and spent an hour coaxing a fever-eyed Briseis out of the broom closet. She could not be dragged anywhere near the front door, so they went out back together and sat in Ben's garden, listening to the distant respiration of traffic and the vicious squabbling of nightbirds.

XII

*A*s it turned out, *saying anything to Ben in the*
following days would have been like trying to subpoena
a quark. He managed to be gone every morning, no
matter how early Farrell made a point of coming down
to breakfast, and the only weekend difference was Sia's
excuse for his absence. Farrell knew his office hours
and twice used his own rotating half-day off to visit him
on campus; both times he was told that Ben had left
ten minutes before. As aware as Farrell had always
been of his own skill at avoiding even the shadow of
an inconvenient confrontation, he had never suspected
that Ben shared the same gifts, and he marveled and
was indignant. *What I do is what I do, but I really
thought better of him. What kind of model is that for
our youth?*

Inevitably, of course, they were both in the same
house on the same evening. They were not in the same
room any more than Ben could help it; but on four
separate occasions, they sat down with Sia to the same

dinner. Somewhat to his own surprise, Farrell let none of those encounters go past without bringing up the matter of the dance in Barton Park, Ben's disappearance after it, and Sia's mysterious and bruising standoff with Aiffe and Nicholas Bonner. He threw in McManus once, partly by accident, but partly because he was genuinely enjoying the new experience of being the relentless Hound of Heaven. *Very addictive, wanting to know things. Lead you into worse ways if you're not careful.*

Three times, like one of John Erne's students, Ben turned Farrell's attack lightly, using as his shield a careless mix of jokes, digressions, and an all but insulting account of overdosing on nut-brown ale and getting clumsily mugged by equally drunk incompetents. When Farrell asked why he had kept his membership in the League For Archaic Pleasures secret, Ben only shrugged, half smiling. "Part of it was Crof Grant, I guess. I couldn't quite see telling you that that fool and I played the same dress-up game. And it was you, too, because you've always had an idea of me that doesn't go with dress-up. As if it would be all right for you to get involved with something like the League, but not for me. I really thought about your being embarrassed for me. Probably why I didn't want to recognize you."

Farrell looked hard at Sia, but the gray eyes under their thick lids were as brutally empty—*or as full of things I can't see*—as Egil Eyvindsson's eyes had been.

But on the fourth evening, the first tentative words out of Farrell's mouth on the subject of vanishings and visitations brought Ben to his feet, leaning across the table to shout a furious confession. "God damn you, Joe, I have seizures! You know about seizures? As in fits? As in roll on the ground, foam at the mouth, swallow your tongue, run into walls? As in start out for work and wake up two days later in the drunk tank, the mental ward, Intensive Care? Any of that stuff ring a bell?" He was stammering and shuddering with rage, and his face seemed out of focus because of the way the small muscles were struggling under the skin.

"Epilepsy?" Farrell's voice sounded in his own ears like a mumbled request for spare change. "You never missed any school. I was the one."

Ben shook his head, interrupting him impatiently. "It isn't epilepsy. No one can tell me just what it is. And I never had it when we were kids, it didn't start until—" He hesitated only minimally. "—until after college." Amazingly he smiled, but it was a flinch of the lips, lasting no longer than the pause. "As a matter of fact, I had two attacks when we were living on Tenth Avenue. Onetime you weren't home, and the other you were busy with some girl, you wouldn't have noticed a UFO. And they were a lot milder back then, the seizures."

Sia had vanished unnoticed, as she could always do when she chose. Farrell said, "You should have told me."

Ben sat down again, his anger exhausted as abruptly and frighteningly as it had flowered. "No, I shouldn't have. I should not have."

"The way you've been ducking and sliding and soft-shoeing around here, you know what I've been imagining? What the hell would have been wrong with telling me?"

Ben was silent, rubbing so hard at the base of his throat that Farrell could see the fingermarks flushing. He said finally, "Joe, this university doesn't yet know how to deal with women asking for equal pay. They tolerate Blacks and Chicanos out of fear—and expect to be praised for it—they flat-out hate gays, and they practically cross themselves every time they pass the one admitted diabetic on the faculty. Try imagining what would happen if they found out I had fall-down fits. I've never told anyone but Sia. I really wish to God you didn't know."

"Oh, for God's sake," Farrell said. He dug into his flan with the vigorous relief of renewed self-assurance. "Did I tell when you wrote that poem to Lidia Mirabal? Her boyfriend, Paco, he practiced a little after-school acupuncture on me every day for a week, but my lips were sealed. Mostly with East Twenty-ninth Street, but anyway." Ben was staring down at the table. Farrell said, "It never happens in class? When you're working?" He took a twitch of the hunched shoulders for affirmation. "Well, there you are, what can they do to you? You're a star, you're a hotshot, next year you'll have tenure and then you won't even have to show up on campus. Come on, if that's all you're worried about."

Ben touched his wrist, so lightly that it made Farrell shiver once, all over. Then he went out of the dining room, and Farrell sat still for a long while, watching the lamplight puddle and run up and down the pepper mill. When he felt the timorous nudge of Briseis's cold nose on his ankle, he looked up to find Sia placidly watering house plants. Her gray-black hair lay loose on the shoulders of the faded Mongolian robe that she liked to wear in the evenings, and from Farrell's angle she appeared strangely youthful, almost childlike, as she moved around the room. Even when he said, "So you knew all the time," and she turned, heavily as ever, to peer at him shortsightedly, he was still as startled and chilled as if the twining dragons on her robe had all lifted their barbed golden heads to seek him.

She said, "I knew what had happened to him, yes, and I knew exactly where he was. But there was nothing I could do."

"I could have done something," Farrell said. "I could have brought him home. In a considerable damn sight better shape than they did."

"You would never have found him. And if you had, there is not a chance in the world that you would have known what to do with him." She never interrupted her work on the plants. "In a way, it was the best thing that those two found him. But the waiting was hard."

"Oh, must have been," Farrell agreed heartily. "Especially knowing exactly where he was and all." Sour as a thirteen-year-old, he added, "If you think I'm going to ask how you came by that bit of specialized information . . . ."

The swift mischief that had stopped his breath at their first meeting sauntered through Sia's eyes and was gone. "From her," she said, nodding at Briseis, who was sitting asleep on Farrell's foot.

Farrell washed the dishes and went to his room. His practicing went badly that night, and he kept dreaming about falling out of boats. Aiffe and Ben were always in them with him, and Aiffe usually wanted to rescue him, but Ben never let her.

From then on, it was most often Farrell who missed dinner, occasionally breakfast, and once or twice an entire weekend. His absences were legitimate enough—rehearsing with Basilisk demanded much more than one night a week, even when no performances were scheduled. As a practical matter, all of the group's arrangements had to be adapted to include a

THE FOLK OF THE AIR

lute; on a more elusive level, there was the whole question of Basilisk itself adapting to Farrell's particular sound and style, and he to the consort's. Farrell expected this, having been through similar rituals before. What he had not quite bargained for were the picnics, nor the impromptu potlucks, beach barbecues, volleyball games, and backpacking excursions, to all of which he was constantly being invited. He complained mildly to Hamid at one point. "Don't they ever stop being *family?* I like the music fine, but the hugging is wearing me out."

"Village thinking," Hamid said. "The League tends to foster that stuff, what with all the baronies and the guilds and the fellowships and such. You encourage people to be thinking in terms of small groups, tribes, that gets real natural real easy, you don't just turn it off." He smiled his long, disquieting smile that showed only the tips of his teeth, and added, "The Middle Ages were like that, of course. You could live out your whole life inside a few square miles."

Farrell said, "They really are good. I have to push to keep up with them. It's learning on the job, too, I'm already playing gigs. We did a private party for Duke Claudio and his wife last week. That was strange, I don't know if I liked it or not. Nobody broke character for a minute, not even when the phone rang or a fuse blew, and they even fed us in the kitchen, the way you did with musicians. Good thing they didn't have stables."

Hamid's grin sharpened. "You wait till you play someplace like Dol Amroth or Storisende." Farrell recognized the names from Tolkien and Cabell. Hamid shook his head with great deliberateness, blowing daintily on his fingertips. He said, "Places like that, you truly get to wondering when in the world you are."

He walked away from any further questions and Julie was only a bit more forthcoming when Farrell went to her. "Households," she said. "There are four or five real ones—four, I guess, Rivendell keeps breaking up and starting over. They're like communes, not even that organized. People sharing the rent, taking turns cooking, shopping, working in the garden, arguing over who changes the cat box this week. We've both lived in a dozen places like that."

"Except that we weren't all playing the same game all the time."

Julie simply laughed at him. "Weren't we? Come on, where you and I lived everybody was conspiring to bomb the Pentagon, or anyway jam up their plumbing. Or it was the great quest for the perfect plural marriage, the permanently correct position on Cuba, the all-time guru, the ultimate compost heap. It was just the same, Joe, just as uniform. And you fit in or you moved on to some other group."

"Did Prester John move on?" Farrell had lately taken to using the name like a depth charge, maliciously toppling it into placid conversation with League members and waiting to feel the water rupture and convulse far below the twinkling surface.

But Julie said only, "I guess," and went on fitting a new cartridge into one of her drawing pens. When Farrell pushed further, her voice abruptly became high and monotonous, whining with tension like an electric fence. "He freaked out, Joe, let it alone. He moved on, right. He overdosed on everything, one more Parnell burnout, all right? Let it alone." There were tears swelling her eyes, shivering on the lower lids, and Farrell went to make tea.

Since the dance, she had not accompanied him to any of the League functions, brusquely pleading either work or weariness. The Lady Criseyde had invited him to play for her weekly dance classes; and once he went alone to a crafts fair sponsored by the artisans' and armorers' guilds, and spent the day talking with ponytailed boys who knew South German plate armor from Milanese, and Peffenhauser's work from Colman's, and with a former chemistry professor whose suits of armor weighed eighty pounds and sold for three thousand dollars. There were two swordsmiths and a specialist in the manufacture of mauls and flails, and there was one who only made the great padded gauntlets that most of the fighters used. Farrell learned that chopsticks were by far the best tools for packing the stuffing down in the glove, and that a one-pound lead sinker made the most successful pommel weight for a tournament mace.

Hamid and Lovita took him to his first tournament, which was staged in Barton Park, though not at the clearing where the Birthday Revels had been held. It was one of the League's rare open exhibitions, and nonmenbers in ordinary dress thronged among the cartoon-colored pavilions, the hedges of bemonstered appliqué banners, and the blazons strung on wire between the trees. Farrell saw Simon Widefarer cut down three novice knights trying to earn their spurs, and King Bohemond defend himself with surprising dexterity in the slow-motion ballet of maul-fighting. Garth de Montfaucon glided victorious out of a roaring mêlée, leaving four of his six opponents hobbling and gasping; and Farrell stood cold on tiptoe to see the ridiculous moustachios prowling down the lists, eyes squinted nearly shut, the lean body humping below the shoulders like a ferret's body, or that of any other creature that found you in the earth by your smell. In the moment of Garth's acclamation, his eyes sought out Farrell in the crowd, and he lifted his sword in mocking challenge. Farrell knew that it was only rattan, but its polished length gleamed in the sun like the real sword, Joyeuse, and he was glad when Garth turned away. *Darrell Sloat. Remedial reading. Doesn't help.*

He did bring Julie to dinner at Sia's house and regretted it before the introductions were over. Strangers, the two of them reacted to each other with the immediate ease of long old detestation. Farrell spent the evening bridging grim silences by desperately teasing childhood reminiscences out of Ben, and in watching Sia probe and test and bait her guest more rudely than he had ever known her to do, while Julie responded with increasingly monosyllabic sarcasm. She went home early with a headache and hardly spoke to Farrell for two days. The most she ever said about that first encounter was, "We didn't want to like each other. Leave it there."

On the eve of the summer solstice, they went together to the greenwood wedding of a psychiatric nurse called Sir Tybalt the Belligerent with the Lady Alisoun de la Fôret, a teaching assistant at the university. The marriage took place at sunset, on a beach where swimming had been indefinitely forbidden because of sewage spills. Basilisk played during the ceremony, which was performed by a barefoot mendicant friar, and Hamid sang *Love Me or Not, Love Her I Must or Die* afterward, with Farrell accompanying him and the costumed guests dancing slowly in a circle around the bride and groom. They then went on to the wedding feast, guided by two Italian mercenaries, one Druid, and two tumblebreasted Elizabethan strumpets who had all managed to crowd into Madame Schumann-Heink. Farrell drove as their tumultuous consensus directed him, further into the hills than he had ever gone, until he fishhooked around a blind curve into a wide avenue dotted with redwood condominium complexes, turned right again at a ranch-style church with a satellite dish on the lawn, and pulled up in the shadow of a canary-yellow castle. Beside him Julie said, "Storisende."

"Sonofabitch," Farrell said softly. "I didn't know they built any up this far." There were banners floating over battlements and gargoyles smirking from the stone-framed entryway. He said, "The Avicenna castles. I've never been in one."

"A bunch of crazies built them in the twenties," the Druid said over his shoulder. "Aleister Crowley freaks, or Theda Bara, somebody like that. Used to steal each other's daughters. I read about it." Farrell helped Julie down from the bus, and she handed him his lute, saying, "Joe, it's a wedding. Just have fun, that's what it's for. That's all it's for." She took firm hold of his arm, leading him toward the yellow castle.

Storisende's four stucco towers were set around a central courtyard, busy and close with trumpet vines, climbing rosemary, overhanging plane and fig trees, a miniature boxwood maze, mossy flagstones, and a fishpond the color of onion soup. The two towers at the back of the courtyard were themselves spired corners of a rambling, tile-roofed house that had apparently changed its mind and decided to be a Spanish mission instead of a Norman keep. The odors of jasmine, wild lilac, and oleander quarreled in Farrell's nostrils, making him sneeze pleasantly. He broke off a sprig of jasmine, placed it in the cross-laced front of Julie's blue velour gown, and kissed her when she looked up in surprise. "There, see," he said. "I'm having fun already."

The marriage feast was going on in both rear towers, spilling back and forth through the main house in a tidal wash of laughter as flamboyant as a magician's scarves, fiercely bawdy wedding catches, and the turned-earth smell of the League's tongue-numbing homebrew. For all its blithely jumbled facade, the castle's designer had done well with columns of sand and lime and air; the stone stairways were all external and the artfully bulging tower walls were thinner than they looked, leaving unexpected space for three stories' worth of wide landings, and round or octagonal rooms as high as lofts, all of them aswirl with men and women whose clothes cast the shadows of great, brawling birds. Farrell drew the lute quickly against him, not simply to shield it from collisions, but to still the voices that rioted in the sentient wood and made it whimper angrily in his arms.

He lost Julie almost immediately to a pair of young girls dressed in the gold-heavy robes of Scythian nomads, who swarmed up to her crying, "Lady Murasaki, the Nine Dukes, all are here, all, hast ever seen such a wedding?" and dragged her off to join in a women's chorus engaged in singing their own songs of carnal counsel to the bride. Farrell roamed the rush-strewn floors at fascinated random, constantly striving to down one full mug of ale before someone's robe or sword hilt knocked it out of his hands. One room was largely given over to a buffet table burdened with platters of conger in souse, beef marrow fritters, meat tiles, friants, numble pie and florentine; in another, an intense argument concerning Senate candidates, couched entirely in the imaginary language of the League—"God's teeth, sirrah, beshrew me, but I'll put it to thee plain, thy man's naught but a mewling, doddering old puppet of the military-industrial complex"—had half a dozen weapons clear of their sheaths by the time the noble Duke Frederik the Falconer could intervene.

A third room did its best to contain the admirers of the Countess Elizabeth Bathory, as she held her own court, clad in nothing much but her two languorous pythons, Vlad and Bela. Lovita Bird, herself dressed entirely in interlaced bands of tooled white leather, was standing to one side, looking contemptuously amused. Farrell eased up to her and murmured, "Come on, Vlad's kind of a dip, but Bela's all right. Or maybe that's Vlad."

Lovita curled exactly half of an exquisite upper lip. "Both of them a sight better-looking than the best day *she* ever saw. Woman's got no more shame than she got shape." She snorted delicately, which Farrell had never seen done.

"Hamid says those snakes are League members. Hamid jives me a lot."

"It's the truth. Associate members, sibyls to the king or some such. Poor old Bohemond, he's got to bring them those lab rats, offerings, and he's supposed to ask their advice on things. Says so right there in the by-laws."

Garth de Montfaucon strolled past with his arm around the bride and a side-glance like a paper cut. Farrell said to Lovita Bird, "You look great in that outfit. Did you make it yourself?"

"I look great in a whole lot of outfits," she said comfortably. "But thank you. Yeah, I made this one, I make most of the stuff I wear here. Keeps me in mind that I'm Amanishakhete Queen of Nubia and no damn bus driver. Can't afford to be forgetting that."

Farrell stared, considering her slender brown arms and small hands. "That's what you do? You drive a school bus?"

"In a pig's coochie, honey." Lovita Bird patted his hand. "Metro Transit, eight hours a day hauling one of those big, whonking, articulated mothers across two county lines and the damn Bay Bridge. Throw them off when they're drunk, they stick me up when they're stoned, call me names when they're straight. You think I could stand that shit if I thought it was real life?"

Aiffe's laughter prickled around the edges of everything, rubbing raw places in the joyous evening. Farrell had glimpsed her two or three times, usually slipping between couples like a memory, teasing either the man or the woman away with her, to dance or to whisper. He had not seen Nicholas Bonner anywhere.

He moved on quickly to sit in a corner with several children, who were playing a strange game, juggling walnuts from hand to hand. All were in full costume, kirtled and tabarded miniatures of their elders, and even the very youngest among them spoke the League talk as fluently as the adults, and more naturally. Farrell learned that they belonged to the three families who made up the household of Storisende; two of them had been born in the stucco castle. As was usual, the girls served Queen Leonora as maids of honor, while the boys went as pages or squires, depending on their ages. All their references centered on League realities, whether they were describing a tournament at "the fair realm of Broceliande in the North"—Farrell thought they might mean Seattle—or merely fussing at one another over the sharing of sticky spun-sugar dulces. Yet when Farrell asked them where they went to school, they fell effortlessly into standard California English, chattering about grades and recess enemies as eagerly as they had just debated the order of precedence at a royal banquet. Farrell found this dizzying, like hitting an air pocket.

At the buffet, while discovering that the thick meat custard called mortrews had enough of a slow-acting, spicy kick to set fire to his teeth, he was accosted by a large, smiling woman, sweetish and powdery as a marshmallow. She wore a full-sleeved, fur-embroidered black robe that touched the floor, a huge, teetering headdress of gauze and wire, and a golden belt with a ring of a good dozen keys that clattered like knives whenever she moved. "Sir Musician, you should be with your fellows," she scolded him gaily. "Musickers are all for playing while their lords dine, to sweeten their digestion with their gladsome airs; it were scandalous anarchy otherwise." She slapped his arm lightly and handed him a turnover in the shape of a crowned swan.

"Lady, my comrades are also at their meat," he answered, pointing out the Basilisk crew with their wooden trenchers as laden as his. Across the room, John Erne's Nisei pupil, the Ronin Benkei, nodded soberly to him, and Lovita Bird waved a jellied eel. The smiling woman said, "Now you are the Lady Murasaki's man, the Knight of Ghosts and Shadows. I am called Janet of Carterhaugh, chatelaine of Storisende."

Farrell, who had often sung the Scots ballad of the young girl who rescued her lover, body and soul, from the power of the Queen of the Fairies, could not help raising his eyebrows. The woman laughed outright, apparently unoffended. "Nay, do I not suit your imagining? Well, I am only recently become the Lady Janet—as late as the Birthday Revels I was still Draja the Tartar, raider and rebel, pitiless enemy of all who dare her mountain fastness." Farrell remembered her, a shrilling apparition in a red wig and gilded leather mail, clutching two spears even when she danced. "But it got so boring," the Lady Janet went on. "Say what you will, there's no one really likes a constant outlaw, and the whole life style is just *dull* after a while. So I packed up Draja, bag and baggage—all her weapons, her armor, all her nasty little gods and charms and endless family legends, *and* her one bloody company formal—and I just sold her to Margrethe von der Vogelweide, who is so tired of being Duke Manfred's operetta duchess she'll take to any hills she can find. And behold, the demure but passionate Janet of Carterhaugh, who defied all Elfland for her love, and dresses *much* better than poor Draja besides." She made him a deep and unexpectedly elegant curtsy and rose winking.

Farrell said slowly, "You can do that? Just stop being whoever you are in the League and decide to be someone absolutely different? You can sell characters, trade them off?" He felt oddly disoriented, almost offended.

"Personas," the Lady Janet corrected him. "Or we call them impressions. Aye, of a certainty, we barter and alter and retire them as we choose, and no constraint but to register the change with the College of Arms." Her sugar-white face grew damply pink as she continued. "I'faith, 'twould be intolerable else. What, should we be bound eternally to the same outworn impression, any more than to a single manner of dress, to one ambition, one mate, one nose? This may be the Middle Ages, good musicker, but it is still California."

A Siamese kitten who had been fearlessly scampering through all the rooms at once all evening bounced stiff-legged up to them to investigate the wonderful secrets of the Lady Janet's trailing hem. She swooped him up to nip fiercely at her chin, telling Farrell, "Behold Sir Mordred, so named because he is so wicked, wicked, *wicked*." The last words were half smothered in the kitten's fur.

Farrell asked, "Does that happen a lot? I mean, are people changing their characters all the time?"

The Lady Janet laughed into Sir Mordred's belly, and he promptly boxed her ears. "Nay, 'tis hardly as common as that. There are many like the Lady Criseyde or the Lord Garth, whose impressions vary not a jot from one Whalemas Tourney to the next, except to grow richer and more sure. But for those of us more fickle, the true delight lies in becoming exactly whom we choose, as deeply as we choose, and for exactly as long. Before Draja, I was Lucia la Sirena, flame of old Castile, and I may well be Marian of Sherwood tomorrow, or Melusine the Dragon Lady, and no one to look twice at me for it. Squire Tancred, Geoffrey of Eastmarch, will you knock it *off?*"

Two of the boys Farrell had been chatting with earlier came hurtling past the buffet, half-racing, half-wrestling, yelling in breathless, hysterical voices, "Caitiff, miscreant, I'll have thy guts for garters!" Sir Mordred snarled, slashed the air indignantly, and tried to climb the Lady Janet's headdress. One boy managed to wave apologetically to her as they vanished under the table; miraculously, they scrambled out on the other side without crashing into the legs or pulling the cloth and trays down with them. Farrell could follow their riotous progress across the room by the wave of robes and gowns being swept hastily out of their way.

"Toenails of the Virgin, a murrain on the pair of them!" the Lady Janet spluttered as Farrell carefully removed Sir Mordred from her hair and set him on the floor. "E'er since Tancred became squire to Cedric the Bowman, the brat's been tormenting my Geoffrey to distraction. Pox on't, but I must needs go deal with the wretched little rug-rats." She curtsied again to Farrell and began to turn away.

"You live here," Farrell said. "What's it like for you, living here all the time?" The Lady Janet looked back at him saying nothing, smiling now. Farrell asked, "I mean, do you eat out much? Do you have friends where you work, do you and your family ever go to the movies, do you take the car in for tuneups? What is it like all the time?" *Why should I be the one feeling like an idiot?*

193

Am I the one with a kid fighting over who gets to be a squire?

The Lady Janet paused and fanned her damp bosom, all the while watching Farrell out of steady small eyes the color of faded denim. She said, "I know how to put quarters in a parking meter, if that's your notion of the real world. I have to know that, because we have no student lot at my law school. I can also balance a checkbook, send out for pizza, and help Geoffrey of Eastmarch with his computer class homework. Does that answer your question, my Lord of Ghosts and Shadows?"

A sudden sharp rise in the noise level made both of them turn quickly to see a burly knight in full chain mail hoisting himself onto the buffet table, kicking a chair over behind him as he did so. He gripped a slopping flagon in one hand and was beginning his speech or his song—it was difficult to be sure—with one booted foot in the frumenty. Even through the redoubled cheering and stamping, Farrell could hear the Lady Janet's squall of outrage as she charged the buffet, reverting instantly to Draja the Tartar. The knight saw her coming, dropped his flagon, and started to climb down.

Farrell drifted on, looking for Julie and trying not to step on Sir Mordred, who kept exploding out of shadows to launch ruthless kamikaze attacks on Farrell's ankles and vanish instantly behind a mounted suit of armor or a half-painted shield leaning in a corner. One of the assaults was providential, diverting the attention of the Lady Vivienne d'Audela, who was just settling in for a good teary chat about her hopeless crush on Hamid ibn Shanfara. Another effectively broke up an impromptu Basilisk rendition of *"When I'm Sixty-Four,"* performed as a serenade to Sir Tybalt and the Lady Alisoun, caught necking in an alcove. Farrell had a serious talk with the kitten at that point, and Sir Mordred promised faithfully to be good, but he lied.

The Lady Criseyde, involved in hasty repairs to the gravy-splashed ruff of King Bohemond, paused to say that the Lady Murasaki had gone out but now into the courtyard, complaining of the noise and stuffiness. A branle was forming in the hallway like a fifteenth-century conga line, accompanied only by Felix Arabia on shawm, resembling a Bosch demon in a genial moment. He caught sight of Farrell and called to him, beckoning over the dozen cowls, plumed berets, and steepled hennins jigging between them. Farrell smiled, waved back, and ducked swiftly across the hall into a room he had not seen before. It was smaller than the others, less well-lighted, with a smell of old neglect about it, as if every celebration since the housewarming had passed it by. Yet there were fresh rushes scattered here, too—*where do you go to get real castle rushes in Avicenna, California?*—and a few tapestries and small rugs taking a bit of the chill from the walls; and by the far wall, directly under the one stone slash of a window, Nicholas Bonner crouched on the floor with a boy who could not have been older than four. They were building a castle of their own together out of red and yellow bricks.

Farrell never knew how long he stood watching them. The room was rarely deserted; he was distantly but continually aware of people, wandering in and out, and of voices joking in the League talk about the perfect concentration of the two children. Neither one ever looked up. Farrell recognized the boy as the Lady Alisoun's nephew and solemn-eyed ring-bearer. Nicholas was teaching him the words for the different parts of the castle as they took shape in clicking red and yellow. "There we are, Joshua, that's the barbican all done. Can you say that, *barbican?*" Joshua giggled and said it correctly. "Oh, very good. Okay, now we have to make a proper postern gate in our curtain wall—*postern*, Joshua, I'll do that one, and you put a few more guard towers on the wall, okay? You do good towers."

He was dressed with casual richness in red and black trunk-hose, puffed like pumpkins at the hips, a short dark-red doublet over a plain white shirt, suede half-boots, and a high-crowned black hat that looked exactly like a soft upside-down flower pot. The angle of the narrow brim hid his eyes. Joshua still wore his ice-cream-white wedding suit, along with the space helmet that had apparently been the price of his performance. He lasted through the remodeling of the curtain wall, but fell asleep while the moat and causeway were being added. Nicholas Bonner laughed gently, almost without a trace of the greedy, prowling sweetness that Farrell remembered, and picked him up so carefully that the boy never stirred. Farrell stepped back instinctively as the golden face turned toward him, but Nicholas was looking down at Joshua and his eyes were still in shadow. Someone across the room was telling someone else how and when to buy silver. Nicholas Bonner began to hum very softly.

A muscular little tail whipped once against Farrell's foot and he whirled, Sir Mordred's ambushes having left him more than a trifle gun-shy. But the Siamese was after wilder game, ignoring Farrell as he stalked past him to move in boldly and openly on Nicholas Bonner's long, graceful legs in their tempting trunk-hose. Far from erupting all over them, clinging like Greek fire for a moment, then leaping away to safety, Sir Mordred sized up his prey in the leisurely manner of a much older cat, taking all the time necessary to unsheathe his claws, blow on them, adjust for windage and elevation, and finally reach out to draw them daintily down Nicholas' left leg from calf to ankle, like a bear marking a tree. And he looked upon his work, saw that it was good—four neat slits in the red hose, and scratched skin showing through—and he sat back, deeply content, and said, *"Rao."*

Nicholas Bonner never stopped humming. He neither flinched nor turned, but continued to cradle the sleeping Joshua. When he raised his head at last—*oh, dear Jesus, what could a little kid ever make of those eyes?*—the champagne stare fixed itself on a point beyond Farrell's right shoulder. Farrell heard a snuffling snicker and knew that Aiffe was there.

She was wearing the blue houppelande that she had worn at the Revels and a sort of gauzy wimple, bulging like a mail sack with her hair. The last time Farrell had seen her close for more than a moment, she had been slumped in Nicholas's arms, as vulnerable as Joshua and far more helpless. Now she was bouncing on her toes, grinning and shivering urgently, the toneless skin truly radiant with something better than health. "Oh, let me," she said like a lover. Nicholas made no response, but Farrell felt a freezing permission pass between them, grazing his cheek like a flung stone. Aiffe pointed at Sir Mordred, now placidly grooming himself, and crooned, "Bad kitty, you *bad* kitty," in a voice as soft as Nicholas Bonner's lullaby. Farrell heard them both in his sleep from that night on.

Sir Mordred looked up in blue-eyed complacency from the technical challenge of washing the back of his neck. Apparently dismissing Aiffe as easily as Farrell, he rolled over and started in on his white-butter stomach. Abruptly his jaws snapped in the damp fur, and he uttered a tiny cry of astonishment and hurt. He licked the place rapidly for a moment; then—with a stilted, uncatlike movement, as though his face were being forced into a bowl of milk—he bit his belly again and again, each time yowling more loudly.

The silver expert said sympathetically, "Ah, poor Puss, poor wretch, truly I've not seen a year the like of this one for vermin. Anyway, you *always* buy when it falls below that price."

Joshua mumbled, "Postern," burrowing against Nicholas Bonner's shoulder.

She can't be making him, they can't be. Sir Mordred was biting and scratching himself frantically now, his cries muffled by his own flesh. Aiffe came to kneel beside him, stroking him and murmuring so gently that her lips barely moved, and Farrell could not hear her at all. But he knew what she was saying; he could feel the words in fire almost as surely and terribly as Sir Mordred, *bad kitty bad kitty bad kitty.* The Siamese fell onto his side, writhing in a circle. Aiffe said aloud, "I guess it's fleas. I don't know what's wrong with him."

Farrell started forward, but Nicholas Bonner looked straight at him for the first time, and it seemed very clear to Farrell that to take another step was to fall off the edge of everything forever, never dying, just falling. *Is this the way Ben feels?*

Then it was over, quite suddenly, because the Lady Alisoun came in looking for her nephew, and Nicholas put him into her arms. Joshua half woke for a moment, clinging sweatily to Nicholas and complaining that he wanted to finish the castle. Aiffe jumped up lightly and went to join them. She stroked Joshua's dangling leg, exactly as she had petted Sir Mordred, and retied his loose shoelaces.

Sir Mordred climbed slowly to his feet, shook himself, and sneezed. He appeared undamaged, but there was blood on his mouth and the blue eyes were dazed and mad. When Farrell tried to pick him up, the kitten bit his hand savagely and ran off, wobbling and tucking his tail like a dog. Farrell watched the group around Joshua until they left the room together. Aiffe looked back at him, grinned until her upper lip disappeared, and stuck out her pink tongue.

Outside in the garden, there were crickets and a big, soft, droopy-looking moon and some bird whistling as if it had human lips and teeth, but there was no sign of Julie. Farrell stood still for a while, breathing the jasmine-slow air and nursing his chewed hand. Then he wandered thoughtfully toward the boxwood maze, which had been designed to represent two linked and initialed hearts, in the Tudor style. It had lately been allowed to go untended until its original shape was as blurred as a cloud formation, but the path into its scrolled center was still open, and someone had pushed through the invading overgrowth before him. Farrell

199

followed the track of broken brambles, letting the lute strings sound loudly, so Julie would know who it was.

She was standing with her back to him, looking up at the silhouettes of gargoyles on the turret roofs. When Farrell put his hands on her shoulders, she said, without turning, "I was coming in"; and then, as the sharp, monotonous cry made them both start, "I hate that stupid bird. I always think it's somebody signaling to somebody else."

"That's your California surfing bird," Farrell said gravely. "Not too usual this far north, but common as dirt, you get down around Santa Cruz. That one's just trying to talk some other birds into coming night-surfing with it. They hate going out alone, because of the elephant seals."

Julie turned, stared at him expressionlessly for a moment, then suddenly began tickling his ribs, fiercely enough to make him yelp and duck away. "Damn you, I *believed* you," she gasped. "Right up to the damn seals, I believed you, I still fall for it." Her fingers were digging into him painfully, almost clawing.

Farrell saw her eyes in the moonlight, forgot his care for the lute and simply put his arms around her, holding her as tightly as he could until she quieted against him. "Tell me," he said. She felt as astonishingly hot as a sleeping child, and he thought, *it could have been Joshua, it could just as easily have been Joshua as that cat.* "Love," he said. "Jewel. Please tell me."

When she looked at him again, her eyes were dry, and her voice was perfectly level, even teasing. She said, "Just sad. All at once, all over, just sad for no reason. The American ailment, it goes away. Now you tell me how you had fun."

Farrell recounted his evening for her, lingering over any event that seemed to have a chance of making her laugh. Elizabeth Bathory's pythons were no help, but his mimicry of knights and ladies arguing in the League talk about bilingual ballots was good for a small chuckle; and when he described the Lady Janet of Carterhaugh trying blindly to peel Sir Mordred off her headdress, he could feel Julie's body easing in his arms and her amusement loosening and warming his own tense muscles. She said in some anxiety, "Your hand's bleeding, there. What happened?"

Farrell took a careful breath. "The cat," he said. "Aiffe bewitched it—Aiffe and *him*." Like the Lady Janet's Tam Lin, Julie changed as he held her, first to stone and immediately after to a bar of soap, skidding through his hands and starting out of the maze without looking back. Farrell followed, his bewilderment quickly giving way to anger. "Jewel, you are going to hear this, you hold up a damn minute."

The path was too narrow for them to walk abreast, and he found himself lurching and half skipping after her, constantly off-balance, his face whipped by dry leaves and twigs every time he grabbed at her shoulder. He caught up with her a bend before the entrance and barred her way. She said, "Let me by, Joe," but she did not try to push past him.

"This is dumb," he said loudly. "You know how dumb this is? Other people can't talk about their sex lives, they can't talk about money, politics, the kids, each other's driving. You and I, we only have two things we can't talk about, and one of them is a fifteen-year-old twit with pimples and magical powers. I never heard of anything so stupid."

Julie said, "I want to go home." She took a step forward, but the California surfing bird whistled again, and she jumped in alarm, and then shouted, "Damn bird, you damn *bird*!" at the top of her lungs. As though her furious breath had reached them, the lights of the wedding feast, seen lilting like birthday candles through the maze's patchy green walls, suddenly shivered and went out. A figure too tall to be quite human, shaped wrongly to be entirely human, was moving between the castle and the maze in a way that was not human at all. Julie backed silently against Farrell, who was grateful.

They heard the hoofbeats first, scraping deliberately on the courtyard stones, and then the voice. "The desire of increasing riches occupieth you, till ye come to the grave. Nay! but in the end ye shall know. Nay! once more, in the end ye shall know your folly. Nay! would that ye knew it with knowledge of certainty. Surely ye shall see hellfire. Then shall ye surely see it with the eye of certainty. Then shall ye on that day be taken to task concerning pleasures." The cold, piercing drone might have rattled in the cavities of a naked skull, but Farrell had heard it before.

Beside him Julie made a little sound like Sir Mordred when he bit himself for the first time. The black horseman was leaning over the hedge, looking straight down at them. When he smiled, the faint parallel ridges rose on his cheeks, like gill slits. "My kingdom is four months' journeying long and four months wide," he said. "In my city, Timbuktu, which is the City of Wisdom, I have as many scribes and scholars as warriors and as many books as I have bars of gold. The throne where I give audience is of ebony, and great elephant tusks arch above my head. Three hundred slaves stand behind my throne. Before me and to my right there stands a giant holding a two-handed sword as big as a man, and to my left my spokesman waits with his mace of office to give my answers and my commands. To the end of my eyesight, the sun blazes off spears and trumpets, armor and jeweled trappings. And I sit in the center of the center of the world and I am not touched. Glorify the Compassionate, the Merciful. I am not touched." As far as could be seen, he was completely naked.

"And that's the other one," Farrell managed to say. "Prester John." But Julie whispered another name and ran out of the maze, leaving him to trail after her once again. The big horse danced heavily away from her quickness, and the black man on his back seemed to be dancing with him as he brought the animal to an easy halt just out of Julie's reach. Farrell heard her call the name again—*"Micah"*—but only the California surfing bird responded.

"Mansa Musa is not touched," the black man chanted. Farrell saw now that he was wearing a pair of dark trousers, glinting and sliding with the moonlight, and nothing more. "In Cairo the Sultan called me his brother and desired to embrace me, as the men do there, but Allah put him away. I handle neither ivory nor gold nor salt, that they may not handle me. My wives come to me in darkness, that not so much as their shadows in the moon may touch my body. Only Allah touches Mansa Kankan Musa."

"It's me," Julie said hopelessly. "Micah, it's me." A tower door opened and closed, sounding very far away, but the courtyard was suddenly crowded with the laughter of people starting home from a party. For a moment, the black man's immense eyes were upon Farrell, brown as old rivers, deep-muddy with decaying secrets, and streaked by thin, luminous currents and the slow backs of crocodiles. Then he kicked bare heels into his mount's thick sides, and the horse lumbered through a judicious U-turn and trotted away past the fishpond, under the spiteful faces of the entryway, and on out into the expensively quiet streets beyond. The clopping echoes bounced back and forth between the condominiums long after the man and the horse were out of sight.

Farrell drew Julie back into the maze, for privacy's sake, and let her cry. He was jealous at first—*no one has ever cried for me that way, and no one ever will, I know this*—but then Julie raised her face, gasping and hiccuping, and he saw clearly how she would look when she was old. "Baby," he said, and began helplessly kissing lines and hollows and wounds that were not there yet, sick with tenderness and fear.

XIII

If you'll look over on your left now, ladies and gentlemen," Farrell said into the dashboard microphone, "we're now passing the South American maned wolf." In his rearview mirror, a dozen faces turned dutifully as directed; two or three others stared straight ahead, meeting his eyes with the wary contempt that certain children always show to magicians. *What are you hiding from me while you let me see this?* Farrell smiled encouragingly into the mirror, but it only confirmed their suspicions, and he sympathized, having a touch of their complaint himself.

"Despite the name," he went on, slowing the alligator train as it waddled past the yard where the two shaggy, cinnamon-toast-colored creatures trotted up and down on deer legs, "the maned wolf is actually a large fox—sort of a fox on stilts, as you can see." He had tried several times to leave the official jokes out of his recitation, but management spies always reported him. "In the wild they live on rodents and insects, but here we feed them chicken and bananas. They'll eat five pounds of bananas a day, just wolf 'em right down.'' Somebody laughed at that one, and Farrell daydreamed about stopping the train and demanding to know who it was.

The day was windy and warm, and children tumbled like bits of burning paper across the path of the alligator train. The sea lions were coughing croupily away behind the aviary, ringing bells and biting their bicycle horn. A young woman, wearing Army fatigues and a purple cartwheel hat, lifted a small boy out of the way and held him easily in her arms while she waved his hand to the train. Farrell waved back. The implacable faces in the mirror followed his gesture that time, to see if that was it.

"On our right," he said, "of course, the elephants. This pair of old scroungers, Winston and Daisy, are Indian elephants—born in Sri Lanka, actually—and the big fellow in the next yard is Mr. Ngugi, and he's from Kenya in East Africa." Winston and Daisy, who had been circus performers, went into their routine on cue, twining their trunks and rearing, yearning with perfect comic precision toward a world made up entirely of cooing, snack-flinging suckers. But Mr. Ngugi had ragged ears and a broken tusk, and Farrell cringed before the darkly brilliant squint six times a day as he slid by in his green and baby-blue train, repeating in the same words the joke about elephants' memories. He made the joke this time, too; but an unaccountable impulse led him to go on, not into his usual thirty-three-second closing speech as the alligator train neared its terminus, but straight into the first lines of his favorite D. H. Lawrence poem:

"The elephant, the huge old beast,
  is slow to mate;
he finds a female, they show no haste,
  they wait
for the sympathy in their vast, shy hearts
  slowly, slowly to rouse . . . ."

He said the lines loudly enough for Mr. Ngugi to
hear, and never noticed the sad-faced bald man who
flushed and began very vigorously to button up his
daughter's jacket, nor the old woman who yanked her
two small grandchildren to their feet, towed them to
the door, and practically slung them off the train, which
was still moving. He halted it between the proper yellow
lines, trying to recall the part about the great beasts
mating in secret, hiding their fire. None of his passengers looked at him as they scrambled down. Farrell sang
the last verse softly into the microphone.

"They do not snatch, they do not tear;
  their massive blood
moves as the moon-tides, near, more near,
  till they touch in flood."

Pleased with himself, he leaned on his elbow in the
round window that was the alligator's left eye and
waved to the young Chicano peanut vendor across the
path. The peanut vendor grinned at him, shaking his
head and drawing a forefinger cheerfully across his
throat. "Abandon ship, *chulo*," he called. "Better tell
me now where you want your stuff shipped on to."

"Jaime," Farrell said, "you really must try to remember about not being in Yuba City anymore. There
wasn't so much as a phooey in that poem—it was edu-

cational and scientific in nature, and all those people got college credit just for listening to it. So did you, of course. Trade the experience in at any night school in the country."

But the peanut vendor shook his head again. "I didn't hear three words of it, didn't even know it was a poem. All I know is you weren't saying those good lines they wrote down for you to say. I hear you doing that thing every day, over and over, you think I can't tell when the beat changes?" Abruptly he scaled a bag of peanuts sidearm through the window into Farrell's lap. "You were doing it different," Jaime said, "you think *they* couldn't tell? Making stuff up on them, more than likely. They hate that, man. They paid for exactly the same show everyone else gets. So not only are you some kind of elephant pervert, you did them out of money. Oh, there will be cards and letters. There will be damn singing telegrams about you, man."

"Next round, *The Bastard King of England*," Farrell said. He stood up, stuffing the peanuts into a pocket of his forest-green jumpsuit, which had been tailored for a larger man and hung on him like a parachute snagged on tree branches. He turned to check the seats for knife slashes, forgotten dolls, bombs, and fallen change. From the last seat in the rear row, with the Petting Zoo reflected in the window behind her, the dog Briseis looked at him.

After a long time, and from a long distance, Farrell heard himself say, "Get down, Briseis. They don't let dogs on the zoo train." *The rear door's open, she must have gotten on that way. I just didn't see her.* He started toward her, but Briseis growled once, so quietly that Farrell froze between steps, suddenly very uncertain of his ability to identify dogs. She stared boldly into his eyes, as he had never known her to do, then leaped to the floor and out of the train in two elegant bounds that were nothing like the movements of Sia's clumping, apologetic old companion. Turning to look back at Farrell, she growled again, and this time it was unquestionably a command. Farrell was never mistaken about commands.

"Wal, Ah swan, Ah reckon the critter wants me to follow her," he said aloud, just to keep the whole affair on the level of a Lassie movie as long as possible. Briseis was loping away, back past the elephants, then slanting off in the direction of the employees' rest-room. She neither slowed for Farrell, nor looked around to be sure of him. He trailed after her, trying to keep her in sight without really running, feeling like the White Rabbit as he checked his watch to see that he had almost an hour of liberty before the alligator train's next appointed round. His supervisor, who mistrusted him, called questioningly as he hurried by. Farrell waved, earnestly yelled back, "Till they touch in flood," and kept moving. *I'm late, I'm late, for a very important date, and I am not dressed for it, whatever it is.*

Briseis surprised him greatly by leading him on his favorite path, down behind the bear cages. Unpaved, too narrow for trucks or the alligator train, it was used more as a shortcut by the zoo staff than by visitors. Farrell liked it for its rough coolness and silence, and for the smell of the bears in the shadows. Briseis was waiting for him at a bend where the path broadened briefly to make room for a low stone fountain, which had become a birdbath by default long ago. The tiny silver hiccup of the water was the only sound Farrell could hear, except for Briseis' deep panting.

Ben's own breath was so shallow as to be inaudible

in the clearing. He was hunched over the fountain, propping himself with his hands in the concrete bowl, his head sunken and turned away, like an animal too sick to drink. Farrell recognized his suit first—the shabby gray corduroy that Ben treasured obstinately for the elbow-patched stereotype it was and wore to work whenever Sia got up too late to protest. Except for the water-soaked cuffs, the coat was unstained, and the rucked-up shirt, missing three buttons, still showed the dry-cleaner's creases. But what was inside the familiar clothes was not Farrell's friend. He knew that before he saw the face, even before the alien flesh, rigid beyond bearing, howled under his hand. He said, "Ben," to it anyway, because he could not make himself call it by the other name.

The stranger replied in a voice that was higher and sharper than Ben's voice, speaking words like the rattling of oarlocks and anchor chains. It was the voice Farrell had heard outside Sia's door on the night when Ben came home, the same voice that had chanted Norse battle songs or nursery rhymes while she and Nicholas confronted each other across their ravaged battlefield, Aiffe. But then Ben—*Egil, Egil Eyvindsson, say it in your head at least*—had been hurt, helpless, unable to stand, or to do much else but glare through Ben's eyes like a madman through steel mesh, monstrously afraid. Now he was facing Farrell with two feet of bird-limed concrete and rusty water between them, testing his strength against the boundaries of this body, making it move. The little, dim scar was stretched dark, and a grin had begun to dance on the clenched mouth, fire along a knife blade. Farrell was afraid for his life then, but he kept his hand on the stranger's arm, for no reason he could ever name, and felt the creature trembling in slow, aching, hideous waves. He held on tight, letting the terrible shivering pass into him.

There is not a chance in that world that you would have known what to do, Sia said. Farrell glanced quickly around for Briseis, but the dog was gone. The stranger was speaking to him directly now; it sounded savagely questioning, *probably something about my executor, or which afterlife program I'm signed up for*. He fell back on his oldest schoolyard gambit, a shrugging, smiling face meant to indicate simultaneous incomprehension and absolute agreement, combined with utter nonaggressiveness. He had never known it to fail, except with Lidia Mirabal's boyfriend Paco, and with Julie.

The next thing he was sure about was being on the ground, unable to breathe. A raging, hammering weight was aboard him, a crowbar forearm crushed his throat, and a sound like trees splitting in a great storm was going on somewhere quite near. Dazed, frantic, he got a knee up into the center of the sound, and the strangling pressure eased slightly. As loudly as he could under the circumstances, he yelled, "Ben!"

A hand scrabbled over his face, feeling for his eyes. Farrell knocked it away, grabbing out wildly himself. His mouth and nostrils were full of musty corduroy, and he felt as though Mr. Ngugi were using him for a fly-switch, but he dug and twisted and worried, still coughing Ben's name, until the stranger grunted and reared up astride him. The wide, rather flashy green tie, *the one I gave him for his birthday*, dangled askew, yanked loose from the torn collar into a knot the size and shape of a Brazil nut, surely never to be undone again. Absurdly, the tie terrified Farrell completely, in a place where the insane assault itself could not go, but it also wrenched him at last to understanding. *Poor son-*

211

ofabitch couldn't get it off, just panicked. Must have thought it was witchcraft, a curse, poor sonofabitch.

"Egil, goddamn it!" he cried, but the berserker only mumbled to himself, turning his head to left and right. Farrell saw where he was looking, heaved wildly with the free upper half of his body, and lunged for the stone lying between two redwood roots. His hand closed on it, but the other took it away from him, almost gently, poising it over him, cocking it so far back that it disappeared behind the corduroy shoulder. Raising his own arms to ward it off, he shouted his old high-school nickname for Ben straight into this empty and blazing hero's face. "Rubberlips! Hey, Rubberlips!"

The stone faltered, started down again, then hung in the air, quaking daintily, like a wind chime. Farrell said, "Rubberlips?" and saw the face begin to buckle and slip, melting into the face of their childhood, soft and wise and secret, the scar dissolving like a star at sunrise. Farrell closed his eyes, out of pity and a kind of numbing propriety—*I shouldn't see this, it's not right*—but even then, he felt Ben's return to the body that still pinioned him, in the same way that he could always feel morning moving up across his blankets, warming his dreams.

"Joe." The voice was small and parched.

A root was grinding into Farrell's back, and he became aware of sweat sliding out of his hair, delicately maddening as fly feet. He sat up as Ben got clumsily off him, swiped at his forehead, and said mildly, "Seizures, my ass."

In the same unfamiliar voice, Ben said, "I'm sorry." Farrell had begun to brush off his uniform, but found himself tidying Ben's torn, dusty clothes, even trying to do something about the hopelessly jammed tie.

"Could have goddamn killed me," he said, muttering like an irritated nanny as he worked. "Seizures. He could have goddamn killed me."

"He didn't know you," Ben said. "Egil doesn't know anybody in this world. Except Sia." Now, suddenly, he was insubstantial, a figure of slowly pulsing ash; the wild power out of time that had answered Farrell's touch a few minutes before seemed to have abandoned Ben completely, taking the marrow of his bones away with it.

Farrell said, "This is Tuesday. You've got a one o'-clock class."

"I do? How'm I doing?" It was the punch line of an ancient vaudeville joke, as much a part of their shared history as music or the Staff Suit they had taken turns wearing on dates long ago. Ben said, "I think I was looking for you. I never remember. How did you find me?"

Farrell told him, and he nodded. "You figure it out about Briseis yet?" He appeared to take silence for affirmation. "Sia used to have griffins for her familiars—panthers, phoenixes. Hell of a comedown to a hysterical dog with a morale problem, but Briseis does all right. In the house, she's just a hassock with fleas—outside, she's Sia's eyes and legs, more than that sometimes. Old Briseis. I belong to Sia, like her, and she has to help me, but she is scared absolutely shitless of Egil. Makes things hard for her, poor old bunny."

Farrell came across the forgotten bag of peanuts in his pocket and offered them diffidently. Ben tore the bag out of his hands and then tried very hard to eat the peanuts slowly. Farrell said, "Jesus. Wait, I've got some more loose ones somewhere."

Ben looked up when the peanuts were gone, saw

Farrell watching him, and smiled amost cheerfully. He said, "Egil will not eat in this world. One of those things you never anticipate."

"I'll buy you lunch," Farrell said. "We have a cafeteria, everyone calls it the Elephants' Graveyard."

But Ben shook his head, saying, "No, let's walk. Please, let's just walk a little."

Farrell put an arm around his shoulder, and for an instant Ben rested totally against him, making Farrell remember how the boy Joshua had slept in Nicholas Bonner's arms.

They walked very slowly back up the path, which vanished under candy wrappers after it circled past the bear cages. Farrell matched his pace to Ben's sidelong caution, and they moved among the baby carriages, the elderly couples, the school children harried into double lines behind their teachers, and the bright figures of older children, only half-tame, darting and patrolling like flights of tropical fish; they spoke hesitantly of dissertations, grants, departmental chairmanships and the transmigration of souls. Three boys were daring each other into leaning further and further out over the moat around the lion yard, and Farrell chased them away.

Ben said, "He's real. That's the main thing. Egil is a real person, right now. He lives in Norway, near a real place called Hamar, and he has a wife named Ingeborg, three children, a younger brother who lives with them, five thralls—okay, slaves—four oxen, four horses, a bunch of truly nasty dogs—"

Farrell interrupted him, resolutely ignoring his use of the present tense. "What time are we talking about? When is all this supposed to have happened?"

"Oh, late ninth century, by the clothing and the talk." The unmistakable teaching lilt was coming into

Ben's voice. "They speak of Harald Fairhair as though he were the undisputed king, so it's since the Battle of Hafrsfjord, whenever that really was. Iceland's being settled, and the Danes are all over the Mediterranean. A lot of Egil's people are teaming up with the Danes now, with Scotland and Ireland and the Orkneys pretty well picked clean. Make it 880, around there."

They were in the aviary, standing before the battered, sinister grandeur of the marabou stork and the king vulture. Farrell had guided them there deliberately, because his supervisor was allergic to birds and rarely came near the building. Ben went on, "He owns his land, maybe a hundred acres, maybe a little less. It's thin soil, but Egil works hard, and he's pretty well off, probably the richest man in the area in terms of real wealth, except for the Jarl, the local lord. Fortunately, he gets on well with the Jarl, they've been friends since they were boys. They usually go viking together, after the harvest's in—it's almost a joint command by now. He's about thirty-eight, thirty-nine. He's a very good wood-carver."

Farrell thought of Sia in the living room and of the blind woman being lured from the tree under the stroking of her knife. He said, "This is the one you did your thesis on. I remember you wrote to me."

"No, that was the Jarl himself. See, the Jarl of Hamar is already sort of half-legendary, even in 880." Ben was patting Farrell's shoulder unconsciously in little hard dabs of his bunched fingers, as he always did when he was explaining something. "He was one of Harold Fairhair's first allies, him and the Jarl of Lade, and there's just a lot known about him because he's forever getting involved in politics—wars, plots, backroom deals, insurrections, the works. A really turbulent scoundrel, but people like him. The skalds keep writing new poems and songs about him."

He grinned at Farrell's look. "Joe, I can't help it, I have to talk like that. He's alive, that amazing no-good, this minute, living his crazy life, double-crossing and flimflamming for the pure pleasure of it, for the game, world without end. I wish to God I could write that thesis again. I thought he was dead, and it makes a difference."

Farrell saw the marabou stork coming toward them, pacing softly, full of a carrion-eater's mincing exaltation. The stained white down of its underbody was molting, and lichenous tufts clung to the great peeling beak—*arms of lawn furniture, left outside all winter*—and to the swollen pink pouch, veined and soft as a testicle. It had astonishingly sweet brown eyes, set in a tiny, naked, pimpled red head like an elbow.

Ben said, "But nobody writes songs or anything else about Egil. I've never read a word, there's not a single reference, I had to find everything out from *him*. Egil's not very glamorous, not theatrical; he's just a farmer, starting to lose his hair, doesn't give more of a damn that he can help about current events. He goes off raiding with the Jarl most years because it's a change from harvesting rocks and trees and there's more profit in it. Like most people. He knows a lot of poems by heart and everything about the weather and a whole lot of little games, like children's games, with stones and string."

"And he can't swim," Farrell whispered, remembering Ben's instants of sudden dreadful terror in the pool. Ben nodded. "That's right, he can't swim a lick—still tends to get seasick, as a matter of fact. He's good with horses, though, and he's a born fighter, a natural, better than the Jarl himself." He gave a harsh chuckle, startling the stork. It thrust out its ghastly head and made a sound like sizzling grease.

"How do you know he's losing his hair?" Farrell asked. The warm wind had shifted slightly, upsetting the smaller birds, who began to blow around their enclosures in clumsy, stuttering gusts. Ben said, "I can see it sometimes. In the mirror."

He was almost chattering as they walked on. "Actually, Egil's had a wild life himself, in his own grumbly farmer way. Did I tell you that he was a slave in Morocco for three years? Married there, had a child, got away when a bunch of Danes came raiding. And he was at Hafrsfjord, and some berserker type put a spear right through him—touched the stomach and went out under the shoulder blade, judging by the scar. He saw a sea serpent once, a kraken, off the Faroes. It had a goat's head, and it stank like a dead whale."

"What happened to his family in Morocco? Did he ever find them again?" But Ben did not hear him. He was rubbing his throat, tugging hard at the skin. "Joe, you don't know, you can't imagine. The smells, the darkness under the trees. They sing a lot, people sound right on the edge of singing all the time. The weather, my God, you hear birds bumping down the roof all night long, frozen dead. I don't think they have weather like that anymore, anywhere, or darkness."

A child running by kicked Farrell's ankle and anointed him with something greenish and wettish. Stopping to wipe his pants leg, he asked, trying to keep his voice gruffly neutral, "What happens? How do you call him, reach him, whatever it is you do? Can you control it?" Ben did not answer or look at him. Farrell let it go until they had nearly reached the Cape hunting dogs' yard; then he burst out, "You don't control him. He comes by himself, am I right? I'm right. Seizures. More like late-period Dr. Jekyll, that's what it's goddamn like." He had not realized how angry he was, nor how profoundly shaken, until he heard his own voice.

Ben turned to face him at last, arms wrapped around his body as if against some dismembering cold beyond even Egil Eyvindsson's understanding. *Nicholas would know. Nicholas Bonner knows about cold.*

"It's not that simple." Farrell could barely hear him, but the dogs broke their endless trotting round and ran close to stare, blotchy tongues dripping out of bat faces. Ben said, "He can't control it, either. He doesn't come because he wants to come."

"A civil liberties issue," Farrell said. His ribs were beginning to feel badly bruised, and his head ached. He said, "Tell me what happens."

The answer was quiet and clear, curiously formal. "I love him, Joe. What happens between us is an exchange, like love. He's alive in his world, exactly as I am in mine. We found a way to trade times, for ten seconds, five minutes, half a day, two days. It's just gotten a bit out of hand, that's all. Like love."

A keeper whom Farrell liked passed by, calling to him what the vet had decided about the rhinoceros's arthritic hind leg. Ben laughed suddenly, the shuddering whine of a saw seized up in damp wood. "Or maybe it's like the Groucho Marx line, how he's got Bright's disease and Bright's got his." He seemed to want to touch Farrell, but could not let go of himself for more than a moment. "Joe, nobody knows anything about being a ninth-century Viking, nobody but me. I mean, how could they? They know the damn verse forms, they know dates, kings, funeral rituals, all the people the

Danes or the Jutes beat up on. But there is nobody else, nobody in the *world*, who can tell you a Viking joke. Just me, do you realize that? You want to hear one now?"

"If it's about the two Swedes, I've already heard it," Farrell said wearily. "I want you to tell me where you go, how you get there, what it feels like when you're there." He glanced at his watch and added, "And I think you should do it fairly quickly, because I have to go drive my little green train." *Even my armpits hurt. I am too old for this, too old for everything.*

Ben said, "Bright's disease." He laughed again, in the old way this time, struggling not to. "Joe, I don't know what to tell you. I'm swarming with memories that aren't mine. Those peanuts you gave me, I ate them here, but I tasted them in another time. Somebody tasted them." Farrell actually felt his jaw drop, which was a new experience. "Things taste so different there, Joe; the light's all different, the constellations, the facial expressions—even whistling sounds different, for God's sake. Feelings. People don't dream the way we do, nothing like us, nothing." His voice was level enough, but his teeth were chattering. He said, "I have his dreams sometimes. I can't wake up from those by myself. If Sia weren't there, I'd never wake up. Nobody would know."

"Is anybody there for Egil? When he dreams you?" Ben blinked and frowned as if he had not heard the question. Farrell said, "Technique, that's what I want. Procedure. Do you say *Shazam*, do you drink something really vile, do you just stand still by yourself and think about Egil in a special way? Tell me, Ben."

The Cape dogs danced hotly against the bars, whining with grim urgency. They smelled to Farrell of blood and horse dung and chocolate, and he wondered whether they could sense Egil, if only as a wrongness, a constant disquieting shiver in their wild logic. Ben stared back at them silently. Farrell saw his supervisor tacking shyly toward them by way of trash-can inspections. "The League. Is that the way it started, being Egil in the League? Is that the connection?"

Ben lowered his arms slowly, watching them all the way down, like the newly oiled Tin Woodman. "The League made it easier. Sort of like a singles bar." It was Farrell's turn to blink, and Ben smiled raggedly. "Common understandings. A sympathetic atmosphere. The luxury of knowing that only certain questions will be asked. But you've got it backwards, Joe. I had to invent Egil for them, as a character, an impression, just to be sure that whatever he did, people would always assume it was still me in my Viking hat. The League gave us a place to meet, you see, a place where nobody could ever think I was crazy. Whatever Egil did."

Farrell stepped back to let a heavy woman with a walking frame pass between them, looking sideways at the dogs and wrinkling her nose. "Give them a bath sometimes, why don't you?" she said to Farrell. "Nobody likes to stink, people like you never think about that."

She was followed by two enlaced adolescents, trailing musk and saliva, and then by Farrell's supervisor, who pointedly looked at his watch, bent slightly at the knees and inquired, "Woo-woo? Chugga-chugga? Ding-ding?"

"Ding-ding right away," Farrell agreed seriously. "I just have to see my friend to his car." When the supervisor seemed disposed to debate, Farrell explained, "He's having dizzy spells—I think it might be something he ate at the Elephants' Graveyard," and left him staring anxiously after them, already settling out of court. The supervisor had worked in better zoos than Barton Park, and the strain had been showing for some time.

"You did drive here?" Farrell asked. Ben hesitated, then nodded. Farrell linked arms with him and started him moving toward the parking lot. "I mean, it's okay for you to drive? Egil's not likely to take over in the middle of an intersection, is he?" Trying to make a joke of it, he added, "You know how California is about expired licenses."

"He doesn't take me over. I told you, it's more like an exchange."

The patient instructor tone made Farrell flush so hotly that the skin of his face felt full of splinters. "Rubberlips, I don't give a shit what you told me. I've seen him three times now, and each time you were long gone, you were busy taking *him* over in the ninth century." Ben halted and opened his mouth to protest, but Farrell hurried him on. "I still don't know what you're really doing, or how you're doing it, any more than that poor sucker Egil does, but I know fear, do you understand me? And I am truly ashamed of you, for the first time in my life, because I've never seen anybody as frightened as that man." *Except one other, the yellow-eyed man who came to Sia's house.* "You ought to be ashamed."

"You asshole, you don't have any idea what you're talking about!" They might have been squabbling over the rules of boxball on a Manhattan side street. Ben said, "I'm not hurting him. I could never hurt him. I love him."

"He was not consulted. Did he ever ask to be loved

out of his own life?" Farrell was trembling himself, shaking Ben's shoulder, peering into his eyes to find Egil's incomprehensible torment. "He doesn't know what's happening to him—he must think he's dying, going crazy, and he *is* going crazy, a thousand years ago. That's an exchange? That's love? That's bloody fucking robbery, Ben."

"Don't spit. You don't know what you're talking about." They had reached the parking lot, and Ben was rocking on his heels as he gazed vaguely along the fish-spine rows of stalls.

Farrell asked, "Why were you looking for me?"

"I don't remember." Ben set off down the nearest row with the confidently off-balance air of a man lunging after a divining rod.

Farrell followed, his voice a mosquito's keen in his own ears. "Let it go. You have to let him go." He touched Ben's shoulder again and was startled anew at the sense of his friend's cindery fragility. "Ben, it's not good for you, either. Whatever you're learning, whatever wonderful things, it's not free. You can't keep doing it, you'll shatter, you'll just dissolve, like him, you will. Ben, I know this."

Ben said, "I can't find my goddamn car." He turned and started back the way they had come, so abruptly that Farrell had to jump aside to let him by. His face was averted, but Farrell saw that one side of his mouth was wrong, dragged up and far back, exposing teeth. He said, "I left it here, I'm looking right at it. Son of a bitch."

They did not speak again until the car was finally located, at the far end of the lot. Ben approached it as warily as if it and he were both strange wild animals themselves. Something in that stiff, exhausted shuffle almost made Farrell cry, and he said, "I'd better drive you home. Both of you."

Ben shook his head and got into the car. Farrell gripped the open window as he started the engine. "What about Sia?" he demanded. "How does she feel about all this, what you're doing? She doesn't believe it's seizures, that takes a silly person like me. Maybe I'll talk to her myself, shall I do that, Ben? Because I don't think she knows the whole story. I don't think Sia would let you go on killing Egil out of love, not if she knew."

Ben looked up at him and then away. His free left hand moved from his throat to his mouth, a fist now, pushing as if he were trying to staunch a mortal wound. "You don't understand. The seizures are the way, the seizures open the way. I never had them until her. They come from living in her house, sharing her bed, being in her thoughts. People aren't supposed to do that, Joe. The gift is too great, we can't contain it, we *tear*. But it's a gift, a blessing, how can you say no to a blessing, even when it wasn't meant for you? Don't worry about Egil, Joe. Egil won't die of it. It's my blessing, after all." The car slid through Farrell's hands, and he was gone.

XIV

*T*he hawk's feet were astonishingly hot. Farrell had braced himself for the skeletal clench on his fist, for the great black eyes considering him as if he had answered some strange want ad—*look away a little, Frederik said not to stare*—and even for the improbably soft breast feathers, smelling first like nutmeg and fresh straw, and then like old, clean bones in the sun. But he had only imagined the power and sharpness of the talons; never the heat shocking through the borrowed buckskin gauntlet, pulsating so immediately against him that he might have been balancing the redtail's snaredrum heart on his skin. He let his breath out at last, and the Lady Criseyde placed her arm behind the hawk's ankles, nudging very gently until the bird stepped back onto her glove. Farrell said, "How beautiful."

"Actually, you're not seeing her at her best," the Lady Criseyde said. "She started molting early this year, just to be contrary, and she's so old and out of shape she probably couldn't get off the ground on a bet.

Could you, Strega?" The redtail said *kack* in a thoughtful way, still debating whether to hire Farrell.

Behind him, Duke Frederik answered for her, "Good madame, five bucks says she takes a rabbit ere Micaela comes anywhere near a grouse." He was adjusting the leather traces on the hood of a huge dark bird, taller and much wider-shouldered than the redtail Strega, with a hulking, ominous dignity that made Farrell think of Julie's motorcycles. The dark hawk was irritable under Frederik's hands, stamping and suddenly rousing every feather with the clatter of a Venetian blind. Frederik whispered and crooned her quiet; then he announced, "Okay, I think we ought to move out. Lord Garth and the Lady Aiffe don't seem to be coming, and the dogs are getting crazy. In the name of King Bohemond and St. Whale, let's roll."

There were nine of them, all in full costume, at the rendezvous point, along with two dogs and six birds—only Farrell, Julie, and Hamid ibn Shanfara had none. To the left, hidden by a windbreak of eucalyptus, the Coast Highway buzzed and muttered; directly ahead, summer-stubbly grassland, parched gray-green and gray-blue, stretched away toward an uncertain horizon. The members of the Falconer's Guild moved in brisk solitude, each one sharing a windowless silence with the hooded creature hunched on his fist. Frederik alone remained cheerfully conversational, paying no obvious attention at all to Micaela, except to stroke her legs slowly now and then. "She's a Canadian gyrfalcon," he told Farrell and Julie. "They're the biggest of the falcons and the fastest. She can't dive like a peregrine, but on the flat, nothing comes near her."

"Weren't they reserved for emperors?" Julie asked.

Frederik shook his head. "Kings. Emperors and

225

popes got to fly eagles. I had a golden eagle once, but I lost him." For a moment his dark, asymmetrical face turned as private as the other faces. "His name was Saladin. I had no business with him. Hamid remembers."

"You going to tell me what I remember now?" Hamid asked mildly. He was dressed entirely in flowing white, turban to sandals, except for the red-hilted dagger thrust into his white sash. He went on, "What I do remember is, you didn't lose that eagle. You let him go."

Frederik did not answer. The Lady Criseyde said quietly, "It's the same thing, really. You're always saying good-bye to hawks; every time you flip them off the fist, you have to say good-bye. It doesn't matter how well you know them—they're never yours to lose or to let go. They'll come back if they feel like it. It's always their choice."

The two pointers trotted along with a sedateness that surprised Farrell, who had never seen a professional bird dog at work. Dry grass pricked through the lacings of his soft shoes as he walked. Looking around at his companions in their cloaks and doublets and trunkhose, cradling their hawks on one arm and their spike-tipped block perches with the other, he felt as if he were part of a religious procession on its way to reenact some vaguely sinister passion, whose lost significance only Hamid knew now. The impression was heightened by the fact that Hamid was telling him the story of St. Whale, the League's patron, who came up out of the sea and walked like a man.

"And St. Whale went up and down, doing great wonders in the land," Hamid half sang in the rough, carrying murmur that he used for reciting League legends.

"For he healed the sick, and he raised the dead, and he spoke to volcanos and made them be still. And he comforted the wronged and the helpless and was their protector. *Hail St. Whale, walking on his tail*." The last phrase recurred constantly, like a refrain.

Julie said, "I don't remember the bit about the volcanos." She was barely in costume, wearing tights, a loose smocklike blouse far too big for her, and an absurd purple beret, the size of a medium pizza, that had been Farrell's once. The Lady Criseyde was letting her carry Strega, and she held the redtail close to her face, which worried Farrell.

"Just now put it in," Hamid said in his normal voice. "Got real tired of him planting apple trees and inventing tofu." He fell back into the ritual cadences of the legend. "Yet behold, the mighty came together, and they said, one to the other, 'Shall it continue so? Shall a sea beast with no understanding have the name of a miracle worker and draw away our subjects' love unto himself? Nay, nay, not hardly, Jack.' But the people said, *Hail St. Whale, walking on his tail*."

A rabbit bolted out of a greasewood thicket under the noses of the dogs, ran frantically paralled to the company for a moment, then vanished unmolested down a hole at the base of a live oak. It was the first sign of life that Farrell had seen in those crackling fields, and he had begun to wonder what the hawks would do for prey. Duke Frederik pointed, saying, "Overrun with them. All kinds of quail, too, and partridges. The guy stocked the place with chukars and pheasants years ago, trying to get the hunters to come out. It never really took—I think we're about the only people who hunt here anymore—but it's a candy store, if you happen to be a hawk." He put his ungloved free fist gently against Micaela's beak. She bit it briefly, but then rubbed her beak on his knuckles in an odd, twisting caress.

Hamid chanted, "Now therefore the great gave their orders, that every knight in the land should ride against St. Whale, and every one rode accordingly, save for three knights who would not do so, for very shame, and these were slain. And they called on every weapon in the land, every sword and spear, dagger and axe and pike, every farmyard cudgel and sickle, that each of them should deal St. Whale a deadly blow. And this was done, except for seven swords that would not be used thus, and those of their own wills bent their blades and indeed became the only swords in human history ever transformed into ploughshares. *Let us hail St. Whale, walking on his tail*." He smiled at Farrell, showing just the tips of his teeth.

Duke Frederik halted on a slight rise, spiking the block perch into the earth as if he were claiming a continent for a king. He placed Micaela on it, but did not remove her hood. The dogs were showing excitement for the first time, leaning hard into their leashes and moaning softly. Farrell turned to see the other falconers swiftly setting up their own birds on their perches; the effect was still uneasily devotional on that tawny hillside. The bells on the hawks' legs shivered in the little hot breeze, sounding like those of a distant caravan.

At this shoulder, Hamid went on, indifferent to anything but story. "Now where St. Whale fell, his martyr's blood soaked into the ground, and strange flowers sprang up instantly, such as had never been seen before. And they blossomed scarlet, with double petals like the flukes of a sounding whale, and they blossom still on that holy spot, every year on the day of the Whalemas

Tourney. And each knight who takes part will wear one of those flowers at his crest, for this is how we remember St. Whale and honor him." Several of the falconers joined him in the muttered refrain. *"All hail St. Whale, walking on his tail."*

The hawks were flown in an order set by Duke Frederik, each turn lasting until the bird had killed. Two of the six—the amiable Strega and a jittery young goshawk—were hawks of the fist, launched directly after fleeing rabbits and quail. The others were true falcons, with longer wings and disarmingly round faces, trained to "wait on," circling almost out of sight of their attendants below. When the dogs, working in turn themselves, flushed prey into the air—"We call it serving," Frederik said—they came down.

Farrell had read often that a peregrine may be diving at two hundred miles an hour when it strikes its quarry. The number had no meaning for him until he first heard the impossible chattering howl of little bells ripping across space at that speed, and first saw a ruffed grouse apparently explode on impact, like a snowball. The peregrine settled daintily down through the swirling feathers, and a grinning, big-footed boy hiked up his monk's habit and galloped forward to claim her. She went with him docilely, which seemed as fearful a miracle to Farrell as the sight of her burning out of pale heaven. One of the dogs was already casting greedily for fresh scent, while a Spanish wizard's prairie falcon had begun its staggering climb into the wind, like a sailor going up ratlines hand over hand. Farrell lost track of her in the clouds, but the wizard unslung a pair of binoculars and followed slowly, taking off his glove and swinging it high to call her closer. Duke Frederik had unhooded Micaela. The gyrfalcon kept her eyes closed for a moment, then opened them so explosively that Farrell stepped back from the dark, living emptiness of her gaze.

Frederik said, "Look at her. She balances between habit and what we'd call madness, and for her there's no such thing as the future. I don't think there's really any present, either—there's just the endless past going around and around her, over her and through her. When I hold her on the glove—" He indicated the leather jesses that leashed the falcon's ankles. "—she's more or less tied to my present, but the moment I let her go, she circles up into her real time. Her real time, where I never existed and where nothing's extinct."

"And where fried pork rinds haven't been invented yet," the Lady Criseyde added. "That bird is not going anywhere they don't have fried pork rinds." Julie was sitting on the ground, sketching Micaela in the act of mantling, right wing and leg extended as far as possible. Farrell stood by her, sneaking side glances as she brought up the shadow of the great wing bones, the precise brown barring of the underfeathers, and the taut splay of the black primaries. Without looking at him, she said, "They ought to be here. It makes me very nervous that they aren't here."

"Aiffe," Farrell said.

Julie nodded. "And her father. He started the Falconers' Guild, he never misses anything to do with hawks. It just bothers me." Her two pencils, alternating rapidly, managed to suggest the curious dusty moth bloom on Micaela's plumage.

"Probably hatching up something nasty for the war. Isn't he supposed to be one of the captains this year?"

"In theory. Something else that makes me nervous is people watching me work."

Farrell moved pointedly aside, further than he

needed to. She had been increasingly short with him since their night encounter with Micah Willows, and he had responded with injured huffiness. He said, "If you mean Aiffe's going to be the real captain, she can't come to the war. Even I know that."

Julie did not answer. Hamid flowed gracefully into the silence, saying, "Yeah, well. That's kind of what the war's about this year." The Spanish wizard, still gesticulating into a seemingly empty sky, stepped in a rabbit hole and broke his binoculars. Hamid said, "The war will be fought to determine whether or not Garth de Montfaucon's daughter can go to the war. Lord Garth issued the challenge last week, and Bohemond gave Simon Widefarer leave to accept. The kings don't fight in the wars, but they have to approve time, place, ground rules, and cause. Bohemond settled on Cazador Island, first week in August."

The wizard's falcon eventually stooped to take a partridge, and the Lady Criseyde went forward with Strega crouching on her wrist. Farrell said hesitantly, "But not *this* war. If her side wins, she gets to come to the next one. If she wins."

Hamid lifted one shoulder. "Considering she's shown up at the last two, it's kind of a fine point." Julie turned to him quickly, startling Micaela, who promptly bated off Frederik's fist, but scrambled back up unaided, hissing and flapping her wings. Hamid continued, "See, if she'd just be a good girl and keep on going in disguise, they'd be so happy to let it go. Like all the other times." He smiled his narrow, alarming smile. "But Aiffe's got something a little else in mind. She may not be anybody's Helen of Troy, but she is damn sure the only adolescent *I* know who's getting to have her very own war fought over her. You think she'll miss that? I wouldn't miss it."

Strega was justifying the Lady Criseyde's earlier cynicism, completely ignoring the rabbits that were flushed for her and showing no inclination to do anything as foolishly wearying as flying, let alone taking prey. She had to be literally shaken off the fist and each time she grumbled along for no more than thirty yards before plumping down abruptly to huff out her feathers and talk to herself. The Lady Criseyde finally picked her up, telling Frederik, "I'll try her again last, after Micaela. Some of us are just spoiled beyond belief." Over her shoulder Farrell saw three figures coming across the field.

Nicholas Bonner was carrying a bird, brandishing it like a torch on a block perch almost as long as himself. Farrell took it at first for a hawk, *damn big hawk too, even this far away*. Then Julie made a sound, and Farrell let himself register the round, concave face, round eyes as big and hard and shadowless as military brass buttons, and the twin tufts that resembled wild, theatrically slanted eyebrows more than horns or ears. It sat motionless, never once hooting or spreading its wings; but on Duke Frederik's glove, Micaela the gyrfalcon suddenly screamed like a bent nail tearing out of a board.

Looking left and right, Farrell saw that every hawk was being hastily hooded by its owner to keep it calm in the presence of the owl. Micaela herself was the only exception. Duke Frederik held her gently against his chest, murmuring her silent, watching Aiffe, Nicholas, and Garth de Montfaucon approach. Somebody complained, "You can't *fly* one of those things. I never heard of anybody flying one of those." Julie closed her sketch pad and came to stand beside Farrell. The back of her hand brushed his, as shockingly cold as the hawks' feet were hot.

Aiffe almost danced the last dozen yards, skipping ahead of her companions to pounce into a deep curtsy before Duke Frederik and the Lady Criseyde. "Pardon, pardon, pardon," she cried in her sweet, twangling whine. "The tardiness was most shameful, yet truly no fault of ours. The great wood-devils are none so easy to come by, search as a poor witch will." She was dressed heavily for the summer day in burgundy velvet that hung like a sandwich sign on her thin frame. Yet she moved with graceful assurance in it, standing up swiftly to fling one arm wide, gesturing toward the horned owl sitting so still on Nicholas Bonner's perch. She said, "My lord, gentles all, will you not now welcome me into your most noble fellowship? I mean, do I have a bird here or do I have a bird?" Behind her, Nicholas Bonner smiled at Farrell like an old friend.

Micaela screamed at the owl again, and Frederik drew his cloak partly around her. "Lady Aiffe, this is more than a marvel." The only change that Farrell could hear in his even voice was a lowering in pitch and an early-morning roughness in the tone. "To hold such a creature as this—"

"Without jesses," Aiffe interrupted loudly. "Take note, everyone, nothing commands my wood-devil, nothing keeps him out in fullest daylight among his enemies, nothing but our agreement." The genuine dignity informing her own voice kept being sabotaged by spiteful delight, shredding into laughter like a torn sail in a storm. Yet when she said, "Now we will go hunting with you," there was the slightest questioning tilt to the words, the smallest tremor of vulnerability, touching Farrell by surprise. *She wants in so terribly.*

233

Duke Frederik said, "We are the Falconers' Guild. Even if your bird might by arts magical be trained to fly from the fist, for there's no owl born could ever learn to wait on—"

"Either one," she challenged him joyously. "Either way. If I bid him circle over my head all the day, at a mile's height or a handbreadth, then circle he shall until I cry *stoop and take*. What would you have him do, my masters? We are at your orders, he and I."

In the silence that followed, the horned owl hooted for the first time, still not moving except to close its eyes. The breeze shifted in the same moment, bringing Farrell the owl's cold indoor smell, *rooms where you put things you don't want to think about*. The Lady Criseyde began to say, "By every form and law of our fraternity—"

But Garth de Montfaucon's voice raked across hers like a slash of brambles. "The law? I founded this wretched guild, and you would read me its regulations? There is nothing in the law forbidding my daughter's bird to hunt with your own, and right well you know it, my lord Duke." He had stepped in front of Aiffe and was glaring at Frederik, his gaunt, tight face twisting like a drill bit. He said, "All that is required, *all*, is that the bird be of age and condition to take prey. There is not a single word concerning species. She could fly a duck if she so chose, and if its disposition were suitable, and none to bar her. You know this."

Nicholas Bonner touched Aiffe's shoulder, and she turned to him. Farrell could not hear what they were saying, but Nicholas was nodding at the owl, grinning his branding-iron grin, while Aiffe kept edging irritably away from him. Duke Frederik repeated, his voice increasingly hoarse and slow, "We are the Falconers'

Guild. The rule is implicit in the name, as it always was."

Someone bumped Farrell from behind, and he turned to realize that the entire company were gradually drawing together, none looking at the next, cradling their hawks against themselves like maimed limbs. Even Hamid had moved close enough that Farrell could see the sharp brown cord jumping in his throat. Nicholas Bonner raised the horned owl's perch slightly higher, and the bird hooted again, spreading wings as black and gray as Sia's hair, wings so wide that the round body between seemed smaller than it was, almost fragile next to Micaela's burliness. Garth de Montfaucon said wonderingly, "Implicit? Nay, what is implicit among such creatures as these, save what they do? What further aristocracy within a fellowship of killers and the lackeys of killers?" Duke Frederik began to answer him, but Garth wheeled away, snapping his fingers at Nicholas Bonner. "My lady daughter's wood-devil will hunt *now*!"

No member of the Falconer's Guild ever gave the same account of the following ten seconds. The Lady Criseyde swore bitterly that Nicholas Bonner had shaken the owl violently into the air, deliberately frightening and enraging it, while Julie remained forever certain that she had seen Aiffe herself calmly ordering the bird like any falconer with a glance and a single curt gesture. The Spanish wizard and the boy with the peregrine both claimed that the owl had flown up of its own volition before Garth finished speaking, though the boy insisted on its having actually hovered for an improbable instant until Nicholas Bonner's cold cry sent it floating to the attack. As for Hamid ibn Shanfara, he said only, "Magic won't cover up stupidity. You don't have to be a witch to figure what's likely to happen if you go shoving a horned owl in a falcon's face. Magic didn't have a thing to do with it."

But what Farrell remembered was Aiffe's hands. Long after time had taken such details as the undersea silence of the owl's strike, the bronze eyes that never came fully open in the midday sun, even when Micaela rose shrieking through Duke Frederik's desperate grasp, and the single dreamy flex of the flowering talons just before they took Micaela by the neck, Farrell remembered the triumph and misery of Aiffe's hands. They had lunged upward with the owl in a clenched glory of control; but when they fell, they stopped at her mouth, palms out, fingers curling slowly, and remained there until the Lady Criseyde finally stood up with the gyrfalcon's blood on her cheeks and the front of her gown. Then Aiffe's hands came all the way down, and she held them flat against her sides, smiling like a queen on view while the Lady Criseyde cursed her. In Farrell's memory of that moment, there was never any other sound, except later, when the owl began calling from the trees.

XV

To no one's surprise or understanding, Farrell's supervisor at the zoo was discovered early one morning in the Nocturnal Animals House, curled up on a ledge between a couple of drowsily annoyed kinkajous. He was given an indefinite leave of absence, and everyone even remotely connected with him was fired within the week, as if sad puzzlement were contagious. Farrell counted himself lucky not to be sprayed with pesticide and applied for an opening that Jaime, the peanut vendor, had told him about at an antique automobile restoration shop. The pay was less than at the zoo, and it meant being indoors more, but he liked the job from the first day, finding it delicately exhausting, oddly comforting work. The shop was close to the campus, so he usually had lunch with Julie.

"It isn't so much anything I do," he told her after a fortnight at the shop. "Mostly I just find parts and stick them on—the owners do the complicated stuff. But the air inside those cars is sixty years old. You open a door and somebody's croquet summer comes billowing out at you. Teddy Roosevelt. Lydia Pinkham."

"It's always the smell," Julie said. "All that hot, prickly upholstery just absorbed everything, sunlight and cigarette smoke, sweaty legs. I remember—when I smell an old Pontiac now, I think about my Uncle Mashi, but when I was little I used to think that Uncle Mashi smelled like an old Pontiac."

Farrell nodded. "Maybe he did. Things get mixed up. The people who bring their cars into the shop, a lot of them look like the people who first bought those cars. It's the clothes, partly, because they have fun dressing up to the cars, but it's the faces more. They keep coming in, right out of those old summers, those brown family photographs. The way the League people look like paintings. I keep seeing them."

"It's what happens in groups," she said. "People who get together because of a hobby or an obsession start to look a certain way. Boat people, backpackers, science fiction types, comic book collectors. Even short-wave radio freaks sort of have a look."

"I don't mean that, " Farrell said slowly. "I think I'm talking about people who mess with time, whether they know it or not. It's like what Frederik said—maybe there's really no present, just the past looping on and on. Yesterday I had to take some of the original paint off a 1912 Taylor, off the door, and all the time I was chipping and soaking and scraping that lovely, tough old paint away, I swear I could feel someone else putting it on. By hand, in a converted livery stable. I know how Frederik feels watching those hawks go up into time. Everything's so close to everything else."

He stopped, leaving a ragged hole in the conversation, through which Julie regarded him steadily and unsparingly. For the first time, he noticed a tiny triangular golden fleck in one brown iris that was not duplicated in the other. *Her hair's not as black as it used to be, in this light. Was it ever?* She said, "Even if I do resign from the League, you don't have to. That's entirely your business."

"For what it's worth, she didn't really mean to kill Micaela," Farrell said. "She was showing off." The Falconers' Guild had effectively disbanded within minutes of the gyrfalcon's death, leaving Aiffe mistress of her father's bylaws and a field strewn with torn rabbits and partridges. "I just don't think she really meant it," he repeated. "What the hell would have been the point?"

Julie said loudly and abruptly, "We have been through this discussion before." She started to stand up, bumped her chair against the one behind her, knocked over Farrell's carrot juice and spent the next few moments helping him to mop it up, all the while snarling, "Didn't mean it? She means every damn thing she does, always has, ever since she learned how to make a boy who pulled her hair in fifth grade pull all his own hair out, snatch himself baldheaded." The tables were as close and crowded as her words, and Farrell heard chair legs and Earth Shoes scraping as customers turned to stare. Julie said, "You really think you feel sorry for her. Poor Aiffe, poor skinny little twit, trying so hard to live up to this absurd, misplaced talent that keeps getting away from her. That's not even pity, that's contempt, and contempt is what gets people killed, do you hear me, Joe? She'll do to you exactly what she did to that hawk, for exactly the same reason. To make you take her seriously."

"I take her very seriously," he protested.

But Julie was a flash flood, never giving him a moment to grab onto a rhetorical tree root or floating log. "The point? The point is that thing you keep missing, the point is power. Power doesn't need to explain itself, power is all about not explaining. Power just does because it can."

Farrell overtipped a grinning, green-bearded waiter and followed her out to the sidewalk where any number of people were patiently tracing the transparent logic of the universe for one another. Julie stalked along ahead of him, shoulder bag flapping like a traffic light in a gale, her shoulders themselves cranked up higher than her chin. Sellers of ceramic whales and stained-glass jewelry leaped out of her way, but a frock-coated street corner mime danced along beside her, aping her furious passage. Julie hacked his ankle when he got too close.

By the time Farrell caught up with her, the strange fury of frustration seemed to have passed, and she walked quietly beside him until they were crossing the campus toward her office. Frisbees climbed languidly over head, *waiting on*, and bicycles exploded silently past their faces, silver-quick as barracudas, giving no warning. By contrast, their riders appeared almost illusory, incidental, having nothing to do with the vicious purposefulness of the bicycles. Farrell said at last, "I don't understand." She turned her head inquiringly, and he said, "I don't even know what I don't understand. Tell me."

Julie turned away to hail a sedately jogging security guard and feed stale cookies to Buddy Holly, the campus's swaggering Toulouse goose, before she answered him. "Aiffe is a lot more dangerous than her ambitions. You dismiss her because all she wants right now is to reign over something called the League for Archaic

240

Pleasures. But what matters, Joe, what matters is how badly she wants it." She faced him, gripping his arms just below the shoulders, digging in hard enough to rock him slightly off-balance. "You know how people say, 'I'd kill to have legs like that, I'd kill to get that job, to get next to him'? Yes, well, Aiffe means it. To wear a crown that looks like a damn sand castle, to lead galliards, to go in to dinner ahead of a lot of fools in fancy long johns—Rosanna Berry would indeed kill for that. Maybe tomorrow she'll kill to be Homecoming Queen."

Farrell said flatly, "I don't believe it. *Him*, yes, her father, like a shot, no question about it. But her, I'm sorry—I've seen her make a total fool of herself, I've seen her embarrass people stupidly and make an owl sort of obey her, and she is running around with somebody she called out of somewhere who should definitely not be here. I'm willing to believe that she can do a great many more things, but I still haven't seen her come anywhere near killing anybody. And if you have, I think you'd better tell me." His voice had grown louder, and he shrugged her hands away, stepping back.

"I keep telling you," she said. "More damn people keep telling you things, it's really amazing."

She walked on toward the medical buildings, and Farrell tagged after her, snarling, "Right, right, don't they ever? And isn't it odd that not one of them can ever give me a straight answer? Ask for the time of day, I'm liable to find out the Duke of Minestrone took it with him when he locked himself in the john ten years ago. Ask for the bus stop, you get a treasure map of a lost kingdom." He knew perfectly well that he sounded like a put-upon adolescent, but he kept on complaining until they reached her office.

There she turned again and smiled at him with a sudden generosity that stopped his breath. *I don't know her. All this time of being friends, and I could make a better guess at what goes on inside Sia or Egil Eyvindsson, or, my God, Nicholas Bonner, than I could about her. Who is she, and how does a speechless foreigner get to meet her?* She said, "In the first place, you've got it backwards about Garth and Aiffe. He can't do anything but bruise you with a wooden sword, but once I saw her do something that was worse than killing, and I'll never forgive her for it. In the second place, old love, you get a straight answer with a straight question. And I don't think you've ever asked a straight question in all your life."

She left him there, outraged denial on his lips and panic in his heart, thinking, *If I don't know her, how come she knows me? Who said it was all right for her to know me? I never agreed to that.* And then he thought, *It's probably too late now. To agree. Probably.*

She did not resign from the League then, but she attended so few of their functions that Farrell was mildly astonished when she agreed to accompany him to a dance in honor of the visiting King and Queen of Hyperborea, the Sacramento branch. The evening passed uneventfully—Aiffe and Nicholas were nowhere in evidence—except for King Bohemond spraining his back hoisting the Queen of Hyperborea during *la volta*. Farrell and Julie came home later than they had planned, singing old rhythm-and-blues songs together for the first time in a long while.

Parnell Street seemed curiously still, a night beach at low tide. The tall black man, swaying in the crosswalk where Farrell had first seen him, looked like a winter-whipped beach umbrella in his dirty striped *djellaba*. He would undoubtedly have fallen, even without the aid of the two shadows who were dragging him down, one almost swinging from his neck, the other kicking viciously at his legs. A car passed from the opposite direction, pulling carefully wide so as not to hit anyone.

Farrell stopped Madame Schumann-Heink where she was, and he and Julie grabbed whatever seemed appropriate on the way out of the bus. Micah Willows' attackers looked up to see two improbable figures charging down upon them, cloaks flying, high boots rattling and snapping on the pavement, plumed hats half hiding lunatic faces, gauntleted hands waving tire irons and crescent wrenches. They had been having enough trouble with their victim's African caftan, which tangled their own hands like seaweed, and it was all suddenly more than they cared to handle, just at the moment. Julie fired Farrell's best lug wrench into the darkness after them, and he never found it again.

Micah Willows' left cheek was scratched and bleeding, but he appeared unhurt otherwise. He lay on his back, not trying to get up, slapping the street with both hands in a slow, measured rhythm. Farrell assumed he was drunk as easily as the muggers had, but there was no smell of liquor on him. When Julie tried to lift his head, he rose suddenly on one elbow, grinning with terrible triumph, as if she had stumbled helplessly into his trap. "The hand that touches Mansa Musa," he intoned ominously. Laughter kept him from completing the sentence. Waving his hand with a leisured, heedless regality, he flopped back on the sidewalk and lay snickering. "You are fucking *doomed*." Julie said his name hopelessly, over and over.

"Can you stand up?" Farrell asked him. "See if you

can get up, all right?" But he was a giggling dead weight, unresistingly impossible to lift and no more likely to stay upright than warm yogurt. Julie coaxed him and wept, and Farrell swore at them both, jealous of her concern and furious at his own jealousy. At one point, after the black man had collapsed for a third time, bringing Julie down hard enough to daze her momentarily, Farrell simply let go of him and walked away. He turned when Julie called to him, anticipating her protest. "I know, I know, we can't just leave him. But he doesn't want our help, the hell with him. I'm going to go call Triple-A or somebody."

"Micah," Julie urged, "is there someone you want us to call? Do you want a doctor, is there someone who'll come and help you? Rodney Micah, damn it, tell us whom to call."

Micah Willows lay on his side with his eyes closed, and Farrell thought that he had fallen asleep. But when Julie pushed his shoulder gently, he twisted and came to his feet in a movement like the slow flexing of water or the deep ripple of a hunting cat. The river-brown eyes had become windows onto a suffering that Farrell knew he had no words for, nor any right to see.

"Yoro Keita," the black man whispered. "Yoro Keita, who commanded my horsemen. Samory, Askia al-Kati, Modibo Toure, who spoke for me and knew a little of my heart. Al-Haji Umar, who was not even of my people, but a Tukulor—oh, Al-Haji Umar!" The blank voice grew stronger, a thin, old, burning wind, shaking down the lost names. "Alfa Hassan ibn Mahmud, much learned in the law—Moussa the singer, Moussa the fool—Sheik Uthman ed-Dukkali, he who spoke to me of Mecca when I could not sleep—Sekou Diakite, Okoro my steward, who was a slave once and could play on the *guimbri*—Bakary of Walata, my good captain—Hamani, Kango, Sangoule the Mossi—" The names fell down around Farrell until he fancied that Julie and he stood half-buried in a ruffling drift of the carved and gleaming syllables, disappearing slowly into a king's grief.

"These are my friends," Micah Willows said. "These will come for me." Farrell thought he was going to fall again, but he stood still, eyes and mouth closed, his face entirely sealed shut, the ribbon-thin body in its torn robe swaying slightly from the waist up. Farrell said quietly, "Mansa Kankan Musa, sir. We'll take you home if we can. Tell us where you want to go."

At that, Micah Willows' locked throat roiled and clicked for a moment; then there lunged out of it the sound that a tree makes, beginning to break in two— a fathomless, shuddering *no*. The black man began to cry out a single phrase, clenching his fists and laying his head further and further back, until Farrell could see the howl clawing through him, trying to tear out at elbow joints, arteries, collarbones. *"Lady help me, Lady help me, Lady help me!"* The words were drowned so deep in rage and anguish that Farrell took them at first for Arabic. Micah Willows turned away from him and wandered slowly up the street, still calling and crying dreadfully, and now beating the heavy rhythm of his words out on his robed body, like any other haunted and helpless prophet.

Julie said, "Please." Farrell went after Micah Willows and took him by the arm, turning him back toward Madame Schumann-Heink. With Julie's help, he half towed, half carried him to the bus, shoved him into the passenger seat and locked the door. Julie climbed into the back and kneeled on the jump seat, holding Micah Willows' shoulders. She asked, "Where are we going?"

"I only know one Lady," Farrell said.

So they drove up through the low hills to Sia's house with Micah Willows dozing between them, dreaming in Arabic, to judge by his occasional murmurings. Farrell told Julie what he knew of Mansa Kankan Musa. "Emperor of Mali, early fourteenth century. It was the richest kingdom in Africa then, and Timbuktu was the greatest city. Poets, philosophers, mathematicians, scientists, they came from all over to study at Mansa Musa's court. When he made his pilgrimage to Mecca, he brought along so much gold the market was depressed for a generation. Some people think the whole Prester John legend started right there—the black Christian emperor, perfect ally against the Turks, if you could just find him. Except he was a Muslim, and long dead by then, and his kid had already let the country go to hell. But they kept on sending out expeditions to look for him."

Julie said, "Micah's League name was Prester John. He was one of the founders." Micah Willows opened his eyes, smiled at them both, whispered, "Fucking *doomed*," and snuggled back down into extinct dreams.

"Yeah, I know that part," Farrell said. "And I'm guessing that Aiffe was fooling around one pleasant afternoon, trying to call somebody through time, anybody, and she locked onto Mansa Musa, pure chance. But she only got the spirit, the soul, whatever, and it lodged in Micah's body, pure dumb chance again. Am I right so far?"

He could barely hear Julie's reply. "It was at the Whalemas Tourney two years ago. When Garth was still king. Micah challenged him, and Garth fouled every way he could, but Micah was winning. And then she did it. She wasn't just fooling around." Farrell reached back to touch her hand, but it flinched under his, clutching Micah Willows' shoulder tighter.

"You saw it happen," he said.

Julie made a sound like heavy cloth tearing. "It was a tilt for the crown, everybody saw it. Everybody in the League knows what happened."

"And nobody wants to know. My specialty." Julie made no response. Farrell said, "By now it never happened at all."

"Oh, by now he was always crazy. Ask anyone." The bitterness in her voice dried Farrell's own throat and nipped at his breath. She said, "He was *never* crazy, not ever; he's not crazy now. He took risks, he was— he *is*—curious about everything, and sometimes he'd dance right on the edge of something really dumb, and I'd get scared and yell at him, and we'd have a huge fight, the kind you and I never have." Farrell started to interrupt, but changed his mind. Julie was crying now. "But he is not crazy. In this whole town full of crazies, he might be the only one who isn't."

When they pulled up in front of the shaggy house on Scotia Street, Micah Willows descended to the curb without assistance, sniffing the midnight air delicately and smiling with a curious drowsy serenity. "Oh, here," he said softly and moved toward the house, floating over the grass like a giraffe, which is a creature made entirely of shadows. Following with Julie, Farrell thought that the door began to open just before he knocked.

She wore a brown dress, as shapeless as Farrell's zoo uniform had been, and less becoming: it made her look thicker and shorter-legged than she actually was and slumped her breasts and belly into one bolster-roll of mashed potatoes. But Farrell saw that she stood in the doorway with the still acceptance of her body that he had only known in a few women who had never in all their lives imagined themselves not beautiful, not even for a single bad moment, in pain, despairing. Micah Willows knelt at her feet and spoke to her in medieval Arabic, and she answered him in the same tongue, soothing and reassuring. But there was something astonishingly close to fear in her voice as she asked, "Why have you brought him to me?"

The question was addressed to Farrell, but it was Julie who answered. "You're supposed to be a healer. He needs to be healed."

Sia said, "He may be beyond my healing. Many things are." She stooped over Micah Willows, and something about her creased bent neck stung Farrell's heart. The twinge lasted until she lifted the black man effortlessly in her arms and carried him through the doorway into her house. Without turning, she said to Farrell, "Joe, call Briseis. *You*, if you care for him, come inside." Julie looked at Farrell and followed her, and Farrell went off around the birdhouses to winkle the dog out of her favorite nest behind Ben's compost pile.

When he returned with a more than usually apprehensive Briseis skulking behind him, Sia and Julie had already settled Micah Willows on a frayed rag rug before the fireplace. Julie moved around the living room as Sia directed her, lighting incense in some burners and not in others. Sia herself squatted beside Micah Willows, touching his face and chest and his sweaty hair, while he held her free left hand, smiling at her with his eyes wide open. She said, "Start the fire, Joe."

The room felt stuffy and overheated, but Farrell arranged logs, newspaper, and kindling without question, tossing on equally obediently the strange spiky bundles that Sia gave him. Most of them smelled bad when he held them, and worse when he added them to the fire—and at least one wriggled in his hand—but each changed the color of the flames, from yellow to blue, blue to blood-red, red to sunset-green, and from green to various shades of purple and gray and slug-white, such as had no business on any hearth in any home. The last packet, and the word she spoke, made the flames turn black and answer her, and Sia, still crouching, turned heavily to face Farrell and Julie.

"None of this circus will help him," she said. "None of this has the least bearing on whether or not I can free him and the one trapped within him from each other. All this is witch-rubbish, this is what that foolish little girl would do, but I am no witch and it will not help." She looked very tired, her cheeks glistening damply and her upper lip showing thin white lines, but she chuckled suddenly—a whispering, fiery sound itself, like hair being brushed. She said, "This is all to comfort me and play for time, because I am afraid. Once I could have healed him by imagining it—indeed, once this thing that has happened to him would never have been allowed, no more than a leaf is allowed to jump back up to its tree. But now I am afraid and I am delaying the moment when I must learn why I should be afraid. So if either of you knows some small spell of your own, we can try that one, too. I need friends, and I have no pride."

She was looking straight at Julie as she spoke.

Farrell asked, "Where's Ben? How come you're still

up this late? Did you know we were coming?" Sia ignored him completely.

Julie bridled, surprisingly flustered, fumbling sullenly for words. "If I knew any damn magic that could make him well, he wouldn't have been like this for five minutes." She looked away from Sia, rubbing her swollen eyes.

The old woman said impatiently, "Oh, more people than not have *some* magic, they just forget about it. Children use it all the time—what do you think jump-rope rhymes are, or ball-bouncing games, or cat's cradles? Where do you think that girl, that Aiffe, draws her power? Because she refuses to forget, that's all it is." Abruptly she sighed and slapped her thighs, pushing herself upright. "But this is not a matter for magic anymore. A vain, silly child played a jump-rope trick on your friend, and now nothing but a miracle will help him. And that is exactly the bloody trouble with amateurs." She beckoned Briseis to her, commanding the reluctant dog step by step until they stood on either side of the silent, smiling Micah Willows. Sia said, "Well, perhaps Briseis can work a miracle. Perhaps we can all work one together. Let's get on with it." She began to unbraid her hair.

The task seemed to take forever, *as if she were unraveling mountains, towers, not hair;* but with each strand freed and brushed out, the living room seemed to grow larger, the walls paling and receding, the ceiling dissolving into starlight. The black flames crouched low, all but extinguished, but Sia loosened and loosened her hair, and the strange starlight filled the room, silvering faces, sparking blue in Briseis' fur, making everything heartbreakingly bright and nothing truly clear. It clung thickly around Sia, until she glittered like a snow-woman, and it filled Micah Willows' wide eyes with dawn.

Farrell had been raised in church but without religion, a compromise pleasing enough to everyone involved. He had never missed God or the hope of heaven, but he had dearly wanted confession to rest his mind, Communion to let him touch something beyond Father Krone's dry, shaky hand, and holy water to taste like starlight. Now, with the room brightening toward some sure wonder, exaltingly unbearable, he managed to think, or say, or neither, *oh, how kind, after all, how kind*. Then Sia shook her hair free upon her shoulders, and Micah Willows screamed.

Even at the moment, Farrell realized that the cry was one of fear, not pain, and that it came through Micah Willows, but not out of him. For all that, it raked right down all his bones, and he started forward as impulsively as Julie. But they would have had to pass Sia, and they could not do that. She stood between them and Micah Willows with her back to them, an immense, shining silence, distorted with strength, no one they knew, no friend of theirs. Briseis rose up on her hind legs, huge as a tiger, and they embraced over Micah Willows' body, crowding into each other so that Sia appeared to have Briseis' pointed, white-laughing head in place of her own. Farrell remembered then the reflection he had seen within the first hour of his first meeting with Sia, and he held Julie tightly and waited for the wonderful thing to happen, as he had always known it must.

But nothing did happen. Sia made no sorcerous gestures, voiced no incantations, called down no lightning, but stood still in one place with her dog's paws propped on her shoulders and a black man threshing on her

251

hearth, each howl arching his back more dreadfully. The starlight in the room began to ebb, and what returned was not good darkness but hot, bustling shadows that chittered like hamsters. A mask over the fireplace was rattling its bronze jaws.

"Ah, well, there, you see?" Sia pushed Briseis down and turned to face Farrell and Julie. "For every action, an equal and opposite reaction—this is true for gods and demons as well as rocket ships. If you bend the universe the wrong way, even for the smallest instant—which is what you would call a miracle—and you lose your hold, the universe snaps back at you, you get something you did not ask for. I was punished so once before." Her voice remained as placidly amused as ever.

Farrell could not remember how to speak. Micah Willows' cries were clawing the inside of his head bloody, and Sia was dwindling as he stared, not merely to her usual size and self, but seeming to lessen in texture as well, so that he thought he could see the black flames and the yammering bronze mask through her body. She hushed the whimpering Briseis with a touch and knelt by Micah Willows once more, murmuring words that were neither English nor the old Arabic. He grew frighteningly still, his breath scrambling and slipping in his chest. Sia whispered to him, "Forgive me."

"McManus," Farrell said. A shadow the size of a pig slid between his legs, then circled back, nuzzling him. He said, "McManus, when he came to the house with a gun. I remember what you did. I saw you."

Sia's surprised laughter sounded like Micah Willows' breathing. "That was no miracle, that was only fear. It is the easiest thing in the world to make human beings afraid—none of us could ever resist it. They do all the work for you, and then they call you a god. But no one can make the universe afraid." A second mask, her favorite, from New Guinea, began to clatter its tusks and sharks' teeth together; she waved it silent, and it spat at her contemptuously.

"Forgive me," she said to Farrell and Julie. "I should never have let you in, never have pretended that I could do anything for your friend. That was vanity, not pity, and I am very sorry for it. Go now. I think you still can."

The pig-shadow had been joined by others, larger, with too many legs. They pressed close around Farrell, pushing against him like Briseis, thick as blankets, smelling like dog food. Far away, on the other side of the shadows, he could hear Julie saying, "Joe, help me get Micah on his feet. We are getting out of here."

"No," he said, as loudly as he could. "He was calling for her, he knew she was the only one who could help him. You love him—" His mouth tasted as rancid as the shadows. "You want him to be like this forever? Even in Avicenna, they'll put him away and give him stuff to keep him quiet, and he'll die. She has to try again, that's all."

"You don't understand." Sia was shaking her head violently, her hair scattering the last remnants of starlight that clung there. "You don't understand. I cheated you because I was afraid, because I knew I would fail, and I know what it means to fail at a miracle. My strength is no more than a wish of what it was, but I did not dare to use even half of it just now, I did not dare. Take him and go, go quickly."

Julie had bent over Micah Willows, working her hands under his shoulders. She straightened slowly, regarding Sia with resentful respect. She said in a low voice, "Because the universe snaps back."

"Exactly as hard as you bend it." Sia gestured around her at the swarming shadows and the hanging masks, all but one of which were clacking and whining hungrily, lunging toward her on their hooks. "This is nothing, because I tried nothing. If I put forth all the strength I have, it would still not be enough to free Mansa Kankan Musa from this time, but the rebound, if you like, the rebound could shake all of us into the middle of next week." Her smile parted the darkness like a sudden sail. "You would not like the middle of next week. I have spent some time there."

Micah Willows sat up, crying softly, "Al-Haji Umar! Al-Haji Umar, I am here! Okoro, Bakary, Yoro Keita, here I am waiting in this place, come and find me!" Julie crouched beside him, holding him as he slumped back, but he struggled weakly in her arms, giggling and muttering, "The hand that touches Mansa Musa." She looked silently up at Sia. The shadows made their faces dim and small; but even so, Farrell saw the long glance that passed between them, deeper than complicity, more candid than easy sisterhood, almost shy.

Julie said, "Please, will you try again? I'll help you."

"You help me?" Sia's answer came so briskly and decisively that Farrell believed forever that she had had it ready before Micah Willows ever knocked on her door. "Child, no one can help me, no one except Briseis, and she can only do what she can do. You are incredibly stupid and selfish—and very brave—and you should go home now, this minute. For some things there is no help, you just go home."

Julie's voice trembled slightly when she replied, but her words were quick and clear. "You said that most people have at least a little magic. Mine comes from my grandmother, if I have any. She was born on an island called Hachijojima and she never learned English, but I spoke Japanese with her when I was small. I didn't know it was Japanese, it was just the way Grandma and I talked. I remember she used to drive my parents crazy, because she'd tell me really scary stories about the different kinds of ghosts—*shirei* and *muen-botoke* and the hungry ghosts, the *gaki*. And *ikiryo*, they're the worst, they're the spirits of the living, and you can send them out to kill people if you're wicked enough. I loved the *ikiryo* stories. They gave me such great nightmares."

Sia was nodding, a drowsy old woman before a guttering fir. "And the goddesses—Marishiten, Sengen of Fujiyama. Did she tell you about Sengen, your grandmother?"

"Ko-no-hara-saku-ya-hime," Julie chanted softly. "She said it meant that Sengen was radiant, like the flowers of the trees. And Yuki-Onna, the Lady of the Snow. I thought she was wonderful, even if she was Death." She paused, but Sia said nothing, and Julie took a deep breath and added, "And Kannon. Especially Kannon."

"Kuan-Yin," Sia murmured. "Avalokitesvara. Eleven-faced, horse-headed, thousand-handed, Kannon the Merciful."

"Yes," Julie said. Briseis plopped her heavy head on Farrell's knee, and he petted her, taking a sad, spiteful comfort in her need of him. Julie said, "I don't remember this at all, any of it, but somehow my grandmother consecrated me to Kannon. A little private ceremony, just the two of us. My father walked in on it, and I guess he hit the roof. I don't know. I couldn't have been more than five or six."

The black flames had gone out almost completely; the only light in the shadow-choked room seemed to emanate from the angry masks and, strangely, from Micah Willows's wracked and scarred face. Julie went on, "All I'm sure about is that I didn't get to be with Grandma so much after that age. I lost all my Japanese pretty fast; and I lost Grandma too. She died when I was eight. She's buried on Hachijojima."

Two shadows nipped Farrell's ankles at once with icy little teeth that left no marks. He flailed them away, but others were moving in, shapelessly aggressive as Julie's Japanese ghosts. Sia asked "Did you ever wonder why she did that, joining you and Kannon?"

"I don't know. Maybe she was hoping I'd be a Buddhist nun."

Sia was shaking her head again before Julie had finished. "Your grandmother was very wise. She had no idea what gift to give you for your life in this country that was already snatching you away from her, but she knew that human beings everywhere need mercy most of all." She turned to look down at Micah Willows for a long moment, then said something almost inaudible to him in Arabic. Farrell had no doubt that she was repeating her last few words, *mercy most of all*.

"Well," she said. In one remarkable movement she stood up, clapped her hands to drive the shadows back, snapped, "Oh, just be quiet!" to the masks—who paid her no attention whatsoever—and turned solemnly around three times, like Briseis bedding down. Farrell and Julie gaped, and she laughed at them.

"No magic, no miracle," she said. "Only an old person trying to get her doddering self balanced properly.

What we are going to do now is absolutely insane and insanely dangerous, and I think we should all get our feet well under us."

Julie said, "Joe, you'd better go. You don't have to be here."

"Piss off, Jewel," he answered, hurt and furious. His voice silenced the masks briefly, and Julie touched him and said, "I'm sorry."

"Understand me," the old woman said, and her own hoarse voice was suddenly so terrible that the room cleared of shadows instantly and Farrell glimpsed the distant, blessed outlines of chairs and chess pieces. Sia said, "I am not doing this for either of you, or even really for him— *them*—nor out of vanity, as I told you before. I am doing this out of shame, because I knew what had happened the moment it happened, and I did nothing. I did not dare to leave my house. I could have called him here to me, but I feared being destroyed if I tried and failed to free him. So I have done nothing at all for two years, until tonight."

Farrell was never sure whether he had actually voiced his mild protest before she cut him off savagely. "Of course it was my responsibility! My responsibility is to see that certain laws are kept, certain gates are only allowed to swing one way. However tired or weak or frightened I am, this is still what I am for. If you insist on trying to help me, you do it out of ignorance, because you cannot possibly imagine what you risk. But I do this out of shame."

Julie asked, "Do you think Kannon will come? What should I do? How should I call her?"

"Never mind Kannon," Sia said. "Try calling your grandmother."

She meant what she had said about balance, ordering

Julie and Farrell to brace themselves in the dark room as carefully as if it were a moving subway car. She even propped Micah Willows against the fireplace as best she could before she turned and said, "Well," a second time. The three of them ranged themselves around Micah Willows, with Briseis trembling next to him and Sia keeping one hand in the dog's neck fur. Micah Willows hugged Briseis's leg, looked up at them all and said, "Fucking doomed. Prester John knows." Nothing else happened for a long time.

The starlight came back first, to Farrell's great joy. He had intended to watch very closely this time, to see whether it was truly bound up in Sia's hair or emanated from somewhere outside the room. But when it was there, it was simply there, making the room float on its foundation, and Farrell too happy to do anything but whisper a welcome and hold Julie's hand. The scent of flowers grew warmer around them as the light spread—*plumeria, the gods smell like Hawaiian plumeria*—making him think of Sengen, beautiful as blossoming trees. Micah Willows, or the king within him, began to moan softly again with inconceivably fearful anticipation, and Farrell had a moment to wonder, *is this how it is for Egil Eyvindsson, each time?* Far above them all, Sia's face was rising like the moon: golden and weary, battered into human beauty by endless stoning. Farrell could not bear to look to her.

Then she said something in a language like soap bubbles that could only have meant, *no, damn it, damn it to hell*, and, as if some celestial wrecking crew had gone to work, jagged pieces of night came plunging through the walls and ceiling of the living room. What Aiffe and Nicholas Bonner together had failed to accomplish seemed to happen in seconds now, as the room ripped itself to pieces like a torn kite in a gale. But the solid old houses and libertine gardens of Scotia Street and the Avicenna lights below had disappeared as well, leaving nothing beyond the shattered suggestion of Sia's home but a sky fanged with strange, hurrying stars and a darkness that was also moving and that went on forever, past any hope of morning. It was the only vision Farrell was ever to have of raw, random space, and he could not keep his feet under him. He crouched down among the tumbling stars, covered his eyes and vomited, thinking absurdly, *I'll never finish sanding that old Essex now, never get home to finish that.*

In a detached way, he was aware that Julie was crying out, somewhere nearby, "Kannon! *Sho*-Kannon, *ju-ichi-men* Kannon! *Senju* Kannon, *ba-to* Kannon, *nyo-i-rin* Kannon! Oh, Kannon, please be, Kannon, please! *Sho*-Kannon, *senju* Kannon!" She went on and on like that, and Farrell wanted to tell her to shut up because she was giving him a headache. But just then the goddess Kannon came to them, so he never did.

Julie said later that she had simply stepped through a hole in space, pulling the endless, meaningless night apart with a hundred of her five hundred pairs of arms and letting it close behind her, but not before Julie had glimpsed the blue-green shores of heaven and the dragons. But to Farrell, it seemed that she came slowly from a long way off and that she entered that place where they were through the one of Sia's masks that had never sprung to nasty life, but was somehow hanging in perfect serenity on no wall, over no fireplace. It was a Kabuki mask, white as plaster; and as Farrell watched, it began gradually to stream with Kannon, dissolving over and over to flow into her round brown face, her flowering arms, cloudy robes, and long amber eyes. Her appearance pulsed and surged constantly, bordering always on forms and sizes and sexes beyond Farrell's imagining or containing. Farrell saw her bow slightly to Julie, saluting and acknowledging her. When she looked at him, he wiped his mouth weakly, ashamed that she should see him so, but Kannon smiled. Farrell wept—not then, but later—because Kannon's smile allowed him to, as it allowed him to forgive himself for several quite terrible things.

He always insisted that he had heard them talking together, Kannon and Sia, in the soap-bubble language, and that he had understood every word.

–Old friend–

–Old friend–

–I cannot help him. I am too tired–

–I will help him–

–You are younger than I and more powerful. You have many worshipers, I have none–

–Illusion. We do not exist–

–Perhaps. But the child called you, and you came–

–Of course. How not? I know her grandmother–

–Yes. Thank you, old friend–

But Sia swore that they had never spoken at all, that there could be no need for speech between them; and Julie drove him wild by describing how Kannon had leaned down to Micah Willows and touched his eyes, actually touched them, and how he blinked and said, "Julie," in a voice she remembered, and promptly fainted. Farrell missed that part altogether, having realized that Ben was hanging far off in the night like Sia's Kabuki mask, peering drowsily across unhealed space at the scene below. Then Kannon bowed again to Julie—who was too busy with the still-unconscious Micah Willows to notice—and bowed low to Sia like the Northern Lights, and went away with the starlight, and Ben came on down restored stairs and crossed the creaky living room floor to Sia. He put his arms around her and held her as tightly as he could.

Micah Willows opened his eyes and said, "Julie? Man, who *are* these people?" Farrell stood quietly where he was, listening to the first birds, and to the sprinklers coming on at the house next door, and thinking entirely about Kannon's smile.

XVI

The war was not optional. Nearly every knight of the League, saving only the combat master John Erne and the King, was expected to take part in it, though the degree of a fighter's activity was for him alone to choose. Farrell knew only that he belonged on Simon Widefarer's side and that he would do something humane and encouraging on the home front. He asked Simon whether making hero sandwiches and teaming with Hamid ibn Shanfara to improvise morale-boosting songs for the troops entitled a man to noncombatant status. Simon guaranteed nothing, but recommended climbing a tree.

The rules of the war were simple and very few. The tangly thirteen-acre island in the middle of Lake Vallejo—a bay and a county away from Havelock—had been ceded annually to the League for the past several years, thanks to a combination of friends in moderate power and a lack of tourist interest in the poison-oak-ridden area. For a week preceding their dawn-to-dusk

262

occupancy, the defending side was permitted to swarm over the island, constructing a web of plywood barbicans and outworks, as well as varyingly symbolic entrenchments, deadfalls, and mantraps, all centering on a primitive fortress, little more than a stockade atop a mound of earth. It was this castle that Garth de Montfaucon's forces would have to take to win the war.

Combat was conducted as in any tourney, with the outcome being determined largely by honor and eight floating referees, four from each side. In the one departure from ordinary League procedures, each party was allowed the use of a weapon customarily forbidden. Simon Widefarer chose the longbow, Garth the morgenstern. In practice, as William the Dubious pointed out, it always came down to swords; but Simon's choice committed the invaders to helmets and serious body armor, despite the special blunted arrows. "That adds up fast, on a hot day. They never write about it, but plain exhaustion must have accounted for as many armored knights as anything else, in the old wars. Look for them to start dropping around two o'clock, three maybe."

"Can we hold them off that long?"

William beamed a bit muzzily. They had been helping to work on the wooden castle all afternoon, aided by a siegeworthy stock of Mexican beer. "Easiest part of it. The thing is, Joe, the defenders always have the edge. There are only three good places to land on this whole island—there used to be more, but Garth spent all week one year bringing in these huge rocks, and he dropped them around so they ripped the bottom out of anything that tried to beach. It'll take them till noon just to get a foothold, and they'll lose a lot of men doing it. They've only got till sundown, and we can keep them away from the castle till late afternoon sometime, with any luck at all."

"Nice house odds," Farrell said. He thought of adding, *except for Aiffe,* but instead he asked, "You're really looking forward to this, aren't you?"

William the Dubious nodded earnestly. "This will be my fifth. I just think it's a great outlet for so much bad stuff—all your aggressions, your violence, phony behavior, the whole thing of choosing sides, winning. I think all wars will have to be like that pretty soon, like ours. Nobody can afford the real ones anymore, but people still have to have them." He caught himself, laughed self-consciously and added, "Okay, *men* have to have them. See, I'm trained."

On the evening before the war, Farrell went with Hamid to a meeting at William's house to discuss plans for the War of the Witch, as it was already being called. Simon Widefarer and most of his strongest fighters were there, arguing like football fans about tourneys past and storied feats of arms in shattering mêlées; and, like connoisseurs of rugs or high fashion, about techniques of shield work and innovations in longaxe combat. There was mulled wine and home-brewed mead, and conversation slipped back and forth across the border between daily speech and the silly, haunting Ivanhoe language.

Farrell fell asleep and was nudged awake by Hamid when the gathering broke up. Drowsily he asked, "How'd it come out? Do we have a game plan?"

"Best game plan in the world," Hamid said. "Pound 'em on the head, stay out of the poison oak, and run like hell when Aiffe shows up. One slick game plan."

Farrell had come to the meeting in League dress—tights, tunic and a laced vest that Julie had made for him—like everyone else except Hamid, who had arrived directly from his post office job, wearing tan slacks, a white short-sleeved shirt, and—in spite of the heat—a narrow red tie, elegant as a serpent. Passers-bys turned completely around to stare at them as they walked down through the sweetly smothering night. Hamid said, "I got to stop drinking that damn mead of William's. You could fly model airplanes on it."

"I understand he's catering the war," Farrell said. "You still think Aiffe's going to show? Simon kept swearing she'd promised the Nine Dukes or some-body—"

"Man, I *know* she is!" Hamid stopped walking. "Simon was just trying to keep their minds off that battle roster Garth sent over. We got them outnum-bered damn near two to one. You think old Garth didn't notice? You think he'd ever let the odds stack up like that if he didn't have a little game plan of his own?" His voice rose and softened into the singing mumble of the St. Whale saga. "Oh, it is going to be a one-woman extravaganza, live from Las Vegas, and when it's over there won't be any more wondering, any uncertainty about just who is the star around this League. And there is to be a death."

They were two blocks further along before Farrell could believe Hamid's last words enough to repeat them. Hamid blinked. "Did I say that? I told you, I have *got* to lay off the mead—it throws me right into my bard routine, and I don't even notice." He was silent for another block, and then he said quietly, "No, that's not true. It just happens like that once in a while, with bards."

"A death," Farrell said. "Whose death? How?"

But Hamid walked on, striding out faster than Farrell had ever seen him, making the red tie lick backwards over his shoulder. "The voice just came out with it, it does that. Pay it no mind."

He did not speak again until they were nearing the Parnell corner where Farrell would turn off toward Julie's house. Then he said thoughtfully, "Word has it that a certain mutual royal friend is no longer on the street. Glad to hear it," but there was a questioning tilt at the end.

Farrell said, "He's in the hospital. Getting over malnutrition, kidney trouble, a spot of anemia, and a couple of those things you get from living out of dumpsters. Also, he's way past time for his regular dental checkup, and he's under what they call observation because he has real trouble remembering who and when he is. But he's doing fine."

"Well, I'm sorry I didn't tell you the truth about him," Hamid said. "I'll be honest, I had my doubts as to how much you could take in." He cut short Farrell's indignant response. "Yeah, I know what you and I saw Aiffe do, but you got to understand, I have also seen more than a hundred intelligent people steadily denying something she pulled off right in front of their eyes. *Unmaking* it, you hear what I'm saying? Changing him, changing Micah, to fit the story, I saw them doing it. Man, he helped found and organize this whole damn League, and two weeks, three weeks, he was just another crazy black man, gone AWOL, gone native, the way they got this unfortunate tendency to do." His voice was shaking as badly as the hand that gripped Farrell's forearm, the enviable, expected grace of being in sudden shreds. "You ever want to see the real witchcraft, you watch people protecting their comfort, their beliefs. That's where it is."

Farrell asked, "Why did you stay in the League?"

Hamid's control was already reasserting itself when he answered. "They needed a chronicler, and I needed something to chronicle. I had my own comfort to look after."

At the corner, he bade Farrell an abrupt good night, turned away, hesitated, and then added, "You know, another reason I had some trouble talking about Micah—I guess you know Julie and he were sort of an item when what happened happened." Farrell nodded. Hamid said, "I wouldn't take it to heart. But I'd say they do have a certain amount of unfinished business."

"It's their business," Farrell said. "That voice of yours, on the other hand, that death tomorrow, I think that's our business. I think we should pay attention."

Hamid snorted. "That voice'll say anything, it doesn't know shit." But his eyes were not mocking when he patted Farrell's shoulder. "Well, we'll pay attention, whatever we can do. That's the thing with the damn bardic voice, it never comes with instructions you can read. Worse than useless. See you on the island."

Julie was sleeping soundly when Farrell let himself in, and he set her alarm clock for a three o'clock summons, sourly certain that she had spent the evening in Micah Willows' hospital room. But when he rose from the bed, she turned over, swiftly wide awake, reaching up for him. "Have a good time," she said. "When in doubt, just surrender. I'll ransom you."

Farrell kissed her, saying, "I know it's dumb, boys playing war games. I just want to see what it's like one time."

Julie said, "Don't apologize, for God's sake. Just remember, not everyone there will be playing. Keep your head down."

She was asleep again when the armored men

knocked at the door. Farrell opened it and saw William the Dubious and two others, all three cloaked from throat to ankle, but ringing softly when they moved. A van, bigger and newer than his own, stood twitching in the driveway. Farrell ducked back into the house, grabbed his lute and the mail shirt that Julie had insisted he take with him, and went outside.

Ben was sitting in the van, dressed in full Viking battle gear, all studded leather and painted steel, with heavy arm rings and a bear-claw necklace. Only the belt-axe and horned helmet were familiar to Farrell. He was badly frightened for a moment, unsure of whom he was facing; but then Ben grinned at him and made a uniquely obscene gesture they had both learned from a Sicilian classmate, and Farrell demanded, "What the hell are you doing here? You said you didn't go to the wars anymore."

"Don't yell," Ben said placidly. "People are sleeping. A little consideration here."

"You had all these papers to grade. You made such a thing out of it—a zillion papers, no time, no time, be working when you get back from the playground, Joe. Embarrassed the hell out of me for even asking you—"

"Grading papers is boring. Wars are fun. Get in, we've got two other knights to pick up."

Farrell lurched into the seat beside him, asking, "Does Simon know? He was throwing a major hissy last night because you weren't coming. Does Sia know?"

Ben said, "Sia sent me to keep you out of mischief. Okay now? Shut up and put that shirt on, you'll need it."

The drive to Lake Vallejo took a little more than an

hour, and the sky was thinning when they parked the van near a concrete-block lavatory and walked the rest of the way down to the lakeshore. Farrell saw a dozen other cars and pickups parked among the cottonwoods and a rowboat plying toward the island, bearing four knights, their cloaks flaring in the dawn wind and their armor the color of the lake. A golden banner with two black swans on it flapped stiffly above them.

It was no great distance to the island, but the boat went back and forth three times before it came the turn of Farrell, Ben, William, and their companions. As a result, they arrived at the plywood fortress just as Simon Widefarer was ending a passionate and furious harangue of encouragement to his drowsy, dispirited-looking troops. He broke it off and led the cheering as Ben, with Farrell following, slipped hastily into the ranks of variously caped and armored men grouped around their household banners. Farrell joined Hamid under the blazon of one Mathgamhain of Cliodhna, but Simon Widefarer took advantage of his position as captain to call Ben personally to his side. He went with odd reluctance, looking back at Farrell to say, like Julie, "Be careful. You hear me, Joe? Be really careful."

Mathgamhain of Cliodhna was well pleased to have both Farrell and Hamid ibn Shanfara in his service. "No lord of Ireland would go to the fighting without his bard and his harper, surely," he said. "And can you play *The Silkies in the Green Sea* for us?"

"We can fake it," Hamid said. Simon Widefarer said loudly, "Nor is there need for any but a dunghilly poltroon to fear the girl. Twice over, both as witch and woman, is she forbidden to set foot on this island today, and it is known to every man that her power may not cross the water. Banish her from your fears, therefore, and attune your souls to victory. For Bohemond and St. Whale!"

"That's running water," Farrell said softly, "not a lake," and Hamid nodded. The last shout drew a sharp answering cheer from the knights—though not as triumphant a one as the sight of Ben had raised—and they wandered off to their assigned positions with some gaiety and swash. The sun was rising now, making their armor seem to slide like water, running crimson, ebbing into silver, eddying black. Three of the men were harmonizing zestfully on *The Agincourt Carol*, their strong, rough voices still clear to Farrell after they had disappeared among the alder bushes.

> *"Owre kynge went forth to Normandy*
> *With grace and myghte of chyvalre:*
> *Ther God for hym wrought mervelusly*
> *Wherfore Englonde may calle and cry,*
> *'Deo gracias.'*
> *Deo gracias Anglia*
> *Redde pro victoria."*

The first attackers did not appear on the opposite shore until the sun was well up. Farrell sat in a tree and watched the enemy knights climbing into half a dozen rowboats and being pushed off toward the island by their barelegged squires. The sunlight on their plumes and visors made them into faceless, fire-headed beings—torch-arrows at the string. Farrell called to Hamid waiting below, "Twenty-six, I make it," and Hamid turned away to report the count to Mathgamhain's lieutenant.

The boats angled away from each other, two aiming

for each of the accessible landings. Farrell had meant to begin staying out of the way, as he felt became an unarmed musician, at the first sight of Garth's forces; but he retreated only a little way as the boats drew in, taking shelter behind the first and slightest barbican, no more than a shoulder-high plywood windbreak tacked hurriedly across a couple of trees. Three knights already crouched there, their helmets beside them on the ground, and each man held a bow. Farrell noticed that two of the bows were wooden, expertly crafted, while the other was of fiberglass, with a sighting device and a rest for the arrow. But it was a knight with a wooden bow who was chewing bubble gum.

Under their motionless gaze, two boatloads of the raiders glided through the gap in Garth's barrier reef to beach among vines. Farrell heard the oarlocks clanking and the boats' bottoms grinding thickly on the shore. The knights began to scramble out, moving awkwardly, shields held high before them. Several had their swords out as well, and most carried flail-crowned maces—the morgensterns—tucked into their belts, the studded heads dangling from chains and wire cables. The heads were supposed to be built up around tennis balls, reinforced with cloth, rubber, and leather; but to Farrell's eyes, they swung a good bit more like icy snowballs with rocks in them. He recognized the foxy brightness of their leader, Brian des Rêves, Garth's closest crony, and heard his soft commands as the detachment pushed forward. The three waiting men chose arrows from their quivers.

Even before they stood up together, fitting arrows and firing over the barricade almost in one motion, Brian—perhaps warned by the rattle of the quivers—had wheeled away, shouting to his knights to scatter, to get to the sides. The blunted arrows clacked off the wooden shields, bonked when they found armor. Farrell would have expected at least five official casualties among the nine invaders, but only one man fell, struck full in—and presumably through—his gorget, and again in the side as he went down. Another knight turned back to help him, was shot in the sword arm, and lunged into the bushes, out of range. The others had vanished; Farrell could hear them shoving their armor through the wiry scrub, moving to outflank the barbican. The defending knights put down their bows and drew their rattan swords, though the undergrowth barely gave them room even to stand on guard. Farrell began thoughtfully to fall back, thinking that Lord Mathgamhain might like to hear *The Silkies in the Green Sea* again.

A thin young man wearing a black shirt and black trousers pushed past him toward the knight who still lay sprawled before the barbican. He carried a clipboard of yellow paper and called loudly as he went, "Ramon of Navarra, arm wound—the MacRae, arm and leg—Olivier le Setois, arm wound—Sforza of Lombardy, slain." The knight sat up, then got to his feet. The man in black said, "Go on over to Glendower's Oak, you know where that is? They've got beer and sandwiches—check yourself off the big roster, first thing." He turned briskly back toward the sudden clatter of swords and garbage-can racket of whirling flails that had erupted behind the barrier. Farrell, easing discreetly away into the deeper woods, got a glimpse of two defending knights standing back to back, each one assailed by at least two men. Sforza of Lombardy marched by, slain in combat and heading for neutral territory until the end of the war. He was whistling softly and snapping his fingers.

Behind Farrell, Hamid clucked his tongue disapprovingly. "Now you see, that man is not serious. The *serious* ones, they lie right where they fall, all day."

Battle had apparently broken out on all three beach-heads. Knights of Simon Widefarer's army went leaping past Farrell, waving their swords and tangling their cloaks in the shrubbery, all hurrying to reinforce the besieged outworks. Simon's lone semblance of a campaign plan involved the archers' keeping off the landing parties for as long as possible, and then giving ground slowly, digging in at every fortification, until it came time for the last stand in the castle and the hope of sundown.

Hamid ibn Shanfara strode the island tirelessly in his white robes and turban, wailing Moorish and Celtic battle songs and constantly inventing immediate rhymed accounts of events that were still going on as he chanted them. Farrell stayed closer to Mathgamhain of Cliodhna, dutifully cheering the Irish lord into every encounter, bearing messages for him and his household, and casting increasingly wistful glances at the refreshment table each time he was swept past it. *That's where I make my stand, boy. Bury me where the braunschweiger'll wave over my grave.*

It was like being at a League tourney that went on forever, without dancing or jugglers. In a certain fashion, matters obeyed the vague rhythms of a real campaign, lurching back and forth between the various outworks and the shore, but continually breaking off for innumerable ritualized and irrelevant personal combats. All action halted in any quarter when it was shouted that Brian des Rêves was blade to blade with

Olaf Holmquist, or that Raoul of Carcassonne and the Ronin Benkei, each with a sword in one hand and a cudgel in the other, were holding six knights something more than at bay in a poison-oak ravine. The rest of it was dust, prickly sweat, squatting boredom, aimless running and ducking into bushes, occasional flurries of pushing and falling down, the bustling of the black-clad referees, and eternally the idiot yells of "Yield thee, recreant!" and "To me! To me! House of the Bear, here to me!" Garth's tactics continued to be no more imaginative than Simon Widefarer's, but it was obvious that no one truly cared which side gained or lost ground—the fighting was all, and Farrell wondered that he should ever have expected it to be any other way.

There was no sign or sense of Aiffe, nor of Nicholas Bonner, and Farrell found himself almost disappointed. Ben was hardly more visible than they, for all his fearsome reputation. Farrell glimpsed him now and then, at a distance, on the trailing edge of some flanking attack or mop-up maneuver; but so far he figured nowhere in Hamid's evolving chronicle of the War of the Witch. Mathgamhain fell at midafternoon, not in battle, but of what appeared to be acute indigestion, and he was followed in quick order by four similar cases and three of sunstroke. Farrell remembered William the Dubious' prediction and would have thought little more of this, but then the injured started coming in. Two had apparently fallen into deep pits that opened beneath their feet; three others had been knocked half-senseless by branches falling from great redwoods. Hamid, skillfully bandaging a victim, looked across him at Farrell and said, "Methinks, man."

"Me, too," Farrell said. But he was hot and grubby and unable at present to think seriously about anything but beer. While Mathgamhain's men were choosing a new captain from among themselves, he wandered away among the trees until he came to a clear-trodden path that he thought led to Glendower's Oak, where the slain and the captive alike went, and where there might be something on hand other than William's stickily dangerous mead. The woods seemed thicker and wilder here, laced with deep, luminous alleys, and the air tasted of old silence. Farrell began to play softly as he walked—a Latin drinking song that Chaucer had known—and presently paused to retune the lute to a more suitable mode. But for that halt, he might not have heard Aiffe's voice directly ahead of him nor had time to lie down by the path among tree roots and long grass. He could not see her, because his cheek was tucked hard against spongy bark and his eyes were shut. He knew beyond the absurdity of it that she would find him if he opened his eyes.

"Nay, this is mine," she was saying, "this is my triumph and no other's. But for the piffling form of it, I'd face them singlehanded, with no knights at my back, no father to serve as my front and weary me with counsel. And no dorky Nicholas Bonner, neither, to tell me what I may and mustn't do. Just me, just Aiffe—gods, what a wonder." Her fierce snicker actually resounded in the lute, and Farrell quickly smothered its tiny answer against his belly.

Silken old laughter responded to hers just as the lute had done. "What, no sweet Nicholas Bonner, then, to nourish your glory? A summer's apprenticeship, and you'll pension me off and make your way alone? Greedy, thankless child, you wound my heart."

"I was never your stupid apprentice," she answered angrily. "You're in this world because of my power,

275

but you've got none of your own—I know that for sure, anyway. And yeah, I do think I've learned just about all you've got to teach me, what do you think about *that*?" The voices had stopped approaching, and Farrell opened one eye a little way.

She was standing no more than fifty feet from him, facing Nicholas Bonner on the path. They were dressed alike as squires in boots, hose, and rather faded doublets, though Aiffe's hair was hidden by a hooded cape, while Nicholas Bonner wore only an owl's feather in his melon-yellow mane. He said, indulgently malicious, "And that little matter of the old·woman who left you drooling in the street? You'd handle her without me?"

Aiffe snorted, derisive and uncomfortable at once. "Maybe yes, maybe no. She's your old woman, your big thing, you handle her. I've got no problem with her, except that she's too strong. I don't like people to be that strong."

Nicholas Bonner's voice was as soothing as sunlit mist. "Well, we're here to learn how strong you are, my own sweeting. This toy war of theirs is your tiltyard, your testing ground—let's see what you can do, then. The small plagues were an exercise; you could have done those in your sleep—in fact, you have." He was stroking her, slipping his hands under the cape. "Time now for something a bit more demanding."

Aiffe sighed and giggled, letting the cape fall from her. "Why do you always want to do this? You don't get anything out of it; you think I don't know? Why do you want it?"

Nicholas Bonner answered her honestly and with something close to dignity. "Dear love, I enjoy exactly what you enjoy, and that is the sensuality of power. There is no other pleasure I can take, even if I would.

Yet each time we couple, you and I, something moves, something is born, as it is with real people. I am well content." When he laid her down on the cape, her small, round breasts butted at him like cats.

Farrell began to crawl slowly backward, away from the path, but he had covered only a few yards when a heavy body pinioned his own, kneeing the breath out of him, and a hand went over his mouth. Ben whispered, "Don't move." Farrell squirmed his head to the side and saw him, face dark with dirty sweat, helmet askew and one of the horns badly chipped. Aiffe was chanting, the cold words whining out of her in the same rhythm with which Nicholas Bonner entered. Farrell watched them, rapt and ashamed, until Ben nudged him and they scrabbled off into comforting brambles. When Farrell looked back, he thought the air was shivering and sliding where Aiffe and Nicholas Bonner lay, *like the air over the classroom radiator, that first school winter. Thought you were going blind at the age of seven.*

"How did they get here?" he asked. "Simon's had people patrolling the shore all day."

Ben shook his head, immediately professorial, even wearing bear claws. "Simon's been watching the only three places where a rowboat can beach. That's not patrolling. Patrolling is when you keep an eye out for things like kayaks. They just slipped in from the Marin County side, easy as you please. Who needs magic?"

The leaves whirred softly overhead, like bicycle pedals, as they made their way back across the island. A Cooper's hawk ripped down through the slanting light, striking for something almost at their feet, then flapped up into an ash tree, where it sat panting hard and staring at them furiously. Farrell said, "That's not just your garden-variety quickie going on back there. That is machinery."

"Tantric sorcery. Sex magic. Really effective if you know what you're doing, dynamite if it gets loose. Sort of like Leg-O's—you can make all kinds of really unpleasant stuff with it. Sia said they'd be using that."

"What else did she tell you?"

Ben shrugged, smiling wearily. "Hard to remember. I mean, she woke me up, dumped me out of bed, damn near dressed me, and shoved me into that van. She kept saying something terrible was going to happen, and I was to stay with you all day. And a pain in the ass it has been, I may add, trying to fight and watch over you at the same time. I haven't been doing either one very well."

Their voices sounded fragile and very far away to Farrell—spider-ghosts scurrying hand over hand up the dusty pillars of light. He told Ben about Hamid's warning and the circumstances of it. "Is that what Sia was talking about? Look, just tell me."

Ben did not answer for a while, long enough for Farrell to become aware that Julie's mail shirt had chafed several raw places on his neck and shoulders. Ben said at last, "She's not always right, you know. And sometimes when she *is* right, it's not in any way you could have imagined. Who knows what Sia means by death?"

The first sending exploded into being as they were informing Simon Widefarer that Aiffe and Nicholas Bonner were on the island. It looked like a raw, bloody stomach with a crocodile's head, and it flew at them on wings edged with tiny mouths. Ben, Farrell, and Simon screamed and fell to the ground, and the creature flashed stinking over them, wheeling back for another go, making the sound of sucking mud. It had ridiculously bright blue eyes.

Half of Simon's forces had been drawn into the plywood castle by now; the remainder—Hamid among them—were either off scouting, skirmishing, or helping to shore up the fortress's rickety outer walls, as Farrell and Ben had found Simon doing. The structure was actually a good deal more solid than it looked, a fact proved conclusively by the time the second and third monster—one half-toad, half-gamecock, the other something like a pulpy *Nutcracker Suite* mushroom with yellow human teeth and a snake's tongue—were streaking and circling low above the castle. At that point, so many yelling knights of the League had jammed through the entranceway and the two sally-ports that the entire castle should have been as flat as a split milk carton; but the walls remained upright, conveniently for the sendings, who perched on them. More and more came banging into being: goat-legged viscera, fanged cacti, huge, hound-faced slugs, creatures like stuffed toys oozing sewage, creatures like tall skeletal birds with fire pulsing between their ribs. Without exception, they smelled of carnivores' excrement; and they kept coming, inexhaustible nightmare hybrids, chattering like parakeets, snuffling like bears. They dive-bombed those who fled; they swooped low to snap and jeer at hysterical knights rolling on the ground; they overran the red sundown, leaving just enough daylight to see them by. *Aiffe's children*, Farrell thought, and thought that he laughed into the trampled brown grass.

Beside him, Ben grunted, "Fuck *this*," and stood up, brushing sendings away from him like gnats. "Absolutely harmless," he announced loudly. "Low-budget special effects, might as well be afraid of a slide show.

Let's get on with the war." He walked briskly toward the castle, picking up a hammer and a handful of nails to work on the weakened frame. Farrell followed, shoving after him through hot clouds of hovering phantasms. He always swore that one of them lit on his shoulder for a moment, and that the stench lingered in the tunic ever afterward. He never wore the tunic again and finally burned it one night, years later, when he was drunk.

"She's very good," Ben said quietly. "If he hadn't been pushing her a bit too hard, we'd have been in big trouble."

"Those things aren't real," Farrell offered cautiously. Ben shook his head irritably, hammering in a corner support. "Not quite, not yet. They will be. Another month, another week. The least little bit over-trained, that's all," He might have been talking about a distance runner. "I certainly wonder what she'll try now."

The sendings kept at it a while longer, increasingly petulant rather than menacing, badgering Simon's knights for attention as the men returned to the castle in shaky, shame-faced twos and threes. A veil was thickening between them and the day they had raided; and by the time Hamid ibn Shanfara drifted in, they had been reduced almost to misshapen pigeons cadging handouts around park benches. Abruptly they twitched out of existence all at once, as if a single switch had shut them down. The late light came back, turning shadows green and gold, showing a good hour yet to sunset. Ben said again, "Now what?"

"Ah, as to that," Hamid murmured in his legend-voice. "As to that, perhaps someone espied two handsome children in the wood, not twenty minutes since, and perhaps one said to t'other, 'Nay, but you'll not do this thing, I forbid it, so.' And meseems the little girl gave him the lie straight away, saying for answer, 'Forbid *yourself*, turkey. This shit is *boring,* and I am about to lose the damn war, messing around like this and the sun going down. Behold and stand back, for I will get myself some real help right now.' But t'other was wondrous wroth, and says he, 'For your life, you dare not! This is nothing for you, this is more than you can yet hold, on my word, sweet sister, on my word.' And it might be she laughed at him, and perhaps some-one heard her say then, 'You have no word, and I told you when I summoned you first that I can handle any-thing I can call. And so I can, Jack, with or without you, I got it *down!*' And it is said that he railed further at her folly, but perhaps not. A bard must say only what he knows." He bowed slightly to Ben and Farrell and began rewinding his turban, amazingly immaculate.

Simon Widefarer was inside the plywood castle, spacing his men thinly along the walls to meet the sunset attack. Farrell was startled to realize how greatly their numbers had been reduced; between losses in battle and a dozen suspicious injuries, Simon was captain only of some sixteen exhausted knights besides himself. At first, he would not part with even one when Ben and Farrell repeated Hamid's tale to him and urged a scouting expedition. "Not if she were coming down on us with all of Charlemagne's paladins. What use is the knowledge now?" But Ben pressed the need fiercely, and Simon finally yielded, saying, "Let *him* go then—" He pointed to Farrell. "—and *him*." He in-dicated the Scots laird Crof Grant, plaided to the eye-brows and topped off by a bonnet like a Christmas fruit-cake, sagging with red and green clan badges, erupting with plumes enough to reconstruct the whole ostrich. Simon said, "I cannot spare Egil Eyvindsson from the defense, but two such will leave us little weaker." Farrell felt as if he had once again been chosen last at stickball.

Skulking through the brush with Crof Grant was a reasonably similar experience to the time Farrell had tried to smuggle a pool table out of a fourth-floor walk-up at midnight. In the first place, Grant's costume refused entirely to skulk, but caught on anything that made a noise, including Farrell; in the second, the man himself never ceased to prattle, in a constant warm spatter of glottals and occlusives, of the countless Sassenach rogues fallen that day to his trusty claymore. Hushing him did no good at all, since he was talking louder than Farrell dared raise his own voice. He was in the middle of a singlehanded stand against three foes armed with morgensterns, armored in crushing youth—"Losh, laddie, gin ye add their years thegither, ye'd hae no mair than my ain"—when they came into a clearing and saw Garth's men waiting silently for them.

To do Crof Grant justice, he said only, "Hoot-toot," before he started running. Farrell lingered for a deadly instant, not out of surprise or paralysis, but because of the five men grouped close behind Aiffe where she stood with her father. At first glance there was little to tell them from the rest of Garth's tattered forces, grim alike with weariness; but Farrell had seen the yellow-eyed man in Sia's house, and he had understood Aiffe's challenge to Nicholas Bonner. *Oh, my lord, she does have it down.* Then Aiffe saw him and laughed and pointed, and one of the strange knights bent a bow at him so fast that he never saw it happen. The arrow sighed in his left ear, sinking itself out of sight in a juniper bush.

Farrell was running by then, half-crouched, hands guarding his face, struggling through blackberry, hemlock, and wild lilac, falling once and having to make sure that the lute was all right, and hearing himself making small noises like a garden hose or a steam radiator that has not been quite shut off. Away to one side, there was an immense crashing and stumbling that must surely be Crof Grant in flight, while behind him he heard only Aiffe's whooping, shuddering laughter. But he knew who was pursuing him as clearly as he had suddenly known who they were: *the real thing, genuine gunslingers out of the genuine Middle Ages, out of the Crusades, the Spanish Netherlands, the Wars of the Roses. Unpretentious, unwashed, unmerciful—the real thing, ready for bear. Lady Kannon, pity now.* At that point, he dodged around one tree cheek-first into another and spun back to the first tree, slipping down against it, still reaching to shield the lute.

He lost color for a little while. When he could stand, three gray people were almost on him. The one closest might have been a pilgrim turned mercenary or a Norman invader of Sicily. Under a steel cap, he had a square, windburned face with flat cheekbones and tufty eyebrows, and his look was so peaceful and humorous as to be called insane. Farrell picked up a dead branch, watching with numb, patient curiosity as the man came on, noting equally the slight bend of the knee, the seemingly loose grip on the sword, and the flakes of dandruff in the pale eyebrows and mustache. The sword had a raw, winking notch near the tip, and the unbound pommel looked like an old brass doorknob. Farrell wondered whether the light reflected into his own face came from the setting sun of Avicenna or Palestine.

He held up his branch as the sword started back. It

moved unnaturally slowly, the knight's lips wrinkling with the same deliberation, his body setting itself for a sidearm blow. Then Crof Grant was trundling between them, grappling fearlessly for the sword and rumbling out, "Fye na, haud ye'er brand for sair shame. Tis a naked museecian, man—would ye harm a sleekit, cow'rin, tim'rous minstrel?" The dreadful bonnet was gone, and his white hair kept falling into his eyes. The knight growled very softly and stepped away from him, moving up on Farrell from another angle. Grant was after him again, partially interposing his slow, shrouded body, "Nay, I say ye shanna'! I say haud! Dinna ye ken League rules, man?"

The sword melted into the side of his throat, and he slapped vaguely at the wound before he stumbled down. Color came back with his blood.

Farrell never remembered how he reached the castle; only that he was not followed, and that he was crying when he got there. Ben held him on his feet and almost literally translated his near-hysterical report to Simon Widefarer, but no one else, except Hamid, seemed to take any of it seriously. He was reassured on all sides that Crof Grant could not possibly be really dead, that metal swords were never allowed in League combat, and that neither captain would even consider enlisting new fighters, once a war was under way. As for Aiffe's monstrous sendings, the minority willing to discuss them at all favored mass hallucinations brought on by uniform minor sunstrokes, such as had been happening all afternoon. Meanwhile there was a last stand to prepare for, and a serious need of heartening music. Hamid looked down at him from a teetery catwalk, saying nothing.

The attack came no more than twenty minutes before

sunset. There was no attempt at surprise; rather, the surviving knights of Garth de Montfaucon's party—still fewer than Simon's forces, and looking even more spent—approached the castle boldly, stepping with a slow, menacing rhythm and chanting grim burdens to keep time. Garth himself swaggered in the lead, but Aiffe and Nicholas Bonner walked unobtrusively to one side in their anonymous squires' dress, followed by the five men she had summoned to her. On the catwalk, Farrell said to Hamid, "That's the one. Second on the left, the short guy." He thought that Aiffe looked anxious and subdued. Hamid said without expression, "I don't want him to be dead. I don't want to predict anyone's death."

"He's dead, all right," Farrell said.

Garth drew his troops up before the outer wall and stood forward, calling, "Now stand well away, of your kindness, for we'd see none injured when the walls come down." Farrell knew that a battering-ram entry was as much a tradition of League wars as ransoms and victory feasts, but no ram was visible among the attackers. Nevertheless, there were knights on the wall who began to back away.

"Steady all," Simon shouted, "Give them no heed, but look to your bowstrings."

Aiffe kissed both of her hands loudly and blew the kisses toward the castle, spreading her arms to wave them on their way. The inner and outer gates fell down flat, and Garth's men swarmed in through the rising dust.

Simon Widefarer and his archers fired frantically into the first rush, dropping a few as they scrambled over the gates. After that there was no free play, even for the morgensterns, and no room for referees. The castle seethed and rocked like a subway car at rush hour; fighting knights were hurled apart, unable to find their combat again, or stumbled together straight through someone else's mêlée, and were cut down by their comrades, as likely as not. For those who fell, there was a very real danger of being badly trampled, and Farrell and Hamid hauled several such as far out of range as they could. They were huddled in a rear corner, Farrell curled protectively around the lute, Hamid jauntily cross-legged, still taking notes aloud. The dust went up elegantly, orange and gray, poising just over the scene like the fighter's breath.

"Here they are," Hamid said softly, and Farrell looked up to see Aiffe's five summonings passing through the ragged gateways, three abreast, two following singly, moving into the battle as delicately as cats stalking a birdbath. Farrell was fascinated to see how much like any costumed bank managers they looked, even knowing what he knew. Hamid said, "All more or less from the same time period. I make it one Norman, one Venetian free-lance, two early Crusaders, and I don't know *what* your boy there is, except nasty." They both stood up as he want on musing. "Wonder how she handled the shock factor. They look pretty cool, considering they surely had other plans for the afternoon."

At the top of his lungs, Farrell shouted the first word that came to him. *"Realies!"* Hamid burst out laughing, but no one else paid the least attention. Farrell yelled, "Real swords, ringers, look out, they've got real swords!" The five men spread out, choosing their targets. The Venetian went for Simon Widefarer, and the one who had killed Crof Grant came straight toward Farrell and Hamid.

Hamid said, "Some day we got to talk about whether it was really necessary for you to do that." The Norman caught William the Dubious with a side cut that doubled him over, then aimed a finishing blow meant to shatter his helmet. The man who had killed Crof Grant blocked Farrell's view. He looked happy and zestful, as if he were meeting dear friends at the airport.

As the sword began to come up, Hamid chanted loudly, "Hate to *talk* about your *mama*, she's a *good* old soul," and danced away to Farrell's left. The sword flickered involuntarily to follow him, and Farrell shoved the lute into the man's face, knocking the steel cap sideways. Everything in him screamed against the idea of using the instrument as a weapon; but he thought about vain, rumbling, ridiculous Crof Grant trying to protect him, and he hit his killer in the head with the lute as hard as he could. The beautiful elliptical back caved in as the man wandered to his knees. Farrell hit the man a second time before Hamid yanked him away from there.

The battle had traveled at least two stops beyond chaos. Whether or not Aiffe had ever understood that her summonings could not be controlled to the point of pretending to kill, that pretending was not in them, it was clear that she had never considered their effect on Garth's own men. Some of his mightiest fighters were plainly distracted with fear of them and seemed positively grateful to be taken early out of the action. Others were astonishingly outraged, turning on their terrifying allies to defend Simon Widefarer's knights from any assaults but their own. Aiffe's summonings struck back without hesitation, and the real swords drew real blood, leaving men on both sides staggering half-blind with scalp wounds, useless sword arms and badly slashed legs from attempts at hamstringing. Farrell himself took a blow across the chest that drove Julie's chain mail deep into his flesh, leaving the ring-pattern visible—and breathing an activity not to be engaged in lightly—for more than a week. *The five of them could kill us all.*

Later, he and Hamid agreed that John Erne would have been proud of his combat students, and that they in turn owed him their lives, though most of them never knew it. Impossibly overmatched as they were against twelfth-century professionals, the moves and defenses he had taught them saved them at least from being instantly hacked down where they stood. Farrell saw a plump boy, his straggly blond mustache thick with blood, fake the Norman off-balance with hip movements as slick as a basketball player's; and he saw one of the Crusaders launch an overhead cut at the Ronin Benkei which would have split a wooden shield and the body behind it as well. But the Ronin Benkei sidestepped and brought his round steel shield up so hard that it slammed the sword out of the Crusader's hand, sending it tumbling all the way to the flattened inner gate. He never did get it back, but made wicked do with a dagger after that. Farrell was always sure that Garth de Montfaucon kept the sword.

There was an immense shouting going on somewhere now, carving a name over and over into the dusty twilight: *"Eyvindsson! Eyvindsson!"* Ben was standing near the gate, roaring and swinging an axe as long as one of the great two-handed swords. His face was the way Farrell had seen it once before, blazing pale, bent with another man's rage out of time and with a delight in rage for which Farrell knew a few dead words. The longaxe whipped around his head, making a sound like a big animal panting, and Ben howled the name as if in awful mourning for himself. *"Eyvindsson! Eyvindsson! Eyvindsson!"*

Aiffe's five summonings made straight for him, and he took them on as they came, in pairs or all at once, sometimes using the axe handle like a quarterstaff to crack their heads and ribs, sometimes driving them before the whimpering crescent of the blade, never giving them a moment to gather themselves for the kind of fighting they knew, but battering them ceaselessly with a toy which could never have broken the skin. Farrell realized later that they must surely have known the terror of the berserker in their own time, and that it was this that routed them, and not so much the fact that Ben knocked the Venetian briefly senseless with one end of the longaxe, then caught the Norman full amidships with the other and drove him out through the gate like a croquet ball. That was the true end of the War of the Witch; the other four simply followed him, professionals cutting their losses. Aiffe ran at them, shouting, but they were already long gone into the darkening air, clearly seeking the place where they had lurched from a reasonable world to this one. Farrell thought he saw them find it, just before the trees hid them.

Yet he was to wonder a little, imagining them stranded here like Mansa Musa, poor free-lances, slurped up onto Parnell Street to roam crazy among the pretend crazies and the half crazies, among the quiet young men dreaming about killing somebody morally. *They might do just fine, what do I know? Maybe it happens a lot more than I think. Probably wind up in Central America.* He never saw them again, nor ever wanted to, but he never quite stopped looking.

Simon's final charge, trapping Garth and his surviving knights between the sword and Ben's axe, was utterly anticlimactic for everyone involved. When the head referee bawled, "*Sunset and hold!*" the plywood castle—dissolving now at all four corners, and with two walls tottering—remained in the possession of some dozen filthy, laughing men sitting on the ground. They raised a cheer, faint and thick-throated and mocking; and Ben became still at last, staring around him with a sick, flinching face, letting the longaxe trail to the ground. The head had been wrenched sideways on the splintering haft, and Farrell saw torn leather windings and a snowy dribble of plastic foam.

There was little sense of celebration. Dead men rose up and dusted themselves, chatting about weapons with their breathless killers, while the two medical students who served as paramedics dressed and bandaged real wounds, increasingly inexplicable. Prisoners drifted in through a deepening mist to arrange ransom terms; some tidying was done, and even a certain amount of dutiful ale-drinking and singing of victory. Aiffe and Nicholas Bonner had vanished with the sun. In time several men went to find Crof Grant.

Not a mark was on the body, nor was there any blood on the leaves where he lay. Ben and Farrell stood together on the island's abrupt shore, watching the first rowboat heave away toward the lights. Nearby, Hamid ibn Shanfara was chanting a lament for all the fallen, as he did each year. "*Gaily went they to the gods, this morning's comrades.*" The saffron shirt gleamed pink for an instant until the shadows took it.

Farrell said, "I kept hoping that somebody from another time couldn't really kill somebody in this one." Ben did not answer, and Farrell felt compelled to keep talking. "Well, Sia called it, after all," he said. "Sia and Hamid."

When Ben turned, his face was fifteen years old, an eggshell of pain. "They called two different deaths," he said. "Egil's gone."

Farrell stared at him. The naked face said, "He's dead. Egil's dead. I felt him die."

Farrell touched his shoulder, but Ben moved away. "You mean, you lost contact, the connection got broken. Is that it?" *Right, Farrell. Of course that's it.* He wanted to put his arms around Ben, as he had seen Ben hold Sia, but he was afraid to.

"I mean he's dead," Ben said, "In his time, his real time, at the age of thirty-nine." Farrell started to speak, then let him continue, anticipating the question. "I don't *know* what he died of. I'll never know. People died all the time back there in the ninth century; thirty-nine was getting on. But I'll always think he died of me. Of what I did to him, what I made him do. I mean, maybe I wore him out, gave him an ulcer, a heart condition, a stroke." His face convulsed suddenly, but no tears came. "I felt him die, Joe. I was trying to brace the gate, and he died."

"That's why you were calling his name like that." Ben was scrubbing furiously at his mouth with the edge of his fist, scouring away the taste of death. Farrell said, "You don't know you killed him. You don't, Ben."

The fifteen-year-old face turned toward him again, oddly swollen and lumpy in the dusk, as if swallowed sorrow had produced an allergic reaction. Ben was smiling slightly. He said, "You see, if I don't know, I'll wonder about it for the rest of my life. If I accept the fact that I really killed him, killed him a thousand years ago, then maybe I can stop thinking about it one day. Doesn't seem too likely, but maybe."

"Will you for God's sake cry?" Farrell demanded. "You're going to hurt yourself if you don't cry." But Ben shook his head and walked away toward a second rowboat about to put out from shore. Farrell stood looking at the water, imagining Aiffe and Nicholas Bonner sliding swiftly along in their kayak, tucked in snugly between the little dark waves. A large seagull followed the rowboat most of the way, swooping low as if to snap up the last herring-bright scatterings of daylight in its wake.

XVII

Crof Grant's death was set down to a heart attack. He had, in fact, a minor history of coronary complaints and had been advised against overexertion. The story made good copy and stayed in Bay Area papers for several days, not so much because of the police investigation, which was unimaginatively thorough, as because Crof Grant's widow threatened to sue the League for Archaic Pleasures for thirty-five million dollars. According to the press, she blamed the League not only for her husband's death, but for most of his life as well, from the decline of his professional reputation to his occasional attacks of gout, his increasing lapses of memory, passed-up offers of better jobs elsewhere, and the general decay of their marriage. "We couldn't *go* anywhere! Half the time I couldn't even understand what he was saying, and then suddenly he's challenging the headwaiter to a duel for being an English sympathizer. The children wouldn't even come to see us. Those goddamn people turned a perfectly good husband and father into the goddamn Master of Ballantrae."

She never got around to filing the lawsuit, but she did hire a private investigator, who took his job seriously. He was visible long after the reporters had disappeared, patiently seeking out and questioning almost every man who had been on Cazador Island during the War of the Witch. His time and energy were completely wasted, in a sense, since the only ones beside Farrell who had actually seen Crof Grant die were presumably back home in the early Middle Ages; but he made people nervous, even so, and there began to be resignations. Too many strange, serious wounds had come home from this particular war; too many men were waking out of too-similar nightmares about fanged flying intestines or trying to talk of the sunset battle, and five faces with no more pity in them than the sunset itself, and always giving up the attempt with the same shrinking, half-imploring shrug. The detective told Crof Grant's widow that he strongly suspected the presence of drugs in the case. She said she just knew it, and to keep digging after those goddamn people. "Sixty-one years old, as much sense as a rutabaga, and they killed him with their goddamn drugs. It explains *everything*."

The reporters came back for the funeral, since it was attended—at the insistence of Crof Grant's will—by a large formal delegation from the League, in full costume. Farrell stood with Julie and a couple of Grant's muttering art department colleagues, watching as the plumes, hennins, capes, kirtles, tabards, gipons, mantuas, roquelaures, and pelerines flashed through the waxy air of the funeral chapel and swept bowing before the coffin. The League gained fourteen new members within the week, more than matching the resignations.

Farrell also appeared to be the only person to have seen Aiffe on the island during the war. Garth's men denied categorically that she had ever led or sorcerously aided them, and two witnesses beside her father swore that she had spent that entire weekend visiting cousins in Cupertino. Farrell told Julie everything that he had seen happen, from Aiffe's tantric coupling with Nicholas Bonner to Ben's rage of despair over the death of Egil Eyvindsson, somewhere around the year 880. Julie listened silently until he finished, and then asked, "What are you going to do about it?" She had wept for Crof Grant with a vehemence that surprised Farrell, who had seen no one else do it.

"Well, I'll talk to that guy she hired," he said, "I don't plan to go looking for him, but when he comes to check me out, I'll tell him what I know. Fair?" Julie seemed satisfied enough, which pleased Farrell. In a burst of candor, he added, "I really hope he doesn't show up, but I'll try to tell him." He truly meant to keep his word.

But the investigator did come to find him at work, and in the end Farrell lied to him, like everyone else in the League, by coffee and omission. "Jewel, it wouldn't have made a damn bit of difference. In the first place, he wouldn't have believed a word of it, any more than the cops—I mean, I could *feel* that—and in the second place. . . . Listen to me. In the second place, what difference would it make if he did believe me? The guy who killed Grant is eight hundred years out of town, over the border. We don't have any extradition treaties with the twelfth century."

As always when she was really angry, Julie looked as if she were about to laugh. "The person who killed him is watching TV, doing a little babysitting for pocket money, and so delighted she can't stop hugging herself. She's getting clean away with murder, and now she knows she can get away with it anytime she wants, because nobody will ever say a word, no matter what they see. You have just personally handed her the whole damn League, from which I have just this minute resigned." Farrell started to protest, but she said, "Joe, get out of here. I really want you to leave me alone for awhile. I'll call when I feel like talking to you again. Go on, Joe, now." He left without looking back, pointedly careful not to slam her front door.

Furious, bitterly defensive, trying himself on her charges a dozen times a day and acquitting himself each time, with no discernible effect on his sadness, Farrell spent the next two weeks either working, practicing with Basilisk for the Whalemas Tourney—the lute back had been expensively repaired, and everyone told him that it sounded as good as ever, but it didn't—or shopping and running errands for Sia. Ben was ill for some days after the war—Sia said it was flu—but then went immediately back to the graduate seminar on the *Haraldskvaeoi* that he had been conducting all summer. He seemed perfectly functional—and completely without spirit, not so much listless as somehow exiled, a squatter in his own body, a refugee enduring one more camp. A student, encountered at Farrell's thirty-sixth viewing of *La Belle Et La Bête*, told him that Ben had lately taken to breaking off during readings to stare at his class out of blankly frightened eyes without saying another word for the rest of the period. "Sometimes he makes these sounds. Not crying, just these *sounds*, in his chest, over and over; I have to leave when he starts doing that. Or he'll start singing, right in the middle of an argument about word position, these crazy old pieces

of Norwegian fishing songs. They're going to find out
about him."

Farrell told Sia, who said that she knew and said little
else. More even than Ben, she appeared to be slipping
into a chilling solitude, neglecting her counseling work,
her weaving, her carving, to stump through the house
in ponderous silence, attended always by the wistful
clicking of Briseis' claws. Her prowling was not at all
aimless; Farrell was entirely certain that she was looking for something real and specific that she needed
badly, but he knew well enough that it would not be
something he could help her to find. Once he woke
knowing that she was standing just beyond the door of
the guest bedroom; but when he opened it, he saw her
with her back to him, gazing so intently at a blank wall
that she did not hear him when he spoke to her. "What
is it, what are you looking at? Sia, what can I do?" She
answered him without turning, but not in any language
he knew. After a while, Farrell went back to bed. He
lay awake for the rest of the night and, if she moved
at all from that spot, he never heard her.

She had not become mute or autistic; when she
chose, she still spoke in connected sentences on subjects
enough to get through most dinners, providing that Farrell cooperated by avoiding any mention of the League
for Archaic Pleasures or the War of the Witch. Their
meeting with the great goddess Kannon under alien,
unbearable stars was also off limits, though she surprised him by asking about Micah Willows, with a faraway flash of her old mischief. "Now I don't want to
find out that he has already rented out Mansa Musa's
room. He is not to be taking in any more boarders,
please."

"He isn't," Farrell assured her, adding without having planned to, "I think he's likely to be a boarder himself pretty soon. I think Julie's probably going to have him stay with her for a bit, after he gets out of the hospital." She had never suggested this to him, but he knew it suddenly to be true.

The two weeks were a bad time. He was lonely for Julie and as deeply afraid for Ben and Sia as if they were his aging parents. There was no one for him to talk to except Hamid ibn Shanfara. Hamid sympathized, but had his own problems. "Whalemas Tourney coming on like the Concorde, and I am not *ready*. Usually got the whole war wrapped up tight by now, your basic epic, full of heroic deaths and family trees, suitable for framing, member FDIC. But this war was hard to get a grip on, you might have noticed that." Farrell nodded. Hamid said, rather gently, "And you better go practice your music. Be a lot of work for us both at the Whalemas Tourney. New king to be crowned, no question about that, and a bunch of squires being made knights, and a whole lot of singing and dancing, and probably a mummers' play in the evening, you know they'll be needing musicians for that. We'll keep ourselves busy and then, after that, we can quit the League." Farrell was silent for a moment and then nodded again. Hamid said, "It'll be time."

There was a convention of horseless-carriage collectors at the county fairgrounds. Farrell went on a picnic with them, riding in the back of his boss's 1904 Packard. The participants wore cloth slouch caps, knickers, long dusters, flowered bonnets and picture hats, gauntlets, high-buttoned shoes, and aviator scarves. They were friendly and talkative, as clean as their spidery little machines, and many among them, both old and young, seemed themselves somehow restored, the dirty precipitations of their usual time scoured lovingly away from them. Farrell noticed that they never strayed very far from the cars, but clung to them physically, as if to seats on a sanctified wagon train. He laughed at that to himself; but when the whole caravan set off on their tour of back roads and small towns, the air did begin to taste wilder and younger, and the country almost imperceptibly to seem less certain, less amenable. Farrell saw a deer, a black squirrel, and—in marshy ground, when the cars splashed across a shallow brook—the footprint of a very large cat. In a while, he became aware that he was looking for jet trails and for television antennas above the trees.

When they arrived at the picnic ground, Briseis was waiting, desperately apologetic but quite firm. Farrell pretended at first not to know her, then took her aside and yelled at her and, as a last resort, tried to seduce her from her duty with deviled eggs and grapes. Briseis wagged and fawned and bounced; and they rode back to Avicenna together in the 1898 Citröen of a cat breeder whose beeper had gone off. On the way, Farrell whispered to Briseis, "This is absolutely the last time you do this to me. How do you think it looks?" He was hoping the cat breeder would not overhear him, but she did.

The front door of Sia's house was unlocked. In spite of the summer heat, the rooms downstairs were small with cold, as if no one lived there. Farrell felt a curious headachy pressure on his sinuses; it had begun as soon as he stepped through the door. He went from one room to another, calling for Sia, and then climbed the stairs with Briseis scrambling behind him. He could not even smell Sia in her bedroom, bath, study or office, and he knew her smell almost as well as he knew Julie's. He went downstairs again and came back up, checking every room two or three times, knowing how still she could sit and how easily he could pass her by. At last, he turned to Briseis and said aloud, "Okay. This house has places I've never seen." Briseis looked at him as boldly and steadily as she had done once before, on the blue alligator train. Farrell said, "Well, you're the familiar around here, you show me." Abruptly Briseis pushed past him and trotted down the hallway that led to the linen closet. It was considerably longer than Farrell remembered when he followed her.

He had long since come to terms with the fact that he would never truly know how many rooms and windows there were in Sia's house, nor where certain corridors went now and then. Farrell knew false walls and secret passages when he tapped them; this was a matter, not of hollowness, but of plenitude, of alternatives thriving in the same space at the same time. The fact of this did not frighten him, as long as he only saw it out of the corners of his eyes, but the concept made him giddy, especially in the attic. He called after Briseis, "Hey, we're not going up to the attic, are we?"

Briseis did not look back. She led him straight into the linen closet—which stretched away around them like a courtyard, smelling of old rainy stones instead of fresh pillowcases—turned right, or something like it, passed through a windowless room that made her extremely nervous, and started up a stairway. Farrell laughed sharply, because Sia had spoken once of a servants' stair and he had searched for it, casually at first, then obsessively, as if pursuing some professionally legendary monster, always a slither ahead of him. *Must start in the kitchen, behind the pantry someway. No, I looked there, damn it. Damn, that dog is definitely taking me to the attic.*

But the stair led down, and somehow sideways, as often as up, catwalk-narrow, alarmingly damp and skittery under his feet. He had given up trying to orient himself in relation to the house he knew; the one certain thing was that the disquieting sense of pressure was growing stronger, whether he climbed or descended. Beginning as a slow closeness in his head, it seemed now to be tightening on the house itself, clenching methodically, until Farrell could hardly move forward through the bell-jar silence. If he stood still for too long, Briseis came back for him, nudging and growling him along the stairway toward what looked at first like a distant street sign, then like the moon, and then like a door with light on the other side, which it was. It opened to Briseis' gasping whine, and the two of them fell through it into afternoon and breath and the presence of Sia, who said, "Thank you, Briseis. You did very well."

She sat in the middle of a pleasant, unexceptional room, in a chair that curled under and around her, its contours altering as she shifted her position. She wore a garment that he had never seen before; night-blue, night-silver, it drifted over her body like the shadow of a cloud, touching her as if it knew her. It flattered nothing, outlining her thick stomach and legs uncompromisingly, but Farrell bowed to her as he had bowed to Kannon herself. A voice that only long-senile Father Krone might have recognized said somewhere, "Great Queen of Heaven."

"Don't be stupid," she answered him impatiently. "I am no queen—no more, never again—and there is no heaven, not the way you mean. And as for greatness—" When she smiled, her face appeared to break and flow with light. "—I sent Briseis to bring you here because I was lonely. Very tired, too, and very frightened, but mostly lonely. Do you think a great queen would do that?"

"I don't know," Farrell said. "I never knew any before." The room might have been the parlor of a country inn, without the moose head and the piano; there were a couple of bookcases, a couple of dusty steel engravings, a worn but genuine Turkish rug, wallpaper patterned with sepia mermaids and gray sailors. Farrell asked, "What place is this? Where are we now?"

"This is a room where I was quite happy once," she said. "Not the same room, of course, that one is gone, but I made it again, as well as I could, for myself. Sometimes this is all I have."

"It's not part of the house," Farrell said.

Her quick headshake ended as a shrug. "Well, it is and then it isn't. It is not exactly in the same place as my house, but it is as much a part of the house as anything else is. Only it is hard to find, even for me. I have spent weeks this last time trying to remember the way back. Briseis was really very clever, and you, too."

"Has Ben ever been here?" She did not answer, and Farrell moved toward the two windows on either side of the still life of apples and wine bottles. Behind him, Sia said, "Be careful. Those windows are my eyes, in a way, and I cannot protect you from seeing what I see. Maybe you should not look out."

There was a castle on the hot, shivering horizon, very far away across wide fields of barley and corn, bounded and traversed by yellow oxcart ruts. The castle was transparent at that distance and looked like sharp soap bubbles. Farrell stepped back, blinking, and the vision vanished, to be replaced by a flowering amber city whose structures made Farrell dizzy and cold to see; and in turn by a tiny three-cornered house tipped far out over a jungle river, where it shone and trembled before dawn. Fish swam through its walls.

"Oh," he said. "How lovely." As if his breath had scattered them, house, dawn, and river were gone, and once again he peered down on barley fields, footpaths and wide-curving streams under a sky like a single pale-golden petal. He saw not castles this time, nor any great manors; and he might easily have overlooked the reed and turf thatches of the little mud-walled huts, except that, as he watched, these ruffled into fire, one after another, opening like waking birds. There were riders galloping past the huts, and men running between them with torches.

He widened his eyes until they hurt to make the scene disappear, but it became steadily more real. Where the riders had already passed, what he had taken for afternoon shadows were black and broken fields; rings of bright flowers resolved into the embers of homes; and everywhere the true shadows sheltered naked children cradling the split, spitted, riddled bodies of other children. Farrell saw a cow trudging in a widening circle of her own entrails, and he saw a woman gnawing eagerly on her arm, while an old man stared straight up into his face *can he see me?* with his mouth opening wider and wider. The old man turned deliberately, then dropped his breeches and bent over, exposing speckled, caved-in buttocks to Farrell's gaze. Turning again, his mouth closed now, he gripped his penis in both hands and urinated shakily at the empty golden sky. The wind tossed the spray back at him, and

303

it dribbled down his cheeks, mingling with his dirty tears.

Farrell whispered, "Make it stop," and, blessedly, the vision began slowly to dissolve. His last sight of the country far below was of a fat woman running, carrying a cat and a feather bolster in her arms. The horseman coming after her was singing a song that Farrell knew.

"Who are you?" he cried out to Sia, and heard her answer inside himself.

"I am a black stone, the size of a kitchen stove. They wash me in the stream every summer and sing over me. I am skulls and cocks, spring rain and the blood of the bull. Virgins lie with strangers in my name, the young priests throw pieces of themselves at my stone feet. I am white corn, and the wind in the corn, and the earth whereof the corn stands up, and the blind worms rolled in an oozy ball of love at the corn's roots. I am rut and flood and honeybees. Since you ask."

The last words were spoken aloud, and, when Farrell could look at her, she was laughing, the Sia of the first morning, pumpkin-plump and cougar-quick, her gray eyes shining with ancient havoc. But this was not the first morning, and he demanded furiously, "Who are you? To show me that and laugh—I thought you were wonderful, I thought you were like *her*." Her laughter moved in the parlor floor under Farrell's feet.

"Like the Lady Kannon? Is that what you thought, that I was a goddess of mercy with a thousand arms, to save a world with each one? No, no, the Lady Kannon really is a queen, and I really am only a black stone. That was my first nature, and I have not changed so much." But the mockery faded from her voice as she regarded him, and she added, "Not as much as perhaps I would have liked. I am stone that has washed dishes, slept in human beds, seen too many movies, but I am still stone. Stone can never be wonderful, I'm afraid."

"Was it real, what I saw? Where was it real?" She did not bother to reply. "There was a woman running," he said. "You could have helped her, anyway. There were so many children."

"I told you, I am not Kannon." The silver ring that held her hair stirred against her cheek, glinting like a tear. She said, "What I did for your friend I did because the thing that had happened to him was against certain laws, as what you saw from my window is not. And even for that, I needed help myself, and I could not have summoned it without that girl, your Julie. I have no power beyond this house—perhaps not beyond this room now."

Briseis whimpered and skulked close to her, clearly not daring either to push for comfort or offer it, but collapsing again within comfort's range, just in case. Farrell said, "Well. I wish I could have seen you when you were a black stone."

"Oh, I was certainly something." The tone was sardonic enough, but her voice was gentle in that moment. She said, "It was nice, I think, the flutes and the smoky prayers and the screaming—a long time ago, that must have been what pleased me. I intervened everywhere, absolutely everywhere, in everything, just to be doing it, just because I could." Her bitter chuckle prickled his skin, as his own music did. "I would have been more use to those children if I had remained all stone."

"I don't understand," he said. "I don't understand how a goddess can lose her power."

She drew back slightly, looking at him with a kind of dangerous wonder, before she smiled. "Oh, very good. I never thought you would ever use that word.

305

Well, with power it is the same for everyone—if you don't want it quite enough, it just leaves you. Power always knows, you see. And gods always lose their power, because we lose our pleasure in it, we all come to want other things, sooner or later. This is where we are different from human beings."

"What did you want?" Farrell asked. "What was it you wanted more than being a goddess?" Sia slipped the silver ring off and began slowly to unweave her thick, straggly braid, as she had done on the night she tried to bend the universe for Micah Willows. Farrell thought, *It's the opposite of that thing the Finnish sailors do. They tie up the winds with bits of string, they tie magic into knots. She's turning it loose, and I'm watching her.*

"Brush my hair, please," she said, "Ben forgot last night. The brush is on that little table."

So Farrell stood behind her strange, flowing chair, in a room that did not exist, and he brushed her hair, as he had always wanted to do, feeling the black and gray sea-weight of it murmur and burn over his hands, feeling the freed winds stretching themselves like cats waking to hunt. Once, showing him how to use the brush correctly, she touched his face, and he remembered lying all one day in a summer meadow, watching a Monarch butterfly being born.

"I like it here," she said softly. "Of all worlds, this one was made for me, with its silliness and its cruelty, and its fine trees. Nothing ever changes. For every understanding, a new terror—for each foolishness at last pulled down, three little new insanities sprouting. Such mess, such beauty, such hopelessness. I talk to my clients, but I can never know how they can get up in the morning, how any of you can even get out of bed.

One day, nobody will bother." She put her head further back, closing her eyes, as he continued brushing; and he saw how, with the small coquettish movement, the ruts and flutings of her throat at once softened and tautened, like stream beds under the first rain of the season. Her hair breathed calmly now between his hands.

"And still you desire one another," she said. "And still you invent and reinvent yourselves, you manufacture entire universes, just as real and fatal as this one, all for an excuse to stumble against one another for a moment. I know gods who have come into existence only because two of you wanted there to be a reason for what they were about to do that afternoon. Listen, I tell you that on the stars they can smell your desire—there are ears of a shape you have no word for listening to your dreams and lies, tears and gruntings. There is nothing like you anywhere among all the stones in the sky, do you realize that? You are the wonder of the cosmos, possibly for embarrassing reasons, but anyway a wonder. You are the home of hunger and boredom, and I roll in you like a dog."

Abruptly she turned, took hard hold of his shoulders, and kissed him on the mouth, pulling herself to her feet as she did so. Farrell, who had wondered often enough what that could be like and flinched slightly in his imagination from the muscular contact, dry as cast snakeskin, found that her breath was noisy and curious and full of flowers, and that kissing her was as shocking and undoing a revelation as the first chocolate he had ever tasted. The chair purred under them, pouring itself across the floor. Farrell sank through the night-colored gown to swim in Sia's absolute welcome with the frightened ease and eagerness of the small four-handed land creature that remembered the sea and became the

307

grandfather of whales. Her breasts were as softly shapeless as he had supposed, her belly as mottled; and Farrell kissed and prowled her, laughing as she did in bedazzlement at such bounty until she put her arms around his neck and told him, "Now look at me, now don't stop looking at me." That became quickly hard to do, but they held tightly to each other, and Farrell never looked away from her, even when he saw the black stone and what lay before it. He only closed his eyes at the last, when her face became too beautiful and sorrowful to bear. But she smiled straight into his head *like someone else*, and all his bones went up in sunlight.

As soon as he could speak, he said, "Nicholas Bonner is your son." They were still joined, still shivering, sprawled together like sacrifices; and she was silent for so long that he was dozing a little when she answered him. "Sleep with a mortal and lose your secrets. Ben wakes up each morning knowing one more thing that I did not tell him."

"Oh, lord," Farrell said. "Ben. Oh, Ben. Oh, no wonder he looks like that."

He began touching his face and peering down along himself, while Sia laughed at him, saying "Don't be an idiot." *Let me remember this, please, when everything else goes let me remember a goddess laughing after love.* She said, "You have not changed. I am not a virus, you haven't caught me. For that you would have to enter my life, as Ben has, you would have to be exposed." She slipped away from him and sat up, hugging her knees. "Nicholas Bonner is my son, yes, or at least that was the idea. No, there is no father, none at all. Is there anything else you would like to know?"

"I would dearly like to know why you still have

clothes on and I don't." The blue-and-silver garment had no buttons, no zippers, no least stain or rumple. He said, "I never saw you put that thing back on."

"It was never off. Mortals should not see the gods naked, it's very dangerous. No, you didn't see me, Joe, you were overexcited. Be quiet and listen." The chair stood up with her, dumping Farrell to the floor as he began gathering his clothes. He kissed her foot as it went by toward the windows. Briseis came and sniffed at him, neither wagging nor whining. He said to her, "We will talk about this later."

Sia said, "I was lonely. It is an occupational hazard for us, and we deal with it in different ways. Some gods create worlds, entire galaxies, just to have someone intelligent and sympathetic to talk to. They are usually disappointed. Others go in for having children—they mate with each other, with humans, animals, trees, oceans, even with the elements. It is all very exhausting and takes up most of their time. But they do have the children in the end. Some of them have thousands."

"And, would you believe it, not one of the little bastards ever *writes*?" Sia looked at him, and he said, "Sorry. I don't know how Ben is at such moments, but I feel like Central Park, or a birdbath or something. So. You wanted a child."

"I am not sure what I wanted anymore. It was long ago, and I was different. Your world existed, I remember that, but it was all fire and water then, nothing else. I had no idea that I would come to love it so much." She paused for a moment. "We have no word for love, you know. *Hunger*, degrees of hunger, that is as close as we can come. If you were a god, we would have been making hunger together."

"So you had Nicholas Bonner," Farrell said gently.

"Conceived in hunger, out of loneliness. Does he know he's your son?"

"He knows I did not *have* him," she said. "He knows I *made* him. Do you understand me?" Her voice was as sad and cruel as wind crawling around the corners of a house. "What he knows is that I made him in myself, by myself, not even really out of loneliness, but out of contempt, such contempt for mysteries, oracles, temples, all those warrens of little half-gods and quarter-gods, that helpless vampire need that illusions have for adoration. I was going to make a child who could exist without fraudulence, who would be a god if nothing in the universe ever worshiped him. Contempt and vanity, you see. Even for a goddess, I have always been vain."

Farrell wanted to go to her as she stood at the window with her back to him, but, like Briseis, he dared not cross the border of her pain. He said only, "Well, he scares the pure hell out of me, but he's not a god. Not if you are."

"He is not anything. You cannot make anything useful out of contempt and vanity, no matter who you are. Nicholas Bonner is not a god, not human, not a spirit of power—he is nothing, nothing but immortal and eternally enraged at me. As he should be. Can you begin to imagine what I did to him?" She turned to look at Farrell, and her face was gray and small. "Can you imagine what it might be like to know certainly that you have no business existing anywhere—that there is no possible place for you from one end of the universe to the other? Can you imagine how that would feel, Joe? Knowing that you can never even die and be free of this terrible not-life, never? That is what I did to my son, Nicholas Bonner."

Farrell said, "You must have tried to—I don't know—to unmake him. You were stronger then, you must have tried."

Sia nodded impatiently. "I could not do it, I was never strong enough. I was exactly like your little witch, just playing with power for every wrong reason and stumbling onto something that would take a miracle to undo. The most I have ever been able to do is to send him very far away, to a place you might call limbo. I don't want to talk about it. There is nothing to do there but try to sleep and wait for someone to summon you by mistake. Someone always does." She chuckled suddenly, grimly, and added, "He always looks like that, by the way. My bodies all seem to be older and uglier each time, but Nicholas Bonner is fourteen years old forever."

"He hates it there," Farrell said, remembering that first long cry of terror in the redwood grove: *Hither then, swiftly, for I'm cold, I'm cold.* Sia nodded, looking away. Farrell said, "Something is squeezing this house like a nutcracker. I can't feel it here, but everywhere else. What's going on?"

"It has begun." Her voice was placid, almost indifferent. "In time, maybe a few days, they will try again to come into my house, and he will try to make me go to that place where I have sent him before. I wonder if the girl is strong enough to enter this room. The house, yes, I think so, but perhaps not here." She took Farrell's hand between her square, stubby-fingered ones, smiling at him, but not drawing him across the invisible line. She said, "Joe, goodness, don't look that way. There is nothing Nicholas Bonner can do but destroy me for the sake of some justice. The dreadful thing is that it is all he can do."

When Farrell continued to stare at her without speaking, she sighed a little and put his hand away from her. "You can go now, Joe. I just needed a little company for a while. I will be fine here, thank you." But she looked all at once like a very young girl trembling with her first real lie. Farrell wanted to hold her, but she turned away again, and he found himself approaching the door, trying to look back. Someone in the room was making tiny, disconsolate sounds; he assumed it was Briseis, and then realized that the sounds were his own.

He had begun to open the door, already feeling the jaws of air beyond closing slowly on him, when she said, "Stay, Joe. I am not fine. Stay with me until Ben comes home."

So Farrell stood at the window with her, and they held hands while the house whined and sang and moaned all around the imaginary bubble of her room. He did not want to look out of her window ever again, but she said, "It's all right, there is only Avicenna out there now, I promise you. Sometimes that is all I see." And she kept her word; the high windows looked down on remembered roofs and streets, parked cars, the bright haze of the Bay, and people Farrell knew working in their gardens, appearing motionless as waves seen from far away.

"I will miss it so," she said beside him. "This hell of a place, I will miss it so much. This fat body, walking mud puddle, deceived by everything, this impossible, ruinous accident of a world, these people who would truly rather hurt one another than eat—oh, there is nothing, nothing, nothing I would not do to stay here ten minutes longer. Oh, I will leave clawmarks, I will drag mountains and forests away under my fingernails when I am dragged off. Such a stupid way to feel. I will be all dirty from clutching at this stupid planet, and the gods will laugh at me."

Farrell said, "When we made love, it wasn't really me, was it?" She did not answer, but held his hand against her breast. "Clutching at the whole stupid planet?" Sia nodded, and Farrell said, "I'm honored," and they waited silently after that until Ben came home.

XVIII

Julie did not call; instead, she came to find him late one afternoon at the restoration shop. Farrell smelled her before he saw her and scrambled out of a rumble seat he was reupholstering, trying hard to look distantly pleased. She stood the car's length away from him, announcing, "I'm still pissed at you, but I miss you. We have things to talk about, and I think you should come home with me and cook us some scallops Marsala. With new potatoes and those nice green beans in peanut sauce, please. But I'm still pissed."

Farrell said, "Well, *I* think you're overreacting and unreasonable; and I think that's a dumb way to wear your hair. Give me ten minutes."

To do her justice, she told him about Micah Willows before he started cooking; to be fair to him, he went ahead with the dinner and threw in a fruit salad with a lemon and yogurt dressing. But it was beyond him to set her plate down in front of her without the scallops

314

bouncing like popcorn, or to forbear from saying, "Just don't start him calling me up for recipes, that's all."

"It'll only be for a couple of weeks," she said. "Two weeks at the most. You ought to know I can't have anyone around all the time for more than two weeks." Farrell dropped potatoes onto her plate like depth charges. "Joe, the doctor said he needs to be around people he knows, somebody he trusts, until he can trust himself to be whole again. Right now, I am about all he's got. His family's back in Columbus, I've been on the phone with them almost every day. They'll pay all his hospital bills, send any money he needs, anything, just so he doesn't come home. He has nowhere else to go."

"A genuine remittance man," Farrell said. "Nicholas Bonner's got the same problem. Right. I'll clear my stuff out of the bathroom first thing."

She caught hold of his arm as he started to turn away and made him face her. "Joe, God damn it, Micah and I have things to settle. We never broke up, he just got possessed." In spite of himself, Farrell laughed outright at the cozy madness of the statement, and she laughed too, shaking her head and covering her mouth for a moment, as her grandmother had taught her. She said "I don't know what it was I felt for him and I need to find out, because I can't stand loose ends. And you and I have a whole lot of business to do yet, because our special relationship happens to be *all* loose ends, and because we have seen things together that nobody but the other one will ever believe. So we have to be really careful never to lose each other, whatever else happens. Do you understand what I'm telling you, Joe?"

"Everybody asks me that," he said. "Jewel, since the day we met, you have never once waited around for me to understand anything. Don't start now, or I'll know you're getting old. Just be careful and call me if you need me, recipes included. Eat your damn scallops, you made such a thing about them."

Julie said quietly, "I am getting old." When he left her house, she held him at the door, looking at him with a strange, angry appeal in her face. "Joe, I'm not going to tell you not to go to the Whalemas Tourney. Just be careful of yourself. Crof's dead and Micah's been damaged, and I don't want to lose any more people I care about. It really does feel like getting old, going bad, feeling my senses shrinking up one by one. You're as weird as Aiffe, in your own little way, but I don't want anything bad to happen to you, ever." She put her head down on his shoulder for a moment and then she stepped back inside her house and shut the door.

In the last ten days before the Tourney, the League for Archaic Pleasures itself seemed to disappear. There were no more classes, no feasts or dances, no more comradely evenings of old music and old stories. Farrell saw only the women of the League on the street, and them almost entirely at two or three specialized fabric shops. Their lords were at home, furbishing up their arms and armor, whacking grimly away at painted four-by-fours in the backyard or arranging hurried private sessions with John Erne. In practice with Basilisk, Farrell found the musicians giving twenty to one against King Bohemond's retaining the crown, with Benedictis de Griffin and Raoul of Carcassonne equal favorites at three to one, and Garth de Montfaucon attracting the long-shot money at ten to one. It was understood that all bets were off if Egil Eyvindsson entered the lists.

"You can't help being interested in it, just from that

angle," Farrell said to Hamid and Lovita. They had been to a silent movie, then stopped for ice cream on the way home. He said, "When it's people you know. I can get six-and-a-half to one on Simon Widefarer."

"Those odds don't mean doodly," Hamid said. "Not in this tourney." Farrell raised his eyebrows. "There's the whole wild-card thing, they didn't tell you? At the Whalemas Tourney the combats don't have to be set up in advance—no eliminations, nothing. Anybody can challenge anybody, and you about have to accept the match."

"Marvelous," Farrell said. "Some back-country baron gets hot for a day, and the book goes out the window. I gather that's how Bohemond won it last year."

Lovita shook her head, making a tiny, subversive ballet out of the simple act of licking ice cream off her upper lip. "That girl got mad at her daddy, 'cause he grounded her or some such, and so she put some kind of protection on Bohemond. I was there. People started getting sick, having accidents, just before they went to fight him. Frederik, old Garth, they couldn't touch him, their swords just came sliding off the air. I was there, I saw it."

Hamid nodded confirmation. "After that was when she really started being Aiffe all the time."

During those days, the strange clench on Sia's house often relaxed for long periods, though it never went away altogether. Farrell was amazed at how easily he became accustomed to the change in pressure, although to walk through the front door was like plunging fathoms deep under the sea, and his head hurt constantly when he was there. But in a short time, it became merely another condition of that unlikely house, like the mockingly mobile windows and the room so far above stairs where Sia waited for her son to come to her. Always, after a slack period, the grip would return with an abrupt viciousness that made the walls twang and the fireplace bricks whimper against one another, while Briseis only touched down once on her way to the backyard. At such times, the house smelled strongly of dry thunder, more faintly of rotting fruit.

Sia rarely left the room upstairs anymore. Farrell set out several times to hunt for her, but Briseis would never guide him again, and he never got as far as the servants' stair. When she did come down, she moved in the house like a bear half-roused from hibernation, focusing on no one living, bumping hard into furniture, if not watched carefully. Suzy McManus could not endure to see her so, but burst into tears each time Sia wandered past without taking any notice of her. Eventually she stopped coming to the house, as client or as housekeeper, though she telephoned every day to ask after Sia.

Farrell saw something like recognition in Sia's face whenever they met, but no acknowledgment of secrets shared, nor of any tender acquaintance. Her eyes were terrifyingly alive, crowded to blindness with the memories of a black stone, and Farrell could not look into them any longer than he had been able to look out through them. In his mind he said to her, over and over, *I will not forget, you will forget before I will,* and once he thought that she nodded as she climbed away from him again, struggling wearily back up to her one safe place, which did not exist anywhere.

Between them, he and Ben worked out a schedule, making certain that she would never be left alone in the house. Farrell had broached the subject differently during another silent dinner, but Ben's reaction was surprisingly swift and precise, and more realistic than his own. "It won't make a damn bit of difference, you know that, Joe. This is not exactly keeping an eye on Grandma so she doesn't fall down in the bathroom. We can't protect her, we can't do a thing for her. We're doing this to comfort ourselves and for no other reason. Just so you know that."

"I know it," Farrell said, briefly irritable. "I know who's after her and what they want—I even know why you can't ever pop your ears in this joint. Have you noticed that it plays hell with the TV reception, by the way? I haven't been sure what you think about lately."

"What I think is that it must take one hell of a lot of concentration to keep this up, even for Aiffe. I don't see how she'll be able to think about the Whalemas Tourney and Sia at the same time."

"I don't suppose that matters very much, either. Nicholas Bonner can." Getting up to wash the dishes, he said over his shoulder, "You're feeling a little better, aren't you? I mean, about Egil."

Ben was silent for almost as long a time as it took the idiot echoes of that question to fade inside Farrell's head. He said at last, "I don't know how I feel about anything, Joe. I mostly know how Egil Eyvindsson feels. He may be dead, but I know him, I am him, he's still real, and Ben Kassoy is something I have to think about and act out. Right now, sitting here, I'm acting, trying to remember how Ben is supposed to hold his face when he talks, and what he does with his hands." He laughed suddenly, adding, "Maybe I could get a grant. I had one when I was studying Egil in the first place." Through the window over the sink Farrell saw two small neighbor children trying to get Briseis to play with them, toddling after her in the smudgy lavender sunset.

Ben said, "Egil was my sanity. The real crazies go to meetings, teach what they love to people who don't love anything, and stand around at receptions for years with other crazy people who never do give a shit about them. And they don't know what anything is, just what everybody thinks it's like. Egil knows—knew, Egil knew what poetry is, and what God is, and what death is. I'd just rather be Egil, but what I'm going to be is the head of the Lit Board next year." Farrell turned to look at him and saw the same lost hunger in his face that he himself felt for other summer twilights and the tall fathers watching from other windows. Ben said, "I was having a good time, Joe. I'll never have a good time like that again. Just tenure."

The schedule was easy and uneventful to maintain, and, as Ben had predicted, completely unnecessary. Aiffe and Nicholas Bonner made no approach to the house, though Ben and Farrell juggled night watches as well as seminars and rehearsals and slept in their clothes like firemen. Sia appeared to notice the new surveillance no more than she noticed anything else human, which made it even more surprising when she insisted that Ben accompany Farrell to the Whalemas Tourney. He tried to make a joke out of his refusal, saying, "You had me dragging after him all through that stupid goddamn war on the island, and he didn't even have the grace to get killed. Enough, already, he can take care of himself."

But there was no arguing with her; she said only, "I need to be alone and I am too tired to make up a good lie for you. Watch those two at the tournament, if you like, and if they leave while it is still going on, then you

320

may come back here. Otherwise, you are to stay until everything is over." She was mumbling from far away, sounding almost apologetic in the face of Ben's anger and distress, but there was no arguing with her.

From the first, the tourney had always begun at noon on the front lawn of the Waverly Hotel. Farrell went in slashed blue trunk-hose and a jade-green velvet doublet; but Ben, going under protest, wore sneakers, jeans, a felt fishing hat, and a ragged denim jacket over a T-shirt bearing a family portrait of the Borgias. "I don't dress up anymore. This is the Whalemas Tourney, I can wear any damn thing I feel like." Looking back at the house as Madame Schumann-Heink grumbled flatulently away down Scotia Street, he said absently, "Like your threads, though. Early Burt Lancaster, very rich period. Very classy."

"Julie gave them to me," Farrell said. "Ben, I know she won't be all right without us, but she'll be the way she wants to be. We have to honor that, just to comfort ourselves."

Ben said, "Farrell, when I want California pieties, you'll be the first I'll ask." They drove the rest of the way in silence, until, nearing the Waverly, he asked a very different question rather gently. "How's she doing, by the way, Julie? You guys talking to each other at all?"

"We call," Farrell said. "Micah sleeps a lot. Sometimes he has terrible nightmares and then he cries for hours. But he knows who he really is and what century he's really in. We progress."

"We certainly do. He's already overqualified to be President. Will she be coming to the Tourney?"

Farrell shook his head. "She's like you, it would take Sia to make her go. And she's got this other person to take care of, and I am being civilized about it. I cannot believe how civilized I am being."

"Um. Egil didn't think much of our civilization, the little he saw of it. He thought it was probably all right, for people who really didn't care a lot about anything."

There was no parking left at the Waverly, and they were lucky to find curb space two blocks away. The great front lawn was sown with pavilions extending in wildflower clumps and surges across the courtyard, past the triton fountain and around to the rear of the hotel, overflowing the ornamental carriageways into the parking lot. The standards and blazons of the high nobles—the Nine Dukes and three or four others—were displayed in a grand arc facing the lists—an open stretch of greensward, bounded only by the lords' pavilions and, at the far end, the gilded double throne—half porch swing, half howdah—in which King Bohemond and Queen Leonora would sit. There were merchants' and craftsmens' booths and the usual small dais for the musicians. Bright skeins of pennons and ensigns frisked up from many of the tents directly to the awnings and window ledges of the Waverly, so that the Tourney appeared to be a true part of the castle itself—a summer dishevelment, a careless unraveling of austere towers. The banner of the League—a crowned golden Sagittarius on a field of midnight blue—floated from the highest turret of the Waverly.

Pushing through a growing crowd of onlookers to step onto the tourney field was a new experience for Farrell. The League staged few public events: outsiders in proper dress were usually welcome at the tilts and revels, but only at the crafts fairs or at exhibitions of Renaissance dancing or medieval combat techniques had Farrell ever seen any tolerance for the casual spectator. "We're not a softball game," the Lady Criseyde had replied tersely, the one time he asked her about audiences, "We're an air, an atmosphere. You don't sell tickets to an atmosphere."

"Maybe so," Ben grunted when Farrell quoted her now. "All I know is, the first couple of years they had to rent the space. Now they get it for free, and all the help they need setting up, and the hotel starts advertising three months in advance. Part of their Labor Day package." The young knights were already banging challenges on each other's shields, hung outside their tents, and the children of the League went scampering across the lists, kicking out at each other like horses in the wind. Aiffe led them, pouncing and spinning with the rest and, when Farrell caught her eye, she laughed silently and turned a cartwheel.

"I'll be damned," Farrell said softly. "Look at that. He really pulled it off." The lists were sprinkled thickly with tiny scarlet flowers, shaped exactly like the upright flukes of a sounding whale. Farrell bent close to touch one and found that it was real and growing, not thrust into the earth for the occasion, as he had assumed. Ben said only, "Happens every year. I have no idea how he does it." They agreed to meet behind a particular pavilion after the opening ceremonies, and Farrell went off to take his place with Basilisk on the musicians' dais. He put one of the scarlet flowers carefully in his cap, remembering the story of St. Whale.

A pair of cornets, cold and sweet and regal, silenced the tourney field precisely at twelve, convoying Bohemond and Leonora to the throne. Basilisk followed with a pavane for the entrance of the Nine Dukes and their households. It went strangely badly, sliding sideways out of the old instruments, twisting away off Farrell's lutestrings, jeering like chalk on a blackboard. Hamid ibn Shanfara was standing nearby, scanning a scroll of music, and Farrell whispered, "What is it? We practiced the hell out of that tune, there's no reason in the world for it to sound like that. This is very weird."

Hamid shook his head. "The Whalemas Tourney is weird, man. Maybe it's the being in public or the challenging of the King, the betting—I don't know. It's just always like this, everything all twitchy and feverish, all day." He was dressed as richly as any of the nobles, in flowing black and gold, with a black turban. He nodded abruptly toward the double throne, now flanked by the two cornet players. "Look at Bohemond."

King Bohemond was clad, not in his Byzantine-cut robe of state, but in armor, with a light blue cloak over him and a great helm in his lap. His round face, always too large and naked for the crown, showed no expression as he looked on Benedictis de Griffin, Raoul of Carcassonne, and Simon Widefarer; but the gymteacher face of Queen Leonora stared at those knights, and at every other, with wide, numbed eyes and a jumping mouth. When the cornets sounded again, she put her hand on her husband's mailed arm. Bohemond never turned his head.

"It really matters," Farrell said in wonder. "She looks as if he's really going out to be killed, and she'll be sent into slavery. Hecuba and Priam, for God's sake."

Hamid rolled up the scroll and stuck it in his sash. "You still don't understand," he said without looking at Farrell. He strode away to stand with his back to the throne and sing St. Whale's blessing in three languages on the day and the Tourney. When his singing ended, the first fighters came into the lists.

None of the early bouts involved King Bohemond. The fighters were boys, new-made knights or else squires seeking knighthood on the field. They circled, they lunged, they left themselves as exposed as the practice posts in the backyards, and frequently they took one another off-balance and rolled to earth embraced, losing their helms. Few of their combats lasted longer than three minutes, and the referee—one Sir Roric the Uncouth, who wore a full bearskin and a pair of plaid shorts—laughed and called jokes to a wincing John Erne as he named the victors. All around the edges of the lists and on the packed balconies of the Waverly, people in jogging suits and tennis whites cheered and clapped indiscriminately and kept trying to get their pictures taken with someone in armor.

But out of those first matches the Ronin Benkei, John Erne's fragile-looking Nisei student, came stalking in armor like jewelry—iron and leather plates laced by cords of amber, amethyst, silver, and emerald into a skin as supple and glowing and adamant as the skin of a dragon. There was gold lacquer on the leather pieces, and a thread of some rainbow inlay dancing through the iron; and two scabbards made of lacquered wood, one long and one short, thrust through his silken red girdle. He wore no helmet but a half-mask of iron, snouted and fanged like a dragon, that covered his face from the bridge of the nose down, leaving his eyes showing like black inlay in his pale skin. He issued his challenges in silence, by pointing with his longsword, which he gripped in both hands during combat. Farrell heard the deepening murmur going among the nobles as they watched the Ronin Benkei scythe down three young knights in a row, battering them effortlessly from every side, like a mountain wind. After the third knight fell, to breathe like an asthmatic the rest of the day from a two-handed blow under the ribs, Farrell said aloud, hardly knowing it, "When did he get that good?"

A yappy giggle, and Aiffe said beside him, "Hey, you talked first. A new era in the relationship." She wore a velvet gown that was brown at the first look, and afterwards more and more charged with shifting foxy goldenness as the breeze quickened and the light changed. There were lilies and vineleaves traced in gold on her gown, and a golden girdle circled her just below her breasts. Her hair was piled demurely over her temples, dressed in a little net with white beads.

"Maybe he got good this summer," she said. "Maybe it was a thousand years ago, doing Zen stuff in the moutains in Japan. You don't know." Farrell stared at her. "Well, you don't," she said. "You can't tell for sure if that's really him behind that dorky thing he's got on. He could be anybody. He could be one of mine, even."

The Ronin Benkei was looking slowly around the lists to choose another opponent, as was his right under the laws of the Whalemas Tourney. His glance halted briefly first on the tense face of Garth de Montfaucon, and then on King Bohemond, who nodded and half rose from his seat, while Queen Leonora looked down, gripping her thighs. But the Ronin Benkei only slid his sword back into its shining scabbard, bowed quite deeply to the King and Queen, and walked out of the lists. Farrell saw him enter a small pavilion that flew neither banner nor pennon.

"I know who you are, anyway," he said to Aiffe. "You're Rosanna Berry and you have to take algebra over this year and you had too many cuts in P.E. and you still break out if you eat one candy bar and you still bite your nails. And a man is dead because of you, and you really think you're magic."

Her eyes changed color. They had been tranquil enough blue-green as she spoke, with tiny darknesses; but now a red gold grew in them, as in her gown, brighter and brighter, though the skin around them went tight and bloodless. She said in a whisper, "You are so fucking right, I'm magic. You wait, okay, you wait, you'll see how magic I am." She bit her finger and ran, and he saw her stand beside her father, who was in the act of challenging the Spanish knight Don Claudio. The breeze furled Garth's short blue cloak hard about his body and then whipped it loose again, so that his chain mail flashed on and off in the sunlight like running water.

Farrell made his rendezvous with Ben, and they moved through the Tourney together, trying to keep unobtrusive track of Aiffe and Nicholas Bonner's own movements. This proved extremely difficult, since Aiffe and Nicholas—plainly by design—hardly crossed each other's paths all afternoon. Ben's civilian dress left him free of spectators' attentions; but Farrell was forever being waylaid and posed with Mr. and Mrs. Bringle of Highland Park, Michigan, and being asked if little Stacy could hold the lute, just for a moment. By the time he broke away, he would have lost Ben as well as their quarry and have to go lurking after any number of plumed hats and tawny velvet gowns before he glimpsed them again. Nicholas Bonner had come in the guise of a juggler and could sometimes be tracked by following children, who came spilling after him as he wandered, weaving four oranges back and forth before his face. Diamonds were painted on his cheeks, and tiny daggers under his eyes.

In the lists, the combats surged one after the other, rolling up and down amid cheers, laughter, the ceaseless clacking of weapons, and the ringing thump of armored bodies falling to earth. Five squires attained knighthood that day; one broke a rib in a greatsword match, and the Irish Lord Mathgamhain broke his right hand in defeating the Tuscan Duke Cesare il Diavolo. Several knights of varying renown challenged King Bohemond; and Farrell was only one of many surprised then, for he rose from the throne each time, handed his crown to Leonora, and fought like a wolverine, swollen with desperation. He cut down not only Raoul of Carcassonne but Duke Benedictis as well, leaping at them almost before they had their feet planted, giving them no time to understand his frenzy of courage. Queen Leonora looked on with her eyes full of tears, as if she faced into a great wind.

The Ronin Benkei never challenged him. He went in and out of his little pavilion like an ancient clock figure and he fought with nobles and squires at seeming random, winning each time. Ben and Farrell nibbled at Cornish pasties, St. Ives beefy buns, and pot herb pie, forgetting themselves in watching two lugger falcons sailing above the highest towers of the hotel, now and then swinging grandly down and away again over the Tourney. Time passed as they did, in gentle, rustling slices.

In the end, it was Garth de Montfaucon who brought King Bohemond down. The combat was brief and unmemorable, except for the fact that Bohemond clearly went into it with no hope at all. Aiffe and Nicholas Bonner were raucously prominent on the sidelines, cheering Garth on, and Bohemond seemed to have his attention fixed more on them than on his contemptuously nimble opponent. When he struck sadly at Garth, Farrell saw what Lovita had been talking about, for the wooden blade turned on the air and Garth was away, laughing. The same thing happened again and again, until the final bustle of swords that sent King Bohemond's helm flying from his shoulders as he toppled slowly to sprawl on his side. When he rose, he bowed to Garth, wearily but graciously, and took Garth's hand between his own in token of fealty.

The roar of acclaim had barely begun before Aiffe was at the throne, snatching the crown from the hands of Queen Leonora and turning to cry, as pitilessly joyous as if the words were literally true, "The king is dead—long live the king! Long live King Garth de Montfaucon!"

As long as he lived, Farrell held that strange moment motionless in his head—a stained-glass window in which a transfigured, bride-faced Aiffe forever leaned down to crown her father, as the falcons banked low above them and Leonora supported her defeated lord. In the background, the nobles of the League for Archaic Pleasures swayed close, painted in forgotten colors and looking on with unreadable, obsolete expressions. It was his last vision of many people he never saw again.

The Ronin Benkei did not fit into the window-world at all. He stood outside, an intruder from another art form altogether in his dragon armor, and he pointed his long, slightly curved sword straight across the composition at the barely crowned King Garth. No one noticed him for some little while; and then there was an immense furor and much archaic swearing, since no new king had ever been challenged within minutes of his accession. Garth's supporters demanded an *ad hoc* meeting of the College of Heralds, but a surprising opposition jeered so lustily at this that Garth himself stepped splendidly forward to announce his acceptance of the match. He waved the crown back into Aiffe's hands, settled his famous black helm once again, and was hardly in the lists when the Ronin Benkei screeched like train wheels and came at him.

Julie's hand was unmistakable in Farrell's, the right forefinger and thumb lightly calloused from years of drawing, the palm as broad as his own, strong and cool. Farrell said, "Where's Micah?" without turning his head.

"Fishing. He's recognized three more people this week, and today they all came and took him out on the Bay. I think he's almost all the way back."

"That's nice." She dug her nails hard into the back of his hand, saying, "I thought you were done being snotty. I came looking for you because I thought you could use some help. Whatever Aiffe's been working up in the lab, the Whalemas Tourney is where she tries it out, always. This one is not over yet."

At Farrell's shoulder, Ben said very quietly, "Damn right, it isn't over. What the hell is happening here?"

Farrell had never seen Garth de Montfaucon defeated in armed combat. For that matter, he had never seen the knuckly-faced man even forced to fight on the defensive; but all Garth's work was defense from the first moment that he struck out at the bouncing, weaving, shrieking, dragon-faced fury that did everything but somersault back and forth over his head, as Japanese demons do. A feint and a flurry, and he was down a leg, kneeling behind his shield—another lunge, almost bending double, and his sword fell silently at Leonora's feet. The Ronin Benkei shouted in triumph, hammering Garth's shield back and back until it thudded against the black helm.

"This is not possible," Ben said. "Aiffe would never let Garth lose like this."

"She did it last year," Julie reminded him, but Ben shook his head, craning forward on tiptoe. "That was different. Why take him all the way back to the kingship and then drop him five minutes later? I don't see her doing that."

"Maybe you're not seeing her at all," Farrell said. Aiffe was clinging to Nicholas Bonner on the sidelines, shrilling for her father as fiercely as ever as he scrambled on his knees to get to the sword. The point of his shield left a line in the earth all the way to Leonora's feet. The Ronin Benkei danced and jeered, but let him reach his weapon. Farrell said, "Her ears are wrong." When Ben and Julie looked at him, he said, "Well, they are. Somewhere in the last hour or so, they've gone all pointy and elfin—very pretty, really, and not hers. Something wrong about *his* ears, too. Quit staring at me like that. I just notice ears."

Like Bohemond before him, Garth seemed unable to concentrate on his opponent, but was yearning in mute disbelief toward the figures of Aiffe and Nicholas Bonner. The Ronin Benkei parried a blind, desperate cut with one edge of his sword, struck the flailing shield aside with the other, and toppled Garth de Montfaucon with a blow that rang on the black helm as if there were no head inside. Leonora's cry of avenging delight could be heard even above the mighty yell of the Ronin Benkei.

Ben was moving before Garth had hit the ground, trampling the scarlet flowers of St. Whale as he forced his way across the lists. Farrell and Julie followed him as closely as they could, holding hands to keep together. Ignoring alike the cheering spectators and the muddy, boisterous throng of warriors trooping to do ritual homage to the second new king of the Tourney—Farrell could see Hamid ibn Shanfara standing on the musicians' dais, coolly improvising an entirely different victory paean from the one he had expected to deliver— Ben marched straight toward the boy and girl who stood watching Garth get to his feet, took them each by the shoulder, turned them to face him and said, "Oh, Jesus Christ, sonofabitch, let's get out of here." His own face was the color of an old sidewalk.

Close to, they looked very little like Aiffe and Nicholas Bonner. Close to, everything about them—age, features, dress, gender—pulled apart into fuzziness and shimmering smudge, a newspaper photograph blown up beyond clarity. They smiled and moved their mouths and made human sounds, and no one else seemed to notice that they were no more human than cream cheese. Looking at them for very long made Farrell feel dizzy and seasick. He thought he would die if they should happen to touch him.

"Simulacra," Ben said tonelessly. "The old Norse wizards made things like that; Egil knew about them. Easy enough to create, but they go bad fast. These will rot away into air by sundown—she only wanted them to hold us here for a while. Worked just fine." He was gripping Farrell and Julie like a pair of hammers, using them to batter a way through the crowd sweeping across the tourney field. Farrell sheltered his lute and kept looking backward, straining for one more glimpse of the simulacra, although he dreaded the idea of their soft, grinning, bloodless images sticking to his retinas. Then the three of them were out on the street, gasping under the parking lot portcullis, and Julie was saying, "My bike's parked on Escalona, I'll meet you at the house." But Ben held tightly onto her arm as she turned away.

"You meet us right here. You are not to go to the house alone." His voice was as gray as his face, so low that the late-afternoon traffic all but drowned it, but Julie looked at him and nodded, and Ben let her go.

She was waiting astride the BSA when they returned in Madame Schumann-Heink. Ben leaned out of the window and called to her. "Take the back road, around the hill." The BSA made a sound like feeding time in hell and leaped forward past the tents and pennons and TV trucks on the lawn of the Waverly. The two falcons were still circling above the hotel, and Farrell could see them in his rear-view mirror long after the blue-and-gold Sagittarius of the League for Archaic Pleasures had sunk from view.

"Why this way? It's no quicker." The BSA was flying ahead of them on the laneless foothill road, dipping in and out of traffic like a darning needle, committing Farrell to a steady flow of criminal offenses just to keep Julie in sight.

Ben said only, "Yeah, it is," the words half muffled by his fist as he crouched forward against the dashboard. His other hand kept coming back to the gearshift, gripping it hard enough to make the rusty metal creak like rope, no matter how many times Farrell slapped it away.

Farrell said, to be saying something, "Those things, those doubles, she did a pretty good job. If she hadn't tried to improve on herself a bit—"

"I told you, that shit is *easy*." Ben's voice was angry and insulting, unraveling like the simulacra. "Sorcerer's apprentice stuff, goddamn training exercises. Will you pass that senile moron now, for Christ's sake?"

"Will you give me my goddamn gearshift back?" Farrell swung out and around a quarter-mile of station wagon, whose driver promptly speeded up, making a three-lane freeway out of the road for a brief but thrilling period.

Beside him, too bitterly frightened to pay any respect to imminent death, Ben muttered, "She is not that good, she is just not that good. Sia could butter the walls with her." Farrell passed a truck and a schoolbus on a blind curve, because Madame Schumann-Heink was at her very best going downhill.

A long string of tarnished-silver clouds suddenly jolted into motion all together, exactly as if a train were towing them. That was the only warning Farrell had before the wind hit, making the VW shudder and boom, *like the time the bear smelled my tuna fish in Yosemite.* Madame Schumann-Heink wallowed almost to a stop until he threw her into second gear and struggled on down the slope, concentrating on nothing but keeping her from going over. The rain courteously held off long enough for them to reach the bottom of the decline and start up the other side; then the trees went out and the windshield turned to cement. Madame Schumann-Heink's headlights only really worked in top gear, and her wipers were overmatched in a heavy dew. Farrell spread himself over the wheel, navigating by the lights coming toward him and silently reminding Kannon that he knew a friend of hers.

Ben was frantic from the moment the rain started, screaming at Aiffe and Farrell alike, while Madame Schumann-Heink rolled and sputtered and chattered her transmission and kept going. Farrell would have missed the BSA entirely if an approaching headlight had not picked it out, almost upside down in a manzanita bush a little way from the road, with Julie trying to pull her legs free of it. He stamped on the brakes, which floored faster than the accelerator ever did, skidded suicidally enough to shake Ben back to functional sanity, and pulled up at last with one tire in a ditch and a great many total strangers honking for his blood. At that point, give or take a little, the hail began.

Julie was soaked, dazed, and furious, but unharmed, swearing in Japanese, as Farrell had never heard her do, while Ben and he carried her back to the bus and dried everyone off with bedrolls and oil rags. "Black ice," she kept snarling, "black ice in fucking September, and both forks bent to hell. Okay, *now* the bitch dies." There was no talk of salvaging the motorcycle; they left it to bleach in the desert and lunged along, while hailstones the size of gumballs flayed the remaining paint off Madame Schumann-Heink. Two side windows blew out, but the windshield held, though Farrell worried more about the engine vibrations as he felt them through the frame. He had driven the ancient VW by the seat of his pants for too long not to know when his seat felt wrong.

The back road followed the eastern frontier of the university, flirted momentarily with a freeway, considered a serious career as a link between Avicenna and the incorporated shopping malls beyond the hills, then shrugged and looped down toward drowsily flowering Scotia Street. The hail was slacking off, but the wind still came clawing out of a sky the color of phlegm. Ben said heavily, "I thought maybe she wouldn't be watching for us on this road. I've never seen her do anything with weather, I didn't think." The last words trailed away into hopeless exhaustion, and Julie took his hands between her own.

There was an explosion behind them, and then another, and Farrell said, "She's good with engines, too. We just blew two pistons." He cut the motor, sighed very deeply, and let Madame Schumann-Heink drift the last three blocks to Sia's house, braking to a stop at the ragged rosemary hedge and the redwood flags leading like invading footprints straight to the place where the front door had been. The carving that Sia had been working on that morning was propped on the back of the living-room sofa. Farrell sat at the curb and looked at it through the hole in the house.

XIX

*F*arrell never knew why he brought the lute with him;
he was not even aware of it until the three of them were
creeping up the stairs. Except for the door, nothing was
obviously missing or damaged, but every room seemed
shrunken, smelling palely of damp dust, as a house
smells that has stood closed for years. Farrell heard no
sounds beyond the scrape of their shoes and the soft
thump of the lute on his shoulder, and even those were
strangely smothered, as if there were no air to bear
them up. *Everything is in that room with her, everything—not just her son and his witch, but all the light
and soul and energy there ever was in this house. We
can't really see the rest of it, because it doesn't quite exist
without her attention. And all her attention is far away
now, in a little low-rent place that I probably can't find
again. East of the sun, west of the moon, with an unlisted
phone number.*

He had counted on Briseis leading them to Sia, as
she had done before, but the dog was as gone as the

front door. So, for that matter, was the linen closet, leaving no least suggestion that it had ever been there. This time it was Farrell's turn to rage helplessly; but Ben said, "There are so many ways," and took them downstairs again, around the back of the house, in through one of the uncountable windows, and up an evasive stair which dissolved into a dim flurry of passages fading off in every direction. Farrell and Julie filed after him along corridors they could not see, around certain doubtful corners that had to be caught up with before they could be turned, and through high, transparent outlines, the color of abandoned spiderwebs, cold to make the blood ache. *I know what these are—the ghosts of rooms she forgot about, just let go when she didn't need to imagine them anymore.* Within those almost-walls, his sense of balance abandoned him utterly, leaving him nauseous and heartsick, holding onto Julie. *How terrible to be forgotten by the god that made you, even if you're just a room. How could you love something that can do that anytime?*

In the end, he sometimes thought, they never did find that last room at the top of the house. It found them. The open doorway seemed to come roaring up to them, visibly slowing down and stopping where they stood. No country hotel parlor waited beyond, but fat, lumbering vines, crowding the frame, beckoning and warning with the same green greed. They had to put their heads down and plow blindly onward, tearing the vines aside and trampling flowers like unpleasant human faces underfoot, until they broke out into a clearing that had nothing in it but sandy earth and stones and Aiffe dancing. Farrell never found another word for what she was doing, but he always knew there was one.

Her movements were nothing like the way she had danced with him or like any galliard or almaine he had ever seen her perform at the League's affairs. On that ground, she was all swirling, filigreed insult; here, dancing alone, she was almost two-dimensional, rigid and thin as a razor blade. Back and forth she went, keeping to a small space, always traveling in a straight line, each razor-quick turn and glide at right angles to the one before, her body gradually writing a precise shape into the air, as if on a darkly gleaming floor inlaid with fiery stars and pentagrams. If she sensed her watchers' presence—and Farrell thought she did—she paid no heed at all, but only danced.

No one, including Aiffe, saw Sia appear. Suddenly there was never a moment when she had not been there, trudging forever across the clearing toward the girl who was calling her out of hiding. She was wearing the disquietingly fluid garment that Farrell remembered, but it murmured over a body that he did not know, one grown impossibly stooped and withered since just that morning. Her shoulders all but hid her emaciated chest. Under the gown, her belly and thighs seemed to have run like candle wax into pitiful drizzles of skin. The gray eyes had gone suet-colored in her shrunken face, and when she mumbled to herself as she slumped along, Farrell saw that her teeth were rotting like cheese. Turning, he saw the silent tears sliding down Julie's face and realized that he was crying, too.

Aiffe's dance never faltered, nor did she speak a word to the wretched old woman standing before her.

It was Nicholas Bonner's angelic laughter that caressed her as he strolled out of the wet, jungly air. *Where are we now, really? In what ghost-garden of her dreams?* "Has it all caught up with you at once, great mother? What, all that majesty tumbled downstairs, all that thunder and lightning shriveled to a sneeze? Did such serene wisdom ever foresee that it must come to this?" He stood beside Aiffe, hands on hips—a child in tights with a Halloween face and a voice that was casting off its assumed humanity, like a tiger bursting from cover. Even his language was melting into a barely comprehensible croon of tiger joy. "How beautiful, how beautiful you are now, what a wonder to see you so. My treasure, my heart, my prize, my mother, how beautiful you are." He reached out a hand to tilt Sia's ruined face toward him; but at the last moment, he drew it back.

Aiffe had begun to move slowly around Sia, not in circles, but in hexagons, octagons, dodecahedrons, weaving straight-line patterns that glazed the air, dimming Sia to Farrell's sight. Nicholas Bonner sang, "But now you must go where I will never go again, to lie down howling in that place you made, that place where you have sent me time and time, and you must wait for someone to call you back to light and warmth and pity, and no one ever will, not you, never. And this is nothing but the least bare justice of the gods, and you know that better than anyone except your son." The old woman shuffled from foot to foot, never looking at him.

"Oh, mother, goodbye," Nicholas Bonner said. Aiffe danced through one last binding figure and raised her arms in a way that Farrell had never imagined. At his side, Ben sprang up and charged, screaming. A vine caught him at the shins, dropping him flat on his face. Nicholas Bonner turned toward the commotion, his laughter soaring as Aiffe's arms came down.

But from the far side of the clearing, in two gigantic bounds and a desperate, yelping leap, Briseis came skidding through the air like a tailless kite in a downdraft. All four legs extended, she crashed full tilt into Nicholas Bonner, who went down harder than Ben and lay where he fell. The stone under his head had not been there a second before. Briseis, half-stunned herself, wandered groggily away into the overgrowth, limping and farting. Aiffe hesitated only an instant in completing her banishing gesture, but Farrell missed it because he was hiding his face against Julie's wet cheek. He kept it there until Sia's own laughter began.

He would have known that sound anywhere, in whatever throat. Young and rough, and as much of the earth as Nicholas Bonner's laugh was of that part of the universe where the stars end, it shook the green vines like a wild wind and set birds fluttering and calling where there had been no hint of any other life in the clearing. Sia said, "The justice of the gods. As old as he is, and he still believes that." Farrell thought he heard Briseis whine, but it was Aiffe.

When he opened his eyes and turned, he saw that she and Sia were standing so close together that they almost touched, and that the air around them was clear again. Aiffe was plainly trying to back away, and just as obviously could not, for the old woman was chuckling gently, "No, no, child, it was your magic that bound me to you. A very pretty spell, beautiful even, but you let yourself be distracted. Magic is easily offended." As Farrell, Julie, and a bloody-nosed Ben stared, her body began to grow round and solid once more, her eyes to focus, her skin to restore itself. She explained placidly to Aiffe, "You see, you would never have let me so near to you if I looked even a little bit threatening. And I am only really good at very close range these days. I think I must need contact lenses."

Farrell realized that she was dancing too, that all her apparently aimless shuffling was taking her in a little sly circle with Aiffe at the center. Aiffe, shaking off her moment of shocked paralysis, glanced once at Nicholas Bonner, who stirred slightly. She said two words in a sweet, curious tongue, made one ugly gesture with three fingers twisted together, and stepped easily away from Sia, pointing derisively at her. "Pathetic," she said. "You think you're such hot shit, but you're just so pathetic. I don't need anybody to help me with you."

For a few moments they circled each other, Aiffe moving in swift, taunting dashes, almost skipping, while Sia swept around her with liquid economy, appearing to partner rather than challenge her. Aiffe kept up a constant picket-fence rattle of mockery, saying, "Old, old, old. You aren't immortal, you're just real, real old, there's a difference." Sia laughed and nodded appreciatively and said nothing.

Julie whispered, "But she's just standing still. She hasn't been moving at all." Farrell blinked, craned his neck absurdly and understood, as suddenly as Aiffe, that nothing of Sia was dancing except her eyes and one foot. The eyes were leading Aiffe, keeping her in motion, forcing her to match her steps to steps that were never really taken. *How does she do that? What the hell are we seeing?* Aiffe was shaking her head weakly, knowing what was happening to her and trying to break free of it. Sia began to sing.

There were no words to the song, and her lips did not open; yet Farrell found himself humming it with her, although he had never heard it before. It was not like the song she had sung to Ben, but it filled him with the same childhood longings, wordless themselves. Sia's sandaled right foot was swinging idly back and forth, the posture and her big single braid making her look like a bored schoolgirl. Aiffe stood still. Her head bobbed slightly in rhythm with the foot's pendulous motion, as did the heads of Julie, Ben, and Farrell, equally hypnotized. The bare, pebbly spot where the sandal brushed the ground was peeling back, was dissolving into mud, into smoky mud, and then into the white-gold madness of lava, as wrong as the idea of looking down at one's own flayed ribs or bubbling lung. Sia went on singing quietly. The raw, roiling wound under her pawing foot grew wider, spreading between Aiffe and her with increasing speed. Farrell could smell it now, like impossibly overheated brakes.

Slow, sleepwalking, teeth bared to the gums, Aiffe raised one hand as high as she could, until it began to spill over with blue light. She gave a rasping, plaintive cry, which was the last thing Farrell heard clearly for some moments. The blue light leaped from her hand and exploded, turning everything in the world to the color of lava. Farrell's vision returned before his hearing, showing him Ben and Julie sprawled on the ground. Aiffe herself was down on one knee, rubbing her eyes.

Sia was standing by her, offering her own hand, saying—once the words swam together in Farrell's head—

"Now, *that* is a long-distance weapon, the oldest of them all. Did my son teach you to use a thunderbolt close to? You should not take him quite so seriously, my dear—there are some holes in his understanding." She turned away, thoughtfully studying the place where the ground had healed completely, the few tufts of grass not even singed. "But you do well, truly. You should never be ashamed."

She kept on turning where she stood, dancing for herself, reaching up to loosen her hair, as she had done when she tried to help Micah Willows. The coarse, grizzled hair fell down differently this time—endlessly lengthening, enveloping her body in a sparkling haze, within which she turned and turned, spinning a chrysalis of light. The thick body seemed to be elongating with her hair, hips lilting languidly, stumpy legs visibly growing slender and graceful.

Aiffe danced zigzags, arrows, patterns like a shattered mirror. Her straight lines probed for a way into Sia's glowing spiral, now beginning to move off slowly toward a rise of ground just beyond the clearing. The sandy earth buckled and flowed under them; trees toppled soundlessly; and the rise became a little hill, with one of the fallen trees replaced carefully on the crest. *Wonder why she changed it from rosewood to a willow. Maybe that's her idea of repotting.*

"Mean old, ugly old *bitch*," Aiffe said, and hurled what Farrell thought was another thunderbolt after Sia. But this handful of brightness boiled over in midair, condensed and coalesced and was a striped snake the size of a pool cue, its skull bursting almost out of its skin with eagerness to strike. It vanished into Sia's hair and was never seen again.

Sia glided on, still spinning her changes, while Aiffe danced around and ahead of her to lean impudently against the willow tree, arms folded. "Just to save you some time, I am really fantastic with trees. I'm just trying to be fair." Sia passed by her, slipping straight into the willow like sunlight. Aiffe made a silly grab for her and drew back, crying out softly in pain, as the rough bark began to shine and tremble. Even from that distance, Farrell could watch Sia's presence moving in the willow, could mark her progress from root to crown, along every waking bough to the tip of each long, trailing leaf, as the tree drank her up greedily. *Damn thing even looks like her now. It is her.*

Aiffe said loudly, "I warned you," but Farrell noticed that she stole another quick look back at Nicholas Bonner, who was trying to sit up. "Merry Christmas to me," she said and abruptly reached inside the velvet gown to put her hand momentarily between her legs. She spoke several words, inaudible to Farrell, then pushed back the gown's sleeves, rubbed her hands together, placed one carefully on either side of the willow tree, and tore it apart. It groaned and squealed and shredded in her grip, flailing its branches uselessly. Aiffe cracked it like a marrowbone, gutted it with her long, skinny fingers, going through it like a bear through a garbage can.

Farrell held onto Ben and said, "Wait. We aren't even here. Wait, Ben."

Within minutes—*are there minutes anymore?*—the hillside looked more like a beach at low tide, strewn with a raging scatter of branches, bark stripped away in damp, splintery sheets, and shapeless chunks of wood, none bigger than fireplace logs. Aiffe's spell-given strength had clearly consumed itself. She leaned on the ripped stump of the willow, her splitting velvet gown heavy with sweat, her breath making the same sounds as the murdered tree. When Sia flowered, chuckling, out of a hamburger-sized chip of bark behind her, Aiffe did not turn.

"Child, enough, let it alone." Sia's voice was infuriatingly kind and amused, even to Farrell's hearing. " We have no quarrel, you and I—how can we? You are a witch, a magical technician, and very good you are, too. But what I am has no more to do with magic than eating ice cream or striking a match. What I am does not die, cannot hate or ever be trusted, and cannot be concerned with your skills. My quarrel is with my son, who uses you as a stick to beat me with. When you break, he will throw you away. Let it alone and I will be your friend, as much as an immortal can be anyone's friend. Let me alone."

Aiffe had wheeled on Sia before her own breathing was quite under control, so her words burst from her in a wet-mouthed splutter of furious contempt. "Immortal? You still think you're immortal? You fat bitch, you fat old walrus, you're dead now, I'm standing here watching you rot." She was slobbering uncontrollably, spitting in Sia's face. "You want to know who's immortal? I walked into your house and I found your secret place and I walked right in there, and nobody ever did that to you before, put *that* up your snotty, fat ass. Oh, you're gone, you are gone, I'm not going to let you stay anywhere. Nick told me, he showed me how I could take your immortality anytime I got ready. I may be a mere fucking technician, but I'm ready, and you are just gone."

Sia never flinched from the blasphemous shower; rather, she put her head back and spun on her toes, like a child playing under an open fire hydrant. Aiffe's saliva became a rainbow mist of jasmine-scented water arching between Sia and herself, even after she covered her mouth with both hands. The mist thickened, hiding Sia completely, caressing and blurring the ruins of the willow tree. Flapping her arms as if she were shooing birds, Aiffe ran straight into it. Her efforts dispersed the haze quickly enough, but Sia and the willow were both indeed gone. Aiffe screamed so loudly that the entire hillside caved in.

Farrell found himself lurching forward, at once leaning on Julie and holding Ben back. The imaginary place where they were went mad around them; the sky was gibbering colors, howling the spectrum; the landscape pulsed from jungle to desert to cow pasture with every shudder of color. *There is still the room where we made love, this is where her eyes live.* Where the littered hill had been, a deep grotto began to take shape, a pool as bright as a cheap toy winking at its heart. Without hesitation, Aiffe scrambled to the edge, threw off her velvet gown, and leaped in. She swam with an otter's theatrical suppleness, constantly doubling on herself to dive again and again, hunting Sia in every least concealing shadow.

Absurd old songs and proverbs straggled through Farrell's head as he watched her. He chanted, "Oh, what a time I had with Aiffe the mermaid, down at the bottom of the sea," and announced earnestly to Ben,

"What that is, that's Neptune's park, ribbed and paled in with rocks unscalable and roaring waters." Ben looked at him with Egil Eyvindsson's face.

Ben whispered, "Oh, God, she never could resist going back to stone."

For all the racket of their fall, the stone fragments had not raised even a handful of foam or caused the tiniest eddy. Now, however, as Aiffe splashed and sported in overwhelming triumph, a deep, slow swirl began to move in the pool, far below her joyously kicking feet, turning the water deep green, then red, then orange, spreading steadily, picking up speed until the entire grotto hummed and sang and thrilled to a yawning note that the three watching could only feel in their teeth and bones. Aiffe understood too late; she clung to a rock and screamed unbearably for control, but the waterspout swept her aside as it surged to full height, spinning so fast now that the immense wind of it tore white holes in the mad sky and hurled Aiffe completely out of the pool. At the top of the spout Sia danced on one foot, whirling against the cyclone's rotation, her arms bent sharply across her breasts and face. Farrell knew that she was singing again, though he could not hear her.

Naked, dripping, half-stunned, Aiffe was already up on her hands and knees, doggedly crawling in a circle, counterclockwise, muttering like a bag lady and scratching blurry marks wherever she found a patch of soft earth. She did not turn when the high, leathery fins and great rough backs began to break the pool's surface. Nor did she move even when the rippling necks with scales as big as bricks lifted jaws that turned themselves almost inside-out trying to snatch Sia down. Only when the waterspout caught fire, blazing up with the breathy hiss of newspaper did she stand and look, gradually raising both fists to hail the impossible castle of flame that hid Sia from her once more.

Her cry was wearily implacable. "On your way, old bitch! I told you I'd never let you rest anywhere! On your way, just keep moving!"

At the sound of her voice, the waterspout billowed out into something momentarily like a human shape traced in fireworks—all sparkling hips and Catherine-wheel belly—before toppling silently in on itself and vanishing, taking the fire with it. Only the wind remained, and it was a different wind altogether, alluringly mischievous as Sia's eyes, playful as Briseis with her trusted beach towel. Like Briseis, in fact, this wind had a toy of its own, one last living ember, no bigger than a penny at that height, but caressed and cozened by the breeze into a tiny nova, soaring over the shattered grotto. Tossed up, carelessly dropped, captured again, it grew brighter and brighter, the brilliance of its little life almost as painful to look at as Aiffe's cries of rage had been to hear.

Far below, Aiffe stood very quietly now, watching the dancing spark for a long time before she began to dance again, very slowly, her movements strangely clumsy, slurred with menace. She kept turning her head far back over her right shoulder as she danced, snapping her jaws.

Farrell had in his life seen more shape-changing than most people. Each time he handled the experience less well; it always left him feeling as wrenched and dis-

349

oriented as if he were the one who had passed through the sweet, nauseating shudder in the molecules, to stumble into moonlight on four feet. He looked away, as always, when it happened with Aiffe, but not quickly enough. Her shoulders hunched and bulked, neck and legs shortening so quickly that she seemed to fall to her knees. The metamorphosis of her head was frightening enough—the bones visibly hollowing and streamlining, but the face itself plunging forward, not into a raptor's hooked beak, but becoming a kind of feathered muzzle, drooling through gray lips. The arms were the worst. They jolted up and out in electrical spasms, achieving magical angles, and Farrell heard them grinding in their sockets as they yanked Aiffe off the ground, even before rust-and-lichen-colored feathers had fully formed. Her feet had turned to huge, yellow-gray talons, arthritically gnarled by their own massiveness. Even the scales on them looked like miniature claws.

Farrell heard Ben laugh and almost failed to recognize the sound. The Aiffe-bird gained altitude like a helicopter, but the very power of its approach blew its bright prey constantly out of reach as it tried to close in. No swallow could have veered and cornered more neatly in pursuit of a gnat, but the ember drifted on, fanned to near-white heat now by furious wingbeats just behind it. The great claws clutched futilely; the slobbering mouth snapped and snapped; and on the ground, Ben whispered, almost pityingly, *"Fool."*

At the same instant, Julie gripped Farrell's wrist and said, "Look down."

Farrell realized that, while they had all been gaping after the Aiffe-bird, the grotto and its surroundings had become a northern European forest, anciently dark with huge oaks, elms, ash trees, and maples, stretching

350

almost as far as Farrell could see, to a snowy void that he looked at once, and then never again. *There is no horizon. There is only where she lets go.*

A little way from where he stood with Ben and Julie, an archer in red crouched under an elm tree, setting an arrow to his bowstring. When he rose, Farrell saw that his face was all of the same white nothingness, except for two pulsing amber absences that were his eyes. The Aiffe-bird tried to dodge the arrow, but it danced after her, tracking her frantic doublings and stooping wherever she fled, until there was nothing for her but to change shape in midair. The arrow flashed between her human neck and shoulder as she fell.

Julie made a little splintering sound in her throat; Ben shouted "Sia!" as if it were no name, but a blessing to armies; and Farrell, being who he was, heard himself deliriously singing snatches of a very old ballad about a king who learned to fly:

"And he flew as high as the steeple top,
And the sun shone gold on his golden crown,
And he flew as high as any hawk,
Till his own huntsmen shot him down."

Aiffe tumbled, sprawling and flailing for a moment, before she righted herself and spoke sharply to the earth below her. The tearing branches leaned aside to let her light nakedness hurtle past, and the ground bulged and rippled up in whipped-cream solicitude, to gather her tenderly into a forgiving green lap, the breath not even jarred out of her. The ember followed her down, fluttering in a rather bored way, and vanished like a snowflake before ever reaching the ground.

Aiffe was on her feet instantly, with the spring of a

351

boxer determined to show that it was a slip and not a knockdown. But the gesture clearly ate up the last of that wild energy that had, in one afternoon, created illusory beings and real storms, hurled thunderbolts, torn rocks and trees to pieces, and broken into a goddess's sky, where Aiffe had flown as high as any hawk. Now she trudged through stillborn spells on stumbling feet, reduced to picking up handfuls of dirt and hurling them into the air, kicking stones and sand away on all sides. Behind her, Sia materialized slowly—lazily—out of the little showers of earth, *the way she arrived out of blood and black stone long ago.* She was dancing as she took shape, but it was a different dance this time, and she was different.

"No more," she said inside Farrell, and with those words the great forest fled, and they were back in the vaguely pleasant little room that Farrell remembered, with the windows full of nothing but Avicenna twilight and an old man and woman laughing on a street corner. Sia was sitting calmly in her elusive chair facing Aiffe, who stared back at her from the middle of the room, dazedly plucking at the velvet gown which had been restored to her. Farrell, Ben, and Julie clung together by the dusty bookcases, while, in the furthest corner, Briseis kept tremulous watch over Nicholas Bonner. He was standing utterly still, arms at his sides, looking only at Sia. A terrible pity swept through Farrell then, and for once he could not turn his eyes away. *What could he be but what he is, nothing but skin and spirit stretched unbearably over a black hole? What could he be but what she made when she was young?*

"No more," Sia said again. Even sitting, she was still dancing, moving only her feet in languid patterns like an alchemist's equations, as Aiffe moved more and more slowly. Sia's hands opened to show that she was holding some of the sandy earth Aiffe had thrown aside—powdery blue-white crystals in her right hand, red-gold in the other. She raised her hands and began to let the crystals drift to the ground. Aiffe screamed, the sound made horrifying by the immobility of her face. Julie started toward her, but Ben barred the way.

Sia smiled. Abruptly she tossed the golden crystals straight up, catching them in her left hand while the blue-white stones were settling gently into her right. She seemed to be playing casually with the crystals, not juggling them, but allowing them to leap randomly from her hands like dolphins or flames, as they chose. Each time this happened, Aiffe half swayed, half lurched a few steps toward her, and then froze again as if the two were playing some sidewalk game together. Sia was singing once more, and this time Farrell understood every one of the dreadfully gentle words.

> "*Proud sister, nothing you believed is true,*
> *Proud sister, everything you know has be-*
> *trayed you,*
> *Head and heart, there is nothing to you but*
> *shadow, nothing but shadow,*
> *you have no friend but shadow,*
> *Sister, little sister, the shadows wait to enjoy*
> *you,*
> *go to them,*
> *go to them,*
> *go to them. . . ."*

With every repetition, the crystals whirled upward, melting together for an emerald instant, just at the height of Aiffe's eyes, then cascading back into order as unlikely as waterspouts catching fire, not one pebble dropped or in the wrong hand. They were spinning steadily faster, and Farrell took a long time to isolate the further moment when they vanished altogether, returning almost too quickly for their total absence to register. Even when he made himself realize that the crystals were dancing through Aiffe's head on their way from one hand to the other, even then he would never have believed what he saw, except for the expression in her eyes, which were all she could move now. Sia sang:

> "Your power is shadow, but a shadow of mercy
>   would have saved you,
> Your knowledge is all shadow,
> but a shadow of understanding would have
>   saved you,
> Your pride is the pride of a shadow, my sister,
> But a shadow's shadow of respect for the gods
>   would have saved you,
> would have saved you,
> would have saved you,
> from the shadows. . . ."

The crystals flared brighter after each tiny, impossible disappearance, and each time Aiffe had dwindled that much more, as if the shining flecks were draining all her substance, emptying her of light and color and will. She was making a sound, nevertheless, a wordless, insect whine that could only have been produced by an adolescent faced with an unimpressed universe. The crystals had begun to form pictures as they flashed back and forth: flickering but distinct visions of horses and beaches, armored men clashing by torchlight—*no, those are headlights, they're fighting under a damn freeway*—boxes of breakfast cereal, boxes splitting at the corners with mysterious hand-labeled jars and packets; buses and television commercials; and a loose-leaf school notebook, filled with magical symbols and diagrams drawn in multicolored felt-tip ink. The patterns looked exactly like Aiffe's dances.

It's all her life, it's Rosanna Berry's life burning out there, moment by moment. It's burning, it's all burning. He understood as well as he was ever to understand anything again that every image the crystals shaped was entirely real, ripped whole out of Aiffe's mind—*that's Nicholas Bonner, I guess that's her mother, that looks like a kid's drawing of trees and maybe a dog*—and that the pictures' glow was literally the light of actual moments being forever consumed. *The way they used to disembowel somebody and throw his guts in the fire right in front of him. To burn a life all up like that.* A scene of naked people coupling and tripling in a field under a horned moon hissed and vanished, to be replaced by Garth de Montfaucon reading aloud from a Dr. Seuss book. Aiffe kept up that whine that made Farrell want to shake her. He said loudly, "Don't. Don't, Sia, don't."

He never knew whether he had truly broken Sia's concentration, bent so absolutely on Aiffe that, in a way, nothing but Aiffe seemed real, nor did he ever allow himself the illusion of having affected Aiffe's fate one way or the other. But the wheeling crystals did falter for a moment, Sia did turn slightly toward him, and in that moment Nicholas Bonner made the only move left to him. Knocking Briseis aside, he sprang forward in a bound that covered half the room—*the laughing golden frog squatting in the redwood grove that first night*—shrieking, "Now, sweet witch, now, save me as I save you, now, now!" and batting madly at the tiny lights swarming around Aiffe's head. Several of the wild blows struck Aiffe herself as she staggered sideways, but it was Sia who cried out.

The crystals blazed up so brightly that even Sia took a step backward. Farrell kept his eyes as wide open as he could, although he saw the world in aching, molten shadows for days afterward. The colors ran and flooded together in a motley bubble shimmering around Nicholas Bonner. Farrell could not hear his scream, but he felt it, like a saw going through the bone. Nicholas Bonner pounded his fists against turquoise, cold, smoky crimson, and great blowing drifts of amber, but he might have been another silent image, burning to ashes with the rest of Aiffe's memory. The bubble tightened around him, and he fell, started to get up, then abruptly tumbled over, curling into a fetal position, knees drawn hard to his chest, head tucked between folded hands, lightning-colored eyes wide as a dead man's. The slack lips were saying a single word, *mother*, over and over.

Sia dawned out of her chair. There was no movement involved, nothing to do with breath and muscle and leverage, only that slow, immense arising in freedom from everything mortal. Farrell tried to look straight at her, to see her truly, but a monster would have been more comprehensible, a black stone more human. What went to answer her son's despair was a shape that

Farrell's senses could not contain and a light that his spirit simply could not bear. *This is why you're not ever supposed to see the gods naked.* So he looked at Julie and Ben instead, and Julie looked back at him, but Ben was far away, moving toward the light.

It took Sia forever to reach the crystal bubble, but forever was no time at all. However long her journey really lasted, she was there while Farrell's ill-used and completely mutinous eyes were still reporting to him that she was crossing the room, was stretching out her arms, and was beginning to say a word that he knew must be Nicholas Bonner's real name. The bubble waited for her, matching her light with its own; but behind the slippery flames, it had already grown thick-walled and opaque, almost hiding Nicholas Bonner. Sia took hold of it.

Rather, she took hold *in* it, for her hands passed straight through the crystal fires and disappeared within the bubble—*how far is she, how far has she gone in there, which is she, which is she?* For an instant, Sia and the bubble were one—a single blinding silence like a star, endlessly devouring itself. Ben was as close to it as his body would let him go, shouting in a language that Farrell had never heard. Farrell had a moment's glimpse of Aiffe with her head thrown back and her skinny arms waving randomly. He was never quite certain whether she had been merely fighting for balance, trying to knit one last reflexive spell together while Sia was unmindful of her, or something somewhere between the two. Julie pinioned her and held her firmly, taking no chances.

Then Sia was there again in the form they knew, her

hands empty, her mouth opening to utter a howl of hopeless pain that would surely rattle the real stars in their courses and shake gods down out of the heavens like scurrying cockroaches. But the cry never came, and Farrell could not breathe for the dreadful wrongness of that denial. The bubble disappeared. Unlike every other picture that the crystals had made, this one was not followed by any other bright vision. It was just gone, and a very old woman was sinking almost weightlessly to a floor no more solid than herself, and the windows were now saying that it was earlier than it had been, not yet dusk at all.

Ben picked Sia up and carried her back to her chair, which altered its shape to keep her from falling again. He was still speaking to her in the strange language that sounded like a storm trying hard to be gentle. Sia's eyes were closed, but her chuckle was as tenderly malicious as always. She said, "For what it is worth, my dearest Ben, my best Ben, you are the only human who ever learned even that much of my talk. Speak it to yourself sometimes, just to remember me." Ben put her fingers to his mouth and whispered against them.

Farrell asked, "What happened to Nicholas Bonner? After what he tried to do, after everything, you were fighting that bubble, those crystals for him."

Still with her eyes closed, she said, "The crystals of time. I did a foolish thing. I meant to punish that girl in the way that *we* punish, that *we* have to punish such pride. I meant to strip her of every memory except that she had offended the gods and must do penance forever." When she looked at Farrell, he saw the huge stone woman with the dog's head once again, and she smiled, nodding slightly. "But time is not mine to control," she said, "only to tease a little. Time is everyone's enemy, especially of the gods. My son got in time's way, that is all, like any child running into the street after a ball. No more to it than that, really."

"But you went after him," Farrell persisted. "You tried to bring him back, you got in the way too."

Sia rested her head on Ben's hand, letting her eyes sag shut again. "And got run over for my vanity," she answered in a voice too weary even for impatience. "There was never any hope, not from the moment he touched those crystals. But he is my son, mine to deal with, mine to banish, and what is between us is between us alone. So I did what I could do, but he will never come back anymore. Time has hold of him at last."

The windows of the room were going out as Farrell watched them, and the familiar white nothingness was stirring beyond. Sia said, "You must go now, all of you, quickly. I will hold the way clear for you as long as I can."

Ben said, "Sia, I am not going." She answered him in the other language, and he turned away and stood staring at the fading walls.

Sia turned her head to find Julie in the dimness. She said, "You are very brave and merciful. Kannon will always come to you in your need." Aiffe stood quietly in Julie's grasp, her eyes terribly tranquil, frowning as if at a pointless question. Only her mouth shivered just a bit—a fishing line taken and run out by something far too massive and wild for its strength.

Julie said, "I don't want her. I don't want the gods ever to help me. I hate the gods."

Sia nodded seriously, even approvingly. "Of course, that is only sensible. *We* are a terrible lot, *we* have no fairness, no honor, no sense of proportion. How could you not hate *us*?" Julie looked away in her turn, and Sia grinned then, momentarily youthful with mockery. "But *we* do have charm, and most of *us* are very good social dancers." Julie did not answer her.

"And sometimes *we* grant wishes that people never know they have made," the old woman went on. She took a ring from her finger and held it out to Farrell. It was gold, the color of new bread, fashioned in the shape of a thick, soft, drowsily coiled serpent with a suggestion of a woman's breasts. The one visible eye was long and empty, a slash of a darkness that Farrell had seen before. Sia said, "It is not magic, it has absolutely no useful powers. It will do nothing at all for you but remind you of me."

"Thank you," Farrell said. He put the golden snake carefully on his left forefinger, where it fitted perfectly. Sia spoke to Ben a second time in her own tongue, but he kept his back turned to her. She beckoned to Aiffe, who stumbled when Julie let her go, but then came forward obediently. Sia took the empty, fearless face between her hands.

"Well," she said, "Let's see. You have conspired against me with my son, you have tried twice to destroy me, and the second time you had visions of stealing my immortality, which is probably the worst kind of blasphemy, when I think about it. In addition to that, you have used your beautiful little gift for nothing but stupid nastiness. You have caused one man's death, another's madness and possession, and you have done worse damage that you do not even know about to people you dragged back and forth across time for the sake of your pride, your play, your revenge. And I am expected to pardon you for no reason but to show off to a friend whose idea of interceding is to tell me that she hates the gods." She began to laugh again, quietly and truly helpless with mortal amusement. "What have I come to, indeed, for my last act in this world?"

Briseis trembled against Farrell's leg. When he turned, he saw that the corner where she had been cowering no longer existed. The door was still visible, but white dissolution prowled on the other side. Sia's voice seemed to be coming more and more from the same void. "This house is falling, and you have no business here. I cannot protect you—if you die before you get out, you really die. Go, go on, this minute."

Julie started to speak, but Sia would not let her. "The girl stays with me, I will do what I can do. What are you waiting for, good-bye kisses? I am done with hellos and good-byes, done with this place, done with you. Get out of my house now!"

Each of them looked back once. Julie said later that she heard Sia say Ben's name, but by the time Farrell stood in the doorway he could barely discern Aiffe in that room where even the darkness was going out. He did see the two steel engravings blink off together and thought absurdly, *oh, that's a pity, she likes those.* Then he was staggering after Ben and Julie down a corridor that was disappearing faster than they could run, knowing with the most casual, distant kind of certainty that they would never find their way in time.

Briseis took the lead, or they never would have found it. They followed her waving gray tail, calling aloud to keep in contact; and though the dog fled before them with unlikely surefootedness, she was constantly forced to double back and double again, as a silent wind of forgetting tore away floors and stairways beneath their feet. Once Julie caught Farrell as he strode off into nothing at all, and once he had to carry Ben in a steep place for a while.

The serpent ring glimmered on his finger with what must have been its own light, but it was not the least help when he pointed it at the oblivion swirling on every side and whimpered, "Avaunt, get thee gone, let us be." *Oh, Sia, remember us another moment, keep us in yourself yet a little.* At the last, they were each running alone, no longer calling, gone from each other as completely as if they had truly vanished. *Would we know? How would we know?*

They never did agree on the exact point where they crossed from Sia's true house into the one they knew. By the time they were even aware of having burst up like divers through hallway, kitchen, and living room, they were out on the sidewalk, gasping and crying and falling down in the wet grass. They huddled together for a long while, the three of them, tending to one another under the casually curious eyes of neighbors come out to enjoy the soft twilight after Aiffe's squall. It was Julie who stood up first to face the odd old house with the roof almost like a widow's walk and the front door missing.

Farrell had known perfectly well that it was not the visible house falling around them, and he knew also that it was silly to expect brick to boil and wood and shingle to convulse with mourning for a struggle and a passing that had taken place so far from them. Even so, he realized that he was vainly, ridiculously angry with the house, in a way that he had never been angry with Aiffe or Nicholas Bonner. "What day is it?" he asked vaguely, and did not hear if anyone answered, but went on staring at the house, waiting stubbornly to see it slump just a little, settling into the shaded ordinariness that it would wear from now on, now that a goddess no longer lived there.

XX

The real problem was the dog.

Aiffe turned out never to have left the Whalemas Tourney at all, but to have accompanied her father to the traditional feast and dance which followed it. Any number of League members could vouch for her presence there, as well as for the fact that she had led the dances all night long, come down with flu the next day, and remained bedridden, feverish and quarantined. Farrell asked Julie, "Do simulacra get the flu? Then who was it who stayed in that room with Sia?" Julie answered only, "She said she'd do what she could do."

In the following days—every one astonishingly warm and lingeringly generous, as early fall often is in Avicenna—a number of small things happened. Madame Schumann-Heink got a new engine, new windows, and her first paint job in a decade, all more or less acquired in a graveyard at midnight. Julie's BSA got two new forks, and Farrell's lute got an entire set of strings and gut frets as the price of its sojourn in a place that was not good for stringed instruments. Farrell himself got Briseis.

That part happened later, just after he resigned from the League for Archaic Pleasures. A certain amount of regret was expressed, mostly by the members of Basilisk and the Blood Countess Elizabeth Bathory. Hamid ibn Shanfara and Lovita Bird were sympathetic and slightly awkward, since they had not resigned after all. Lovita told him, "Honey, you have no idea just how much weird shit I will endure for the sake of having someplace to dress up. I'm sorry, I got to be somebody besides that damn bus driver now and again."

Hamid said wryly, "Little bit addictive, the *griot* business. Down at the post office, they don't have much room for a person wants to be an entire group memory all by himself."

Farrell said, "Individuals have memories. Groups have forgetteries."

Hamid laughed outright. "Tell me the difference. There's no law against anything that child did, there's no way to prove anything we saw, and there is damn sure no undoing any of it. Might just as well make up a poem about how old Crof Grant died in battle with ten million trolls, tell stories about Prester John getting taken up to heaven by St. Whale. Just as likely as what really happened, and it sings better."

"But everybody knows the truth," Farrell said. He felt mired in priggishness, and Lovita's dimple did not help him.

Hamid said, "That's why there's the League, babe."

Sia's lawyer—a short, dashing woman with a few too many pointed white teeth—called Ben and Farrell to her office to read them Sia's will. It had been drawn up several years before Ben ever met her, spoke nowhere of her death, but only of a possible disappearance, and left everything to him, with the exception of Briseis. Not only was the dog left specifically in Farrell's care, but a remarkable number of clauses went into making it clear that, if Farrell refused to accept Briseis or attempted to get rid of her at any time, the entire bequest to Ben was to revert to a trust administered for the purpose of feeding the ducks in Barton Park. Farrell yielded without a struggle, but with curious misgivings. "She could see the future," he said to Ben. "If you can see the future, you don't just do things."

"She saw part of the future part of the time," Ben said. "I think she liked it that way."

Farrell had spent the first days after Sia's departure hovering around Ben like a Gray Lady, trying to help him deal with a loss that Farrell could neither share nor truly imagine. But in fact, as the fall passed, Ben went about his life with a quiet decisiveness, teaching his classes, keeping office hours, going dutifully to faculty meetings when no escape offered itself, working on his overdue skaldic poetry book on weekends, and even going swimming with Farrell once or twice a week. He spoke of Sia from time to time, gently and with affection, as if remembering an old lover now safely married to an eye doctor. Farrell knew just enough about grieving to be alarmed.

They walked all the way home from campus one evening, taking advantage of the last softness in the air, cheerfully debating aspects of the class struggle involved in the coming World Series between Seattle and

Atlanta. Ben interrupted the argument to ask abruptly, "Why do you keep looking at me the way you do? Is something falling off?"

"Nothing," Farrell said. "I'm sorry, I didn't know I was staring."

"Every damn minute, weeks now. This isn't the Island of Dr. Moreau. I'm not going to revert, start running on all fours."

"I know that, I'm sorry. I guess I'm just waiting for you to start breaking furniture." They walked on in silence for some time, meeting no one, listening to music from lighted windows, until Farrell said, "In the end, it's none of my business—"

"Of course it's your business; who else's damn business is it? Don't get all humilified on me." He paused, and then said in a quieter tone, "Do you remember when she realized that she couldn't save Nicholas Bonner? I mean that one exact moment?"

"When she opened her mouth and I thought she was going to cry everything to pieces, just shout all of it down. But she never made a sound."

"No, not a sound. If she had, if she'd let even the least little bit of that sorrow out, we'd have been lucky to go mad. Most likely, we'd have turned into something that could endure to hear her—stones, air. She ate that pain to save us. That's what destroyed her, you know."

"I don't know that. I don't know anything about her, except that she's a goddess and immortal, and you're not. You're supposed to scream."

"Oh, I will. But not for a while yet." He smiled at Farrell then and touched his shoulder. "You do know how it is with really little kids, when they get hurt or really upset? That long, awful moment before the howl?" Farrell nodded. "That's where I am right now. I can't even get my breath to cry, but I still have to live."

Briseis met them halfway down the block, ignoring Ben entirely to dance and yap around Farrell as if she were a much smaller dog, running between his legs and all but snapping at his ankles. Ben said, "Well, somebody sure knows an authority figure when she sees one."

"It's not funny. Don't encourage her. Ever since we told her about the will, she's been getting nutsier by the minute. Knock it *off*, Briseis," he ordered, as the dog leaped up to him. "See that? That's not fawning, she never licks my face, she just looks at me as if I know where all her puppies are. Wake up in the night, and she's standing right by the bed, *waiting*. I hate to tell you, but if she keeps this up, the ducks are going to get your house. Briseis, God damn it!"

They stood outside the house for a few minutes, watching timers turn lamps on and off. Ben said finally, "You still talk about Sia in the present tense. I always notice."

"I think of her like that. Hell, I dream about her most nights. The strange thing about that is, we're always out of the house, going shopping, working in the garden, just walking down Parnell. Don't you have dreams about her?"

Ben shook his head. "I can't afford to, Joe. Sometimes I think she's really dead, sometimes she's just gone somewhere I don't know how to imagine. But it doesn't make any difference, it can't. Where she is, she's done with me, the same way she's done with Nicholas Bonner. He was the real reason she hung around the human shape, he was her responsibility, but he's gone, and she's done with all of us, she meant what she said. And I still have to live."

Farrell's unease deepened with the autumn, putting him at vague but constant odds with everything. His dreams of Sia persisted, companionable and undemanding in themselves, but more and more leaving him angrily bereft each time he woke to look up into Briseis' foolish, urgent eyes. The dog took to following him to work, which was bad enough but manageable; the people at the auto restoration shop liked her and fed her bits of their lunches. But the second time she dragged the blankets off him in Julie's house at three in the morning, he came up reaching for her throat, and it took all of Julie's efforts to make him stop yelling and throttling Briseis. It took a good deal longer for him to stop trembling, even when Julie held him.

"I wouldn't say this to everybody," she said, "but I suspect you're getting a message." Farrell huddled in a chair, glowering across the bedroom at Briseis. Julie said, "I think our friend wants to talk to you."

"Not me. Definitely not me. Ben's her man, and you're her friend, practically a second cousin. I'm the straight man, the dummy—I'm Briseis, when you get down to it. You don't make long-distance calls to Briseis."

"We're all her Briseises. What else could we be to her? Tenth-rate material, cheap styrofoam, meant for packing cartons, not to be depended on by a goddess.

But she didn't have any choice, she was stuck with us and, damn it, she could have done a lot worse for familiars. Maybe we couldn't be much help, but we must have been some, because she's sending for you again. And if she wants you, you have to go."

"Go? Go where?" Farrell sat up, and Briseis ran into the bathroom, rousing the white cat Mushy, who won the ensuing two-rounder by a TKO. Farrell said, "Jewel, I couldn't even guess if she's on the bloody planet anymore. And it's not just *where*, it's *what*. She could come back as the Pocatello National Bank or a manhole cover in Kuala Lumpur. I would not know."

"Briseis would. She left her to you for a reason." Farrell snarled. "So would your ring, probably. Look at the way it's shining right now."

"It just does that. It's not any good for anything, it's just supposed to remind me of her." Julie smiled and spread her hands. Farrell said heavily. "Even if. Even if I quit the job and pile my stuff in the bus one more time, and sit Briseis on the dashboard so she can point where she wants me to go. Even if I'm that crazy. What happens to us?"

"What always happens to us," Julie said. "It just took longer this time. I'm very glad it did." She patted the edge of the bed, and Farrell came and sat next to her. They were quiet together for a long time. She said, "I told you before, we'll always be together because we've shared something we'll never be able to share with anyone else, and our other lovers will always be jealous. But neither of us wants to live with anyone. You know that's true, Joe. It happens to be one of the big things we have in common."

Farrell said, "We waited too late. There were times for us long ago, I remember them. We could have been an old couple by now."

"An immortal is summoning you on a quest, and you're sitting here mumbling domestic fantasies. I'm going back to bed."

Farrell put his arms around her. "When they bust me for vagrancy and mumbling in Pocatello, will you come and get me?"

"As long as you tell me when you find Sia. You will find her, old buddy. Nobody else could, but you will."

The morning that he set out was glass-crisp, not rounded off with fog but sharp-cornered, making him sneeze when he inhaled deeply. Ben helped him pack the last of his belongings into Madame Schumann-Heink, where Briseis had insisted on spending the night. He said very little, and Farrell was the one who volunteered, "This is lonely. Leaving's never been lonely for me before. I'll miss you."

"I'll miss you a lot," Ben said. "I know you're going on my quest, and it feels really strange. But I can't go with you."

"Of course you can't. You've got your work, you've got a whole life to keep together, like Julie. She sent for me because I'm the one who's still just messing around."

"That's not the reason." Ben petted Briseis, speaking directly to her. "Tell your mistress that I will love her all my life and that I'm as angry as I can be at her for leaving me when I needed her. I know it's presumptuous and insulting, but you tell her. You tell her I'm angry." Briseis licked his hand, and Ben said, almost inaudibly, "Tell her I do speak her language to myself."

Farrell drove Julie to work for the last time. Neither of them spoke at all. They held hands all the way, even when Farrell had to shift gears. When he parked near her office, she got down by herself, walked around to the driver's side and pulled him halfway through the window to kiss him. "Be careful," she said. "You're the only one I've ever had."

"The only one what?" There was no way to avoid asking the question, and they were both laughing when she replied, "Ah, if we only knew that. Wouldn't we be somewhere then?" She kissed him again and walked away without saying good-bye. Farrell found this oddly hopeful and reassuring, since he had never known Julie to say good-bye, and they had always seen each other again.

"Pilot to navigator," he announced to Briseis. "Which the hell way?" Briseis bounced her paws on the dashboard and whined in the general direction of the Bay. Farrell waited until Julie was out of sight, then put the bus in gear.

Leaving the campus, he spotted a red-haired man in a three-piece suit who looked like a game-show host, standing next to a hot-pretzel barrow, screaming out his timetable for the arrival of the Antichrist. Farrell said to Briseis, "Look at that. They're all over the place, preaching to muggers in the rain, converting fire hydrants, absolutely crazy as jaybirds. But they have to do it, they have to tell people what God tells them, they're all on quests, too. And here I go sliding on by, just as easy and civilized, and nobody knows I'm asking a dog to tell me which turn-off I take to find our goddess. A remarkable thing."

Passing a high school that looked like a Moorish airbase, he drove slowly, growling at the adolescents who drifted across his path without ever looking up, clearly rendered invulnerable by their Walkmans. Four girls in long skirts were coming toward him, walking abreast, advancing like a curtain of bright rain. One girl was Aiffe. She walked in the middle of the group, giggling and fooling, leaning on one friend to adjust her sandal, on another to yelp with laughter, shoving them with her hips and flinging her arms over their shoulders. Farrell heard her whoop, "But he's so *dorky!* He thinks you get hot if he bumps up against you on the lunch line!" The yellow-brown mane flared constantly across the faces of her companions.

Farrell shouted, "Lady Aiffe!" several times, but she did not turn until he tried calling her by her real name. Then she turned, frowned, hesitated, said something to her friends, and crossed the street as he pulled to the curb, blocking a driveway. Briseis whimpered impatiently, but he got out of the bus and stood waiting as the girl approached him.

"Hey," she said, "The old Knight of Whatever. Ghosts and Dragons." She might have been a little paler than the child who had changed herself into a bird; otherwise, she looked no different at all. Farrell said, "I heard you got sick after the Whalemas Tourney. Are you okay now?"

Aiffe looked briefly puzzled, then nodded. "I was sick. I'm fine now. I was really sick." The recognition in her eyes went no further than his face; there was no indication that she connected him with any event beyond the Tourney. "I was pretty delirious," she said. "I don't really remember a whole lot."

"Do you remember Nicholas Bonner?"

Her face went utterly blank, empty past pretense. She had never heard the name before. She said, "Actually, there's a whole lot of people in the League I don't know anymore. I'm not as much into that whole thing as I used to be."

"Your father still is, though."

She laughed, hugging her book bag and leaning against Madame Schumann-Heink. "Grownups have *time* for that stuff. They don't have to do computer science homework and try out for plays. Hey, we're putting on *Arsenic and Old Lace*, I'm going to be one of the old ladies." She chattered on, while her friends fidgeted at the end of the block and Briseis yawned and sighed in the bus. Farrell interrupted her at last.

"I didn't mean to make you late," he said. "I just want to ask you one thing." Aiffe waited, her smile only slightly wary. Farrell asked, "What did she say to you? In that room, putting your mind back together with everything else coming apart, what did she say?" He had meant to keep his voice conversational and unthreatening, but Aiffe took one small step backward. "Come on, you have to remember that much," he coaxed her. "Even if you don't remember how you got there, or what was going on, you have to remember being there with her, she must have talked to you. Did she say where she was going, what was happening to her? Will you tell me what she said, God damn you?"

There was a moment when he was absolutely certain

that some part of her, some red-gold fleck in her eyes, understood perfectly what he was saying and sat back laughing at him, *like Nicholas Bonner in the redwood grove.* Then the same eyes were full of bewildered tears and she was lunging away down the street to her friends. Someone uniformed enough to be a security patrol was starting toward Farrell, and he swung back up into the bus and got himself and Briseis out of there. In his last sight of Aiffe, the other three girls were consoling her and hugging her; one was even trying to brush her hair.

The snake ring glimmered against the steering wheel as Madame Schumann-Heink approached the freeway. Briseis had her head out of the window, apparently watching sailboats on the Bay. Farrell said, "Pilot to navigator. South is Mexico, north is Canada. Let's hear it." Briseis' nose and tail indicated the turn-off.

DEL REY PRESENTS

PETER S. BEAGLE'S

Fantasy
&
Magic